SPEAK FOR ENGLAND

Speak for England

James Hawes

Jonathan Cape
London

Published by Jonathan Cape 2005

2 4 6 8 10 9 7 5 3 1

Copyright © James Hawes 2005

Grateful acknowledgement is made to: IPC Media Ltd for permission to reprint
images from the *Eagle Annual* Number 7 © IPC Syndication; Quartet Books
for permission to reprint an extract from *The Abolition of Britain*
by Peter Hitchens; Macmillan for permission to reprint an extract from
The Lost Tribe by Edward Marriot

First published in Great Britain in 2005 by Jonathan Cape
Random House, 20 Vauxhall Bridge Road, London SW1V 2SA

Random House Australia (Pty) Limited
20 Alfred Street, Milsons Point, Sydney,
New South Wales 2061, Australia

Random House New Zealand Limited
18 Poland Road, Glenfield,
Auckland 10, New Zealand

Random House South Africa (Pty) Limited
Endulini, 5A Jubilee Road, Parktown 2193, South Africa

The Random House Group Limited Reg. No. 954009
www.randomhouse.co.uk

A CIP catalogue record for this book is available from the British Library

ISBN 0-224-07302-8

Typeset by Palimpsest Book Production Limited,
Polmont, Stirlingshire
Printed and bound in Great Britain by
Mackays of Chatham PLC, Chatham, Kent

The second of five siblings, James Hawes was born fifteen years after VE Day, in the month JIGSAW (the Joint Intelligence Group for the Study of All-out War) decided that 'the Polaris submarine system seems in every way compatible with the British character'. The Gloucestershire Regiment sponsored his application for a Commission while he was at Oxford, but he withdrew and has often regretted it. He has held lectureships in German literature and history at universities in Ireland, England and Wales, and has published four previous novels as well as an academic tome, *Nietzsche and the End of Freedom*, which sold two hundred copies. He is divorced and has a son. They live quietly in Wales.

The idea for this story came out of a conversation with my brother Robert, who also made many helpful suggestions later on. Dan Franklin's enthusiasm, when it was still no more than this idea, was extraordinarily supportive. Stephanie Cabot's encouragement was beyond price, her notes saved me from many embarrassments, and she found the book from which the depiction of cannibal raids and human butchery in Papua New Guinea is taken (Tim Flannery, *Throwim Way Leg: tree-kangaroos, possums and penis-gourds – on the track of unknown mammals in wildest New Guinea*, New York, 1998). Nerys Lloyd's comments were swiftly insightful, as ever. This book is dedicated to her, and to my parents, Maurice and Janet, who quite apart from everything else, were wonderfully helpful in giving me details of the world into which they brought us children.

A telling speculation persists amongst certain now-frail ex-members of JIGSAW (the Joint Intelligence Group for the Study of All-out War) regarding the February 1958 disaster. That ill-starred **Comet IV**, carrying what *The Times* of the day called 'the best and brightest of our youth' (as well as Sir William Penney, Chief Superintendent of High-Explosive Research at the Ministry of Supply), disappeared without trace en route to Australia shortly before Britain's planned Grapple Y thermonuclear test on Christmas Island (the follow-up to the Grapple and Grapple X explosions of May and November 1957). Certainly, the official response to the crash was curiously muted in comparison with that to the three **Comet I** losses of 1953 and 1954, the last of which had seen Britain's most prestigious warship, the aircraft-carrier *Eagle*, cut short a flag-carrying visit to Naples in order to search for wreckage. The rumour runs thus: the debacle of Suez and the disastrous revelations concerning Burgess, Philby and Maclean had so rocked U.S. trust in the U.K. that our Secret Services might have had good reason to head off an investigation which could reveal (i) that we had used a commercial airliner to transport H-bomb parts and (ii) that this unwarlike subterfuge had been uncovered by the ever-more confident Soviets and dealt with in a decisive manner. Like all such speculation, however, this is almost certainly more entertaining than it is true. The low-key governmental response to the 1958 loss was more probably just the instinctive expression of a general national despair at yet another example of Britain's inability to keep up with the U.S. in any significant field. True, the **Comet IVB** beat the Americans by three weeks to inaugurate a non-stop London–New York service in 1959, but that victory was meaningless: within the year, BOAC was buying 707s and 'Supermac' was begging ignominiously for Polaris to replace Britain's much-vaunted (and extremely expensive) V-Bomber force, which had in truth become obsolete almost before it became operational. The eagles and trumpets were indeed fled the skies.

Richard J. Simpkins,
Comet Falling: Britain's Jetliner and the End of Empire,
London, 1998.

– We pray here. He looked up, almost vertically, to the mountain.
– This is where it speaks to us.

Ever since our arrival I had wanted to talk about the mountain. I was unable to pinpoint it on my map. I had aviation charts, the best available, but over the whole area was a white square marked 'obscured by cloud'.

Edward Marriot,
*The Lost Tribe: A Harrowing Passage into New Guinea's Heart of
Darkness*,
New York, 1996.

Breakdown might be defined as occurring 'when the government of a country is no longer able to ensure that its orders are carried out' ... in a word, through breakdown of *morale*.

JIGSAW,
'Note on the Concept and Definitions of Breakdown', June 1960,
quoted in Peter Hennessy,
The Secret State: Whitehall and the Cold War,
London, 2002.

I

SURVIVED BY A SON

Papua New Guinea, Boxing Day

—Keep the line straight, Marley, said the battle-hardened officer, warmly but firmly. Brian Marley stopped blubbering, helplessly obedient even now. He blinked hard several times, shivered convulsively throughout his soaked and emaciated body, then wiped a forearm and backhand over his face, smearing a mixture of blood, sweat, tears, snot, leeches, mosquitoes and various other small, repulsive, salt-licking, blood-sucking, flesh-eating arthropods (many of them uncatalogued and endangered) a little more thinly across his nose and mouth. —That's more like it. Right then. Trousers up and let's show the buggers how an Englishman dies.

There were in fact no Englishmen apart from himself, present or correct, no officer in command of anything and no one to show. Marley was alone in the hellish forest, talking to himself, slumped in a sagging heap, trousers round his knees, forty-three and about to die.

—Can't, he gasped.

—Now see here, laddie, you still *tried* to get your trousers down and if a man can still be bothered trying to get his trousers down, even if he doesn't quite make it in time, then there's still some fight left in him. So no excuses.

—But I won, I won the show, I've got two million pounds waiting in England, this is all so . . . bloody *unfair*, he whimpered again, as if he might yet appeal to something other than the uncaring jungle. The sheer injustice of it all made the helpless tears start again in his eyes.

—Unfair, man? Who ever said it was *fair*? We're here

3

because we're here. Does it mention *fair* in the Good Book or the King's Regulations? Does it buggery. Come on now, Marley, trousers back on, pick up that damn camera and we'll say no more about it.

Marley pawed feebly at his trousers and looked blearily around to locate the bright yellow, waterproofed, shock-resistant, digital satellite camera which had been his constant companion for the past six weeks and which now lay pathetically in the stinking undergrowth. A yard away. Too far to reach. Even if he could hold it steady. Too late for that now.

He groaned softly and heard the dead, echoless sound of his own lonely voice, damped by the soggy, rampant greenery as effectively as if he were sitting in a sound-proofed studio. His head rolled backwards of its own accord, smacking itself hard against the rock wall. He hardly noticed the blow. Yet another nameless insectoid horror, far too big and with far too many legs, wandered across his face, but he only even bothered to brush it idly away when one of its feelers actually began to probe his nostril. He scarcely cared. Death seemed a welcome friend, a mere cessation of horror, a quiet slide into a warm, dark river . . .

—So you're going to die? What do you want, man, the ruddy VC? Every mincing little pox doctor's clerk and every arse-licking shopwalker is going to die. You're one of the lucky ones, for God's sake. How many of the poor sods on *Hood* got the chance to know they were sorting things out for their son and heir? And to leave him a message? Eh?

—Yes, yes, yes, OK, mumbled Marley to his invincible other self. Anything to shut the mad bastard up.

He waited for the next shivering lurch in his body and, when it came, allowed himself to slump sideways, using the small momentum he thus gained to fling out his right arm, so that he could hook two fingers into the grab handle of the camera. He caught hold, dragged it in and cradled it to his panting chest. Then he began the long, seemingly impossible process of hauling himself up on to his feet.

—That's the stuff, Marley!

Marley did not know *why* he had started talking like this to himself, since he had never been anywhere near the Army. But he remembered *when* the voice had begun. It had suddenly come to him, out of nowhere, at the end of the first week, after his seventh unbearable, sleepless vigil in the forest (the days were horrendous, but the nights beggared belief), when he had been on the verge of quickly giving up on the chance of winning *Brit Pluck, Green Hell, Two Million*. That morning, the helicopters had come down to offer the six contestants for the first time the (of course) dramatically televised and (naturally) well-strung-out choice: were they *really* going to stay for another week in the soaking, sauna-hot, pitch-black forest, amid the unbelievable racket of a trillion oversized insects flying, hunting, mating, killing and eating each other (many of them evidently also partial to large, hairless mammals)? Or would they choose instead to fly straight off home, to warmth, sanity, medical care and the consolation of many tabloid interviews? Marley had hesitated, pen in sweating hand, as he looked at the legal waiver which they all had to re-sign each week, before the helicopters left them here again. Live in front of the cameras, he had almost cracked. What chance did he have of winning? Why not give up now, before too much vileness had been endured for nothing? Why pile new, public shame and failure on to the old, private mess of his life?

—Well? Watcha say, Bri'? You comin' home? Fancy a nice warm bath and a nice cold beer wiv me an' the girls, do ya? Decision time, Bri' ... Home for Christmas or Hell in the jungle?

5

Marley remembered the impossibly flawless white teeth in the wide-screen smile of the inane presenter as she had posed the question. He remembered her breasts shoving out against her ludicrous pink T-shirt (*NFR* it had said, in spangly letters distorted by the uplifted, surgically enhanced flesh beneath; he had wondered what the hell that meant). He had almost given in. But at that moment of decision, the insane, military voice had come into his head.

—She's not so dumb, Marley. Trying to make you crack. Get those eyes off her tits. Think of your boy, man. What's another week?

Before Marley had been able to decide, the choice had been made for him. One of the other competitors, a sporty little hairdresser from Edinburgh, had run out from the undergrowth towards the helicopters, screaming and weeping, almost beheading herself with the still-spinning rotor blades as she flung herself into the arms of the smiling TV presenters, still gagging convulsively and unstoppably from having awoken to find a cockroach the size of a mouse clambering about inside her mouth. Talk about a fab start to the series! And so, since only one of the six competitors could leave on each flight, the first to fight his or her way on board being given the place, Marley had been forced to stay on anyway.

From that evening onwards, he had instinctively allowed this bizarre voice inside his head free rein. At first, he had merely used it when talking to himself, but soon he had found himself using it when speaking to the camera which was continually transmitting the horrors of his daily life here back to the 24/7 viewers of *Brit Pluck, Green Hell, Two Million*. He knew that he was clinically mad, talking to himself like this. He was perfectly well aware that it was nuts. But the Voice had kept him going that night, when he had almost wept for home, and it had continued to do so while all around him were gradually but utterly losing their minds and the contents of their bowels. By the time of the second chance to leave, a week later, he had fallen utterly under its spell.

One by one, his rivals had given up, their greed for money and their lust for that modern sainthood, media fame, finally giving way under the unspeakable, crawling, winged nightmare of the rainforest. Each had at last taken the helicopter out in a state of total mental and physical collapse (great telly!). Brian Marley, however, obeying this ruthless yet avuncular parade-ground voice, had even kept up his shaving. It seemed that in pre-emptively embracing lunacy rather than trying to stay sane in a place utterly hostile to human life, let alone civilisation, he had adopted the right tactics.

A fortnight in, failed contestant number two, a handsome young accountant from Bromley whose hobby was skydiving and who had appeared to lack any emotional existence whatever, was forcibly airlifted out because he had become so preoccupied with attempting to dig out with his fingernails the subcutaneous worms infesting his legs that he could not even remember his own name for the cameras, let alone re-sign the legal waiver. That had made good viewing, as had the psychic trauma displayed the following week, when the third would-be double millionaire, a big-boned Lexus saleswoman from Belfast who had been brought up in tinker caravans and had seemed unbreakable, was found eventually, by tracing her radio-location beacon, sitting up a tree doing a very convincing imitation of a bottle-blonde orang-utan. Only his radio-location beacon had saved the fourth member as well: a chatty DIY expert from Yorkshire, he was found almost lifeless in a swamp, one arm lost to crocodiles and incurably insane.

The Great British Public was finding this theatre of

dissolution and collapse as irresistible as Victorian clerks had found tales of Empire: Channel Seven's viewing figures were breaking records which had stood since the days when people had only had two stations to choose from.

After five endless weeks on nothing but salt, bread, water and vitamin C tablets, Marley's body weight had come down to approximately eight stone and the fight for the two million pounds had come down to precisely himself and a bald, divorced, middle-aged schoolteacher from Swansea whom Marley had long realised was his chief danger because what on earth did a bald, divorced, middle-aged schoolteacher from Swansea have to lose? Any sane defence department would recruit entire battalions of bald, divorced, middle-aged schoolteachers as semi-suicidal shock-troops. Throughout the sixth week, Marley and this Welsh schoolteacher had sat or staggered about in the jungle, observing each other's decay warily from as far away as possible, each carrying out in private his by now almost hallucinatory chats with the spellbound audience back home. The stern Voice had kept on giving its military orders and at last, at last, it was the schoolteacher who had cracked.

How clearly Marley could remember the moment, the glorious moment, when the choppers had come down once again and the schoolteacher had crawled towards the landing place, blubbering gratefully, already clearly doomed to lose his left leg to gangrene. Marley had stood and watched quite happily, assuming an At Ease position, saluting the two helicopters in a nonchalant manner. He knew the rules. He was now the sole remaining competitor, he would sign a final legal waiver, they would cart off the destroyed schoolteacher from Swansea and leave him, Brian Marley, there for one further week, a whole week utterly alone, just himself, his mad instructions to himself, the forest, his camera, water (no bread or vitamins for this last week) and many spare batteries. And the two million pounds to hold out for. They would also leave him an emergency beacon with which he could summon them at any time, a permanent temptation to forfeit the prize money. But Marley had known he would not use it. He had watched the helicopters hover slowly down towards him. He had shaken his head amusedly at the frantic waving of the teacher from Swansea, who, having yielded at last to pain and despair, now seemed possessed by the terrifying idea that his rescuers might now turn mockingly around, fly off and leave him here to die after all.

—I want my pension, see, Marley, my pension, I've paid into it for so long, so *bloody* long, all those years with all those *little bastards*, oh yes, it's a very, very good scheme really, nothing in the private sector can compare, I'll even be able to *eat out* once a week or so, you know, so long as I keep saving the newspaper tokens. You go ahead and die here if you want, Marley, I'm getting that bloody pension, I am, and I'm *going home for Christmas*!

—Absolutely, Marley had nodded, smartly. He was invulnerable, for he had no pension at all back in England, and if he did not win here, Christmas would be merely a long haul of duty and guilt. Free of hope, he had known no doubts. One more week of mere physical torment in this place was nothing, nothing at all, compared to the vast lifetime of shame and regret that surely awaited him back in his so-called home . . .

. . . *the thudding wind from the rotors was cool and steady, he could see them coming down, as clearly as if it was next week already, here they came to waft him back in triumph, alive, clean, rich, sending him to embrace his mother and little son in time for a real Christmas after all, and then to take Consuela Martinez in his arms, in an England where at last he could be truly at home . . .*

9

—Put a sock in it, Marley.

—Eh? What? Marley opened his eyes and found to his wailing dismay that he was still alive, still alone and still dying.

—No good to anyone, remembering that sort of stuff. All gone now.

—No, croaked Marley. —No good to anyone now. All gone. Not going home.

All gone, yes. Several perma-grinning young presenters and two entire TV crews had perished, along with all the water, vitamins and replacement battery packs, as well as the emergency GSM beacon, when the two Channel Seven helicopters, vying for the best shots of this climactic point, had managed to collide some fifty feet above Marley and the blubbering Welshman as they came down to land. Marley had watched in disbelief, and at first in something like rage, as the double wreckage had hung impossibly, for whole seconds, like two vast iron dragonflies frantically mating, then plunged towards him, landing plumb on top of the landing site's radio-location device and the wretched schoolteacher.

Marley had not had time to dive for cover. He had been flung back by the blast and half baked by the sudden bloom of appalling heat that followed in its wake. He had fled wildly, trailing smoke from his smouldering clothes, along with every sentient creature for miles around. When he had dared to return, he had found that no one and nothing had survived. It was at this point that he realised his own radio-location beacon was no longer on his wrist. After twenty frantic minutes he had found it where he had fallen when hit by the explosion: melted, deformed, destroyed. He had calmly sent a long clip of footage out on his digital camera and had then stood there amid the smouldering wreckage and the mummified, twisted bodies for several hours, more in numb disbelief than

10

anything else, expecting every moment to see rescue helicopters approaching. But none came. His camera could
only transmit, not receive; he had no way of knowing who,
if anyone, was getting his film. Again and again he had
sent forth pictures and sounds into the empty, pitiless skies
above the small clearing (*Where are you? Surely you can
see the smoke?*) until the horrid forest night had fallen with
its usual awful, equatorial speed. As the last light faded,
Marley, frantically scanning the fast-darkening patch of
sky above his head for any sign of approaching aircraft
(*Hello? Look, I think you should hurry up*), had finally been
driven from the crash site by nightmarish hordes of enormous, slavering crocodiles, drawn out of their depthless,
Jurassic swamps by the scent of flame-grilled Western
flesh. Trying to send yet another camera message
(*Gentlemen, I suggest you beam me aboard*), he had almost
waited too long: in the end, he had escaped those lunging,
prehistoric jaws only by a despairing scramble up into
trees filled with horrific, thigh-wide snakes, unbearable
clouds of mosquitoes, hordes of ticks, armies of leeches,
vast, clattering moths, small but inconceivably deadly
frogs and spiders the size of dinner plates. In the hideous
blackout of the night, he had clambered, yelping with
pre-human terror, from branch to branch by handhold
alone, sometimes brachiating helplessly and uninten-
tionally through the yawning darkness. Then he had fallen
at last, expecting death, but had slid instead God knew
how far down a muddy ravine, climbed blindly, staggered,
blundered crazily again through the forest, and had finally
collapsed into a shivering half-sleep, wedged high in the
crook of a large, slimy tree.

For three days, entirely without food and with only
filthy swamp water to drink, he had tried to find the
wreckage again, knowing that some rescue mission would
be mounted eventually, but it had been no good: he had

somehow become trapped in a steep-sided gorge where his camera could find no signal. And he simply had no idea which way to go: the forest was so impossibly dense that even the mile-high pyre created by the destruction of two well-fuelled choppers was completely invisible a mere hundred yards off. Twice he had thought he heard more helicopters, high up above the sightless canopy of leaves, but he had not been sure, amid the hideous, incessant whirring of insect life, if they had been real or not. He had no way to attract them in any case. A dozen times he had tried to climb the enormous trees and reach the light, but without claws and a prehensile tail it had been a physical impossibility. Each time he had fallen or slid trembling down again, quite sure that only certain death lay that way.

Yesterday, it had got worse. Yesterday the rains had come.

Earth-shaking thunder in the inhuman, unseen heavens above, the insane battering of the downfall on to the forest canopy a hundred feet over his head as endless lightning flashed beyond the dark roof of leaves; waterfalls cascading down between the trees. At first he had rejoiced at being able to drink again. But then he had noticed the swamps rising all around him with impossible speed. He had bludgeoned his way madly through the forest, deafened and blinded by the deluge, raging with fever and terror, wild with hunger and despair. By the time the downpour stopped, he had found himself trapped between a swiftly rising, crocodile-infested morass and a colossal, near-vertical wall of rock.

And so now, today, here he was, standing at the foot of an awe-inspiring cliff that blocked off the world and the sky, lost, alone and dying. It was, strangely, the being alone that seemed most impossible to bear. If there had been a hand, any hand really, to stroke his hair while he

12

died, he would have died gladly and on the spot. Well: we are all surely born to die, the wretched and the great, but perhaps none of us is equipped to last for long alone. So at least thought Brian Marley, with wild deathbed clarity. As he stood and tried not to sway in front of the camera, he was now assaulted by visions not of escape, but merely of a happy death, images pornographic in their luscious, gold-lit, yearning intensity: a man in a four-poster bed, candlelit, surrounded by his children and grandchildren; a man in a mountain tent of animal skins, attended by shamans and weeping relatives; a man in a water-filled shell-hole being given a last cigarette by his comrades. Most bizarre of all: a man in a hospital bed, holding newborn baby twins, with his five-year-old son and young wife beside him, attended by a competent young doctor preparing a big syringe of some gold-tinted, gleaming opiate, a respectful accountant standing by with reassuringly thick wads of insurance documentation, and a priest of some nondescript but mighty denomination, murmuring into Brian Marley's ear, on his warm deathbed, last rites which no priest has ever said but all, perhaps, have really meant. Simple, gentle words which seemed to consist largely of the repeated phrase:

—*Well done*, Brian Marley, well *done . . .*

Marley came to and found himself awake, unsaved, alone. He also found that he had automatically begun to lie down in the sodden filth.

—Not yet, Tommy, not yet, he barked to himself through creaking vocal cords.

His mission was clear and simple: to record his last message, and then to climb. Just to climb, until he found a signal or fell and died first. Perhaps he would find a ledge to die on, up there, somewhere beyond those hated, sun-killing treetops. If he could, he would cram himself into the rocks, tie himself to branches with his belt, send off his message and die. The birds would get him, of course, but at least, that way, they would eventually find *something* of him. He recoiled in illogical horror at the thought of lying down in the stinking filth and simply returning to that liquid, primeval matter as rotting meat for crocs and leeches. Better a sky burial. His last act would be to defy the forest which had killed him. To reach at least the light.

—That'll show the buggers, eh, chaps? So let's get on with it.

—Get on with what?

—Dying, Marley, dying. It's what we're here for, old man.

—Yes, of course.

All his agony and terror was now replaced by a simple wave of animal exhaustion. The logic was inescapable. He was mere hours from death at most. There was, therefore, no hope. Which, in a strange way, was better.

—Come on, come on, chest out, belly in and all that rot.

Marley tried to stand up straight, unsupported by the rock, but his arms and legs felt as though they were composed of wet, cold spaghetti; his guts seemed to be a mass of sodden old tennis netting that might at any time simply drop rotting through his loosened pelvis; his head was a monstrous, liquid-filled, lolling weight upon a ludicrously skinny pole. His eyes were more and more determined to roll backwards into his skull. Even the fetid tendrils of the forest seemed an inviting bed. He began to drift away from the rock wall and to sway back downwards again towards the warm, green filth . . .

—No you don't, Marley.

—What? What?

—You forgetting something again? For God's sake, Marley, what do you call that damn thing in your hand?

14

Marley looked down at his right hand.

—Oh yes, camera, he croaked.

—Exactly. You've still got your boy to think about. Biggest privilege a man can have. Chance to show him what you were made of, show him how you took it. Leave him something to be proud of. Last letter home. And don't give me any of that telling-the-truth bollocks. Only spotty little teenagers and German bloody philosophers are interested in the truth. The truth is for the Lord God Almighty to know and for you and me to shut up about. Give the poor little sod something good to remember his daddy by, that's what we want, isn't it? So pull yourself together, man. Just this one little job to do, then I'll let you sleep till the Archangel Gabriel blows his ruddy trumpet.

Marley blinked. Yes. A message to his son. A chance to make a last impression on the world, to leave some mark of himself behind. He would be more than scattered bones in mould. A picture in oils, a carving in marble, an enamelled vignette on a gravestone. He would die humanly, with a name and a face, not as an unknown beast.

—That's it, laddie, get set.

Marley had one little son, Tommy, to show for all his forty-three years on earth, for some twenty-four years' regular enough sexual activity with various women. Not a great hit rate, perhaps. Not much, compared to an Orthodox Jew in New York, a reasonably successful Kalahari bushman or a proud, penniless farmer in the mountains of Afghanistan, maybe. Not exactly the stuff of which empires are won, built up and peopled, true. And yet there was, or at least so it seemed to Brian Marley as he prepared unexpectedly to die, every difference in this world and the next between an obituary that finishes with *he leaves no children* and one that concludes *he is survived by a son*.

15

—Good man, Marley, that's the spirit.

As for Consuela Martinez, what could he say to her? Nothing. He hardly knew her, except as an impossible dream. He had only ever kissed her once; to leave a message for her would be simply laughable. So he would not. He would save the private, impossible dream of her eyes, her hair, her mouth for his last breath, his last thought. He had read somewhere that Hell or Heaven are defined simply by the last image created in your dying mind: if that last vision is bad, if it is fearful, rancid, sour and bitter, then your life has been a logical and inevitable progression to Hell; if it is suffused with light, love and hope, then Heaven is gifted to you automatically. Perhaps. At any rate, that was the only hope he had, so that was the way it would be: he would now record his last message to his son, then climb towards the sky until his camera found a signal. He would press SEND and, knowing that his last words were flying off, digitally encoded and thus almost eternal, towards some unseen circling satellite, sure now that his little boy would have something from him, he would hug his dream of Consuela tight, let go, fall and die.

—Right then, let's give them something to write home about, chaps.

Marley somehow hoisted himself to his feet again. He braced himself arse-wise against the rock face. He noted a small, knurled tree some three feet in front of him. He breathed deeply, and after some seconds of looking down at his right foot, located the nerves that connected this foot, unlikely as it seemed, to his brain. He asked the foot to move. It did nothing. He concentrated harder, glaring wildly at his torn and rotting boot. At last, his foot shivered and left the ground. Marley quickly grabbed hold of what remained of his calf muscles with a mental arm and swung the foot forwards, then immediately commanded that side of his body to follow the impetus. It worked. His body swayed towards the tree and his right arm, almost of its own accord (*well done, that right arm!*) caught the thin, slimy trunk of the tree and held his weight. With his left hand he now stuffed the camera into a likely crook of branches. It held tight. He lowered his head and slowly pushed himself away from the little tree. Gradually, wheezing, he straightened himself up. He was now looking at the camera. It seemed wedged at the right height. He shook out his creaking, bony shoulders, braced his weight on his shivering hips, and stretched out both hands. He saw them, his old man's hands, make landfall on the camera. He forced them to stay still and quiet on the warm yellow plastic. Then, with infinite care, he instructed his right hand to hold the camera fast where it was, while his even feebler left hand was sent off to remove the precious lens cap. It fell from his shaking fingers, and was immediately lost for good in the calf-deep mush underfoot. Marley did not care. This was the last time he would use the lens cap; he felt like some cowboy hero opening his whiskey and throwing away the cork. It would not be needed in this universe again.

Making sure once more that the camera was firmly placed, Marley took a painful, careful step back from it, feeling for his footholds in the slimy half-ground. He slipped, grunted, caught himself, and stood straight again, held backwards on the hard stone. Through the eternal clouds of fat, black mosquitoes and ghastly, swarming sweat-bees, he looked into the camera's blank, black eye.

In it, he saw, reflected in the awful green half-light of this terrible forest, a terrible figure: himself, unrecognisable. A stranger, wild, mouth agape, face eaten away, being eaten away further even as he watched by a thousand nameless mouths, hair stuck in blood-caked, dung-like wads to a head which was already halfway to a skull. Dying? Christ, he was already rotting away. He could not show this to his son.

—For God's sake, man. Look at yourself. You're a bloody disgrace. Shut that mouth for a start. Sergeant Major, I'm surprised at you, letting this man give a last message to his own son in this state.

Marley willed his mouth to shut, and eventually saw it do so in the dull reflection. He felt as triumphant as if he had just commanded some distant cybernetic jawbone to close, by mental impulse alone, before a disbelieving crowd of scientific journalists. Encouraged, almost ecstatic at this proof that his mind could even now exercise some kind of dominance over his biodegrading pre-corpse, he scrabbled his hair into a remote semblance of a humanoid parting and tried frantically to imagine the son he was about to talk to.

It was not Tommy as he was now, a mere three years old. What possible good is there explaining anything to a three-year-old? Three-year-olds just have to be told that God is in His Heaven, Father Christmas is up the chimney and everything is all right. So who was Marley talking to? At what age do boys become human? When could Tommy ever understand? Boys do not become human beings till about twenty-six, ask any car-insurance number-cruncher. OK then. Tommy at twenty-six, listening to him over a quiet beer in a good old-fashioned pub. A man listening to his own father, and learning. How old would he, Marley, be? What year would it be? Marley grew dizzy at the sound of the science-fiction dates that came out, which he would now never reach.

An insistent peeping, too regular to be that of some unknown animal or bird, pulled Marley back from the brink of fainting once again. It was the camera, pleading electronically with him for more life. PLEASE REPLACE BATTERY PACK it blinked hysterically. Marley cackled viciously at this spineless bit of high-tech whingeing.

—Fat chance, old boy, he laughed. —Better ask the boffins. Oh, sorry, forgot, the boffins bought it, didn't they? Ha!

Marley slowly stretched forth his finger to press the record button on the camera. But as soon as he touched it, he withdrew his finger in sudden, electric panic.

A new fear seized him, a ludicrous, absurd fear which was somehow more deeply terrifying than all the horrors of the forest, a fear which he now knew had been lurking in the unswept crevasses of his mind for as long as he could remember, waiting its moment, prowling through all his life in a dark jungle, stalking him.

How was he going to speak?

How did he, himself, Brian Marley, really speak?

Marley blinked in quiet panic while the dank, deadly forest all around him seemed to hold its panting breath and wait.

What did his real voice sound like? Not the mad military voice that had been ordering him around, of course. That was not how he wanted his son to remember him. That was not really him.

But then, what was?

The ridiculous, falsely enthusiastic, carefree voice he used to his boss at work? No. That was a blatant lie. What, then? The accent he put on in tough pubs when he was trying to disguise how middle class he really was? Or the accent he tried in scary restaurants when he was trying to disguise how middle class he really was? The chipper tone he assumed when reassuring his mother vaguely that everything was going to *work out* somehow despite his apparently complete failure in life? The ludicrous, shameful, sub-Oxbridge drawl he had learned to

19

use at college and still fell into with his old college friends? The would-be semi-transatlantic twang that always began to infect him after a few days spent with Americans? The risible faux-Irish throatiness that he affected when he sang folk songs in allegedly authentic theme pubs to impress his foreign women? The bizarrely unreal, Spanish-influenced rhythms he had started falling into when talking to Consuela Martinez?

Which? How? Who?

Marley's body stood frozen before the soaring rock face, but his mind staggered with internal vertigo as he stared into the endless, meaningless blackness of his own self. Where his voice should have been, where *he* should have been, there was nothing but a dizzying void.

Yet he had to speak, here and now, or die in eternal silence. By the time Tommy could understand this, Marley's bones would be dust. This would be all that was left. Digital immortality or eternal silence: it had to be done and it had to be done right and it had to be done right here and now.

—Pull your socks up, Marley.

—Piss off! You're not me! Marley cleared his throat and his mind desperately.

With his shivering finger poised over the button in case he should miraculously hit the authentic tone of himself, he tried to begin speaking to his real three-year-old son at the imagined age of twenty-six, across the gap of twenty and more post-mortal years.

Christ, if only he was Irish. They knew how they sounded. Or Scots. No problem for them. Welsh, what-ever. Anyone who knew exactly what they were supposed to sound like and just did it without thinking. Someone who knew exactly who they were. A Geordie, a Scouser, even a Brummie for fuck's sake, there, see, *for fuck's sake*, that was not him, that was not how *he* spoke, that was something to do with Ireland or Australia or something, that was someone else, that was learned, taken on, taken up, borrowed. A caveman, that would be real. A lump of unthinking primate. He would just look at the camera and smile and wave goodbye. He had nothing to say to his little son because how can you say anything true if you don't even know that the voice and the words you are using are yours? He had nothing to leave. He would just lie down here in the jungle for a bit, ah, that was better already, he would dissolve gratefully away into nothingness. Daddy says goodbye. Daddy is waving goodbye, goodbye . . .

—Daddy, he said aloud, imagining Tommy's voice mourning him.

He opened his eyes with an inaudible snap and found himself lying on his back, looking through thin, dry, dappling leaves at the blinding sun as it hung just clear of the mighty, rearing cliff. The light did not hurt his eyes. He blinked again.

—Daddy, he said again, carefully, listening to the sound with ears suddenly cocked. —Daddy.

That was it. No sound of lies or pretence. The small tone was pure. It sang. Daddy. Marley stared up into the fiery light above him and swallowed with infinite care, fearful of disturbing the crystalline gyroscope of his humming vocal and mental cords. He could hear quite clearly the clicks of his own disbelieving eyelids, blinking.

—Daddy, he said again, and pressed his right middle finger to his temple, just above his brow, where he seemed to have felt some secret resonance, as if to fix that tone and timbre tight at a distinct physical point. His finger still jammed hard against the thin skin and flat bone, he slowly, very slowly, got to his feet. He raised himself up, feeling each vertebra unwind cautiously.

At last he stood once again, silent before the camera,

his finger locked tight to the point on his forehead where he had felt that echo of some tiny but undeniable truth about himself. *Daddy*. He closed his eyes. Time ceased. He breathed, deep and slow and wide. In the endless spaces of his mind, the word grew and created a still region of peace. *Daddy*. He summoned up all the thoughts and insights he had gathered here, in the sleepless, lonely weeks. Unconsciously, he nodded to himself, as a prisoner kneeling at the block might nod to the headsman. Time it was. He opened his eyes and stretched out the index finger of his left hand. The camera's soft-feel switch clicked sweetly. The lights came alive, blinking. Reluctantly, it seemed, the little miracle of space-age manufacture, sitting here in this timeless forest like some incomprehensible object from an unimaginably distant alien star, signalled that it was, however briefly, ready once again to immortalise the voice and face of what would soon once have been Brian Marley.

—*Daddy here*, he began. —*Not much time now. I, well, I, er, look, I'm sorry I missed Christmas with you, sweetheart. But really, I just wanted to explain to you why you haven't got a daddy. A dad. For God's sake, pull yourself together, man, OK, OK, there, I'm trying, I* . . .

And so he eventually pulled himself together and stood up straight again and, in the end, despite several bouts of uncontrollable collapse in his guts and heart and tear ducts, he managed to tell his son what he thought his son should know, about him and about living.

Then, dying, with his precious camera strapped to his belly, which itself felt like it was sticking to his backbone, he climbed up the sheer purple rock face of the Wall.

He climbed in a strange ecstasy of pain and exhaustion, and as he climbed, he knew that this feeling of omnipotence, of absolute trust in the grasp of his weak hands and the grip of his ragged toes, came simply from a scorn of death. He climbed like a wild boy in a tree, to whom the question of how the hell he is ever going to get down again has simply never occurred and who therefore never bothers to look down and thus has no inkling of fear. This freedom from all future he found exhilarating: he was simply going up and up and when he stopped being able to go up that would be it. There was nothing to harbour his strength for now, no second thoughts and no bets to hedge. He was climbing and that was all, as he was climbing he climbed, nothing more, he was pure deed at last and had never felt so utterly, completely alive.

—That's the way, laddie, *per ardua ad astra*, eh? Do not despair for Johnny head-in-air.

Marley stopped, clung to a vine and, without looking down, turned the camera on for perhaps the twentieth time. NO SIGNAL AVAILABLE it said weakly. So he turned it off again and climbed on. No signal yet, perhaps, but at least the air was fresher here, the suffocating breath of the forest had left him and his lungs worked freely again in the sunlit air. For the first time in weeks he saw the world without a permanent, speckly, dancing filter of mosquitoes. He breathed in the cool light and the blue silence, stretched out his hands one after the other, to their utmost reach, the absolute limits of their strength, and found there were still reserves to call on. He had escaped the darkness. He was heading straight towards the sun on a one-way ticket. From somewhere deep inside his mind, as if uncovered, like a fossil in sand, by the erosion of his life, a strange picture formed in Marley's mind. A long-forgotten image of a man in his position, a spaceman climbing a mountain. It reminded him of days as a sick child, for some reason. Marley climbed on, keeping the rhythm of his death-clamber without missing a beat, and, as if obeying this merciless beat, the mists of his mind cleared and with extraordinary clarity the original of his vision burst to the surface from the measureless deeps of his forgotten past:

On and on he climbed, stopping, checking his camera, shrugging, climbing again. As he climbed, as his body strained and tore to its uttermost limits, his mind wandered free, reeling idly backwards and forwards through the endless vaults of his long-lost, unclear memories. Through this mist, he climbed and climbed and climbed.

After some immeasurable period of timeless time, it might have been a mere half-hour of solid climbing, it might just as well have been half a day, Marley saw, a few dozen feet up and to his right, what looked like a ledge, the sudden out-sprouting of substantial bushes and moss which must indicate a rootable place. There seemed to be a cleft, a tiny gorge in the rock face beyond. A gap for a signal to get through, perhaps? And he needed a rest. He began to swing himself upwards, hand over hand, towards it.

But it was as if the mere sight of a possible goal, a tiny shred of something even distantly related to hope, was too much. With mad, high-altitude clarity, he realised that his strength really was at an end now, at any minute his body was simply going to give in, shut down like a machine, let go of everything and fall. Suddenly, he had to fight the desire to look down, and his heart jumped sickeningly as the sense of what lay below almost overwhelmed him. By the time he reached the lip of the rock he was almost gone. A final gasping swing of his shuddering legs brought his knee, and then at last sufficient of his body weight, on to the ledge for him to scrabble up to it, roll over and then flop down on his back, gasping in the hot, bright rays, chest heaving, heart open, ready for the end at last.

He lay there a while in his snug nook and cranny, his cloud-high, sunlit deathbed.

Blindly, he felt for the camera. He rolled feebly over, away from the infinite precipice, towards the cool shade of the bushes, so that he could lie on the thick carpet of bright green moss and raise the camera towards the endless bowl of the sky, as if the tiny length of his arm might somehow make all the difference in the world, might summon forth a signal from the brilliant, uncaring ether.

The camera flickered into life. And then, impossibly, the signal indicators blinked and said: BATTERY LIFE REMAINING 2% READY TO SEND.

Not daring to breathe, Marley stretched forth his other hand to press the button that would send his pre-recorded, dying message flying through the stratosphere, that would ensure that his voice and face would be preserved for ever in a digitised eternity and in the living memory of his little boy . . .

Then he fell.

The ledge was, it turned out, not a ledge at all but merely the lip of a steep, sharp, knife-edged scarp disguised by the felty moss. Down went Marley on the other side, with a small yelp that sounded more like a feeble protest against some minor injustice than a cry of mortal fear.

The next few seconds were a whirling blur of surprise, of half sliding and virtual free fall through trees and shrubs large and small. Marley shielded his eyes with both arms by some deep instinct until after several endless moments of this painful descent, he finally took clean off and away from the rock. He had just enough time in the air to consciously embrace this as his last moment of life before he crashed down through a tall clump of hard bushes, landed with a thud that seemed to dislocate his entire skeleton, rolled several yards under the transferred momentum of his impact, and finally came to a dead stop.

For a long time he lay there, winded, aware only, through his closed eyelids, of the orange heat of the sun.

Quietly, incredulously, his nervous system started to reboot itself from the stunning crash and to scan itself for information as to its current status. He began to register a hardness, a stony lumpiness under the back of his skull. He shifted his head with great care, like a desperate patient, half asleep, trying to get more comfortable on a thin hospital pillow without waking himself up. He stopped. There was no doubt about it. The ground under the back of his head was firm, not swampy and soggy. He smelled strange, heady, woody perfumes and hot dust. Slowly, he began to move his fingers, investigating this impossible solidity beneath him. He softly worked the nails of both his hands and felt that the soil was thin, dry, rocky. He was, it seemed, no longer in the hated jungle.

Since this was clearly nonsense, he simply lay there for some more time, eyes still closed, licking his cracked lips. The sun moved imperceptibly across the orange screen of his non-vision as he drifted in and out of consciousness. Amid the heavy, herbaceous smells he heard insects, but these were mere background noises, friendly punctuations of the stillness, soothing even, after the hideous, non-stop, crawling, munching whirr of the rainforest. At length, he found the dullness in his mind clearing of its own accord, like shreds of fog lifting in a sunlit valley.

Without in the least actively wishing to think about anything at all, he started to consider the impossibility of his present situation. He first wondered whether it was the absolute proof of his death. He weighed up the now rational possibility that the Bible was, in fact, literally true and that he had died and landed in some hot, dusty ante-room to judgement, an oasis between the Tigris and the Euphrates perhaps, or on the banks of the Jordan.

There was now, however, a different noise, a noise so thoroughly impossible that Marley immediately decided that he was not just possibly, but very certainly dead. He opened his eyes slowly, wary of his first look at this unexpected afterlife.

He was at once blinded by the luminous white clouds that filled the sky above him. Quickly, instinctively, he turned his head to one side (thus incidentally proving to himself that his spine was still working) and so found himself staring at a small hedge-like tangle of some unknown bush or shrub with flowers of a violent red. It gave off the heavy scent that filled the air. Through it, Marley could see nothing, but he could hear that sound again.

Interesting, thought Marley's brain. He had never played cricket with a real leather ball and real bats and so forth; he had never even watched a real cricket match with any conscious interest (apart from in the pub, the last hours of Botham's Victory in 1981, of course). Thus he had never actually heard the fabled sound of willow on leather, nor the ripple of polite, knowledgeable applause from a small English crowd. And yet somehow, he knew instantly that this was exactly what he was hearing.

Cthwock! clappetyclappetyclap.

—Well played, Hawkins.

Marley breathed and smiled. So this was what death was like, after all: a warm homecoming to something we have never truly known but yet missed all our lives, the end of all that strange, shadowy homesickness and yearning that haunts us all our years like the long, still shadows on a lonely summer evening. A comfortable, final, opiate dispensation of the acquired imagination. He let his head roll back and closed his eyes again. Goodbye, goodbye, goodbye . . .

. . . At this point there was a sudden loud rushing and crackling in the bushes, and before Marley's dazed hearing could triangulate itself enough to register that whatever was causing this noise was heading straight for him, he received a smart blow on the left ear and shot upright in pain.

Beside him lay a very old but quite undeniable cricket ball.

Without thinking, almost more surprised that he could sit up than that he should have been hit on the ear, here, by a cricket ball, he picked it up and was thus holding it, looking at it dumbly, when a tall, lithe, tanned, blond, blue-eyed youth of perhaps fourteen came bounding through the bushes, dressed in long, once-khaki shorts and a white cotton shirt, both heavily repaired. When he saw Marley he stopped dead and stared. Before the amazed young man could speak, Marley upon some instinct tossed the cricket ball to him; he caught it with a neat and pure reflex, his eyes still fixed on Marley.

—Well held, croaked Marley.

—I say, are you English?

—English? Of course I'm bloody English, said Marley.
—Lieutenant, have this idiot boy put on a charge.

Then his mind and spine gave way simultaneously. His eyes rolled backwards into their sockets, his shoulders fell, his head met the hard ground with a stony thump

28

which he seemed to hear rather than feel, and he began to float-fall, smiling inanely, down a long, dark, grateful shaft, hearing as he fell these last, impossible words:

—Golly! I say sir Headmaster sir over here sir. I think it's an Englishman!

II

GET RICH OR DIE TRYING

England, Seven Weeks Earlier

Brian Marley finished his cold little Spanish beer and put the glass down slowly, so as to appear relaxed and so as to delay by one final second or two the awful moment when he would have to say goodbye to Consuela Martinez, which was also the moment he would have to try to kiss her, to risk the almost certain shame and failure of trying to kiss her.

As the beer glass settled undeniably on the table, leaving him with no further excuse for inaction, Marley feverishly recounted to himself all the little signs he thought he had spied in her over the past weeks: those minute variations of her walk, of the way she held her head, of her eyes and hands, that had seemed, when he added them all up in the long nights, to say that it was not impossible. And after all, she had come out with him for this drink. But then he weighed this circumstantial evidence dispiritingly against the certain facts that she was ten years younger than he was, that she was beautiful and admired, that he was her teacher for God's sake and that she was in any case going home to Argentina in a few weeks' time. The scales tilted firmly: hopeless. And yet he had no choice, because if he did not try to kiss her now, he would never try again, and that meant he might as well give up for good, because he had never expected to feel this way ever again at his age and he was sure he would never feel this way again and . . .

. . . And so he swallowed and then looked boldly at her. She seemed to be reading her beer bottle carefully, as she told him about her father.

Her father, it seemed, liked the English. Her father especially liked RAF pilots from the Second World War, that was why he had grown his proud moustaches. He loved to visit the Royal Air Forces Association in Buenos Aires and was always glad to talk about his battles, to the BBC especially. Recently he had escorted the Chief of the Air Staff of England around the Fuerza Aerea's College at Cordoba and had reminisced about that unforgettable day when he had sunk that big English warship off Las Malvinas. Air Colonel Martinez, she said, had often been invited to RAF messes to discuss the war and fly 'shotgun' (as he apparently delighted in calling it) in their two-seat planes. The young English pilots loved to watch that famous tape from her father's cockpit camera, to hear him crying, twenty years before, as young then as they were now, ¡Gringo de la mierda! ¡Por la patria! as he plunged suicidally through a wall of tracer bullets, Sea Slug missiles and Triple-A, to see the cannon shells from his Mirage splash and burst into the water before they tracked in to ignite the under-gunned, top-heavy, soft-skinned frigate.

—God, yes, I remember seeing that, said Marley.

—That was your father?

—Yes. Always he say to me, Daughter, what other nation would understand me when I raise my glass and tell them that I am happiest to have destroyed an *English* warship?

—Well, yes, I suppose.

—So that is my father.

—Right.

There was no putting it off any longer. The silence must not be allowed to outgrow this moment. Marley had rehearsed his next speech in many night-time daydreams (dreams which he had always dutifully forbidden to go any further than this first moment). He knew very well what he was going to say. And if he did not say it now he would never say it. Right, then.

—I, um, I was thinking, you know, about the, er, the Oxford and Shakespeare weekend, next weekend, I mean, the class trip.

—Yes? She looked up at him. The shape of her dark eyes made him feel dizzy with hopeless longing.

—I mean, you *are* coming? It's just, I saw, I happened to notice I mean, that your name wasn't on the list.

—I think yes I come. You are our teacher on this trip?

—Yes.

—I am not seeing your name on the list for signing.

—No, I wasn't sure, you see, because of my son. But I am now. Sure, I mean. What I mean is, look, yes I'm definitely leading the trip next weekend so are you coming?

—I am signing up for it tomorrow.

—Good. Oh good. I think it'll be very . . . nice.

—Also I think.

—Right. Well, look, Consuela, I am having to go, sorry, no, that's wrong of course, don't say it like that, what I meant was *I've got to go*, to get my son. I'm taking him away this weekend. So I can be free next weekend, you see. For the trip.

—You are a good father I think.

—Ha. I try. Um, right. Charlie, can you put them on my tab, please? Got to go. Bit short of cash.

—Right you are, Brian, smiled the cool young bar owner.

—You are taking your son far?

—No, just Kent.

—Ah yes, this garden of England.

—But I'll be back for the class on Monday, of course.

—Yes.

—Right.

And so then he kissed her. He did so rather more quickly and rather more blushingly and rather less smack on the mouth than he had planned over the past few weeks, but still, there was no real doubt about it. He had kissed her, and at least partly on the mouth. And she did not look shocked or disgusted or amused or any of the other things she could have looked like. Instead, she looked as if she were still waiting, as if he had not really kissed her yet at all. So he got up a bit more hastily than he had planned and banged his knees on the table much more than he had planned and only turned round to wave once before he was gone.

—I have other margarita, please, Charlee, called Consuela Martinez brightly, reaching for her little leather purse.

—No worries, said the cool young bar owner. Beside him, his cool young wife noisily put a Deep Chill-Out Trance compilation on the CD player and lit another joss stick vengefully.

—Full price for her now, she snap-whispered.

—How can I? She's been here for an hour with Brian.

—And he bought the drinks. Which *he* gets half-price. Which is why he comes here.

—Well, I can hardly just double the price for her now, can I?

—Why the hell not? That's the whole *point* of giving Brian half-price drinks, for God's sake. So he'll bring his students here, so that *they* can pay *full*-price, cool? Didn't think she was your type. Not thin enough, I would have thought. Too old. Thought you preferred to give our profits away to the thin young wasted ones with pierced navels. Like at Glastonbury last year.

—Oh, for God's sake, not that again.

—Don't worry, I counted the tofu burgers you gave away that second afternoon, and it was *always* to the thin little whacked-out, smackhead ones. I mean, sorry, but since when exactly is this *Brian* some friend of ours? He brings in the punters, that's all. Just another scabby bloody Foreign Language Teacher. You know what they're like.

All perverts. Suppose you're jealous of him, are you? Me, I never trust a man who only fucks foreign women.

—OK, OK, Happy Hour is officially over.

Consuela Martinez drank her drink (¡it was too expensive!), then she left the bar and walked down to Trafalgar Square and sat by a big bronze lion and wrote a postcard to her father. When she had posted it she went down Whitehall to look at the handsome guardsmen on their horses, so English in their shining armour that they had frozen completely over into utter immobility, like statues in a museum of ancient warfare.

*

—Sorry, sorry, murmured Marley absently to the countless unknown people who shoved past him as he escalated clankingly up from the bowels of the cold earth and out into the grey November light of Shepherd's Bush Central Line tube station.

—What you on, mate? demanded someone, and Marley, looking round as if waking up, realised that he was standing on the wrong side of the steps and smiling idiotically. Curing the first part was no problem, a quick sidestep put paid to any further escalator rage, but the second bit was more difficult because the smile on his face, far from obeying his command to behave itself, kept on trying hard to escape his control completely and burst out of its cocoon as fully-fledged laughter or even song.

He had done it. He had kissed her. He, mere Brian Marley, had kissed the gorgeous Consuela Martinez. Incredible. Since his divorce he had had only a couple of meaningless little flings, but now he had kissed Consuela and had not been scorned and his whole life felt backlit by an emotion he had almost forgotten: hope.

He shuffled forward dreamily amid the crowd, lost in this half-remembered sensation. It was like the sun on his face. He suddenly remembered being a newspaper-delivery boy in the seventies, pushing a vast old creaking pram stacked with Sunday newspapers across a frosted-over park at dawn, the universe almost monochrome, grey–blue–green and dusted white, the streets around piled with uncleared, frozen rubbish bags, the newspaper headlines that joggled before him shouting of strikes and despair, but he feeling the first, weak yellow rays of the sun warming his cheeks, hearing ducks calling from somewhere through the unfrosting world, his head filled with vague dreams of girls and colleges and the vast, unknown life to come. Sheer hope.

He was so far away from Shepherd's Bush and here and now that when a little old lady stepped neatly out before him, half blocking his path, he noticed her so late as to almost walk right into her.

—Oh, sorry, he murmured. She smiled up at him. Dimly, he realised that she had blocked his path quite deliberately and that her delicately painted eyebrows were making a hopeful, chirpy little effort especially for him. —Oh, sorry, um, can I . . .? he began. Then he saw that she was shaking something at him. A collecting tin. He looked down and saw her little cardboard tray of little red artificial poppies. She smiled again, with a slight, inviting, almost coquettish upward sway of her tray. —Oh, oh yes, of course, laughed Marley, and patted his hip pocket instinctively.

Changle-chink went the coins in Marley's pocket and the happy new world about him collapsed in spectacular ruin. He blinked, and suddenly Shepherd's Bush tube station was no longer suffused with the golden, dawn light of his mind, but lit with nasty, grey neon.

—Would you like a poppy? sang the old lady, confident in her leading question.

—Aha, he said, smiled wanly and dug blushingly into

38

his pocket. Feigning a stuck hand, he sifted feverishly amid the body-warm metal tokens, trying to make sure that when he brought his hand out again, he did not dredge up, along with the general shrapnel, any of the four two-pound coins which, he now recalled with horrid certainty, were pretty well all he had left.

If he gave her one of *those*, it would mean another trip to a cash machine this afternoon so as to buy his son, Tommy, tea in a café, and he did not want to go to a cash machine before his next month's pay cleared on Monday, because if he went to a cash machine today it would merrily ask him if he wanted to check his balance, which, even if he managed to resist looking at the dreaded non-balance, would inevitably make him think about the fact that his next cheque, even when cleared, would not so much as cover his running debt. And then, far worse, there was always the lurking, sweat-inducing, nuclear possibility that he might already have reached his new improved overdraft limit (*Why Wait? Get It Now With A Personal Credit Extension!*), and that the machine would simply laugh in his face when he asked it for still more as yet unearned cash. In which case he would only be able to get Tommy a McDonald's Happy Meal somewhere on the M25 and then he would have to sit and watch him eat fat and salt and sugar and feel guilty about feeding his little son fat and salt and sugar and secretly wish he could afford some happy fat and salt and sugar for himself too. Christ. Yes, and Christmas still to come . . . He simply *had* to make his stupid little flat nice for Tommy, for their modern, jolly, post-divorce Christmas. And then it was his mother's seventieth birthday, he had to do something special for *that*, when was he finally going to be able to do something really good with her, take her away somewhere really nice, whatever, did he think she was going to live for ever? And worst of all: next weekend he was going to be in Oxford with Consuela Martinez and she had just let him kiss her and he had, absolutely *had* to be able to spend merrily with her, not to try to *impress* her, no, she was not like that and nor was he, he just dreaded the greasy horror of pretending to check what looked nice on the menu in the restaurant window while secretly looking straight at the prices. He had been doing that all his life, literally and figuratively, he was *not* going to go, yet again, through the ghastly routine of saying he was *not really hungry enough* for a starter himself, that the house wine was *probably fine*, that he did not *really like* pudding, not with her, not this time, this was different, this *had* to be different, this was . . .

—Thank you *so* much for stopping, sang the old lady, swiftly fixing the little plastic-and-paper flower to Marley's lapel with her small hand. He saw the cling-film-thin skin over her pale veins. He pictured her standing there all through the uncaring day. And at that very moment a tall red bus, a real, proper, old, open-stair, conductor-manned bus, trundled slowly eastwards past the station entrance, towards the West End, right in front of him. Its reflecting lower-deck windows treated him to a swift flicking series of full-length images, like a child's thumbnail cartoon: himself, standing in the entrance of the neon-lit station, a man in his early forties, of normal English height and appearance, wearing a tweed jacket, a plain cotton shirt with no tie, blue jeans without ridiculous design features, dark socks and rather expensive brown leather shoes with proper laces and soles, his hand struggling absurdly in his pocket as he stood before a smiling little old lady jangling a hopeful tin as she collected alms for ancient, maimed soldiers.

Shame flooded him. Of course the old lady had picked on him, she had seen a normal, decent poppy-buying Englishman who wore this sort of thing without thinking about it. She was not to know, any more than Consuela had known, that his jacket was second-hand and the whole get-up was actually just his wretched quasi-uniform, the rig of all established Teachers of English as a Foreign Language from Bournemouth to Bangkok. They could not tell that he was only still in England because he was now a part-time single father with a three-year-old son and, since he could not abandon his son, he could no longer do what your normal TEFLer does whenever things get too tough or too real, i.e. flee to some new foreign country where he can play the English card again. Nothing showed that he was not, in fact, a happy, easygoing Englishman who was working at the London English School in Piccadilly simply because he loved teaching people his beloved English language, but a wretched failure who could think of no other way to pay the bills.

The big red bus passed by, the flickering picture show finished, and Marley was left there, standing beside the old lady, staring out at the street and staggering inwardly as he saw his own life in sudden, merciless, arc-lit clarity. He had kissed Consuela Martinez under completely false pretences and now he was hoping to sleep with her under them too. He was nothing but a liar and a cheat and an arse.

—Any contribution will do, said the old lady, a touch pointedly.

—Ah, he said. It was no good. He could no longer bear the shame of trying *too* obviously to select what he brought out from his pocket, so he just grabbed whatever was there, hoped, slid out his hand and revealed a palmful of coins. He looked down. Nestling atop a small scrap heap of blatantly useless and patently ungiveable copper coins, all four of his big two-pounders grinned up at him, silver and gold, bereft of any cover and quite undeniable.

—Ha, said Marley, and gave up after a brief but hopeless

battle. He clinked one of the fat, heavy coins into the collecting tin. McDonald's it might have to be, then.

—Thank you, smiled the old lady, and then, as street-wise in her own way as any seller of the *Big Issue*, and far more confident in the selfless justice of her cause, she was already shifting her eyes and smile while the iron was hot, grasping this vital moment, like street sellers everywhere do, to see if any of the other hurrying travellers who had seen the little drama of Marley's yielding might be fixed by her gaze and shamed righteously into following suit.

—Ha, said Marley again, this time to no one, and hurriedly joined the stream of pedestrians. The little poppy now stood in his lapel, pinned just at the fading lower edge of his vision. It mocked the low pretence of his existence. After a few paces, he stopped dead in the busy street, like a man who has just walked into an unexpected lamp-post, causing a small chain reaction of collisions and outraged remarks on the crowded pavement behind him. Apologising to one and all, *sorry, I was, um, sorry, oh, excuse me*, he wrestled to maintain some kind of control over his tail-spinning existence. He tried desperately to limit the damage and avoid a catastrophic depressurisation of his life, but the memory of that kiss mocked him, a tiny feather of bulletproof truth brushing across his lying lips. He had done it all right. He was her teacher and she had trusted him and believed in him and he had lied and he had kissed her. True, he might *get* her (the word made him cringe) by lying. And yes, the impossible might, *might* happen (well, it might, impossible things did happen, life on earth existed in an endlessly wheeling, infinite, frozen universe, for example). She might, impossibly, *might* want to stay in England with him. And then? Aha! The thought of his flat in Acton, the only thing he had been able to afford after his divorce, and which was now, in the *ongoing downturn* (as the Chancellor of the Exchequer still insisted on calling it) worth scarcely what he had paid for it last year, made him shudder as it always did. He could already see the dismay in her lovely eyes as he opened the highly secure but unutterably vile white plastic door for her, and displayed the reality of his existence . . .

No, no, no. He took out his phone and called work, hurrying before his cunning second thoughts could inveigle him into a fine and rational debate which, as they knew from long experience, they would almost certainly win.

—Hi, it's Brian here. Look, I'm really sorry, childcare disaster, you know, I'm going to have to drop out of taking the Oxford and Shakespeare trip next weekend. I know, I'm really sorry, I'm sure someone else'll do it, they all need the money. OK. Thanks. Sorry again. Yeah, see you Monday.

He killed the phone and stood there in the street. There. Right. Done. The right thing. He made a mighty effort and shouldered the door closed on the hopeless memory of Consuela Martinez's eyes. The locks and firewalls of his mind creaked, but then snapped shut and held. There. He breathed deeply, then began walking swiftly down the little street towards his mother's flat near the BBC.

That was how his mother always described it, *near the BBC*. It reminded Marley of some aged German farmer's wife blushingly admitting that she had once nearly touched Hitler's coat, or a shrivelled Russian grandfather with a wind-beaten, drink-beaten face, modestly describing the day he had stood quite near to Stalin in his youth. Marley's mother had never worked for the BBC, or been on it, or even into any of its buildings, and she spent a surprisingly large proportion of her waking hours denouncing its recent productions, but she had banned 'the other side' for most of Marley's youth (the early part of which had still been black and white) and she still maintained a quasi-religious belief in the power of this and other state organisations.

State organisations had won us the War and now they were how we were going to *get on*. The ration book kept you healthy and the BBC kept you informed and the Labour Government meant that your parents would never go back to the Means Test. You were evacuated by the State to safety during the Blitz, worked hard and went to Grammar School (your parents had to scrimp just to buy the uniform) and got an education you could never have otherwise afforded (thanks to the 1944 Education Act) and then went to a University you could never, *ever* have afforded (thanks to the State Scholarships) where you mixed with people who actually had that strange thing you had perhaps heard of in novels or in the stories of your relatives who had been in service, a *private income*, you quickly learned to speak properly, of course you did, everyone did, you couldn't *not*, and then you got a job with the State in the BBC or the NHS or Education or, in Marley's mother's case, the Civil Service, a highly respectable, well-paid job in the days when mere accountants were quite distinctly the social inferiors of Grammar School teachers and a chequebook was a weighty privilege. You married a tall, pipe-smoking man who had been an officer in the Navy (thanks to the odd National Service commission for the rare Grammar School boy who had both a useful electrical engineering degree and a decent backhand return). The two of you worked and saved and got quite a nice flat in 1957, in the days when Shepherd's Bush was just about respectable and mortgages were daring, mysterious things awarded after many interviews in private rooms with watch-chain-wearing Building Society Managers. The State was giving you a leg-up, letting the deserving rise, rewarding hard work. The lazy, feckless, beer-and-soccer people would keep on dancing and drinking and shouting abuse at their referees, while the chinless, useless public-school drones would wither in the White Heat, dissolve away into the dustbin of history as their big houses and unearned incomes were justly taxed out of existence and their public schools righteously deprived of their absurd charitable status. Leaving your own children, the heirs of Victory, inevitably to rise as the new elite of cultured technocrats, the Radio 3-listening lawyers, theatre-going doctors, book-loving lecturers and polyglot mandarins of, say, 1984. Merit and Education would out. And perhaps, by having a flat *near the BBC*, one might even help irradiate one's offspring more directly, if more mysteriously, with the mighty, beneficent nimbus of State Power.

Marley, having passed the BBC by some three hundred yards, thus arrived in Godolphin Road, W12, the site of his entire youth. Between the ages of twenty-two and thirty-seven he had been here no more than once or twice a year, keeping in touch by postcard from various countries, but since his return to England with the newborn Tommy, he had been coming once a week at least. He walked slowly along the pavement, eyes down, as if scanning for some long-lost clue to his own life, a map scratched forty years ago on a wall, perhaps, or a forgotten name carved into bricks.

—Hello, darling, sang his mother from the top of the stairs which led down from street level to her flat. She was apparently fussing with her wheelie bin, but Marley knew she had been waiting for him. He was late *and* he was not going to stay long. A sharp twinge of guilt pinched his heart.

—Hello, Mum, said Marley.

Marley's mother sallied broadly forth, a maternal

45

galleon in full, tweedy sail. She embraced him hard, squeezing him to her vast, cologne-misted breasts. Absurdly, for he was at least a foot taller than she, he felt himself completely enveloped. He smelled the powdery dryness of her short, self-cropped, snow-white hair and the rough, warm cloth of her jacket. He squeezed back, and felt again, as he had started to feel recently, the alarming bones beneath her substantial but loosening flesh. He tried not to shy away from the barely repressed, laughingly disguised heat of her affection, swayed secretly away from the burden of her sole devotion. All his life her love had threatened to overwhelm him with a sea of debts that could never be repaid.

In 1967, Marley's father had left them and gone to Australia. Marley's mother had spoken of this only once, on the memorable day in the mid 1970s when she had discovered spunk-glued socks beneath her fourteen-year-old son's bed.

—Don't overrate sex, Brian, she had said merrily. —Sex isn't that important, you know. People can manage perfectly well without sex. The way people go on today you'd think that nothing else mattered. Your father left us because he met a little Norwegian au pair with a miniskirt and was terrified in case he missed out on *free sex* and *swinging*.

—Ah, gulped Marley, fourteen, overpowered by guilt yet overwhelmed by the image.

Apart from this, Marley had merely gathered over the years that since the sixties had not swung noticeably for thirty-odd-year-old single mothers without inherited money, his mother, encumbered with his beloved self, had had little hope either of a decent second marriage or of fair and meritocratic promotion. For the little boy himself, his father's sudden departure from the scene left only a distant memory of loss, a blank vignette, haunting still sometimes when going alone to bed, of a bearded, smoke-shrouded figure picking him up for the last time, trying to explain something which could not be explained. He dimly recalled having cried —*Sorry, Daddy, I'll go on the Scottish train next time!* for he had recently annoyed his father by refusing the chance to go on the last trip of the Flying Scotsman because this would mean missing the unrepeatable appearance of the Daleks in the new *Dr Who* adventure. Then his father had driven off for ever in his maroon car that smelled of leather and warm oil. Young Brian had, for some now measureless time, tried to contact Daddy with his *Lost In Space* walkie-talkie set (*Authentic! Transistorised electronic! Range up to 500 yards!*). And then he had given up and life had gone on and that had been that.

After this decisive setback, Mrs Mary Marley (she kept the name) had undertaken no renovations of either her life or her flat in Shepherd's Bush. By the time young Brian was safely placed in the Grammar School in Hammersmith, leather satchel on back and polished shoes on the State's natural class escalator, the seventies had begun and she found herself, with no less astonishment than everyone feels at that moment, forty years of age; she resigned herself to her progressively less respected Civil Service work and to pursuits which involved Quakerish friends, meetings about Africa and (until 1989) penfriends in East Germany to whom she wrote in the idealistically conceived and now, with the worldwide triumph of English, utterly pointless world language, Esperanto; her hobbies did not include a new male about the place nor any foolish and pointless expenditure on new furniture and suchlike consumerist fripperies. As a result, her quiet home had remained mothballed in the mid-sixties, and her affections had been concentrated purely on her only son.

The only physical evidence Marley had of his father was a photograph. This photograph was in black and white, framed, and showed a Naval unit marching self-consciously, with shouldered rifles and curious white ankle leggings, across the flight deck of an aircraft carrier. The picture was titled, in fading letters of handwritten, once-black ink, *Green Division, HMS* Eagle *Malta, Coronation Day 1953. God Bless the Queen.* Mrs Marley kept it hanging in a prominent position near to her better pieces of china, well away from the various expensively framed photographs of her son posing before well-known cultural artefacts from several continents. Whenever she had a visitor whom she suspected of social condescension to a woman who had only reached Executive Officer Grade 4 by her retirement and who lived in a mere flat in Shepherd's Bush (however near to the BBC), she would skilfully bring the conversation around to this photograph. The visitor would then in the nature of things peer politely at it and ask which one was her son's father, to which Mrs Marley would reply, as if absently, in gay triumph:

—Which one? The one in the front with the bloody sword, of course.

—Oh. Oh, yes, of course. Do you know, Mary, I think I *will* have another sherry.

Shortly after his eighteenth birthday, when Australia was still a place from which young people fled at the first opportunity, when the flight still cost you a whole term's Student Grant but there were still Student Grants to blow on such things, Marley boldly asked his mother directly for information, and, having got it after a horrid battle, the only war he had ever had with her, had gone off two weeks before the start of his first term at college, to find this fabled man with his high boots, his beard and his sword.

He knew he had found the bungalow in the modern

48

suburb of Brisbane when he saw standing in the drive, gleaming in the unnatural sunlight, the maroon English saloon which he could still smell and hear in his dreams, now for ever saved from the rusting winters of its homeland. He walked quietly up and patted it cautiously, as if it were of gossamer rather than hot steel and might crumble into archaeological dust at his touch. A tall, shy, clean-shaven man in late-middle age came out of the house.

—She's a 1957 Magnette, said this man, proudly though a mite guardedly, in a pronounced Antipodean accent. —Only one previous owner, too.

—Yes, I know. You bought it to celebrate me being born.

Marley looked up and saw a leather-tanned, strong-jawed blonde woman in her late forties looking at him from the kitchen window of the house. Even before he raised his eyes to meet his father's, he realised with a lurch of vertigo that he had, vaguely, insanely, expected to meet the fabled young Norwegian woman here, the sexy, swinging hussy who had tempted his father away from his mother. In some deep and darkling recess of his hopes, he had madly associated this visit with the hope of losing his virginity before his new life in college began. Even before his father recovered the ability to speak, the question what the hell was he doing here and what on earth did he expect had begun to form in young Marley's mind. Then his father did indeed say something.

—Oh Jesus Christ almighty. Look, shit, um, er, Brian . . .

And then this shy man hastened down his drive and, without even holding out his hand, shiftily whispered that he, Brian, the long-lost son, must pretend to be his, his father's, long-lost *nephew*, because his, his father's, Norwegian-born wife did not *actually* know about his,

Brian's, existence and it wouldn't half *make a scene* with her and his three beefy, tanned, Brit-scorning teenage children. Marley, his hand still on the sun-baked maroon metal, felt his heart freeze over, like his jaw froze over when at the dentist's, but he just nodded, glad of any secret alliance with his father, even though it was directed against himself.

At first, he confidently expected a secret, late-night, man-to-man, fist-fighting, whisky-driven revelation of loss and love as his reward. A private audience with his absent father, a cathartic showdown that would set all things clear and put him on his feet for life. But as the lies and the wretched, meaty dinner dragged on, he slowly realised that he was going to get no closer to this unknown Australian man's emotions than finding out that Frank Marley, who apparently had an irrational and incurable fear of flying, had come out by subsidised emigration ship, MG saloon and all, and, since the sea voyage was so long, not to mention punitively expensive, not to mention completely defunct in any case nowadays, had not the slightest intention of ever going back to England, which was, his family all agreed, utterly buggered up anyway.

—I mean, all those *strikes*, Brian. God's sakes.

—Ya, und this seventeen-per-zent inflation! And the rain! Ho! You eat more meat?

—You actually *like* that Punk Rock shit, Uncle Brian?

—Hey, you reckon England's *ever* going to win another rugby game, Uncle Brian?

—Maybe this Margaret Thatcher'll sort things out, Brian. But I doubt it. Far as I can see, the place is just a tired old dump and that's the end of it. Maybe they managed not to get blown to bloody pieces in a nuclear war and take us all with them, but that's about it. You know that's why we left England, er, Brian?

—Because of nuclear war?

—We all thought it was *when*, not *if*. Didn't you know? Christ, I remember holding you in my arms, I mean, you know, when I was visiting your mother, my sister I mean, yeah? Right. Where was I? Yeah, I was holding you in my arms, at my sister's, and watching a telly screen about the size of a sheet of dunny paper, trying to find out if Harold bloody Macmillan and J. F. bloody Kennedy and Nikita sodding Khrushchev were about to blast us all to buggery or not. That's partly why we came here, mate. Right, Gudrun love?

—Ja, ja. So Brian vot did you say your father does?

—This and that. He's away most of the time, I don't see much of him.

—Right, well, um, listen, shit, sorry, all, I clean forgot I promised to meet Stan Young to sort out the hook-up on his caravan. I'll have to rush. Won't be late home, love. Er, sorry about that, Brian. Love to talk. But I guess you'll be wanting to be on your way. Big country, lots to see in just one week.

—Yeah, Uncle Frank, better be on my way.

And so the now wiser Brian Marley had grabbed his ex-army rucksack and bade the useless, relieved Frank Marley a merry goodbye at the door of the bungalow. He had come prepared to confront a heartless lothario, a mythical figure who had (totally unforgivably) ruined his mother's life but who had (rather fascinatingly) done so out of wild sexual desire. Instead, he had found an inglorious figure who managed to unite the three qualities which every eighteen-year-old youth finds most repellent in older men: he had been frightened, he had been wrong, and he was married to an unattractive old woman with wrinkles.

—Oh, look, Brian, one thing.

—Yes?

—Sit at the front on the way back.

51

—What?

—In the plane. Sit at the front. Cough up, boy, no matter how much. Statistically, you got more chance of surviving. Don't bother about trying to get a seat near the wing exits, no one *ever* gets out of those. You know where the fuel tanks on a plane are? Right: in the wings! That's why they put all the rich buggers up front: more chance of getting out alive, simple. Not that anyone's got much of a hope anyway, if one of those things goes down. And you can forget all that shit with life jackets, I mean, really, Brian, can you give me a *single attested example* of anyone ever being saved from a jet-plane crash by a life jacket? For Christ's sakes, can you please just show me on a map where *exactly* a jet is going to crash-land in water between here and bloody Perth? It's balls, boy. Just balls to make you feel good. Just to fool you. Oh, they are bloody unnatural things, take it from me, I'm an engineer! Christ, think of it, sitting there with the fires of hell blazing away twelve feet from your arse in a cigar tube stuffed with kerosene and only a skin of aluminium this thick, *this* bloody thick, between you and instant bloody cremation. And the whole bloody thing straining away to get off the ground, eeeeaaaah!, at the absolute bloody maximum of every mechanical tolerance because it was designed by a bunch of bloody accountants, mate, that's why, yeah, to cost as little as bloody possible and still *just about* defy gravity, with wings *so* small that without a hundred thousand pounds of thrust per engine the thing is about as aerodynamic as a bloody dead dingo. Christ almighty, Brian! One rivet pops out, just one little piece of cheap sodding Taiwanese tin *that* big, that was probably knocked in with a two-pound hammer by some brain-dead sixteen-year-old apprentice last thing on a Friday afternoon while the foreman was sloping off for a fag, and boom!, every poor sod on board is queuing up for harp lessons. Not me, mate, not Frank Marley, not on your life, boy.

—Frank, pliss, you vill scare your nephew.

—Sorry, Gudrun. Sorry, Brian. Just, you know, I, it's . . . Right. Better go then. To Stan's, yeah. Well, good to see you, er, Brian. Safe flight. Sit at the front, boy.

—Thanks, Uncle Frank. Good to see you too.

Then Marley had gone out, got drunk for a week in Brisbane with anyone he could find to drink with, wished he had never come, wished he had never seen his father without a beard, wished he had never tested his dreams, wished that his father had died rather than gone away. Then he had flown home to the reality of England and college.

And now he was in his forties and divorced and broke and his mother was letting him into her flat, for sherry.

Above Marley's head as he walked through her narrow hall a steady, dull, insistent *doomph-doomph-doomph-doomph* began to thud from the flat above. Then, just as suddenly, it stopped.

—The new couple upstairs, just practising for tonight, said Marley's mother. —They'll start properly at about midnight and go on till four.

—Christ, said Marley.

—Don't bother going up, darling.

—Oh, OK, said Marley gratefully.

—They won't listen and there's nothing anyone will do about it so there's no point causing a scene. They don't mean to be unpleasant, they're educated, they're about twenty-eight and they have lots of money and no children and they just seem to think it's normal. I'll be fine, I'll sleep in your little room tonight and I have earplugs. How *is* darling Tommy? You *do* look tired, you poor thing. Are you getting the weekend off for once? What, you've got him *all weekend*? Oh, that woman is the end. How can I help, darling? He's perfectly old enough for me to look

53

after him occasionally now. Here we are, cheers.

—Just a small one, Mum, I've got to drive.

—You *poor thing*.

Marley fought back a powerful wave of self-pity. He felt the secret, strong, desire to just for once, just for five minutes, be allowed to slump and moan and complain and imagine that if he did so loudly and convincingly enough, someone else could sort things out for him.

—Oh, I'm fine, Mum. Cheers. Good to see you.

—And it's lovely to see you. You know Tommy is welcome to stay here absolutely any time you need a *little break*.

Marley's mother had an almost superstitious veneration for her son's 30 per cent part in rearing his own child. In proportion, as she had cast her ex-husband (and by extension, male-kind) as hopelessly addicted to self-indulgent pleasures, so she considered her own son a saintly martyr to paternal duty. She ascribed this to Marley's innate or inculcated moral qualities (for both of which she could rationally claim some credit) rather than to modern Child Support legislation. She had also managed to reinterpret Marley's life with a cavalier disregard for cause, effect and chronology, so that his undoubted failure to make anything of himself despite having gone to Durham University for God's sake (she had long given up any real hope of him getting *an interesting job* of some kind) was entirely due to *that woman's* having more or less *inveigled* him into getting her pregnant and then *virtually* leaving him as a single parent.

—I've dug some of your old annuals and toys out from under the stairs, so I'm well prepared for him. Look, here we are, I'm sure he'll adore them. Remember them?

—I didn't know you kept these.

—Well, it's a good thing I did. Look. The *Eagle* annuals. *The Valiant. The Victor.* How you used to love them. Look:

your Action Men. So convincing, that German Army uniform, isn't it? And the Australian jungle soldier with his little flame-thrower. I've kept them all. I saw some Action Men in the shops the other day and I thought of Tommy, but they're so *garish* and *American* nowadays, aren't these much better? I can't think why they changed them. All these little plastic soldiers too. The Eighth Army, the Afrika Korps. You used to love putting them up and knocking them over with marbles, do you remember? Of course, it's all those ghastly, violent computer games these days, isn't it? Oh, and here are your *Famous Five* books, you used to spend whole days reading these, do you remember?

Marley remembered. He gazed, stunned, at the old leather trunk full of books and toys, the now undeniably collectable relics of his own past which he had neither seen nor thought of for over three decades. The dates on the spines of the annuals alone filled him with a sudden, powerful melancholy: 1965, 1966, 1967, 1968, those wonderful, summer-filled years when you could ride a bike, read all day, and build a whole kingdom in a cock-eyed tree house, untroubled by pimples and sweaty, half-understood yearnings. Some of the annuals pre-dated Marley's own birth, let alone his reading age, thanks to his mother's sensible habit, ingrained by years of rationing, of laying in stocks of Poorly Presents whenever she spotted a jumble sale: after all, your child still got Dan Dare and all, but it cost you sixpence instead of 10/6d. Marley took the *Eagle Annual* of 1965 from the box and weighed it in his hand, as if it might somehow weigh more, or perhaps less, than it seemed; as if the past obeyed subtly different laws of mass and volume.

Holding it again, he was overcome all at once by the extraordinary feeling that this was somehow far more real than whatever he had been doing for the past thirty-five years. The decades reeled in seconds before his eyes, years of living and working and travelling and worrying and loving and losing, but it all seemed to have no substance compared to this. He could absolutely recall reading this very book while sitting at the top of the stairs to this flat, in the sunshine, with 'Yellow Submarine' playing from every doorway but their own (his mother did not allow pop music), watching the hot street with half an eye for a purple car that would never return. And there was something else. Something forbidden or threatening. With absurd caution, he let the book open at its own volition and found a picture which had haunted him all his life. There were several of these images locked away in his mind from those years: a bubble-gum collecting card given to him by an older boy, called 'Fiery Death' showing a German screaming as he was flame-throwered by grinning British soldiers; a strange line drawing of a hideous witch, so hated and feared that the infant Marley had scribbled frantically and vainly over that whole page of *The Golden Treasury*; one particular episode of *Star Trek* with a night-mare-inducing monster that had turned from attractive woman to hideous, flesh-eating alien while men were kissing it . . .

As he stared at the *Eagle Annual*, 1965, his mind folded space and time up together with dizzying ease. Sitting here now in his mother's living room, he could clearly remember the last time he had remembered seeing the picture he had first seen when sitting here in his mother's living room twenty years before: he had been in the middle of nowhere in Ireland, in the late eighties, having a car fixed, when the garage owner had run out shouting, —*Lads, Jesus Christ, did you hear the news? Kiev has just been nuked!* He remembered looking up, expecting to see the sky criss-crossed with vapour trails, and thinking of

56

this very picture with the numb terror of someone who has just heard the knocking of inescapable, childhood fate:

—And the *level of the language*, of course, is so much better than in those dreadful modern comics. I'm sure he'll love them too.

Marley shook himself out of his private loops of inter-time and returned to the present. He listened without hearing. He knew that he should try to tell his mother that while he personally would love to have the books and that they were certainly *worth taking care of* (he carefully managed to avoid thinking the unthinkable) he did not, in fact, very much want her to start looking at them with Tommy. He knew she thought that all children should be reading fluently by four years old and guessed that if she sat down with Tommy and these books she would follow the cartoon strips word for word with her index finger as she read to him. He tried gently to hint that he would probably get Social Services calling round to see him if his ex-wife and the kindergarten teachers found Tommy telling them about stories in *Daddy's books* about redskins being wiped out by cowboys, turbanned tribesmen being routed by Maxim guns, Boy Scouts defeating the evil schemes of slant-eyed Malaysian terrorists, entertaining black people called Mambo and Jambo who spoke pidgin English and chirpy commandos mowing down buck-toothed rice-noshers (*Banzai! Arrgh!*), square-headed sausage-eaters (*Achtung donner und blitzen! Urgh!*) or out-of-work ice-cream salesmen (*Mamma mia! Aieee!*).

It was all water off a duck's back, of course, and so, after listening to a brief lecture on the inexplicable insufficiency of her pension, the crying need for Identity Cards and the sad degeneracy of the BBC, Marley kissed his mother again to bid her goodbye until Sunday lunchtime, when he would return from his old college friends' house in Kent with little Tommy. His mother recalled these old college friends having visited many years ago (as penniless students, Marley's friends had found a floor in a flat near the BBC very handy) and asked after them.

—What do they *do* now?

—They've got an ironing business in Kent.

—Oh, well then.

—They make lots of money.

—Well, if you want to *take in laundry*, darling. And what about that Grant? Is he still a Trotskyist poof?

—Well, he's not a Trostkyist any more. He produces half the stuff on Channel Seven.

—*Channel Seven*, indeed. Well, even the BBC has gone to the dogs, so I don't suppose it makes much difference, these days. Didn't that hard-faced little woman in jeans somehow get a job in the BBC? She was some sort of Trotskyist too, wasn't she?

—Tamsin. She's Grant's business partner now. But she doesn't wear jeans any more, she always wears black. And she's always appearing at New Labour things.

—Exactly. Sexually incontinent men who call themselves homosexual because they're just too shy and quivery to get a decent girl, and careerist hussies who say they despise bourgeois morality because they simply have no morality at all.

—Er, sorry, Mum?

—It's people like *that* who decide that programmes for seven-year-old children should be full of teenagers who can't talk properly shouting at the camera and films of girls with hardly any clothes on miming sex. Well, dear, it's certainly not the *seven-year-olds* who decide what to make and put on, is it? And it isn't we licence payers either. Oh well, I suppose your Grant had a *little friend* to give him his first job, and no doubt that Tamsin girl wasn't above *being nice* to a few men. It all seems very unfair on normal people like you, I must say. Never mind, darling, I'm sure something will *come up* for you soon.

—Ha, laughed Marley, wondering if he should carefully explain to her that at his age, and with his CV, there was no spectacular retroactive justification of his life waiting just around some nearby corner or other. —See you on Sunday, Mum, he said instead, kissed her and smiled.

*

Some five miles east of Brian Marley, the three most powerful men in Britain, all of whom had spent their entire adult lives zealously plotting and planning and climbing various more or less greasy poles in order to be here now, were turning their vast experience to the vexed question of Monetary Union. The Prime Minister was strumming his guitar absently, trying to work out those tricky but effective augmented (or was it diminished? he could never remember which) bits of the chords to 'Crazy' while he looked doubtfully at the plan which his Press Secretary and his Best Friend (currently Without

59

Portfolio again) had laid before him some twenty minutes previously.

—A referendum straight after Christmas? Are you sure? asked the Prime Minister at last. —It's a *bloody* big step.

—It'll certainly write your name in the history books. Again, I mean, nodded his Best Friend, solemnly.

—But I thought having a referendum was, y'know, a *Tory* policy.

—Well, exactly, said his Best Friend, with angelic patience. —That's what we *do*, remember? It'll dish them completely.

—Aye, laughed his Press Secretary, —not that the puir wee saps need fixing ony more than they're fixing themsel's.

—But I mean, well, I was just thinking, would we really *win* a referendum?

—Trust us, said his Best Friend, a little wearily. —It's all watertight. The Scots and the Welsh and the Northern Irish will all vote For because they all think they'll get enormous EU subsidies. They know how well the Irish have done out of it and we'll give the Nats a free hand to remind them.

—Sorry, I've forgotten: will they *really* get huge subsidies?

—Of course not. The Irish only got so much because of the Germans and the French liking them. The Germans like the Irish because they're the only country that doesn't go around dropping hints about *invasions* whenever the Germans get fed up with paying for everything and the French like the Irish because they think liking the Irish will annoy *us*. No, no, the French want all the subsidies to go to Poland and *those places* now, to make sure they toe the line. The Welsh and Scots won't get a thing. But they don't realise it, of course.

—Heh heh, stupid wee Tartan Tory fuckers.

—So you see, we don't have to worry about winning

in England, because whatever happens in England won't matter anyway. When the results come in, we'll break the vote down country by country. Three countries to one in favour. Then we point out that Lisbet is Queen of *several nations bound together by indissoluble links of history and rhubarb* and all that stuff. She *loves* that sort of thing, believe me, and she'll say it on the telly if we ask her. That'll shut the yellow press up. Can't be seen to be going against dear old Lisbet. Then we simply explain that Britain *as a whole* clearly voted for Monetary Union. And you do that speech I gave you about *How Can England the Champion of Freedom Ride Roughshod over the Democratic Wishes of Our Fellow British Nations?*, you know the one.

—Oh yes. I was practising it just the other day actually.

—Aye, gie it the auld *People's Princess* treatment, boss.

—Mmm. Do you know, I was actually amazed to find that this was written by Willie Nelson?

—Wullie Nelson? Never, boss.

—Was it really?

—Oh yes, definitely. Look, and you're *sure* Monetary Union is a good thing?

—Well, how can it not be? If it gives more power to people like us?

—I suppose. And you're *absolutely* sure the Americans are for it?

—They know we'll always be their best friends, sighed his Best Friend. —They want us running Europe for them.

—The Yanks fuckin' love you, boss.

—And they know Croatia and Lithuania and the Czech Republic and Poland and, well, you know, all *those places*, will be on our side. They all want American bases desperately.

—Aye. They're scared shiteless of the Russkis, they dinnae trust the Jerries and they couldnae gie a flying fuck about the Frogs.

61

—And the Americans *will* let us keep Trident? I mean, look, obviously I wish we didn't *need* to have Trident, we all wish that, but the fact is, in this world, it's not *about* what we wish, we simply *have* to have it, don't we? And writing my secret letters to the Trident captains that first day after we won did make me feel, sort of, the *responsibility*, you know. A bit like Churchill, really. And it makes us, well, the Top of the Table in Europe, doesn't it?

—Yes, yes, yes, we can keep Trident. Obviously, we'd still have to ask the Americans before we ever *used* it.

—I'd never *want* to use it, of course. But these Rogue States, y'know. The President was saying to me just the other day, well, it was *night* here of course, I actually did have to get up out of bed to talk to him, but I'm sure he'd simply forgotten about time zones and that sort of thing, and anyway, he was saying to me . . .

— . . . of course. But we have to ask the Americans now anyway.

—Oh yes. I forgot. Oh well, I suppose even *Churchill* relied on the Americans, secretly, from right at the start, didn't he?

—Of course he did. By the way, I think your little finger goes like *that*, actually.

—Wow, yeah. So you really think we go for it?

—I do.

—Well, and for fuck's sake, boss, wha' are folks goin' tae do if they're *no'* happy with it? Eh? Vote Conservative at the General Election?

—Ha ha ha!

—Heh heh heh!

*

—Absolutely, said the plump, blond, florid Editor of the *Intelligencer*, gazing down at the book on the aged Senior Editor's desk. There was nothing much else he could say, really, since the Senior Editor had been completely and, well, *absolutely* proved right yet again.

—You see, said the Senior Editor, patting the fat volume, —I *know* our people, Harry. Those idiots at the *Paper* think that just because the Party is such a God-awful wreck, our sales will fall. On the contrary. Our people buy us precisely *because* the Party is such a cock-up. Just now, the *Intelligencer* is all they have left. We're even winning readers from the *Paper*, you know. And no bloody wonder. I mean to say, how many people in this country actually *live* in Islington? How many of us would give a damn if every bloody Britpop artist and young stand-up come-dian jumped off some ruddy cliff tomorrow? Not very many. How many people over twenty-one want to know about the latest Club Nite in Brixton, God save us? Not very many. Most people still settle down at about thirty and have children. I mean, how many of us are actually homosexualists? Eh?

—Well . . .

—I don't mean chaps who happen to have buggered or been buggered for God's sake, that can happen to anyone and it damn near happened to me on several occasions at school, in both variations come to think of it, and no doubt it happened to you at Eton too, no no no, I mean *habitual sodomites*, you know, chaps who wreck their whole lives because they've become addicted to Guardsmen's backsides or dockers' cocks? Eh?

—Um? Sorry, what was the question again, chief?

—How many of us are actually like that?

—Well, not many of *our* readers.

—Exactly. Most of us are normal and those normal people are our readers. I knew they'd like it, you see? Instinct.

It was a large, handsome coffee table book which, on the Senior Editor's personal whim, had been published in time for the Christmas rush last year. The owner of the *Intelligencer*, who lived in Bahrain for reasons of tax, had allowed this book to be brought out on the grounds that it would cost him nothing much at all to do so, for it consisted simply of reprints of various obituaries of military men (many of them friends of the Senior Editor) which had already appeared in the *Intelligencer* anyway and of which he thus already owned the copyright. Indeed, there had been several small paperback collections of these already published. But those had been modest books, mere throwaway stocking fillers. This was a blatant celebration, a weighty, hardbacked monument clearly designed to outlive its purchasers.

Opposite each obituary, with its formal wartime portrait on glossy paper, appeared a historical photograph of the fight, or at least the theatre of action, in which the late man had gained his most notable decoration, together with photographs and brief biographies of comrades who had not survived, all placed in context by maps and scholarly notes about the course and significance of the battle in question. A hymnic foreword had been provided by a formerly postmodern novelist of international standing. The resulting volume was called *Best of Breed*, it was splendidly produced, substantially priced and had taken the entire book trade by surprise in becoming the runaway hardback bestseller in the vital pre-Christmas period. No marketing investigation had yet been able clearly to establish whether *Best of Breed* was being bought mainly by elderly people to read wistfully to themselves or by young people to laugh at ironically with their friends.

—But then, d'you see, irony is just yearning in disguise, isn't it, so it doesn't really matter, does it?

—Absolutely not.

The owner of the *Intelligencer* was clearly going to make some several million unexpected pounds out of the deal and despite the complications this was causing to his tax-minimalisation strategy, he was happy, so the Senior Editor had that week decided to stay on for yet another year, much to the irritation of the florid, blond, plump Editor, who was anxious to make his mark while he still had his blond hair and thus, though florid and plump, also counted as *young*. He rather fancied the chance to make the *Intelligencer* a bit more, you know, *lively*. He loved the Senior Editor dearly, of course, owed him everything, but, well, what was it the Bible said about there being a season for all things? Recently, he had begun dimly to understand how the future Edward VII might have felt about matricide in, say, the year 1895, or how Charles might be feeling now, for that matter . . .

—Instinct, the Senior Editor laughed. —I *feel* it sometimes, you know. I mean, I say, you know this M25 thing?

—Yes, actually.

—I saw it the other day from a pal of mine's little aeroplane. I looked, do you see, just *looked*, at all those poor buggers spending their lives driving round and round like bloody lemmings, permanently half knackered and *bloody well* fed up, decent, normal chaps and girls who never wanted much really except orders they could understand, mortgaged up to the eyeballs, worried sick about their kids and schools and pensions and just about ready to grab hold of someone in Westminster by the balls and ask them exactly what the *hell's* going on. *Those* are our men and women. *Our* tribe.

The Editor shuddered as he thought of small businessmen from Wokingham and of those terrible women from terrible places whom one sees only at Tory conferences. If only his readers were just a bit, well, *sexier* . . .

—And good, sporty girls.

—Eh? Sorry?

—We need more good, sporty girls. You know. New

Zealand type. South African, perhaps, and no reason to worry about a little touch of the tarbrush, often helps a girl's looks in my experience, not to mention her spirit, better than those horse-faced bloody Yank girls with too many teeth. Or the good old English sort, you know. *Miss Joan Hunter Dunn, Miss Joan Hunter Dunn.* Not too bloody skinny and not seventeen. About twenty-one. Oxbridge blue. Or cellists, you know. Always loved a girl with a cello, don't know why. Sort of girl you could take anywhere, fit for anything. Alexandra Devonshire's daughters, say. You know. Good stock. Give your poor buggers on that M25 cock-up something to cheer them up, eh? They don't ask for much, you know. Just something to make them feel that someone's got a grip on the tiller and everything's all right. Sporty girls in summer dresses, with cellos. That's the ticket.

The Editor revived somewhat as he thought of his new assistant. He would be surprised if she played the cello, but she was very sporty. Her attitude to sex was rumoured, indeed, to verge on the healthy.

—Absolutely, he said, and stared dreamily out at the dark, rain-lashed Thames.

*

—Dadddddy! screamed Tommy, and Marley, straining his eyes through his age-scratched, rain-smeared, oily windscreen to scan the pelting hell of the black, wintery M25 ahead of them, felt his brain lock in helpless despair and guilt.

It was all his fault.

He had forgotten to allow for the insane battle of getting Tommy away from the bottom-of-the-range private kindergarten near his ex-wife's flat on a Friday afternoon. Tommy's kindergarten was patronised by ordinary, struggling, nannyless people for whom the maths of Earnings vs Private Kindergarten only just added up. Like Marley, they actually had to cut their workdays short, losing money they would notice losing, to get here early in the hope of not hitting the M25 in the rush hour on a vile Friday afternoon in November: they arrived in warlike and resentful mood, each secretly convinced that if they could only grab their offspring and get away just that vital *little bit* before everyone else, they would make it to wherever they were going before everyone else in the South-East of England could get in their way.

Marley, like everyone else, had double-parked and had stood in the rain for ten increasingly nervous minutes amid the other parents, swapping false little smiles as they all waited, on sneaky watch for traffic wardens, straining their necks so as to catch sight of their children as soon as possible and wave to them, merrily but force-fully to *come on now, darling, come along, quickly now*, so that they could be first away from the school. They did not actually shove each other's kids bodily out of the way in the dash, but it was close. Marley had managed to get Tommy pretty fast today, had swung him up and around and on to his shoulders over the heads of many other children, just missing kicking several rival parents in the teeth with his son's small but solid shoes, and had made it to his car almost in pole position, but it had still taken him twenty solid minutes of nudging in, cutting up and edging out just to escape the rain-lashed streets around the school. These few narrow, residential avenues were the daily battleground of fake-tanned, faux-blonde women in undentable Malaysian four-by-fours with bull bars fitted just to make absolutely sure that if they hit anyone else's child they would be sure to kill it, insanely harassed working mothers wearing charcoal suits designed for women with rather more in the way of shoulder and much less in the way of bum, in small but

67

sneaky French cars which bore the warning scars of years of this warfare, and outraged, pre-apoplectic males in repmobiles who had been morally blackmailed or legally compelled to clock off early to get here, thus losing them deals, undermining their status and banishing them from the vital Friday post-work drink and flirt. Each and all of them clearly believed that their precious time, their incredible dutifulness, their stress levels, the importance of their careers, the vital ceramics class or guitar lesson for which little Hugo or Letitia might be late, or simply their employer's lease on a this-year's-plate Mercedes overrode any consideration of legality, never mind courtesy, forget communality, and that they alone knew of, or had the right to use, the latest cunning rat run or supposed short cut. A psychic barometer placed near to the kindergarten would have imploded beneath the pressure of the secret but limitless mutual hatred, or fused solid with the sour, cancerous aura of naked but impotent self-interest. If the handgun laws of Middle England had been those of the Midwest, several people would certainly have ended the day being shot in the face through their half-tinted windows as they yelled inaudibly and gesticulated unmistakably at one another for ruthlessly backing-up, ten-point U-turning, blatant lane-blocking or whatever else it was that they had just also done themselves or had every intention of doing themselves if they got half a chance.

And so by the time Marley made it on to the M25, everyone else in the South-East of England had got there as well. And now Tommy needed a poo. Between Junctions 22 and 23 of the M25, at five o'clock on a pissing wet, bitingly cold, pitch-dark Friday afternoon in November. Which meant that instead of spending his weekend with his mother in the warm, womanly comfort of her quiet flat in Ealing where he lived most of the time,

Tommy had been gratuitously taken by Daddy straight to Hell.

—Daddddddy!

—OK, OK, we can stop here, look, that's it, it's fine, we can poo here, just keep it in two seconds longer, sweetheart . . .

Tommy did not have a pull-up nappy on his bottom because Tommy (being three and therefore, in his own mind, far above pull-up nappies) had been prepared to make a stand-up fight of it. Marley had not wanted the weekend to get off to a bad start, so he had given in and hoped for the best. And now Tommy's poo was coming out into his pants and he was hysterical and there was no way they could make it to anywhere with a toilet no matter how suicidally, or indeed infanticidally, Marley drove.

He scanned all his greasy, spattered mirrors, craned his head to see behind him, and at last dared to slide his elderly, non-ABS-equipped, pre-airbags, vulnerable little Japanese car leftwards between the lines of manic traffic, flashing his headlights and blasting his horn, and so at last stopped on the side of the motorway.

—Christ, Marley gasped aloud, in relief at having made it.

—I can't help it, Daddy! cried Tommy.

—No, no, no, sweetheart, not you, come on, it's fine, it's no problem . . .

Marley popped his own seat belt quickly off, twisted round and leaned over from the driver's seat at a spine-wrenching angle to pick at his son's multiple harness, but soon had to give up in the face of modern Infant Car-Safety Technology.

—Bloody stupid things, he managed to say internally, rather than shout out loud. For God's sake, when he was Tommy's age he had sat on the floor, unseated and unharnessed, and played in the back of his father's MG saloon, in one of the footwells either side of the prop-shaft tunnel. He could still feel the rattle and hum, still smell the oil and leather and warm, dusty carpets . . .

—Hold on, sweetness, stay in your chair, one sec, just one sec.

Marley was by now straddling the handbrake and half stuck between the front seats, facing rearward, towards Tommy; he hoisted himself painfully out again and gave his own door handle a backhanded flip. The car's driver door was instantly whipped away and banged back against its hinge stops, shuddering. In a second the temperature inside the car dropped by twenty degrees as icy spray whirled into every corner of the cabin.

—Jesus Christ almighty, shouted Marley to no one, and slid arse-wise out of the car, skinning his shins as he went on the bare, battered metal of the door frame.

Now the full gale of the rain and the mindless volume of the M25 rush hour hit him like a freak wave in a cold sea: it raced up the back of his shirt and made him cringe in instinctive, primeval loathing, like a slug nosing salt. He twisted round straight again, faced into the shattering roar and the slashing rain and staggered to both feet. He stood there for a moment, paralysed, his face flayed, and stared disbelievingly around at the hurtling doom all about him. Then he flung open the rear door to reach in and grab Tommy. He saw in his little son's face the impact of that grey wave of chill sound and light: sheer terror. A vast articulated lorry roared from nowhere out of the halogen-blinded blackness and the world ended for an infinite second or two as forty tons of murderous steel blasted past three feet away, sending up clouds of freezing spume to engulf them. The little car, a pathetic cockleshell of thin-pressed steel, rocked helplessly. Tommy screamed in mortal fear.

—Ahhhhh!

—Come on, said Marley, with determined breeziness, fighting off Tommy's clawing hands and shoving hard against his little tummy so as to open the parachute-style buckles fully at last.

A merciless midwife of despair, Marley now hoisted his little son, kicking and screaming, into the vile rain and the squealing darkness and the terrifying blasts of the lit-up cars and lorries. Nothing in evolution could possibly have prepared Tommy for such sights and sounds. He was beside himself, beyond all thought and language, screaming, insane and blind, as Marley forced him to lean against the freezing metal crash barriers and squat on the wet, black roadside and do his tiny shit into the endless, raging, death-filled night. As he shat, piteously, Marley had to hold on tight to him, for fear that he might simply break and run, like a crazed animal, into the four lanes of roaring oblivion that were charging incessantly past them well within spitting distance. He felt his hands squeezing through his little boy's soft, flawless skin, down to the small, fragile bones. Quite suddenly, he wanted to cry into the disguising rain.

At last, the shitting and the screaming were done, and Marley hugged his son back into the car, trying feebly to shield him from the rain with his own sodden body. When Tommy was safely locked back into his child seat, whimpering for his mummy, Marley shut the back door and stood outside the car for a moment, besieged by the rain and noise and lights, despairing, a lone, wet, bedraggled old male primate in a world of screaming iron, gazing hopelessly up at the ghostly penumbrae of the rain-shrouded sodium lights, as if at far-off, uncaring gods. Then he blinked, dragged himself back to reality, slid his damp way back into the car, smiled at his bawling son, chirped, —OK then, let's go!

71

with insane jollity and edged out into the monstrous blare of traffic once again.

As he rejoined the normal flood of car-culture insanity, Marley reminded himself that he had to calm down, drive carefully and be sure not to kill them both. If he wanted to drive off the hard shoulder of the M25 straight out into onrushing lorries, he should do it another time. And why not, another time? The life-insurance people could never prove it had not just been a normal accident, been suicide. That way, at least, Tommy would be set up for life. Marley, after all, was quite literally worth more dead than alive. Perhaps he should get a removable sticker for the back window, to be slapped on to the glass whenever Tommy was not with him: BABY NOT ON BOARD TODAY PLEASE RAM ... Yes, but not today. Right. Wake up. Marley re-adjusted his spiralling brain to M25 Night Survival Mode and set himself the task of singing Tommy to sleep.

Once, an old, very happy and heavily child-blessed jazz singer in a pub had told Marley that the children of the sixties were the first in the whole history of mankind to have been brought up without God and lullabies, so no wonder they were so messed up. Marley did not want Tommy to grow up messed up, but since he had been brought up to not believe in God he was limited to the lullaby bit and since he obviously did not know any English lullabies, he sang Scots and Irish lullabies instead.

—*Speed bonnie boat*, sang Brian Marley, and —*It's straight I will repair to the Curragh of Kildare*, he crooned, an Englishman alone with his small, exhausted son, in the bleak, black night, on the most hopeless of roads, this strip of hated tar. —*Bonnie Charlie's noo awa'*, he chanted, and then, —Christ almighty! he yelled, grabbing at the wheel in heart-clenching panic as he was bracketed from behind by multiple full-on headlights and blasted by a high-powered, outraged car horn. He had somehow drifted over to straddle two lanes, forcing a vast, speeding Ferrari to lurch horribly around him, skimming the right-hand kerb, flashing and blaring and slaloming alarmingly across the soaking roadway.

The Ferrari's lights shimmied crazily as it screamed past, doing at least 120: Marley, frozen at the wheel, watched the two red blocks of its rear lamps dance sickeningly from side to side among the other traffic for a good five hundred yards, setting off hoots, brakes, warning lights and flashes, before they finally settled down again and merged into the lunatic normality of another hundred little tin boxes flying insanely through the wind and rain and darkness, every driver centrally locked into a private cocoon of metal and plastic, most of them listening to some jabbering radio presenter, each of them a mere sneeze from eternity.

—You mad bastard! screamed Marley.

—Ahhhhhh! yelped little Tommy, shocked awake from his lullabied reverie and instinctively assuming, as the small heir of three million years of human or proto-human evolution, the vast majority of which had been spent in the African savannah, that his father's scream was a warning of either a large feline, a pack of canines or a rival hominid clan, intent on killing and/or eating him on the spot.

—I hope you get a bloody heart attack and die! yelled Marley at nothing that could conceivably hear him. The presence of what *might have been* was so tangibly solid, the unnerving sense of an alternative universe close behind him so strong, that he very nearly expected to look into his mirror and see, receding at impossible speed, his own car, with himself and Tommy inside it, strewn wrecked and smouldering across the motorway.

—No, Daddy, please I don't want my heart to be attacked! wailed the only person who had, or who could possibly have, heard Marley's curse.

—No, no, darling, not you, not you. Not you. Him. Oh God.

—Why you want God to die, Daddy?

—No, no, OK, it's all right, sweetheart . . .

*

Inside the big, red Ferrari, Channel Seven TV's most-favoured producer, Grant Brodie, forced his right hand to relax its clawlike death-grip grasp on the steering wheel, willed his shoulders to sink back to something like normal, and required his back to return to the seat. He nervously checked all his large, bright mirrors and his even larger blind spots. Then he remembered to breathe. Having done so several times, he cautiously moved his left hand down to press the buttons on his wheel-mounted CD controller, killing the Old Skool remix of the *Brideshead Revisited* theme which had been sweeping the clubs in the last weeks and which, just now, had almost wafted him unawares to a sudden and violent death. As he did so, he realised that he was still clutching his phone in this hand and that the voice on the other end of the phone was still bleating tinnily away at him.

—Grant, are you still there? it buzzed. —Grant?

—Christ. Yes. Just about. Fuck it, Tamsin, I nearly just bloody died.

—I know, it's *serious shit*, isn't it?

—No, you idiot, I mean I almost bloody crashed. Another two feet and I'd have been lying in a bloody box this time next week, mainlining formaldehyde in the middle of a bunch of snivelling queens singing Bellini and Judy Garland.

—But Grant, everyone knows you *hate* Bellini and Judy Garland.

—Would that have stopped them? Don't *ever* give me news like that again when I'm driving in the fast lane.

74

—Well, how on earth am I supposed to know when you're driving in the fast lane?

—Tamsin, I *always* drive in the fast lane.

—Oh yes.

—Except when I've nearly been killed because someone called me in the fast lane to tell me we're in the shit. What the hell do you mean we've *lost* one of our contestants?

—The fat nurse from Basingstoke. She's bloody *pregnant*.

—What? Fucking bitch!

—I know. It just showed up on her medical.

—Bloody over-oestrogened cow.

—There's *no way* we can use her now. The lawyers say it just can't be done.

—But we need six of them. It's all set up around *six* of them. We're taking them out there next week. It's in the Christmas schedules. Channel Seven has already spent a fortune setting up its own real-time interactive betting arm specially for this. Remember the penalty clauses if we don't deliver?

—*That's* why I called you in the fast lane, darling.

—Tamsin, we have got to sit down *first thing* tomorrow with a list of replacements.

—OK, OK, your place, *first thing* tomorrow morning.

—See you at eleven then. So stay off the powder tonight, won't you, Miss Nosebag?

—Chance would be a fine thing. My Icelandic painter is being a *complete* wanker at the moment. He wants me to *have a baby* with him, so he's given up boozing. He's so *boring* when he's sober. At least when he's drinking you sometimes get a window of about ten minutes between loss of emotional inhibition and loss of motor control. Oh well, I suppose if a girl wants a hetero man she always has to allow a little autistic licence. Do you know of anything exciting going on?

—Exciting? If only, darling.

—Oh Grant, I'd love to feel *radical* again, just once.

—I know. I remember when it felt *wicked* to be cruising at 2 bloody a.m. You were bound to meet interesting people because everyone else was in bed. Now everywhere's full of camp little insurance men off their tits all night long every night who you can't even *look* at without them launching into positively mathematical descriptions of how they want you to do what to them with which implement.

—I blame cheap uppers. God, my first gram of coke at college cost more than I pay these days, and that was nearly, well, that was a long time ago.

—Wasn't it? Do you know, Tamsin, sometimes I get this spooky feeling that we're all allowed to do anything we want whenever we want these days because actually nothing any of us ever does these days will ever matter to anyone.

—God, Grant, you're depressing. I think you should come back to Soho right now.

—Fuck you, you mad little gobshite!

—Sor-*ry*, only joking.

—Not you, *him*.

—Who?

The *him* was the driver of a small, rusting, decal-covered GTi filled with leering young men which had just veered in, two feet from his front bumper. He could see them cackling back at him. Incredibly, the bass from the little car's hypertrophic sound system was briefly audible even here, inside Brodie's fatly insulated Ferrari.

—Grant? Hel-lo?

—Look, Tamsin, this is ridiculous, I've got to go or I'm going to die. See you tomorrow at eleven. *With lists.*

*

The air inside the little old rusting white Golf GTi which had just given Grant Brodie his second mortal scare of the evening was thick with sweet, speedy, compost-heap skunk smoke and its plastic interior panels shuddered with the over-amped bass beats of 50 Cent's *Get Rich Or Die Trying*. The occupants of the car were all pallid white males of seventeen or eighteen. They had spent the morning lying about on hire-purchased sofas in their broken non-family homes, playing video games involving mass death and pornography or watching adverts for things they would never be able to afford which they were told would infallibly make them happy; they had spent the afternoon pumping weights and doing a boxercise class in the local council-run gym, preparing their bodies for physical demands that life would never make on them: now they were going out to have some *fun* in their car. This car functioned in their testosterone-drenched mental world not as a means of transport, but as a weapon of male display, whose low status must be compensated for by their own suicidal bravado in flaunting it: only thus could they hope to impose their sour adolescent spoor on a disrespectful world. As they approached, now, the brief, dizzy, daring height of their strength and spunk and muscle/fat ratio, they were still left outside the big Club of Life, gazing in at the bright windows and watching balding old gits of thirty-odd getting the hot, low cars, the tall, cool girls, the endless white sands and the fuck-palace lofts. Half a billion years of pre-social evolution cooked in their veins, united now with the mass-advertised cry of the modern youth market: *get it now while you are young and fast*. In order to show which sub-tribe they belonged to when they were in otherwise classless places where the music was so loud that no one could ever hear anything anyone said, they were all dressed in various prominently branded pieces of gear from the US badmeister Steve 'Skagga' Tombs's NFR

77

clothing line. On their big T-shirts, their baggy pants, their caps, their anti-CCTV hooded sweatshirts and their air-cushioned trainers, that was all it said, NFR, which of course stands for *Not For Resuscitation* and if you don't know it means that without being told then ha ha excuse me please you old cunt who gives a flying fuck what you think about anything anyway, eh? Eh?

—Scared that old bald fuck in his Fefuckinrrari shitless!

—Yee-hah!

—That car should be fuckin' *ours*, mate.

—Old cunt.

—Turn it up so every old cunt can hear it.

—Tha's more like it. Serious fuckin' bass. Pass that fuckin' smoke then, ya cunt.

*

In her small hotel room near Paddington, Consuela Martinez was reading books about England, which she had bought from the New Non-Fiction table of a large bookshop in Oxford Street. She read of vicars and tea, of Morris Minors and farmers, of the quaintness of inventing an outdoor game that takes five days in a country where it always rains ho ho and of the fact that one of the oldest Oxford colleges is called New College ho ho ho.

She put down her book eventually and drifted into a dream about her father's big old antique dresser. A tall, dark oak cavern filled with English clothes, English shoes, Dunlop Maxply tennis rackets signed by Rod Laver and dress uniforms of the Fuerza Aerea (made by Gieves & Hawkes), into which she used to walk and hide, half believing, from having read English children's literature, that she might gently push her way between the heavy-hanging, man-smelling coats and jackets into a magical world of princes and pageants. Her slow, sleeping breaths

78

filled with the childhood scents, reproduced flawlessly now by her miraculous brain, of wood polish, shoe polish, leather and tweed. Deeper she dreamed, of a stable yard in a green land, a tall, blond man, his rough, woollen-shirted arms enveloping her slowly, irresistibly, crushing her safe like a big oak tree, her long skirts lifting as if of their own accord . . .

Outside, the thudding music, the revving cars and the guttural chimp-howls of London's youth greeting one another did not disturb her dreams.

*

Marley's old college friends were gathered around the Aga in Sevenoaks.

They had been friends since the early 1980s. At eighteen, being among the few people who in those days went to universities, they had each vaguely expected to do something or other sort of memorable. After college, they had all hung about for a few years wondering exactly what it might be, then got safe and steady jobs. Now they were in their forties. Their parents were all still more or less alive, their marriages all still more or less holding, their children all still more or less infants, and none of them had so far suffered any worse tribulation in life than the odd bout of looming debt brought on by eating and drinking out too much, going on holiday too often and buying pretty well whatever they wanted whenever they felt like it. They were all currently standing around, drinking red wine in a somewhat guarded fashion and warming their bums in pairs on the rail of the host's Aga. Since the golden age of their kind of safe and steady job was gone (few of them had any serious share options), they mostly had houses which were too small, too modern and too well insulated to have real Agas without baking everyone to death. A couple of them had recently installed one of the new official fake ones, which consisted of a thin sheet of artfully pressed, embossed and enamelled metal, representing the front of an Aga, surprisingly realistic and fitted with the vital, authentic, bum-warming chrome towel rail (heated by concealed electrical elements). These were sold by mail order, exclusively in the *Intelligencer*, to those Englishmen condemned by undistinguished birth, unfortunate investments or unwise marriages to houses below their imagined station, so that they might at least have something to warm their buttocks consolingly against as the evenings fell. However, the particular old college friend who was hosting this weekend owned a business which collected ready-washed but unironed laundry from most of Sevenoaks and employed Albanian women to iron it in a roughly converted barracks in Maidstone, so he could afford a real one and a house big enough to put it in, so he naturally had.

The old college friends' wives were retiring gratefully to bed. Having taken a maternal (if somewhat condescending) pity on Poor Divorced Brian, they offered (as he had hoped they would) to include Tommy in tomorrow's proposed Wives-and-Kids trip to some nearby child-friendly National Trust house called Chitterlings (—*The family still live there*, one of the Wives had chiruped, *it's so lovely, the Beauveys, Lord Maidstone's family, it feels so . . . lived in*). So that was all right. Marley could now get drunk tonight with his old friends and they could all conspire in the helpful fantasy that their true lives still lay in the future, that the vague radiations of their dreams could still pass for genuine hope, and that their gossip on matters cultural and political was of any significance to anyone.

With the womenfolk gone, they all began to drink properly. For some time they reminded each other of the bold and carefree things they had done at college in the days when grants still existed; of how they had hated Mrs

Thatcher and had *very nearly* cheered when the IRA almost blew her up; of the wild Bohemian days when, after college, they had all for a couple of years systematically abused that benign arrangement from the post-war years, designed as a safety net to save honest working people and their blameless families from destitution in time of economic woe. They laughed at the memory of how it had been so ludicrously easy to get one's dole and one's housing benefit, while working out exactly what glittering career lay ahead of one, that *not* simply to trot along and pick up one's free money had seemed a sure indicator of congenital idiocy. Yes, they had been pretty wicked, all right! Then, after a slight pause, one of the old friends got down to the real topic of the evening.

—So, um, what's it like, Brian?

—What's what like?

—You know. Divorce.

—Singles world, Brian.

—Out there again, Brian.

—In the mix again.

—Free.

—So? What's it like?

—Oh, you know, said Marley.

—All those foreign girls, eh?

—Ah, said Marley, and looked at his wine. *Consuela.* The Tesco's Finest claret suddenly tasted like old fridges and Marley felt the surprisingly urgent desire to throw it across the room and howl like a wolf. —Hmm, he said, instead. —Actually, I just need to, you know, the loo, just a sec . . .

In the thankful, unjudging silence of the lavatory, he sat heavily down upon the closed seat, backside still glowing with Aga-induced warmth but heart gripped with the cold and merciless tragedy of existence. He considered his future. It was all too clear. The Personal Columns

81

were his only refuge now. A modern solution to a modern problem, why not? He had skimmed them often on quiet Sunday mornings, those little ads where every girl is Attr and every man is Tall and everyone has a GSOH. Perhaps there he could tell the truth? Well, at least, nearly . . .

M 42 tall unbald multilingual prof hmwnr dvrcd (but flly rcvrd!) p/t fthr of blvd (*eh? boulevard? no, that was no good*) beloved son (3), seeks upbeat hppy (*no, that might be read as* hippy) happy F 30–38 (if poss solvent) for grwn-up rltnshp inc kids if u have kid already fine maybe even better for instant Big Family (no big families = no big stories!) ok ok just begging for Normality really I know we are all supposed to be oh-so-happy with our little flats and our one-z-fun pre-cooked meals and our white grave-goods piling up on 0% credit but I've written this and you're reading it so we both know that's all lies so let's be honest for once and look why not just do a nice little enlightened arranged deal to save ourselves both from wishing we had made (more?) kids when we were young instead of wasting our lives on our so-called careers and dooming ourselves to spend the next thirty years desperately keeping up the fantasy that we have not in fact blown it for good and made our very own easy-to-clean Hell. Please include recent photo. All replies answered before Christmas unless old/fat/ugly/stupid/neurotic. BOX NO 42½

—Oh God, sighed Marley. Christ, why had no one older and wiser told him to do law at college? That was all any career adviser should ever be allowed to tell anyone: *do law, do law, do law.* Still unable to face his old friends again, he picked up the top book from the pile of the usual lavatory-reading matter. It was a heavy volume called *Best of Breed*. He flipped it idly open, and found himself reading about an incident at the battle of El Alamein, in which a man with moustaches and big shorts had won the VC commanding his men as they held out all day, cut off, against panzers.

Though by now fainting with loss of blood from his head wound and occasionally hallucinating that he was defending a harbour from enemy ships, Turner insisted that he be kept up to date by a running commentary, and upon being informed that three successive shots had scored hits, he cried, 'Good work, a hat trick, a hat trick!'

Marley stopped at these words, mid-page. He knew the story. He had heard it before, years ago, so long ago it was as if he had always known it. He closed his eyes in disbelief as the cover of a *Victor For Boys* comic (*every week, only 6d*) flashed up before his eyes, telling him, aged perhaps six or seven, of the glorious Defence of Outpost Snipe. No, it was impossible. He turned back a thick, glossy page in the weighty book. The hard wooden seat of the lavatory seemed to fall slightly but swiftly, dropping his stomach as if he had just breasted a humpback bridge rather too fast in an old car. He was right, Outpost Snipe it was. What the hell was this? Why was his head filled with names and battles from twenty years before his birth? Stunned, he read on about other men in ridiculous shorts doing extraordinary things. Malta. Italy. Normandy. Arnhem (*'the counter-attack was pressed home in the finest style with bayonet and grenade, irrespective of casualties, throwing the SS back in confusion'*). Almost all of them struck some deep, soft-tolling bell of boyhood memory inside him . . .

—Hey, you dying in there, Brian?

—Oh, God, sorry, just, you know.

Marley hastily feigned noisy wiping and washing, pulled the chain and then, using his well-known nicotine dependence as a further excuse for solitude, swooped for another fat glass of wine from the kitchen table before going straight on through his old friends and out into the garden.

Apart from the eternal hum of the distant M25, all was peaceful here. Marley sheltered gratefully from the rain beneath a small tree, lit his cigarette and glugged his wine. The alcohol began to seethe and tingle in his brain. He looked back, hidden in the darkness, to observe the lit-up kitchen and his friends gathered around the Aga. Forty-three, Christ. What had he and they done? He could not stop the obituaries from rearing up mockingly in his brain, reminding him of how he had laughed at all that sort of thing in *Monty Python* and suchlike. And what exactly had he managed, pray, with his life, with this one, unrepeatable shot at existence? What attacks on anything had he ever pressed home in style? What hostile forces had he ever thrown back in confusion?

BRIAN MARLEY (no decorations)

Brian Marley, who died last weekend during a hastily rearranged trip to Oxford (and Shakespeare) in circumstances which are still unclear but were almost certainly more ludicrous than tragic, never risked his life for a friend, his heart for a woman or his health for adventure. Born at the start of the sixties, into unparalleled peace and prosperity, Marley went to college, where, inexplicably subsidised out of general taxation, he was able to get drunk almost every night while espousing a variety of then-fashionable causes, none of which involved him in any personal discomfort and most of which were later shown to be

84

fatuously wrong-headed if not actually nurtured by the KGB. Graduating with a completely useless Humanities 2:1, he travelled widely over the next two decades, teaching English as a cut-price street-walker for the international American language, chasing foreign women, missing out on several domestic property booms but not noticing the years passing. At the age of 38, he had an affair with an Englishwoman, Celia, whom he met abroad, presumably as the result of undiagnosed homesickness. This led to her unintended pregnancy and their subsequent marriage. Unable to settle in the reality of England, he was divorced soon after their return (no third party was involved) and thereafter occupied a small flat in Acton where he kept his unimportant collection of second-hand tweed jackets. At 42 he fell absurdly in love with a young Argentinian woman and, knowing he was doing the wrong thing and abusing her trust, but lacking the moral fibre to escape the general mendacity of his life, hurt her deeply and ended up alone anyway and serve him right. A disappointment to his mother, he is survived by a son, Tommy, who learned at an early age to despise him.

—Oh sod and bugger, said Marley softly. Then he stubbed out his cigarette on the tree trunk, drained his glass and turned back towards the kitchen to get more wine.

Before he reached the door, however, a shadowy figure plunged out of the house and into the garden, shouting into its phone, its overgrown turn-ups flapping in the rainy breeze, a chain jangling loose from its belt to its hip pocket, sucking on a very large and very stiff gin and tonic with all the abandon of a man who should by rights be snorting fat lines of cocaine in Soho. Even before this person's features caught the light, Marley knew that of all his old college friends this could only be Grant Brodie.

—No, no, no, Tamsin, you *total* airhead, we *can't have* anyone who was *ever* in the army *or* has had mental treatment, you know the rules. They've got to be normal. Normal boring bloody straight people with jobs and mortgages! Oh fuck, look, I'm coming back to town. Get yourself straight. Christ. Oh, hello, Brian.

—Trouble? said Marley to the yellow-tinted, sightless shades that turned on him in the gloom.

—Programme just went pear-shaped. Give us a fag then.

—I thought you'd given up.

—I give up every day, darling. Till the sun goes down and the notion of actually *wanting* to live an extra few years seems quite absurd.

—I know what you mean.

—I doubt it. What, you, the happy-go-lucky boy?

—Boy? Forty-five next big stop, not happy, not feeling lucky and not going anywhere.

—Yes, nasty, isn't it? I'm forty-four next month. I was going to have a big party but then it occurred to me that after forty, every birthday party is merely a rehearsal for one's own wake. We will not make any new big friends, we already know all the people who will come to watch us being buried or burned. Look, here they all are, just killing time really and calling it a party. Another bloody *party*. And in aid of what, pray? Mere seduction and oblivion. I shall have no *real* parties. No birthdays to arrange, no Christmas stockings to fill quietly at night. I shall have no degree ceremonies to attend or sports days to cheer. No brides to greet or give away. I shall never christen a child, let alone a grandchild. Oh, I shall go to a few hundred more *parties*, no doubt, but the next ancient human ceremony at which I shall be of undoubted centrality will be my own funeral, whether it's in thirty years' time or next week.

—Ah.

—*Ah*, indeed. The authentic English reaction to any emotion. Oh well, must be off, Brian, you dear Aga-arses are very nice, but town calls me back. Tamsin's incapably coked up already and I stand to lose several hundred thousand pounds on Monday morning if I haven't found someone who's perfectly normal and vaguely middle class and passably lucid but so absolutely desperate they'd risk their life for money. It's harder than you think, I can tell you. Anyway, I want some cocaine.

—I'd do it.

—Well, I haven't got any here, so bad luck.

—No, I mean I'd do anything for money.

—No you wouldn't, darling, you're just a sweet lightweight. Farewell.

—You all think that, don't you? Well, I'm not, right?

—Dear me, Brian, what on earth is this? Un-English behaviour?

—Today I realised my life is nothing but a heap of lies, so the only thing left for me to do is keep half-sober and earning until I can sort Tommy out and try not to be too depressing when he's around so I don't mess him up before he leaves home. And by then I'll be nearly sixty, so that'll be that and I can go to the pub one afternoon and stay there for ever. And if I ever get to the Pearly Gates, all I can hope for is that St Peter might say, *OK, Mr Pantomime Englishman, today I'm in a good mood. Tell you what, how about we just pretend you never even existed*? So there. Right. More drink. Drive safely, Grant. And I hope you find someone for whatever it is.

—Wait. Let me tell you about my programme.

—Sorry, I don't really want to hear about your exciting career just now, Grant.

—We're going to drop six ordinary Brits into the last

unexplored jungle on earth, and see who lasts the longest before they go screaming bonkers or die. Or get eaten.

—Eaten?

—Actually, between you and me, the cannibalism has more or less stopped now, I think, though you never know. They still keep on finding little tribes who think white men are just a legend and the world stops over the furthest mountain they can see. And eat each other. So I'm not sure about the cannibalism bit, though obviously we're going to milk that one for all its worth, but yes, the dying could be very real.

—You can't do that, can you?

—Well, yes, it *is* pushing the envelope, but underneath the edge of the envelope is where the money hides. And everyone will have to sign a very clear legal document that says they can't sue, *whatever*. We'll film that business live, of course. Nice build-up, you know the sort of thing: *Now you are quite sure you realise what this means, are you?* Gap. Dark music. *Absolutely sure?* Gap. Darker music. *You could die, you know.* Synthesised trumpets. *And you're still ready to sign?* Music builds. *You really want to go for it?* Then handshakes, weeping, congratulations, smiling presenters, the usual. Then off we go to Papua New Guinea. Our helicopters will come at the end of every week, but if anything goes wrong in between, hard luck. And to be honest, of course, we're rather hoping that someone *will* die. On camera, live, on Christmas Day if possible. Big first for reality TV, as you say. Not *you*, of course, Brian.

—Me?

—Well, you see, I thought perhaps you might like to have a go.

—Oh yeah, me against SAS men?

—No, no, no, we're not *allowing* anyone like that.

—I'm not a celeb, Grant.

—Exactly. That's the whole point. This time we're just going to show very ordinary, normal British people, well, *falling to bits*. No voting. No interviews. No stupid group tasks or anything like that. Just six Brits with little digital satellite cameras, each alone in the jungle, seeing how long they can last in hell with Christmas coming. And millions and millions of people betting millions and millions of pounds on the result. That's where the real money's going to be, you see.

—Do you really need someone?

—Someone's just bloody dropped out and we start next week. A forty-odd-year-old English teacher not in terribly good shape, sorry, but you really *aren't*, would be ideal. You have *got* a mortgage, haven't you?

—Got one? It's killing me.

—Good, good. And to be honest you're so, well, so bloody *English*, Brian. We've got our regulation chatty Welshman and bolshie Scotsman and charming bloody Colleen and plain-speaking Northern git already so we don't want any more of *those*. We need someone else from real *England*. The prize is two million pounds, by the way. Tax-free.

—Bugger me.

—I'll pass, but thanks. And guaranteed fame, of course.

—What, and you just have to last the longest?

—Well, not quite. When it's down to one person, remember, it's almost Christmas by now, well, this one person can either take £100,000 and get on the chopper, or else choose to be left all alone for a whole week, *over Christmas*, with their camera and lots of batteries and salt tablets and a crate of water and fuck all else except an emergency beacon. We thought £100,000 was quite clever, enough to tempt people home but not really enough to change someone's life for ever, these days. What do you think? The people who bet on the last contestant can

89

choose, too: they can take each-way odds right then or keep the lot on the nose. If our champion holds out another seven days he gets the two million quid and his punters get the full whack. But if he calls the choppers in before time's up, if he misses his little interactive chats, for any reason at all, mental or medical, he gets *absolutely nothing* and nor do the people who bet on him. Great telly, eh? Greed versus fear and weakness, essentially. Oldest drama in the world. You know, even if you didn't win, you'd be in all the papers for a week or two. And think of it this way: at least you'll have a few weeks off the fags and booze, and frankly, how the hell is either of us going to manage *that* any other way? Are you OK, Brian?

Marley could feel his skin growing cold, and guessed he must have turned white. Something had suddenly churned his guts, sucked all his blood away from his flesh and nerves, dragging it in primeval tides, safely into his inner organs. It was adrenalin, that unmistakable hit of self-made chemicals, a mainline cocktail of fear and longing that had been brewing up in his heart ever since he kissed Consuela Martinez; that burning ice that can suddenly race up your veins and chill your scalp, that tells you darkly and deeply that the unusual sound you have just heard is nothing else than the knocking of fate on your very own private door.

—Well, well, well, you're serious, aren't you?

And Marley could only nod.

*

Consuela Martinez nodded, looking down at her cappuccino coffee in the students' café at the London English School. Marley got ready to open his mouth. He was well dug in and prepared for this speech. He was going to speak to her long and slow and low and solid as a rock, full of certainty and future, the way every lover should always speak.

Then she looked up. Marley felt a spiritual vertigo seize him as he looked into her eyes, those eyes as deep and dark and mysterious as the well of a ruined castle, where he would be sure to drown in big seas and rip tides of emotion.

—It's, you see, look, the thing is, um, he said, having cleared his throat with some difficulty.

—Yes?

—I, well, you see, the *reason* I can't take the Oxford and Shakespeare trip, it's, look, I just wanted you to know that I was really looking forward to it. Oxford, I mean. And Shakespeare, of course.

—I was looking forward to seeing England, with you.

—Yes. Oh, hi, Graziana, hi, Shukiro, be with you in just a minute.

—You are too busy to take us on the Shakespeare and Oxford trip?

—No. Yes, I mean. I'm, look, Consuela, I'm, going away for a bit.

—You are leaving our class?

—Yes.

—Oh. That is a pity.

—Is it? I mean, yes, it is, isn't it? The thing is, um, what I wanted to say was, well, I'm, I'm sure they'll have another good teacher for you. Someone better than me. Younger, I mean, ha, more, more fun, for you. To show you Oxford.

—And Shakespeare.

—Yes, him too.

—You will be away a long time?

—Um, about six or seven weeks. I might be back before Christmas but I don't really know for sure. I hope not, actually.

—You are teaching somewhere else?

—God, no. I mean, of course, I love doing this, my

91

teaching, here, I mean, with you, and the others too of course, it's just, something else. A sort of, a sort of big chance for me.

—That is important.

—So, will you, that is, your, er, your course carries on here after New Year, doesn't it?

—If I return.

—But you must.

—Must I, Brian?

—I mean, because your English is coming on so well, of course, and if you don't come back, well, I, you, you'll have thrown it all away. Your English.

—Yes.

—Which would be a shame.

—Brian?

—Yes?

—After Christmas, when you come back from your big chance, will you come back to teach us here?

—Well, I'm not really sure. About the teaching, I mean.

—Oh.

—No, no, I mean, God, yes, of course, I'll come back here. To visit. The class. And you. And see, how things are. With your English. And things. Yes, yes, OK, Kazuo, what is it now?

—I have filled in my registration document, oh my teacher. I hope it is correct.

—Right, right, let me ... yes, that's fine, fine, ah, but look, you've got the date wrong here, Kazuo, ha ha. That should be 1977, not 1987, you *can't* have been *born* in 1987, ha ha. Oh yes, sorry, of course you could. Sorry. Yes, that's fine. Very good. If you could just tell the others I'll be there now. Great. Oh bugger, look, Consuela, I just wanted to tell you, yes well, I'd better go, my class, you know.

—Yes, you must go. They are hoping for their teacher.

—Waiting, Consuela, waiting.

—Oh yes. It is confusing. It is the same word for us in Espanish: *esperando*, they are waiting, and hoping, and expecting.

—Yes, I know. I've always thought that was, sort of, well, nice.

—Yes. So now you will go away and I will be waiting and hoping and expecting to see you again. Is it a nice joke, Brian?

—Very. Very nice. Right then. Um, so, I'll, I'll see you in seven weeks. I hope. Or wait, ha ha. Goodbye then.

—Till we see again.

—Yes.

Marley got up, skilfully managing almost not to get his legs tangled up in his chair, and left quickly.

After he had gone, Consuela sat for a long time over her untouched coffee. A single fat tear gathered on her dark eyelashes until it grew too heavy and fell. She saw it splash down through the damp crust of brown sugar, the chocolate dusting and the milky froth, then watched as the sweet foam slowly folded back, leaving no trace of her teardrop's salty passage.

*

Little Tommy's tears streamed down his face. He did not turn his face aside, in the prideful, self-preserving, hopeful adult way, but kept straight on to his father's face, eyes wide open, as if unconsciously insisting that Marley should see clearly just how much hurt and despair he had once again brought into the world. Marley, unable to bear it, answered this timeless call of loneliness and bereavement in the only way it can be answered, in children or in adults, by lifting up his little son and hugging him tight. Eventually Tommy recovered the power of speech.

—Why might you be away for Christmas, Daddy?

—Well, look, it's a bit complicated, Tommy. I might be

back in time. But Father Christmas will come anyway. And I'll definitely be back after New Year. And things will be much better then, said Marley, hugging his son even closer and looking over his tiny shoulder at the woman, now more and more a stranger, from whose womb his boy had struggled. —Much, much better.

—*Six weeks?* she mouthed, silent, furious.

—Peut-être sept.

—*What the hell's going on?*

Marley was not going to tell her. He was not going to tell anyone. But behind Tommy's back he made the timeless, finger-rubbing sign that said: *lots of money.*

—O-K, she sighed.

*

—I'm going away for a bit, Mum. I might miss Christmas. I've got a big chance.

From the upstairs flat, the manically exact *thudda-thudda-thud* of computer-generated music had started once again.

—I always knew something would *come up* for you, darling, said Mrs Marley, without further question, as if she preferred to keep her son's big chance in the happy, abstract realm rather than run any risk of dissecting it and revealing it to be neither very big really nor in all honesty much of a chance. —Don't you worry about me, I'll be fine.

—Cheers, Mum. Marley raised his sherry. As he drained it, he looked once more at the frozen, black-and-white figures marching for ever across the long-scrapped aircraft carrier, and at the bearded, booted man carrying the upright sword.

III

FORTY-FIVE YEARS ON

You see, my friends, we each *sub*-consciously imagine our Self to exist at the height of its powers. Our bodies decay, but our minds are proud, and insist on anchoring us at the time of our youth, our strength, our maximum *impact upon the world*. On awakening, I myself frequently have, for some seconds, difficulty in ridding myself entirely of the happy illusion that I am approximately twenty-five years of age, rather than approximately three times that old [*laughter*]. This is no doubt a trick of psychological health, but does it not mask a deeper truth? *Sub*-consciously, yes, we will always be strong young people, but what of the *un*-conscious? What of the half-remembered influences of our very earliest youth? We are our parents' children in every meaning of the word, for the world into which they brought us was theirs, not ours. In reality, we may all be old [*cries of: no, no; speak for yourself, Carl; laughter*]. In our *sub*-conscious, we all are young and full of hope. But perhaps in our *un*-conscious, in that secret engine-room of our Selves, we are all forever small children, still ruled by the assumptions and prejudices, the fears and the visions of the last generation. Like those well-known generals, we cannot *help* fighting the previous war. No doubt this is fine in a world in which nothing changed but the seasons and where the wisdom passed down in laws and stories was vital to our own lives. But today we are all little Columbuses, setting out onto uncharted seas, our fathers' useless maps thrown to the four winds. Our psyche cannot keep up, it lags a generation behind, hugging the known coasts of a flat but homely earth. And that is why, perhaps, our modern lives so often feel to us like mere dreams as we follow our forefathers into eternity [*laughter; applause; cries of bravo*].

Carl Jung, impromptu speech, shorthand notes taken by Professor Charles 'C. O.' Nicholson during a dinner in Jung's honour given at the Royal Society, London, 1960.

January in England

Christmas gone now, a mere unlovely, unsettling shadow on the bathroom scales and the credit-card statement. Winter unleashed and hitting hard, a polar blast hailing on down from the overmelting ice floes, roaring over fish-stripped, ship-swallowing seas, whipping cold sleety salt in the faces of green Celtic sea cliffs and grey Nordic fjords, barrelling on across the blood-soaked old Continent, where every ploughable field, each grazeable acre and any defensible townland can recall in its stones and its bones the scream of legions, the thunder of guns, the crunch of armour.

In Northern lands and landlocked Eastern plains, the inhabitants draw gloomily upon whatever stocks they have laid up, mental and physical, against the icy, suicidal, hard-drinking darkness; around the more blessed Mediterranean, the annual billion litres of suntan lotion, piss and shit has finally dispersed again into the panting, rainswept waves, hotels and restaurants begin lazily to be renovated and restored against the hoped-for spring. Somewhere between these two extremes of latitude and hence of lifestyle, in the lowland portion of the largest island of a mid-sized archipelago set out north-westwards of the Eurasian land mass, a flat, overpopulated, once-mighty country plonked halfway betwixt the widowly caution of oft-raped Europe and the bumptious, newly outraged virginity of the New World, another Sunday morning dawns without much hope.

Across this land, England, the sun is a mere yellow weakling, skulking in grey-green clouds, easily outstared without shades, shadowless. Featureless weeks of this to come, the chances of anything but sleet and wind-blown rain between now and Easter slim to nil. In the heartless urban centres, pedestrianised to death, chewing-gum splotches march as far as the eye can bear, unscrubbable witnesses, like scene-of-crime stains of grey, lifeless blood on greasy concrete slabs, as if the entire population was gunshipped from the skies three days ago, ambushed in the midst of untroubled consumption, mown down, raked up, hastily stacked in flat-pack coffins and dumped by the truckload in machine-dug graves. Leaving only grey fluorescent peace in the shuttered malls: feeble chain-store neons, like street lights wrongly programmed, glimmering weak in grim daylight above the steel-grilled windows, seeming low on power from pointless nightlong brightness, calling out desperately to a nation which has been living discreditably off intangible earnings and notional equity for rather too long now and is starting to become dimly aware of a long overdue calling to account, of the day of piled-up reckoning that is to come: *PAY NOTHING TODAY LAST CHANCE SAVE SPEND SAVE AGAIN TODAY PAY NOTHING AT ALL NOUGHT PER CENT TILL THIS YEAR NEXT YEAR SOMETIME PAY NOTHING SAVE NOW DON'T MISS WHY WAIT CLOSING DOWN FINAL NEVER NEVER MUST END LAST DAYS*, identical temptations plastered in thinly disguised hysteria across the virtually indistinguishable centres of various so-called cities from Plymouth to Newcastle.

Air Colonel Achilleo Martinez of the Argentinian Air Force, however, had landed not in England, but in London, the undisputed capital of Northern Europe.

He was entirely unworried by (and indeed, professionally viewed with approval) the substantial military hardware on display around Heathrow these days. There may be those who argue that such parades of standing military strength sit ill with Anglo-Saxon traditions of freedom, but Air Colonel Martinez was not among them. He did not admire England for its supposed liberalism and so-called good manners. ¡No! He knew that the English had to behave like the English because if they did not make themselves behave like the English they would be madmen, the terrors of the earth. Before the English became English they were pirates and barbarians. Now they were pirates and barbarians with fine manners and woollen suits. They fooled the world. ¡But not Air Colonel Achilleo Martinez, ha ha! No, no, he admired England not for its alleged liberty but for the historical fact that England always managed to end up on the winning side. As far as liberty was concerned, Air Colonel Martinez agreed with Goethe that a little Unfreedom is better than a lot of Disorder.

In any case, as he now emerged from his taxi in Piccadilly, substantial and antique baggage again in hand (he despised wheeled plastic cases), he had no intention of allowing a small thing like reality to trouble him on his visit to London to console his beloved daughter on the loss of her Englishman.

¡Of course not! Who does? Who allows the vile deserts full of tower blocks which surround Madrid to dampen their joy upon arriving at the Prado? Are the thankless miles of concrete-blocked nothingness a problem for Paris? No, no, we each have our own destinations and expectations, and so long as our San Marcos still defy the waves, we will simply not notice the ghastly landward approaches to our Venices.

To Air Colonel Martinez, London was a walled city whose boundary posts, Pillars of Hercules beyond which he had not the slightest desire or reason to go, were the British Museum, Oxford Circus, Westminster Bridge, the Aldwych, Buckingham Palace and Marble Arch. Its focal point was the United Services Club, where his room had been booked tonight through the offices of a friendly RAF wing commander. And since he entertained the rational expectation that he would find these deep and significant things unchanged, he had been entirely untroubled by the suggestion that anything superficial might have altered.

¡His poor Consuela!

Ah, he had seen the programmes she had recorded, of Mr Brian Marley in the jungle. Yes, he had spoken like a true Englishman, no wonder he had seen off the gutless rabble of his opponents. A man. A man with a son, Consuela had said. Air Colonel Martinez sighed. They had kissed just once, his Consuela had said. ¡A pity they had not made love! A child for his Consuela, to console her, a grandchild for himself to hold. A half-Argentinian, half-English grandchild. A fine mixture. Of course, it would have been even better if she had married him first, but he could have forgiven that. With daughters you know who your grandchildren are, in any case. Ah, here was Whitehall. Yes, nothing had changed. That was good.

*

—So, I mean, that's OK then, is it? The results of the referendums? Referenda? OK, do you think?

—Fuckin' great, boss.

—Absolutely fine.

—But, um, the majority *against* in England was, well, I mean, you know, ha, *pretty definite*, to be honest. Wasn't it?

—Aye aye, aye, but what about in *Britain*, boss? Heh heh!

—You see, counted *by country*, just like we said. Scotland, Wales, Northern Ireland, all *very* strongly in favour. So in fact *Britain* voted decisively *for* the euro, three to one. A very substantial majority.

—Heh heh!

—Yes, I suppose it does sound pretty, you know, *convincing*, when you put it like that, doesn't it?

100

—Very convincing indeed.

—So now we just have tae win the General fucking Election. Then we can do anything we like for another five years anyway whatever any wee bastard says.

—We *will* win, won't we?

—Well, how ridiculous, of course we will. *Our* voters will never vote for *them*, so all we need is twenty of *their* natural seats to vote for us again. I've already told the Chancellor to cut income tax in the Budget, by the way.

—Oh. Oh, thanks. So, um, does that mean we're going for early May?

—Of course. And I think we should get tough on crime again, don't you?

—OK. What about the, y'know, *causes* of crime?

—Oh, I shouldn't worry about that bit.

—Heh heh!

*

—Pity about this Marley fellow not making it, said the Senior Editor. —Sounded like quite a chap. Are we running anything about him? All the little rags are.

—Absolutely. I'll send someone round to see his aged mother. She lives near the BBC, they say.

—How ghastly for her. All those wine bars full of skinny, barren harridans in black coats and shaven-headed catamites in ridiculous trousers. Oh well. Must toddle, if anyone needs me this afternoon send my car to the United Services, will you?

—I'm sure we'll be fine, Chief.

—Yes, I'm sure you will, Harry.

*

Mrs Mary Marley held her grandson on her ample knee. Though her adult life had been lived in times of wary peace, she had in childhood dodged stuttering V1s in

101

Cricklewood, heard the boom of anti-aircraft guns, felt the thud of anti-English bombs, seen houses burning, smelled death as she was hurried schoolwards past last night's new-made ruins and watched in silence as cups of tea were brought, clinking dully on cheap saucers, to the pale recipients of dreaded telegrams.

She had drunk her own cups of tea, and wept her own, private tears and felt her womb cry out against the time-less wrongness of a child dying before its parent. Now she was herself again, and she watched with a certain degree of wartime scorn as her former daughter-in-law wept public tears of gratitude.

—Mum's got to go to work now, Tommy, sniffed the child's mother.

—We'll be fine, won't we? retorted his grandmother.

—Can we play with Daddy's little soldiers again?

—Of course we can. And we can read Daddy's books.

—I don't know how I would have managed without you, Mary. I suppose the TV people will pay up soon, but until then . . .

—Of course you would have managed. Everyone does. But that's what families are for, my dear. Off you go now. Oh, and don't forget, my dear, you *are* divorced, you know.

—Bye bye, Mummy.

—Bye bye, Tommy (*sniff*).

—Granny?

—Yes, my darling boy?

—I wish Daddy wasn't dead, Granny.

—Of course you do, darling. And so do I. We'll miss him. He was a nice man. But I'm afraid it's hard cheese and we'll just have to get on with it, won't we? Now, let's see where those soldiers were, shall we?

Mary Marley took her grandson's little hand and led him to the old leather trunk full of Brian's old books and toys. She felt warmth flowing through her own cold hands at the feel of living, strengthening flesh again, the touch of trustful futurity, the smooth certainty that life, a life connected directly and undeniably to hers and indeed now dependent on her, was growing, going on, walking at her side again taller each day. She had missed that feeling for years. But now she had it again. It was better than having Brian, in a way, what with having to worry all the time about whether something would ever come up for him. Yes, they would be just fine.

*

—I don't care if we *don't* find him, Grant. The longer we *don't* find him, or his body, the better the story. We'll break 25 million viewers tonight for the start of *Brit Pluck 2: The Rescue Mission*. And Brian was *such* long odds at the start, God only knows how much Channel Seven Betting has stashed. We are *so* made.

—Poor Brian, though. We *were* friends, Tamsin.

—Well, yes. But think: you've set his child up for life. He'll get the two million quid now.

—Yes, that's true. It was really all for his son he was doing it, you know.

—God, how cheesy.

—I suppose. And for love, believe it or not. Not a bad way to go, really.

—Speak for yourself, Grant. I'd rather go with a big fat line of coke just hitting my brain and a handsome German man about to fuck me stupid, if it's all the same to you.

—Well, yes.

*

—Here, George, OK if we switch channels? I wanna see that jungle rescue thing.

—Remember that stuff before Chrimbo?

103

—Ha ha ha! Them choppers, fuck!

—Fuckin' righ'! Ka-fuckin'-booom!

—See the face on tha' fuckin' stupid TV bitch when she knew she was fucked?

—Ha ha ha!

—Fried all them fuckin' tarts an' poofs proper, eh?

—Fuck aye. Might happen again, never know. Pints all round, Macksie?

—What you fuckin' reckon? How come you always *asks*, like, when it's *your* round? Fuckin' set 'em up.

—'Magine that poor bastard left out there all on his own, like.

—Greedy old fuck.

—He migh' be alive, mind.

—Dying out there. All on his tod. Fuck. He lasted it out, fair play to him.

—Mad old cunt.

—Wonder if they found 'is body, like. 'Magine the state it'll be in now. Fuck.

*

Brian Marley's body was still.

It had for some time given up on thrashing and twitching about, and now lay panting softly of its own automatic accord, streaked in gentle rivulets of cooling sweat, while Marley himself, his ghostly, disembodied, unconscious essence, snorkelled comfortably about in the half-lit darkness, roaming gently, timelessly and weight-lessly through dim reefs of memory or premonition.

His unanchored soul was vaguely aware of sunrises and sunsets coming and going with unusual speed and was occasionally even half conscious of his own physical body lying, it seemed, on a bed under blankets, but whenever he felt himself about to rise finally towards the bright blue surface, he allowed, or rather softly, softly, ever so

104

softly, commanded himself to sink down again towards the restful dark.

This time, his slow fall back into the sunless world of pure dreaming was accompanied by an image of snowflakes whipping towards him, out of the blackness, against the windscreen of an old car, the thin, silver, whirring wipers clearing only small black arcs in the white powder outside. As Marley, through his childhood eyes, stared at this forgotten memory, the endless snowflakes hypnotised him until he lost focus and the windscreen faded out. The white specks were no longer snow falling, but onrushing stars, he was the captain of a starship warping for ever through a universe which smelled curiously of old carpets and warm oil. He embraced his dizzy fall towards infinity, hugged unconsciousness back close into his arms with all the instinctive desire of a half-sick child yearning to prove to himself and his mother that he needs a day off school, a day that can be spent not at a small desk, under constant threat of the teacher's anger for his sheer incorrigible daydreaming, but in leafing again through well-known pages, *This Eagle Annual belongs to Brian Marley Christmas 1966, Love from Mummy and Daddy; This Victor Book For Boys belongs to Brian Marley, Christmas 1968, Love from Mummy.*

—Mummy, he murmured.

—Hello there, Jungle Jim, laughed a female voice.

—Are we all sitting comfortably? Then let's begin, whispered Marley to himself, as exhausted and relieved as the captain of a Trident submarine on hearing BBC Radio 4 again after a nerve-racking day-long signals blackout. He pulled the blanket tighter. The familiar soft itchiness snuggled around his earlobes, the beloved panel of silky smooth material which topped the blanket slid along his cheek. Someone else's hands pulled the bedclothes back a little, tucked him tighter in.

Home at last, then.

He permitted his eyelids to flicker briefly open, just to check. Three inches from his nose he glimpsed, in that little instant, the grey wool of the blanket and a small, square sewn-on patch which he knew well, had always known well: the Wool Utility mark which he had seen so often on his mother's blankets and nowhere else. Beyond this, his snapshot glance registered the unmistakable spine and lettering of an *Eagle Annual* among other books on a small bookcase.

Everything was all right, then. He was at home, waking up. He was not lost in a vile jungle, dying and dreaming that he was a child back in his mother's flat, but was, in fact, back in his mother's flat and dreaming that he was lost in a jungle and dying. Perhaps it was even better than that? Perhaps he was in fact still a child? That would be nice. That would be very, very nice, to be seven or eight again. Or six, even. I think I shall stay six for ever and ever. Hello again, Daddy. That would be nice. Perhaps everything had not yet actually happened. Perhaps this time, he would go on the Flying Scotsman and Daddy would not be cross with him and not go away. Perhaps it had all not yet gone wrong.

Gone wrong?

What?

Who?

How many years?

What had gone wrong for how long for whom?

He did not know. Yet he was quite sure, in some dark well of his being, that it was so: *things had gone wrong* for this person, whoever he was. Injustice had been done; failure had been known; despair had been visited. He did not want to know any more. Whatever had happened to whoever, it did not matter now. It had never happened.

His decision was final. It was Saturday again now, a Saturday in the mid 1960s. A long Saturday with his mother and father all to himself. A strong hand holding each of his little hands, swinging him up into the air at every third step, Jump Jimmy Crow, laughter and chatter above his head, an infinite Saturday of pigeons, parks and galleries, of sherbet flying saucers and crisps with packets of salt, of big red buses with jolly conductors, ending in a breathless rush, carried high in delicious, jogging fear on strong male shoulders (the animal feel of tweed against his little thighs naked in short trousers, the atavistic brush of a beard against his tiny calves) as they all hurried to be back in time for *Dr Who*, to hide in joyous terror from Daleks or watch open-mouthed as hopelessly brave British Soldiers fell screaming before silver robots emerging from sewers into Trafalgar Square, murderous shop-window dummies jerking into terrifying life or half-seen monsters lurking in the London Underground itself. Or perhaps they were burying Sir Winston Churchill today, and that was why he was off school? Or was it evening, was he being allowed to stay up late for the black-and-white football at long last, to watch Georgie Best demolishing Benfica? Or had they all gathered about the flickering set to see men bounding impossibly across the moon?

Breasts.

Two small, softly freckled and impossibly lovely breasts were swinging gently, bralessly, inside a thin, almost transparent, half-unbuttoned blouse right before his eyes, as whoever it was finished tucking him in. Marley's head cleared with a rush of blood that seemed to empty his entire body except his brain and his cock, and he instantly knew that he was not an innocent child, whatever else he was, and this was not his mother. He looked up and found himself staring into a young woman's smiling, merry blue eyes.

Her hair was short and blonde, roughly cropped in tight curls, her skin tanned, her teeth white, her eyebrows unplucked and there was not a sign of make-up on her

107

face. Her strong, rough hand was around his own. She seemed to be not merely human, but a vision of Life itself.

—Welcome back to the land of the living. I'm George.

—Ckcrchar, said Marley.

—It's Georgina really, of course, but everyone calls me George.

—Glrrrg, said Marley.

She moved to shift Marley's pillow, and under her blouse he saw her young breasts moving freely again. Now fully conscious and hence aware of shame again, he swiftly shifted his gaze upwards.

Above him was a faded, green-painted wooden ceiling. Stronger, whiter sunshine than Shepherd's Bush has ever known glared into his face through small wooden sash windows. From somewhere nearby came the sound of a referee's whistle, the unmistakable *thoomph* of a rugby ball being kicked hard and high and the cries of a pack of youths in full pursuit, encouraged by deeper male voices.

Marley felt panic rise in his throat, and froze. None of this could possibly be true. He had obviously gone completely and utterly insane.

—Is he alive, Miss? called a young boy's voice.

—Yes, Hawkins, he's alive, said the girl.

Marley looked cautiously around, deeply scared of what he might find, and saw a boy of about ten, blond, tanned, dressed in large shorts and an ancient, much mended white cotton shirt. On his head was a school cap. He was sitting cross-legged, barefoot on bare floorboards near to Marley's head, and had evidently been cleaning an old but well-cared-for rifle: now, he had stopped to stare up at Marley. Marley blinked back at him. The girl strode smoothly, barefoot, hips briskly swaying, to a wide-open green-painted door which stood swinging in the breeze. She called out into the bright, yet strangely diffuse, sunshine beyond the door.

—Tom, I say, Tom?

—What ho, George? answered a voice from some distance away.

—He's come round. Better get the Headmaster.

—Righto, George. Right, you lot.

A referee's whistle outside blew a single long and piercing blast. Marley swallowed with great difficulty and then lay slowly back on his little bed, grasping the cold iron frame with whitening fingers, as if the creaking metal springs might give way at any moment and plummet him down into some limitless abyss. His heart bumped hard at his breastbone with the terrifying certainty of total madness.

He looked down at the boy again. The boy was twirling the small bolt which acted as the weight on the end of the string of his rag pull-through and looking up at him, fascinated, expectant. Another boy in identical clothing, brown-haired and darker-skinned, rampaged into the shed and slid into place beside the first boy. They both stared at Marley.

—You *are* English aren't you sir? chirped the first boy.

—I'm Hawkins by the way and this is Crompton Minor it was Beauvey who found you *he* said you spoke English but you never know because he's such a chump are you sir are you English?

—Auerghhh, said Marley.

—Gosh if he *is* English that means the Head was right all along then, said the second boy.

—Of course he was right Crompton Minor you Bolshevik ass he's the Head he's always right.

—Ow sorry Hawkins.

Marley now looked around himself in quiet but absolute panic. He found he was sitting on an ancient iron camp bed in one corner of a large, wooden, plank-built hut: beside his head, fixed to the wooden wall, was a framed picture:

THE DAM BUSTERS ARE BACK

.... with

VULCANS

of course!

No. 617 Squadron, the most famous wartime unit in Bomber Command, is back. This squadron, which breached the mighty Ruhr dams in World War II, has now re-formed, and is equipped with the RAF's most potent bomber — the Avro Vulcan.
It represents a great advance on 617's wartime Avro Lancaster. A single Vulcan, carrying nuclear weapons, has greater hitting power than the total bomb load of all 7,366 Lancasters produced during the war.

FLIES ATLANTIC IN THREE HOURS
A Vulcan of No. 617 Squadron, R.A.F., has crossed the Atlantic in 2 hrs. 59½ mins. It covered the 1943 miles from coast to coast at an average speed of 649 m.p.h., while flying from Goose Bay, Labrador, to Waddington, Lincs.

A. V. ROE & CO. LIMITED MANCHESTER. Member of Hawker Siddeley Aviation Division

At the far end of the hut was a small raised stage. Above its centre, two crossed bamboo staves carried a large Union Jack and an Australian flag of exactly equal size, the reds aged to pink, the deep navy shades faded to sky blue like the ragged, blood-rusty colours of regiments long amal-

110

gamated or disbanded, hanging in the still, dusty, wood-polished air of a quiet English country church. Between the banners hung a framed and faded portrait of the young Queen Elizabeth and her dashing Duke of Edinburgh. Below this picture was fixed a carved and scrolled piece of wood, a memorial inscribed with many names.

He looked towards the open door of the hut, where the backlit figure of the young woman stood, leaning against the door frame, arms folded, face to the hazy sun and back to him. Beyond her, outside the hut, Marley could see a sunlit plain, a flat savannah no more than a mile across, bordered by towering cliffs. The light flooding this plateau was bright, warm and high, yet seemed curiously muted, its shadows soft, its rays not blinding. Marley blinked out into this strange illumination and could make out a small complex of wooden huts. Some twenty yards from the door he saw one of what was clearly a pair of rugby posts. The woman looked round at him, without shifting her weight from the door frame, and smiled. The short curls of her blonde hair glistened in a dull halo around her small ears, and darts of blue laughed in her eyes.

—Are we waking up, Jungle Jim? she asked.

Unable to find any remotely appropriate reply to this question from this apparition, trying to hold on to the laws of possibility and thus reality and thus sanity, Marley swung his head around away from her. In the opposite wall of the wooden hut were two green-painted sash windows. Through them, he found he could see, outside, the same golden, grassy, almost treeless plain, except that on this side the sheer mountains were even closer. Atop the soaring, rocky peaks glittered the incredible, stellar whiteness of an equatorial glacier, from which seemed to stream great ribbons and washes of white mist. And at the foot of these mountains lay, twisted but still gleaming in the sun, the dead-eyed, skeletal aluminium shell of a four-engined jet liner, its nose crumpled, as if it were a giant silver paper dart, straight into the face of the rock.

Marley stared at the wreckage of the plane. From some dizzy well of his boyhood, *locate and cement part no. 32 (cockpit canopy) to fuselage assembly*, his brain miraculously and instantaneously located, selected and dredged up a salient Fact from the billion apparently useless filed-away Facts with which the RAM of the male cortex is stuffed from birth. In the same insane way that he could still, or rather still simply *did*, without in the least wanting to, identify a 1969 Ford Cortina E at three hundred yards in his rear-view mirror or tell a picture of a Panzer III or Spitfire I from a picture of a Panzer V or Spitfire XII at a single unconscious glance (why? why? dear God *why*?), he found that he now knew, with absolute, absurd and somehow terrifying certainty that the ruined aircraft he was looking at was a De Havilland Comet IV.

Marley stared wonderingly at the long-dead plane wreck. Amazing as the sight itself was, it was an inner vision, called up by it, which stunned him with the cavernous pre-echo of lost remembrances darkly surging into view: *his father's hands, helping him build that very model aeroplane, his father's voice speaking softly, his father's hand trembling . . .*

Then this murmur from the dark well of the past was crowded instantaneously out by a babble of voices and a crowd of feet coming quickly nearer in the here and now. Marley swung himself back round to stare at the doorway again in something approaching blank terror. Who knew what demons his evident insanity might conjure up next?

The footsteps and voices approached the open door.

Marley jumped back halfway under his blanket as five or six children's faces appeared at the same moment in the small window nearest to him, pressed to the glass, gazing at him fixedly. Then came a smart but polite knock on the wooden wall of the hut beside the open door and a man of about his own age, barefoot but clean-shaven, short-haired, dressed in an ancient blazer and long shorts with turn-ups, stepped into the hut past the young woman, unlit pipe in smiling mouth, hand held out.

—What ho, George. Hello, old chap. How are you doing? Hawkins, finish cleaning that ruddy rifle and put it away. Boys and guns, eh? I'm Devereux, Tom Devereux. Housemaster. So you lot made it at last, eh? Well done. How's England?

Marley gazed mindlessly at the large, firm, tanned hand that was held out towards him. Then he looked helplessly up at the bright blue eyes. The eyes narrowed slightly and the hand was smartly withdrawn.

—Hmmm, said the man.

—Ckrekrch, said Marley, and reached in desperation for the tin mug of water beside him. Behind the man, the doorway was now crowded with youthful, expectant faces of both sexes and various ages.

—Well sir *is* he sir is he English?

—Frankly, Hawkins, I'm not sure.

—If he *is* sir does that mean we beat the Reds in the end sir?

—If he *is* sir are we going to England now sir?

—Can we go to the cinema in England sir?

—Can we go to the Oval sir?

—Can we go to Twickenham?

—Can we go to Brooklands?

—I said stay *out*, Johnson-Smithers. Out, the lot of you.

—Ouch gosh ow sorry sir.

—Sorry about them, the little buggers are dead keen on hearing about the old place. Me too, of course. I was born here as well. We only know about England from the pictures and articles in the Books from the Flight, you see. Well? Found your tongue yet, old chap?

—Please sir he doesn't *look* English sir I mean not like in the pictures.

—Mmm. Let's see, shall we? Crompton Minor, bring me *The Peoples of Mankind*, will you?

—Yes sir.

Marley watched in silent, dreadful fascination as the boy ran over to the small bookcase in the corner of the room, where Marley had first glimpsed the *Eagle Annual*. On it were ranged a large Bible and a small selection of other volumes which Marley, with mounting horror, also recognised at once: alongside the *Eagle Annual* number 7 (in which Marley was unnervingly sure he would find a certain particular Dan Dare story) were the *Eagle Sports Annual* 1958, *I-Spy*, the *Boy Scout Annual* of 1958 with its Girl Guide counterpart and the *Wonder Book of How and Why*. From this bookshelf the boy selected a large tome entitled *The Peoples of Mankind*, which he now brought back to the man.

—Thank you, Crompton Minor. Now we'll see, eh? Now, where was it? Ah yes, here we are. Hmm. Hard to tell, the shape he's in. English? I don't know about that. But he's Fair White all right, we can say that at least. Of course, boys, these pictures are merely a general guide, you know. What do you think, George?

The book was passed over Marley's unmoving head and past his wide, terrified eyes. As the young woman took it, he saw the page at which it was opened.

ENGLISHMAN.   NEGRO.   COOLIE, SOUTH INDIA.   CHINAMAN.

114

FAIR WHITE. DARK WHITE. ANCIENT EGYPTIAN. JEW.

—It *is* rather hard to tell, Mr Devereux. Though I'm pretty sure I heard him say *are you all sitting comfortably then I'll begin* just now, and that's the same way the Headmaster always says we should start the stories for the little ones, isn't it?

—It is, George. Of course, boys, the very fact that he made it here, up the Great Barrier, solo and without climbing gear, *suggests* he's English, or at least a colonial of British stock. And they count, really, of course.

—Sir sir sir go on sir ask him who won the Boat Race this year sir.

—Have the Aussies got the Ashes back sir?

—Are we beating the Welsh at rugger these days sir?

—How are the Jaguars doing at Le Mans sir?

—Ask him if it was our V-bombers that beat the Reds sir I *bet* it was.

—Have we got a colony on Mars yet sir?

—Is Charles King now sir?

—Look here, you shower, I said leave the chap in peace, he's pretty knocked about. And anyway, we don't even know if he *is* English yet.

—But sir sir Beauvey said ow yow sorry sir . . .

—Beauvey is a thickheaded oaf who eminently deserves a good clip round the ear at every possible opportunity on mere principle, Hawkins. As are you all, as are all boys of all races in all places at all recorded times in history. The Headmaster's on his way over, so you'd better pipe

115

down or you'll all cop six. Ah, here he is. Now we'll see.

The crowd by the doorway parted in laughter and cries of mild pain, the boys hastily doffing their caps, as they made way for a man somewhere between sixty and ninety, tall, clean-shaven on the chin but with splendid, snow-white moustaches bristling around almost to meet his short, sharp, salt-and-pepper hair. His eyes were the greenest and the most alarming Marley had ever seen. He was dressed in long white trousers and an ancient cricketing jumper that was more darns than jumper; he walked barefoot and carried in one hand a schoolmaster's cane, visibly frayed by time and use, which he swung briskly at the height of his own knees, idly and indiscriminately cutting a path through the thighs of the yelping, giggling boys and girls: in the other hand he held a strange, bright yellow object which Marley seemed to half remember from somewhere. Behind him, Marley could see several men who seemed to be somewhat younger, and behind them another group who he guessed might be about his own age. The children were finally driven off by a last group of adult men in their late teens or early twenties. All of the men were clean-shaven, and all wore blazers.

—Well, Devereux? demanded the white-haired man.

—Not sure yet, sir.

—Hmmph. This is some sort of damn clever miniature camera by the look of things. Suppose he could be a Yank. They always take all sorts of gadgets with them everywhere, can't do without them, the silly buggers. But you said he talked about a lieutenant, Beauvey? Are you sure, boy?

—Yes sir quite sure sir well nearly sure sir.

—You see, George my dear, the Yanks don't *have* lieutenants, they have *lootenants*.

—Do they, Headmaster? How funny of them. And I'm almost certain he said *Mummy* yesterday.

—Yes, George, but that could have been *Mommy, Mama,*

116

Mutti, Mamma. They all say that, you know, at the end. Remember that, boys, d'you hear? I've seen many men die, white, yellow, brown, black and most of the mixed-up stuff in between, good men, some of them, had to help out a couple of my own chaps, too, when they were trapped halfway out of a Sherman that was brewing up in Normandy. Where was I, George?

—Mothers, I think, Headmaster.

—Ah yes, thank you, my dear. Yes, all these dying chaps. And who did they all want, eh? Not their wives, not their sweethearts. Always their mothers, at the end, always their mothers. Remember that, boys. Let me try then. Make way. Now look here, old boy, we need to know if you're English or not. Simple enough question, eh? So come on, out with it, name, rank and all that sort of thing.

Marley stared blankly at the bright green eyes. They seemed to call to him from a dream, from some place he had never been but knew well. But he could not answer. He did not know. He did not know anything except that he himself was clearly and horribly insane. The man thwacked his cane menacingly against his thigh.

—Damn. Beauvey, come here, boy. Are you *quite* sure he said he was English?

—Quite sure sir you did tell me you were English didn't you sir tell them you did sir go on sir or they'll all think I'm an ass and the other chaps'll rag me something rotten and the Head'll give me six *please* sir do sir I'm Beauvey remember sir I found you during the Boxing Day match.

—Do try, Jungle Jim.

Marley looked at the desperate boy and thought very hard. He wanted to help the boy. He looked at the white-haired man. He very much wanted to placate those bright green eyes, to make them soften and approve. He looked at the girl. He very, very much wanted to please her. She nodded gently, raised her eyebrows encouragingly. Marley took a deep, shuddering breath and raised one emaciated arm.

—*Beau-vey*? he asked slowly, pointing a trembling finger.

—Yes yes that's me he understands Headmaster sir I told you Mr Devereux sir.

—He could be just parroting, sir.

—Ye-es. Come on, old boy, you said *Beauvey*. Well?

—Come on, wounded soldier. Here, let me sit you up a bit.

Marley let her sit him up a bit. She retreated a couple of steps. He looked around the room, his mouth working soundlessly. They were all staring at him. He closed his eyes, but instinctively held up a hand in a gesture that begged for patience and silence. In the darkness behind his eyelids, safe from the impossible visions around him, he considered: *Beauvey*. He had heard the name before. He did not know where or when. But out of the dim swirlings of his mind emerged not a thought, not any conscious identification with the world, but merely a phrase, a sentence, a shape of words without meaning. When it finally made it out through his mouth, it did so with a stunning clarity, in a voice which Marley did not recognise at all but which, somehow, was deeply his own:

—The, the, the Beauveys still live at Chitterlings, you know.

A cheer broke out around the hut. Marley fell back heavily in his bed, panting with the effort this had cost him, flicking desperate glances up at the white-haired, green-eyed man, to see if he was pleased. To see if the girl was happy with him. She seemed to be. She hurried to mop his brow.

—Well done, Jungle Jim. So you *are* English!

—He *is* English sir I told you so sir gosh sir I say sir my grandad said *his* father back in England was going to have to give Chitterlings up to pay his taxes because of the socialists and . . .

—Quiet, quiet, Beauvey.

—Ow ouch sorry sir.

—Devereux, George? A word in your ears, chaps.

—Yes, sir?

—Yes, Headmaster?

They spoke in lowered tones, directly above Marley's head. There was something terrifyingly comforting about it, as if he was now completely without responsibility for his own life or anything in it. The old man with the green eyes would decide everything.

—Now look here, I want the children kept away from him. All of them. They're going to get too damn excitable. Could make problems for morale. We've got to know what state England's in, and if they know we're here, before we can decide whether to play this one off the front foot or the back, eh?

—Yes, sir.

—Of course, Headmaster. I'll look after him here.

—Good girl, George. What I don't understand is, if England's made it, why the devil haven't the locals heard about it? They haven't said a thing. They'd know, somehow, it'd get garbled the way the silly buggers garble everything, but they'd have heard *something*. For all we know, England could be a radioactive wasteland, we could simply be holding out in some corner of Australia or New Zealand. No, no, we've got to find out before we let the chaps get all worked up about going home. Otherwise things could fall to pieces here.

—Absolutely, sir.

—Yes, Headmaster.

The man and the woman quickly and efficiently emptied the hut, shut the door and drew the blinds. When all was secure, the Headmaster turned again to Marley.

—Well, but here you *are*, eh, old boy? I'm Quartermain, Head of this place. So you climbed the Great Barrier, eh?

That's what we call it, d'you see? Good man, confess I didn't think it could be done, hell of a thing, God knows how many chaps we've lost trying to get down it. How many d'you think, Devereux?

The younger man looked over at the names on the wooden reredos beneath the royal portraits and squinted.

—Lost having a crack at the Great Barrier, Headmaster? Oh, I should think thirteen or fourteen, one way or the other, over the years.

—Is it really? Is it? Well, well. So many, eh? Good chaps. But *you* made it, eh? Good show. Well?

—Well what? said Marley.

—How is England, man?

—England?

—Come on, the children are all gone, you can speak up now, man. What happened? Was it very bad? When did it finish? Did we win? Have you got back-up coming? Where are the rest of your chaps? Down in the jungle?

—The jungle? Oh no, not the jungle, please, I don't want to go back there, oh my God, the rest, oh Christ, they're all dead.

—Dead? All of them? Did the Reds get them?

—Our helicopters, they crashed, they burned, I ran, I . . .

—Bad luck. Never trusted choppers myself, old boy. So look here, is England . . .? But Marley's shot-blasted brain could take no more. He swooned back and fell rolling from his bed, unconscious upon the clean-scrubbed boards. The last thing he was aware of feeling was an arm beneath his neck, the strong arm of a girl called George . . .

*

—Father, you see, I simply do not believe he is dead. I know he is not.

—Ah, Consuelita, you are like your mother! When I crashed off South Georgia they gave me up for dead. All

120

except her. I lay in the water thinking of her, for two days. Yes, her thoughts kept me alive. And Our Lady of the Sea, of course. Until the English *fished me out*, ha ha! like a frozen piece of salted cod. Ah, hot, sweet, British Navy tea and rum!

*

The miracle of reviving strength; the simple marvel of the recirculating blood; the wonderment at every touch and smell and sight of the world again. And yet, where was he? Who was he? Marley had experienced unnerving dislocations of consciousness many times when hung-over (especially when waking in the mid-afternoon from a lunchtime drink), those horrid feelings of timelessness, placelessness and emptiness, but this was different.

If this was madness, how comforting it seemed, how strangely well known, how curiously reassuring. It was very close to pleasant, in fact. His mind had simply given up the unequal struggle, leaving his body to assert a more ancient control. Just for once, his body was flooding his mind with demands, not the other way round. For years, his overwrought, hyperprimate brain, stuffed on every waveband with the frenzied gibbering of the third millennium, had been plaguing his poor, stress-racked body with sleepless worries, fears, plans and hopes. Now his simple, ancient flesh and bones and blood were sending out wave upon wave of self-made narcotic hormones, pheromones, serotines, all of which carried one easy but powerful message to his burned-out consciousness: *Look, you had a try and you couldn't hack it so will you shut up for God's sake, give it a rest, just let me, your body, get better.*

Marley's brain obeyed gratefully, shut up, shut down and went into power-saving hibernation mode. It carried out all its root functions and duties, but little more: his heart beat a touch more strongly every day; his lungs rose and fell a little more deeply with each passing night; his stomach managed larger spoonfuls at every attempt, eventually even small bowlfuls, of the soups made from gamy meat and curious vegetables which George brought to his bedside.

Mainly, though, he just slept, until, after some incalculable period of days, the Headmaster and Devereux came in to see him again.

—Look here, old boy, said the Headmaster, —you seem to be pulling through and we simply *have* to know. How is England? Are they coming for us? Will they search for you? Some of our chaps thought they heard choppers down over the jungle. Well?

Marley looked again into the green eyes. He had lost all fear of them now. Down there in the deadly jungle, his body had passed through pain and horror to a numb state of mere exhaustion and acceptance: so, now, his mind had gone beyond all terror at its own crumbling and had decided simply to observe the happenings of this impossible world, as if looking down on it all from some pleasant nearby planet. He simply smiled back at the green eyes, happy to give pleasure where he could do so, but quite unafraid.

—Sorry? Will who search for me? I'm afraid I just don't know.

—Don't suppose you've remembered your name?

Marley shook his head apologetically but firmly. He knew that he had *had* a name, yes, and that he had a past, but somehow he just did not care to remember these things. If he allowed his eyes to glaze and to wander inwards, he knew that he could eventually find the way to this name through the dark thickets and thorny tangles of his bruised mind. The path to himself was clear to him, the trackway to the gate of memory. But he suspected that it led only to a big, rusty iron door, more like the door to a musty vault than the gate to a bright garden. This rusting door was set in a high wall of old, crumbling brick, topped with broken glass, set in a tangle of rubbish-filled, wet, dull brier. A firm push would open that iron gate, he knew, but something told him that whatever was beyond it, it was not a happy place. It reeked of guilt and failure and hopelessness. The thought of what might lie beyond made him shiver. He did not want to go in there. So he turned away from the gate inside his mind, focused his eyes fully outwards, stared back into the bright green eyes and simply smiled at the expectant faces looking down at him.

—I told you, I don't know anything. I'm very sorry.

—Well then, what ruddy regiment are you? Surely you can remember *that*?

—Me? A regiment? Am I?

—Well, it bloody well sounded like it.

—Perhaps I am.

—Damn it all man, nearly fifty years I've held this place together, waiting for someone to get through to us from England, waiting every day, watching young chaps grow old and fine girls turn grey, just trying to stop the place going to the dogs so that one day we can all go home, to England. And now you're here and after all that time you can't tell us the first blasted thing about the old place. Good God, man, I've a mind to . . .

The green eyes flashed and Marley felt the instinctive fear of them again, of these eyes that had, he somehow knew, seen much of death.

—Please, I'm sorry, I'm trying, don't send me back to the jungle, please . . .

—I don't think he *can* tell us, sir. Shock.

—No, no, of course, you're right. Sorry, old boy. Oh damn and blast it all to hell.

The Headmaster let go of Marley's arm. Marley shrank away under his blankets again as the Headmaster and Devereux stood in close and low conference.

—What are we going to do, sir?

—I don't know, Devereux. I really don't. Even if there *are* other chaps out there, with choppers, and even if they do search for him, there's absolutely no guarantee they'll find us up here. Bugger that cloud cover.

—If only we had a working radio, eh, Headmaster?

—Well, we haven't. You, whatever your damn name is, have the boffins back home found some clever way to spot chaps from high up, through cloud?

—Sorry? Have the who found a way to what?

—Sod and buggeration. How much ammo have we got left, Devereux?

—Three dozen rounds, sir. Enough for another two seasons' hunting, assuming they're all sound, but that's our lot. There's a couple of the younger chaps, the ones that think they heard the choppers, starting to say we should fire them in volleys next time anyone hears anything.

—No, no, they wouldn't hear us unless we actually *hit* the buggers. Hell of a racket, in a chopper. I've seen chaps screaming and blazing away like ruddy dervishes trying to attract choppers, never did the slightest good. Very bad for morale. And if we waste all our ammo for nothing and they *don't* hear us, which they won't, what then, eh? Then we're really in the soup. Damn it, Devereux, it's a big decision. We've done pretty well up here so far, one way or another.

—Thanks to you, sir.

—I just did my bit, Devereux. Let me think. Yes, there's no doubt about it. We'll just have to move out. *We'll* have to find *them*.

—Move the whole Colony down into the forest, sir? By the Gate?

—Of course, man. Can't sit here on our fat backsides now we know there are still Englishmen out there some-where. We've got to make contact.

—Yes of course, sir. Shall we start right away?

—No, no, Devereux, think, man. The rains have come
on down there now. We'll have to sit it out one more wet
season up here, gather supplies.

—A big hunt, eh, sir?

—Absolutely. We'll need all the supplies we can gather
if we're going to get the children through the jungle. And
some of the poor little sods won't make it. It's the children I'm worried about. The ranks behind, and all that.
And we need to think of morale. Always a problem,
morale, once the chaps think they're going home. No one
wants to cop one just when they've made it through the
slogging match and the show's as good as over. We need
to keep the young bloods in check. The hunt'll be good
for them.

—Not the hunting season yet, of course, sir.

—Well, this time we'll just have to make it up as we
go along. How long will it take us to cross the gorge?

—My chaps can throw up a rope bridge in two days.

—Good show. Right then, let's go and muster the chaps.
And as for you, old boy, whoever you are, get well ruddy
soon, will you? Sooner the bloody better.

—I'll try, er, Headmaster.

Then they were gone, and Marley closed his eyes
again.

He spent the next few days in the warm, luxurious,
languid half-sleep of someone who has just been transferred from intensive care, who will soon be again receiving
visitors at normal times and who can look forward confidently to the day when that rather unnerving hospital
wristband is no more than a gentle reminder held up by
a fridge magnet, a half-ironic memento mori, looked at
less and less with every passing day and at last put out
unthinkingly with the rubbish. He lay and ate what he
was brought and slept when he felt like it and read idly
now and then, with the guiltless, instinctive knowledge

125

that he had every right, medical and moral, to do bugger all for a bit.

At night-time, George came to bring him extra blankets and tuck him in.

That was the best bit. The nights were surprisingly cold: each evening, as the equatorial sun plunged swiftly below the mountains, ceasing to bathe the blinding glaciers in light and heat, the clouds seemed to melt into a mere inky mist, through which could occasionally be glimpsed patches of a pure, depthless black, untouched by artificial light, vertiginous with stars that hung so brightly, in constellations Marley had never seen before, that for the first time in his life he fancied he could truly see the cosmos soaring above him in three endless dimensions. George's head, a sweet shadow looming against the uncurtained window of the hut, silhouetted against these unknown stars, was the last thing he saw each night, as he sank without delay into restorative, exhausted oblivion . . .

. . . Ah, to be *tucked up* again, at long last to be smiled at by blue, breezy eyes that held no secrets and needed nothing . . .

One still afternoon, it might have been the third day, it might have been the sixth, or the sixtieth for that matter, Marley was lying in his now usual semi-dormant state, idly reading the *Eagle Annual* for 1958, which he found he knew well. The sense of the vastness of the forgotten world inside his head was somewhat dizzying as he turned page after page, knowing pretty well exactly what was going to happen next to Harris Tweed Secret Agent and Dan Dare Space Pilot of the Future.

Pleasantly stunned, and more than ever convinced that he was only dreaming about being here (or perhaps, dreaming that he was dreaming about being here), Marley

126

finished his Dan Dare story, turned a page or two idly, then gazed blearily at the Secret Grip with which Jim Laker had defeated the Aussies in 1956. Something about this picture called him. As he stared at it, his eyelids began to close, he felt his fingers close in ghostly memory of a heavy, too-heavy, too-large cricket ball, his little hand in a larger hand, a laughing voice in his ear, a pipe stem pointing out this same illustration, a strong, loving ruffle of his hair, a tickle of beard bristles on the back of his little neck . . .

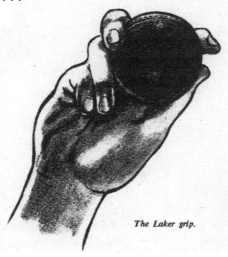

The Laker grip.

127

—*Cthonk!*

—Well played, Eagleton.

The younger boys were playing cricket outside now. Marley turned his book the better to catch the light from the pale sun, so as to fully appreciate the fine line drawing of Britain's Plutonium Factory, which was confidently predicted to produce power so cheaply that by approximately 1972, the Housewives of Britain would get their electricity virtually free, while incidentally ensuring that our defences had enough hitting power in case of need. This was followed by a comic strip about valiant Highland Rebels in 1745 (in which it was pointed out many times that the Vile Redcoats were mere German Hirelings rather than True Englishmen) and an informative article (it seemed very well thumbed) about how to pitch a tent.

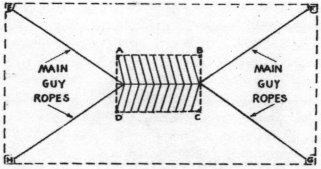

Pitching a tent is an easy matter, even in a gale or at night, if you have previously noted the measurements of the two rectangles ABCD and EFGH.

He was interrupted by the entrance of a substantial figure of about sixty years of age, in darned but flowing robes and a clean though battered dog collar.

—Hello, old boy, said this man.

—Hello, Vicar, said Marley, without meaning to.

—Ah! You recognise the old cloth, then? Coming back to you, is it?

—Not really. I just thought you must be the vicar. Aren't you?

—Well, the chaps usually call me Padre, actually. You know, Army style. After all, I'm not the vicar of anything, ha ha. Just the chap who reads the Bible at Assembly. And looks after the choirboys, of course. Anyway, yes, where was I? What are you reading, eh? Ah yes, the *Eagle*. Very useful, those books. Don't know what the Founders would have done without them. The hunting chaps use those drawings to make their rope bridges, for example. Well, now, I think it's about time we got you up on your feet, don't you? Fight the good fight and all that, eh?

—No, said Marley rebelliously.

—Ah. Don't suppose you've remembered your name yet, eh?

—No, said Marley, smiling but firm. —Sorry. I'm sure it'll come, though.

—Remember what you were doing here?

—Sorry.

—Were you sent to find us?

—I don't think so. But I'm glad I did.

—Rather. I suppose you *are* C of E?

—Oh yes, said Marley without thinking about it at all. For a second he saw, smelled, heard an old church, was perhaps eight again, standing in an itchy shirt, shorts and tie, waiting for the organ introduction to end. —*For all the saints, who from their labours rest*, he sang gently.

—Ah, aha, one of my favourites!

—I think I'd like it at my funeral.

—Well, you'll be glad to know that's not why I'm here. You're much better, you know.

—I *feel* much better.

129

—Good, good. But no doubt you're curious. About the Colony, eh? Must be a bit of a shock for you, eh?

—Yes, I suppose it is.

—Bit of a shock for us too.

—I suppose it must have been.

—The Headmaster always said that England would pull through one way or another, even if it was only in Canada or New Zealand. A great man, a great man. We would all have gone to the dogs without him. I was just one of the boys back then, on the Flight.

—Ah? said Marley, feigning distant interest with the gracious condescension of the incontrovertibly bedridden.

—I was due to go up to Christchurch the following year, '59. Organ Scholarship. I would rather have liked to have gone to Christchurch. But the Lord moves in mysterious ways and perhaps now I shall see it again at last. You an Oxford man by any chance?

—Sorry?

—University? Oxford?

—I don't know. Oxford? That's funny. The name rings a bell. Colleges and quadrangles?

—Yes, that's it!

—But I know it. I know it well. I remember I was, sort of, showing people round it.

—Perhaps you're a don? You know, a fellow of one of the colleges. Do you think?

—I don't know. That sounds as if it would be nice.

—I'll say, old man.

—I don't think so. But I did go to university somewhere. I can't remember, I'm sorry. I think I was probably drunk most of the time.

—Ah, Oxford, then.

—Perhaps. I know I've got old friends from university. All this is something to do with one of my old university friends. He's a poof.

130

—Is he really? *Is* he?

—Yes, and another one of them takes in washing.

—Takes in washing? A university man? Good God, poor chap.

—He takes it to Albanians in a barracks in Maidstone.

—Maidstone, occupied by the Albanians? University men doing their washing? Good grief, this will kill the Headmaster. But how did you get out here then? Who sent you? Is there a resistance movement?

—I can't remember, I'm sorry.

—Albanians, dear God, poor England. Perhaps we shall have to stay put out here then.

—Well, it does seem very nice here.

—Yes. Nice. Exactly the word. It *is* very nice. Of course, we were so damned lucky.

—Were we? I mean, were you?

—Well, I'm no whizz on stats, old boy, but I don't think many crates get shot down like that over mountains and most of the chaps and girls on board just walk out, eh?

—Shot down?

—Red fighter. MiG-17 the Headmaster said, and I'm sure he'd know. Or was it 19? It'll say in the Book, of course. Anyway, there he was, saw the swine clearly, dived on us out of nowhere, absolutely the Assyrian coming down like the wolf on the fold, gunfire, hell of a bang, part of a wing gone, flames pouring out, down we went. Nearer my God to Thee and all that. Rather brings out the latent papist in one, I have to confess, no pun intended. Don't know how on earth the pilot kept control of her at all, but there again, he'd flown Lancasters all through the last show, back from Berlin on two engines with half his crew dead and all that, DFC and bar, so I suppose he knew a thing or two. So yes, anyway, down we went, with the Headmaster standing there, absolutely standing there like a rock, telling the boys and girls to stop crying and brace up like Englishmen and

131

Englishwomen and prepare for impact. Of course, he wasn't the Headmaster then, just the Games Master, but we boys all looked up to him like anything, because of his MC of course, and he simply took charge there and then. So, there we were, going down fast and –

—But *why* did they shoot you down?

—Well, quite. We were just a jolly gang of boys and girls on our way out to the big Commonwealth Public Schools jamboree in Adelaide, absolute non-combatants, I mean, you can hardly call a public school Officer Training Corps a fighting unit, can you?

—I suppose not.

—But I imagine the godless Red bastards, pardon my Aramaic, thought anything flying the Union Jack was fair game in wartime.

—But, sorry, I don't understand, I mean . . .

— . . . Yes, it *was* rather a miracle, I suppose. There we were, going down fast, straight towards the mountains. I could see the glacier peeping through the clouds. It's very beautiful from up there, you know. Angelic, rather. I knew my geography a bit and so I knew there are only three equatorial glaciers in the whole world and I remember quite clearly thinking, oh well, at least we're going down somewhere a bit, well, you know, *sublime*. Then the Headmaster got on to the microphone and made the most wonderful speech, I can still remember it word for word, after all these years. He said, *Sorry chaps, looks like this is it, better say our prayers before we hand in our lunch buckets. Pity we didn't get to do our bit but some chaps just don't and there's an end to it. But you're a good set of chaps and girls, and don't worry, England will pull through again, she always does, and our V-bombers will give those Red buggers what for.* The next thing we knew we were right down among the mountains, clouds all around us, into Thy hands do I commend my soul and all that, next stop the Pearly Gates. Then suddenly, whoosh, out through the clouds and down here and rattling across the ground like billy-o. And most of us made it. Absolute miracle, really, you're right. Quite restored the old faith. Poor chaps up in the front of the crate all bought it, of course.

—Daddy always said the front of an aircraft is the safest part, said Marley, for no reason he could identify.

—Did he? Did he really? Was he in the RAF? asked the Padre hopefully. —Can you remember? Do try, old boy, we're so *very* keen for you to remember. We're dying to know about England.

Marley frowned to himself. Shreds of memory whisked across the empty but untroubled plain of his mind, like the single strands of a web, almost invisible except when the sun caught them and glanced off, which had brushed his cheek on some forgotten, bright September morning, a day when tiny spiders all around were hatching, spinning, catching the wind . . .

—The RAF? No, I don't think Daddy was in the RAF. But he was something to do with planes. I had a photo, I must have lost it. Wait a minute, *I* know. He was in the Navy. Yes, he was on an aircraft carrier. It was called the *Eagle*. Like this book, you see. I remember that. He had a sword.

—Well, he would have, wouldn't he? And?

—I'm afraid that's it. Sorry. That's all: he had a sword and a beard and he once told me that the front of a plane was the safest bit.

—Well, I dare say, normally, but not when the nose of the plane goes straight into the foot of a cliff, as you've no doubt noticed it did.

—No, I suppose not.

—Damn bad luck on them after the way they'd got us down but I suppose they'd had a good innings one way or another and we still toast them every year on the Queen's birthday and one day whatever's left of England will hear about them. And so here we were. And you're right. It *is* nice here, isn't it? I was never in Kenya. Were you?

—Kenya? I don't think so.

—Ah. Well, the Headmaster was there for a bit, licking the locals into shape, and he says the climate here's just like the best bits of Kenya. Perfectly fine for white men, not like the bloody jungle, eh? But *you* know all about that. Dreadful place. So, ah, what were you doing there? Remember, do you?

—I don't want to go back there. I don't want to go back to the jungle. The Headmaster won't send me back to the jungle, will he?

—No, no, no question of that, old boy. Stay calm.

—I can't remember anything!

—Shhhh. It'll come, old boy. We did try to make it through the jungle at first, of course we did, well, I mean, we had to *try* to get back to England, or Australia at least. Had to try to do our bit against the Reds, didn't we?

—Did you? I suppose you did.

—Some of the chaps tried going down the Wall, the way you came up. None of them made it. God knows how you did it.

—I came up. I suppose it's easier coming up.

—Yes, I suppose it is. But our chaps were trying to get down, you see.

—I'm not going down.

—Of course not. Saw a couple of them fall myself. Good chaps. There *is* another way down, just one, a pass in the cliffs, we call it the Gate, I'll show you when you're better. That's how we stay in touch with the locals. But it leads straight on to a vile mudslide a mile long, and at

134

the bottom you find yourself right in the middle of the very ghastliest swamp you ever saw. We only send the strong young chaps down there now, in the hunting season. They'll be down there now. Of course, we tried to get out that way back at the start, all of us, I mean, we had to try to get back to England, to do our bit, but it was hopeless, you know how awful it is down there, we were covering a few hundred yards a day, no more, it was the rainy season, like now, we had no quinine, the crocs got some of us and –

—Ahh! The people in the helicopters. The dead people. The burned people. The crocodiles, yes, the crocodiles ate them, too . . .

—Shhh, that's enough, old boy. That's better. Quiet now. Anyway, there we were, dropping like flies, hopelessly lost and, worst of all, the locals were hanging about snapping up stragglers. To eat, you see.

—Eat?

—Oh yes, they're all cannibals round here, given half a chance. Some worse than others, but all of them rather too partial to the odd forkful of another chap. You were damn lucky not to end up boned and rolled and served up with whatever the heathen little devils have instead of Yorkshire pudding. The Headmaster only just got most of us back in one piece, back then. Bad time, that first few months. Remember it clearly. Lost a lot of chaps. Malaria, infections. Thought we were all done for. Burials every other day. But the Headmaster kept our chins up till we got on our feet. We still expected rescue, of course, back then. But no one came. The war, naturally. So then the Headmaster decided we'd better get ourselves set up for a long haul and sit tight and just keep the side up here, in case England needed us later, after the war.

—The war?

—Was it *very* awful? I suppose they got London? How did people behave? Did morale collapse? Surely not. But it must have been pretty bloody if it took you so long to get here. Was it? Was the fallout terrible? Did you come from Australia?

—I'm sorry, I'm feeling a bit, I'm all, I don't understand, I don't feel very well, I'm trying but I can't. I just can't. You won't let the man with green eyes send me back to the jungle, will you? Not to the crocodiles and spiders? Will you? You won't let the cannibals eat me?

—Ah, George, there you are, I was just . . .

—George, please, tell him, tell the man with green eyes I don't want to go back to the jungle, I don't know anything about any wars, I won't go, I like it here, it's nice here, I just want to read the books, I can't remember, will you tuck me in please, I . . .

—There, there, Jungle Jim. Put a sock in it, will you, Padre, for Heaven's sake. Can't you see he's not up to it yet?

—Sorry, George. I was just seeing how he is, you know.

—He's getting better but he needs some peace, is how he is.

—Yes, of course. Well, look, old man, any time you fancy a chat, yes. Well. I'll be off then. Come to choir practice, we can sing that hymn of yours if you like . . . Toodle-oo then.

—Oh George. I remembered the crocodiles.

—Shhh. Don't mind him. Frankly, I don't know why on earth we have to have one of Nature's bachelors wandering about the place in a nightie droning on to the chaps and petting *that* sort of boy, but the Headmaster says it's the way they do things in England, so I suppose he must be right. Do they really have that sort of thing in England? Sorry, there's me doing it myself now. I suppose we're all just a bit worried now the hunting

136

chaps are all away. I mean, it's not usual for them to go out in January, and the Headmaster hasn't run with the hunt for years now, so he must be planning something big. But I'm sure he knows best. He always does. Everything will be all right. Now, no more questions. Let's just rest, shall we? You've done enough.

—Have I, George?

—Yes. You just rest now.

Rest.

The word itself seemed like a tiny lullaby.

Rest.

Marley held George's hand and let all the air out from his body in a long shudder that seemed to release all pain. He was allowed to rest. He had done enough for now. She had said so, she, this unknown, strong girl with a cool hand on his brow which helped him slide so easily, smiling, into untroubled sleep. He had done enough, at last.

—Thank you, Marley smiled. He drifted softly back downwards, lead-weighted, into sweet oblivion. —You know, George, he murmured, as he sank into the happy darkness again, —I do remember that. Vicars. Yes, the Headmaster's right, we do have vicars in England. We have them on the radio every morning, *droning on, droning on, droning on* . . . George?

—Shh now.

—Goodnight, George.

—Goodnight, Jungle Jim. Rest now.

—Yes, rest. Rest.

*

—Was it *you*, was it *really*, Air Colonel? I say, I wish you'd told me you were coming to Town, I would have brought one of my chaps to interview you for the *Intelligencer*, you know, twenty years on, pals again, all that. So it was *you*, eh?

137

—Yes, it was I, Sir James. And I shall say to you with all my heart that I am most proud to have sunk an *English* warship.

—So you are, by God. I remember the footage. Damn fine thing, though of course I wish our AA gunners had got you first. Well, well. And this is your daughter, eh? Hel-lo.

—Hello, Sir James.

—What a grand girl, Air Colonel. Well *done*. Too many pale bloody city girls about these days for my taste. And what a jolly dress, such a nice change from skinny girls in black. But you look sad, my dear.

—Her friend, Sir James. Her English friend. He has died in Papua New Guinea.

—I do not believe my Brian is dead, Sir James.

—Women, Sir James!

—What, not that chap on the telly? Don't watch much telly myself, but I heard about him on the wireless. Now now, my dear, don't cry. He sounded like a decent chap. Bit eccentric, but then so were Paddy Leigh Fermor and all that sort and they did their bit and more when it came to it. Well, that settles it, you *must* join me for dinner. Do say you will. My dear, you'll sit next to me, eh? Well done, my dear Air Colonel, well *done*.

*

—Come along, Jungle Jim, said George, as she firmly parked an old bath chair beside Marley's bed.

—I don't want to, said he, rebelliously.

—Well, hard cheese. Time we got you cleaned up. So good for morale. Anyway, you smell. As dear old Matron used to say: one can only get by for *so* long just faffing about.

—Faffing?

—Yes, you know: Face, Armpits, Fanny and Feet.

138

—Ah, said Marley, trying to concentrate on thoughts of George's face and feet.

—Let's get you out of your pit then. Fun, the old bath chair, isn't it? It belonged to a bigwig on the Flight, some sort of civilian top brass from the Ministry of Supply, it says in the Book. He was up at the front of the plane, so he didn't make it. But his bath chair wasn't, so it did. As you see. In you get. That's the way.

And so Marley processed for the first time out of the hut which had been his half-lit refuge and into the bright, soft light of the world outside, steering the ancient cane bath chair, pushed by George.

He was very aware indeed of her breasts a small distance behind his ears. They called to him in ancient voices. He tried to force himself to think about other things. The trouble was that there did not seem to be any other things there: shorn almost entirely of memory, his mind was a mere weightless plaything that was drawn this way and that by whatever gravity was nearby. Such as the old boys' annuals he had been reading. Such as George's breasts.

—What do you think of the place, then? she asked.

Marley gazed around. He now saw the reason for the curiously diffuse effect of the sunlight here. It was because of the layered cloud streaming endlessly down from the glacial mountain to the west of them. This luminous white mass swirled a mere couple of thousand feet above their heads, ripped and shredded by winds at various heights, but always with at least one sheet screening the sun.

—Jolly, our sky, isn't it? said George, shoving him wobbling across the uneven, hard ground. —And jolly lucky for us, I suppose, in one way, or the Founders would all have frazzled. It half clears every night, that's why it's quite chilly in the mornings, which is also good for us because it keeps all the ghastly little insects down. I suppose we would all have got malaria otherwise, but

139

the little horrors can't take the night frosts we sometimes get, and anyway, it hardly ever rains here so there's no water for them to breed in. Of course, there's water for *us*.

Marley could now indeed see a small but powerful waterfall which fell from among the towering cliffs into a rocky pond no larger than a heavyweight garden inflatable pool, sending clouds of spray into the air. The pool drained into a dark cleft, where the water tumbled away again into the ground.

Beside this tiny lake stood a strange, beehive-like structure, evidently constructed of baked mud and sticks, about ten feet tall and with a low, round-arched entrance. It looked like an ancient tomb. Beside it, two girls of perhaps eight years old were tending a bonfire from which a boy of about ten was carefully taking red-hot stones with a pair of metal sticks and placing them inside the hut.

—On the other hand, George continued, —I suppose all that cloud means that no one can see us from the sky, even if things are back on their feet in England. We see things flying high in the night, among the stars it looks like, the Science Master says it may be space rockets, and we always wonder if they're English. Are they?

Marley scarcely heard her. He was growing absurdly yet quite inescapably aroused as his bath chair, propelled by a beautiful, strong, unseen young woman who spoke in an accent which, somehow, he had never heard but was perfectly at home with and which for some reason he found strangely exciting, jolted him across the bumpy earth. What was it about the way she spoke? Why did it make him feel as if he was lucky to be with her? As if everything she said was somehow worth more? He could not work it out, but the simultaneous messages of physical powerlessness, exalted position and sexual desire made him feel like an Arab prince, deprived by a life of excess of the ability to walk, but not of his libido, being wheeled by a young blonde princess towards his carpeted, veiled, lamp-lit tent . . .

—What? Oh, um, sorry? he said.

—No, no, my fault, you're not ready yet. Of course you're not, you poor thing. You so nearly went, you know, it was that close. But now you're coming back. Plenty of time to talk about England. Right then. Shave first, then bath-time.

—Shave?

—Of course. This isn't the Navy. No beards here. There you are. Careful, it's Swedish steel and Tom Devereux keeps it terribly sharp.

Marley's fantasy bubble was pricked by the appearance of a cut-throat razor as well as by George's matter-of-fact tones. He looked up, a strategic error which brought his face into virtual contact with the buttons of her blouse.

—Can you do it yourself, do you think?

He tried to focus on the polished, glinting steel, but could see only, at the height of his own eyes, the impossible smoothness, the unbearable curves of her skin between the buttons. He wanted to moan. But he said: —I'm not sure.

—Better let me do it then.

So he let her do it. George walked away and Marley sat back in his chair and closed his eyes, trying not to think about sex, concentrating on studying the interesting play of the dull orange light that flooded through the membranes of his eyelids. After a few minutes his radar picked up her returning footsteps behind him. His hackles rose in harmony. Then, to his surprise, he felt the soft creaminess of soap on his face, and her hands rubbing it

141

into his beard. The unexpectedness of it short-circuited his sheer desire.

—Yes, she laughed, —we have quite decent soap, the Founders took years to get the right recipe, they say, but thank God they wrote everything down in the Book, so now the girls make it by the wagonload from ashes and fat and plant oils. It seems to be a sort of mild antiseptic, too. That's better. Now head back and hold still. Don't move.

—I won't.

Marley sat still as the slim, deadly steel glided, twanging, across his throat and jugular, around his mouth, about his chin, over his cheeks, slicing away grimy hair and, it felt, the layered years. He could feel George's firm breasts, unmoving against his shoulders. He kept his eyes fixed on the soft skin in the crook of George's elbow, forbidding himself from thinking about her breasts as the blade flicked and sung around his face. He could not escape the deep, lunatic certainty that death would be the sure and certain punishment for any transgression. But he could also not help feeling her nipples against his shoulder blades and her fingers beneath his chin. And he could do absolutely nothing to stop himself from smelling, beneath the woody, fruity scents of the soap, the sweet, sweaty, salt-and-smoked paprika of her unshaved armpits.

—My Englishman, she said softly, contemplatively, her mouth so close to the top of his head that her voice seemed not to carry through the still air to his ears, but to vibrate like a deep, dark whispering flute within his skull itself. —How old are you, Jungle Jim?

—I don't know. I think I'm about thirty. No, that's wrong, I must be forty.

—Well, I much prefer a man of about forty. The young chaps are *such* puppies. Just want to have a bash at everything in sight if they were allowed to. Which they aren't of course, not until they get their blazers. The Headmaster keeps them busy with sport and hunting. Anyway, I prefer the older chaps.

—Ah.

—There. How does that feel? Nice?

Marley stroked his own face. It felt better than wonderful, as if his skin were new-minted, shining, elastic and young again, glowing with life and hope and future.

—Yes, very. Very nice. Thank you.

—Bath-time now. Or rather, the steam lodge. The Headmaster knew about them from his time in Malaya. It's a wonderful tonic. All ready, Jameson Major?

—Ready Miss Harcourt, said the sweating, fire-reddened boy and the two girls in unison.

—Well done. Right, Jungle Jim, in we go.

—But . . .

—Come on, up we get.

She hoisted him gently to his feet. He grasped her arm like a sick old man, scared of falling, reddening with the shame of his fear. He steadied himself, almost tearful at his own wretched weakness, and shook her arms away petulantly.

—That's the spirit, she cried. —Just like Douglas Bader.

Marley tried not to feel absurd pride at her praise. Feet carefully planted, he straightened his back cautiously and felt his height increase by a good six inches. His chest felt lighter, his breath came more easily.

—In here? he asked, pointing to the low, dark, rounded archway.

—Can you make it, do you think?

—Of course.

—Well, I'd better go first.

He watched her squat easily down, stretch out her body and slip through the dark hole like an otter. He looked around. The two girls and the boy were watching him gravely, with that curious knowing look of children who do not actually know what the hell is going on but know very well that it is something they are not yet meant to know about.

—Need a hand? she called out from inside, her voice sounding miles away now.

—I'm fine, croaked Marley.

—Take your time, no hurry.

He looked at the small, dark, rounded doorway. It seemed a very long way down and the darkness beyond it seemed very dark. With great care, he bent his spine and lowered himself to a somewhat painful kneel, then to a crawling position in which he felt slightly absurd and strangely vulnerable.

He was about to start moving gingerly forward towards the beckoning darkness when a small pile of female clothes, flung from the entrance, landed around his face and shoulders.

—Oops, sorry, called George, from her distant, muffled planet.

—Ah, said Marley, unable to think of anything else to say. The touch of rayon on his cheek, the weird, cold, flat smoothness of it sent him spiralling back in time again towards the half-known past. Without wanting to, he could smell her skin-warm knickers. He lowered his head, as if in surrender, and the clothes tumbled silently to the ground in front of him, a cascade of unbearable womanliness. He could not go in there. Not with her. Not the way he was feeling. But there was no escape. Desperately, he played for time.

—So, should I, I mean, get undressed out here?

—*Pas devant les enfants*, she replied, laughing.

—Oh yes, right.

He blinked several times, then gave up. Trying hard to

think of nothing, he crawled over the pile of her clothes and into the dark, warm hole.

As he got his head and shoulders inside, a wall of heat enveloped him and the sweat burst instantly from his face and neck. With his own body filling the passage, he could see absolutely nothing inside the hut.

—Come on, she laughed from nowhere. Her voice was now clear, slightly magnified and utterly disembodied in the dome-like, unseen space above him. Fighting back an animal terror at the formless black, he took a breath of the hot, dry air: it felt like a cloud of thick red gas. He dragged himself further in, terrified of the inevitable moment when his hand would come upon her naked body. Instead, it was her hand that stopped him, her hand on his shoulder. It was cool and very heavy.

—Mind the hot stones, she said. The cool hand guided him firmly, placed him securely and signalled him clearly to stop where he was. Then it went, and he was alone again in the darkness. But he could feel her near him, a blacker blackness in the black.

—There. Togs off then.

—Right. Um, right.

He fought with his clothes awkwardly in the darkness, not daring to stretch out either hand or foot too far as he stripped, in case he accidentally touched her and she mistakenly thought he was grabbing at her. He closed his eyes in exhausted concentration as he struggled idiotically with his trousers.

—Need a hand there? she asked merrily.

—No, God, I mean, no, I'm fine. There.

He opened his eyes gratefully as his left foot slipped at last from his underpants. Now he could begin to see, by the small shaft of light coming in through the rounded door.

—Chuck them out, said she, and without looking round,

he hastily flung his filthy clothes out into the brightness.
—Jameson Major?

—Yes Miss Harcourt? (Marley could hardly hear the boy's voice from inside the hot, dull cave.)

—Get the girls to boil that lot in soap, will you?

—Yes Miss Harcourt.

—Now, come and lie down.

—Right.

Marley prepared himself mentally before he turned his head, telling himself that all he was going to see was a naked young woman. Perfectly normal and natural. Then he turned his head and saw George, naked and young and womanly, smiling quietly at him in the soft shadows of the light from the door and the slow, red glow of the stones. The sight hit him like a karate chop to the throat.

—There's a moss bed here, come on.

—Um, right.

Suddenly he could feel on his skin the forest, the dirt, the near death. He felt he smelled like old meat. He scrambled quickly across the space to the bed of mosses beside her, horribly conscious of his balls dangling absurdly as he crawled. Speedily, he lay face down on the ground, hoping that his cock would tuck itself safely up between his legs, praying for relaxation.

—First, we'll just get hot for a bit.

—OK.

Marley got hot. The sweat trickled from his scalp and his shoulders, sliding in big, tickling droplets down the sides of his neck to form a small pool in the small of his back. As he lay there, he tried with all his might to blank out the presence of this beautiful, slim, strong, naked young woman lying just beyond his reach. But 400 million years of evolutionary programming and a single lifetime's Englishness were making it tough.

146

Then she stirred decisively beside him. Instantly, Marley's defences were crushed and swept aside. His chest locked tight to hold still his jumping heart. He lay there on his front, muscles held tight, cock in a state of painful mutiny against the unyielding moss bed, staring out wildy into the red-hot, half-lit darkness, not daring to blink in case the rustle of his eyelashes should give him away. His entire silent body felt as though it were covered in tiny sound-and-motion sensors that were scanning the shadows with that ancient sixth sense, desire.

There was no doubt about it. She was moving towards him. She had stood up. He heard her sinews work and the moss breathe softly. He detected the slight wave in the hard, still, hot air that had been created by her rising. He heard and felt the soft padding of her feet. Closer. The tiny increase of heat from the nearness of her body. She was right beside him now. Then he felt the soft vibrations of the earth as one footstep came down on the other side of him. Only one. He strained his secret radar in disbelief. There was only one possible calculation. She must be straddling him, standing over him with legs apart. He swallowed with great difficulty, vertiginously aware of what must, in that case, be some three feet above his back. Silence. He could hear her breathing high above him. He felt as utterly vulnerable as a fallen warrior on some prehistoric battlefield: he clearly felt the soft place between his shoulders where she was about to plunge her bronze spear.

Her sinews flexed softly, audibly again. A shadow of body heat closed on the small of his back. Then, incredulously, he felt her kneel down, felt the firm, soft warmth of her thighs on his hips, felt the soft hairs of her mound idly waft across his buttocks. His cock was trying to force his buttocks upwards or bore itself into the ground. Something had to give . . .

. . . then a powerful, painful scraping surged the length of his spine and jerked him awake.

—Ow!

—We do it like the Romans used to, you see.

—Do what? gasped Marley, unsure if he should now have visions of vast orgies or horrible tortures. Or both.

—Scrape ourselves down with rib bones. Wonderfully effective. We don't have any olive oil, sadly, she laughed.

Marley now lay in disbelieving heaven as she washed his shoulders and back. Concentrating on not getting a hopeless erection again and thus ruining it all, he forced himself to focus all his nerves on what was actually happening, not what his wretched fantasies might impossibly want to happen. To be in the Moment.

Marley felt and felt and felt and ceased to think. He was not himself, not a man with a past and a future, he was merely a surface, a hollow geodetic sculpture of skin and bone, a vast galaxy of minuscule electromagnetic impulses that lit up here and there in infinitely tiny supernovas as they whisked and jetted across and along the feathery, vibrant web of his nerves. His entire world was the soft, sliding vortex of her soapy hands on his hair, his neck, rubbing his shoulders, massaging, pressing, squeezing, then the firm long scraping strokes, almost painful but at that strange balancing point where almost painful means infinitely pleasurable, scouring his skin, sloughing away all grime and aches, shelling off hope and worry, failure. He was aware of her body astride his back, but it did not feel like urgency or longing, it was merely as though the whole of his pelvis and his groin had turned to hot, soft wax. He felt the rib bone scrape softly again in broad swathes down his back, draw swooping circles on his shoulder blades and down his sides, smooth, long, combing motions up his legs, as if she were inscribing secret, sweeping, hieratic symbols

148

and signs on his living skin. Everything was being cast off, stripped clean and washed away, made clean and new . . .

He felt her hands again, her strong, smooth soapy hands, moving in soft patterns down his neck, his shoulders, his back, his lower back.

His very lower back.

Lower.

Between his legs.

Marley opened his eyes wide in panic.

Her hand soaping his arse. His balls. His cock. Her arms now rolling him gently over. His erection impossible to hide now. He sat up, as if by doing so he could bow in shame and conceal himself.

—I'm sorry, George, I didn't mean . . .

—Oh, don't worry. It's perfectly natural.

—Is it?

—Well, isn't it?

There was a long pause, a heavy silence in the dark and in his heart. And then she leaned slowly forward and nibbled his ear. Her strong hand closed from nowhere around his cock.

—My wounded soldier. My real Englishman, from home.

—George.

—When we get home, will you show me England?

He stroked her thick, short blonde hair softly and marvelled at the smoothness of her cheeks, the smallness of her skull, the beauty of her little ears, the pale down on her upper lip. As he did so, she rolled him slowly on to his back again.

—Trafalgar Square, she murmured, as if intoning some great and secret mystery, —Horse Guards, Whitehall, the Houses of Parliament.

He felt the damp, warm moss underneath his arse, her

149

thighs at his flanks, her hand guiding him up, shoving gently through the soft lips, inside her now, sliding inside her as if it, this, he and she and them would go on for ever.

—Windsor, Oxford, Stratford-upon-Avon, she whispered. She moved above him, a dark shadow of beauty, face half lit from the diffuse brightness outside.

—The White Cliffs, the White Horse, Stonehenge.

She pushed him down again and now almost lay on top of him, it was she who was moving and pushing now, she who was sliding into him, not him into her.

—New stock, she panted. —From the old country.

—George, oh George.

—From England. Oh, Hadrian's Wall and Offa's Dyke, Ullswater, Long Mynd, Simmon's Yat.

—Oh George.

Marley did not listen and did not care. As she recited the book-read names of England, her chant to her unknown homeland, he simply chorused her name again and again, like a prayer. He spread his arms like wings and began to cry out, long and low, as his body found a sudden new rhythm and began to melt into hot liquid and cold fire.

—The Tower, Tower Bridge, many-towered Camelot, Tintagel, Glastonbury, Avalon, Land's End, John O'Groats, John of Gaunt, this other Eden, Covent Garden, Holborn . . .

—. . . George . . .

The tone found itself; the chord resolved; the deep note held and sang. Marley opened his eyes wide in deathlike joy and saw her suddenly sit up straighter again, arcing her young, strong back, opening her mouth, a darker darkness in the half-light, feeling every little ridge and ledge inside her, the top of him thumping up against soft muscle deep inside; he looked at her face, searching, longing for light to see it better, screaming in all the agony of life and longing, coming, coming coming howling, the tight jet of spunk rushing up like a racing tide from way inside his thigh muscles, taking half of his life with it as it surged in pulses that felt as though they would never stop. As he came, he grabbed her face with both hands and gazed wildly into the dark of her dark blue eyes with a dizzying whirl of feelings: fierce desire, hard joy, triumph and gratitude and utter disbelief, and he saw her eyes glaze and break focus, watched her young, unplucked brows furrow, and then was staring down into the endless blackness of her open throat as she threw her head back and he cried, —George, George, George! and she cried, —White City, Shepherd's Bush, Holland Park, England, oh England! Oh!

*

—Which one was your husband, Mrs Marley? asked the young reporter from the *Intelligencer*, staring at the faded picture.

—Which one? Mary Marley laughed merrily. She rather liked this young man, though she had of course made a point of saying that she herself read the *Paper*, had always done so, and would never, ever buy his Tory Rag. —Which one? The one in the front with the bloody sword, of course.

—Of course, Mrs Marley, sorry. Stupid of me. That's very good. That's very good indeed. Oh, um, just a small one this time. Oh. Well, ha, thanks. Cheers.

—Although the *Paper* has gone to the dogs recently.

—Would you mind terribly if I put that down?

—Shout it from the rooftops, please do.

*

—Aaah! cried Marley, as the ice-cold waterfall, tumbling down from the impossible, equatorial glacier thousands

151

of feet above them, engulfed him. George shoved him hard, he fell forwards and the deep, freezing pool swallowed him up. He had still been half asleep as she had led him blinking and staggering, knees still uncertain, out into the sun again. Now he arose, blowing and bellowing from the merciless cold. —Bleurgh, oh God, ow, wow, oh George!

—*Pas devant les enfants*, she grinned, as he tried clumsily to embrace her, and she skipped out of the pool, quickly wrapping herself in an ancient, threadbare towel and holding another out to Marley. He took it with amazement, recognising the brand name from his childhood.

—This must be nearly fifty years old.

—Make do and mend, she laughed. —There were plenty of towels and suchlike on the Flight, thank goodness, though I don't know how much longer they would have lasted. But perhaps we won't need them, now. If England's made it, I mean.

Marley emerged gasping and electrified from the cold water. He took the towel from her and grinned. She grinned back. Her eyes shone into his, and his mind and heart were totally open to her, laughing, smiling. He gazed in wonder and adoration at her water-dropped hair and face, and without plans or intentions or second thoughts he reached out to touch her face. Her lips seemed to be reeling him in gently but irresistibly towards her . . .

—Here, she laughed, and tossed him a pile of neatly folded, utterly faded, once-khaki clothing. Marley caught it without thinking, and felt ancient cotton, worn so long it was almost polished, smooth and thin. A label inside the shorts bore the legend MADE IN SOUTHERN RHODESIA.

—It came with the Flight, of course. But decent stuff lasts if one takes a bit of care, doesn't it?

—I suppose it does.

152

—Put them on, then.

She whipped the towel from his body, spreading it in the same motion to cover the sight lines to the giggling children. Marley struggled into the shorts and shirt. The legs of the shorts almost reached his knees.

—Good fit, said George. —You look almost human. Uniform suits you, but then, it suits all men, doesn't it? Here, my turn, lend a hand. She swung round, handing him one corner of her own towel, and slipped skilfully into a short dress which had once had a bold pattern of large red flowers. —Decent again, she laughed. —Now, you look as though you can walk.

—Yes, I think I can, said Marley, testing his bare feet on the hard ground. —Actually, I feel wonderful. Like new.

—Remember anything now, Jungle Jim?

—Everything. Every second.

—No, I mean about the war and England.

—No, said Marley happily. He did not remember anything and he did not want to remember anything. The gate stayed closed. No past, thank you, and no future either. He just wanted to stay in this little garden here and be with George now.

—Oh well, I'm sure it'll come back.

—Can we go back inside the sweat lodge?

—No we can't. I'm going to show you round.

—All right.

—Climb up here and you can see the whole Colony.

She led him up on to a large rock some twelve feet high, she bounding up like a young dog, he scrabbling unmanfully but happily up behind. Panting absurdly, he arrived at the flat top of the sun-warm stone and stood beside her, grinning again, irradiated by the sheer life that seemed to blaze softly from her.

Before him, basking in the strange, shadowless light, stood a panorama of order. Lines of small huts, their roofs

153

made from huge banana leaves, made two dead-straight avenues, in the centre of which stood three larger huts and a single ancient tent.

—Recognise it? she asked.

—Recognise what?

—The layout.

—No. Should I?

—Doesn't everyone do Latin in England? I thought they did.

—I don't know. What's Latin got to do with it?

—Well, the Headmaster says it's based on a Roman legionary fort. We've got volume five of Caesar's Gallic War, the bit about England, well, *Britannia* I suppose they called it then, and there's a description of a legionary fort in it, with a picture, so the Headmaster told all the Founders to copy it. And so they did. The tent's the Headmaster's, of course. He prefers canvas. Such an old dear, we all love him. There's the main hut, that's where you've been resting. We call it the Aula Max. Come on, time to show you round.

Marley scambled back down the rock behind George, and they walked across the dry plain towards the encampment.

—Where the hell did you get the huts?

—Oh, the Founders had them on board the Flight, in sections. They were going to set them up in Australia for the big Commonwealth Public Schools' jamboree. The little one next to it is where we make the penicillin.

—The what? asked Marley, staring dreamily at her throat.

—You know, the super new drug. The Founders had the *Wonder Book of How and Why* with them, luckily. One of them was the Chemistry Master. Before he died he managed to work out how to make a sort of penicillin from old taro flour.

—Before he died?

—Yes, of something that wasn't *quite* penicillin, the Book says.

—Which book?

—The Book. Our Book. Oh, sorry, of course, you don't know. We write everything that happens down in the Book, you see. The weather, how supplies are holding up, how we're coping, what the locals are up to, births, deaths and marriages, obituaries, anything good that anyone does, who wins the games, who did well on the hunt, everything really. The Headmaster reads from it every day at Assembly. It's so we don't *forget*, you see? He always says that's the real difference between us and the locals. They forget. They're clever chaps in their own way, of course, when they're not too busy eating each other or messing about trying to please their absurd little gods and shamans, and they can learn pretty fast too, but then they forget things, because they can't write so they can't really pass it down. It all gets muddled up into funny legends and myths. They think anything that happened before the oldest man in the village can remember is sort of *prehistoric*. So each lot of them have to learn it all again and again. Which is lucky for us, I suppose. But *we* don't forget. We write it all down, and we remember. So we know all about England, even though there's only half a dozen of us left who have ever seen it. We haven't *forgotten*. And that also means we know how to do things like make penicillin. Which was a good job for you, Jungle Jim.

—Can we go back to the steam lodge now?

—Well, well, you *are* all bright-eyed and bushy-tailed. Stop that.

—OK, said Marley happily.

—That's better. Golly, are all the men in England like you?

—No, said Marley firmly.

—Ah, so you *do* remember now?

—No. I just know.

—Dear me. Well, perhaps we *can* go back into the steam lodge later. *If* you behave.

—I'll behave. Do you know, George, I read something once, I don't know where, that said you could tell when you were really happy because if you were, you wouldn't mind if this single moment would be repeated for ever and ever. If now was for ever, I mean.

—What a funny thought. Oh well, at least we know that England's still there. We should be able to make it, one way or the other. See that little wood over there, in that fold of the cliffs? That's the way to the Gate.

—Oh yes, the Padre said something about that.

—It's where the hunting chaps go down to the forest. It's terribly dangerous, they say, otherwise we could all go down that way. Of course, I don't know myself, because it's out of bounds for the kids and us girls.

—Out of bounds? Why?

—Why? Well, I don't know. It just is. Because the Headmaster says so, I suppose. Only the hunting-age chaps are allowed into the woods. I'm sure they'll take you there later. The Headmaster calls it the Gate Club, he says all chaps just need somewhere they can be with other chaps. He says most chaps in England have clubs and suchlike, where only chaps are allowed to go. All the books talk about them too. The Headmaster always says the first place he's going when we make it back will be his club, in a place called Pall Mall. I always think that sounds terribly funny, don't you? Pall Mall. Have you been there? Have you got a club?

—I can't really remember. I think I did once go to a club where only men go, with a friend of mine called Grant. But I don't think I liked it very much.

—Well, I'm sure you'll like the Gate. Now, here's the junior boys' history class going on. What ho, Mr Givvens.

—What ho, George, said a middle-aged man wearing a mortarboard and gown over his shirt and long shorts as he addressed a dozen boys sitting cross-legged before him. —What ho, old man, feeling better? You *look* better. We're on Nelson today. Now, boys, can you tell our new friend what is England's mission? All together now.

—To civilise to protect the weak to spread freedom sir.

—Very good. And no one did more for that great cause than Horatio Nelson. Crompton Minimus, if you had picked your nose in that manner as a ship's boy on Horatio Nelson's quarterdeck, he would have given you a dozen with the cat o' nine tails. I, however, am more merciful, and from me you shall merely get two with this.

—Ow ouch sorry sir.

—Who can tell our visitor the date of the Battle of Trafalgar?

—It was 1805, said Marley, taken unawares by a small, scuttling byte of memory which wriggled past his block and through the gate.

—Splendid! cried the history teacher.

—Nelson's flagship was the *Victory* and he died at the moment of triumph, shot by a French musket ball. His last signal was 'England expects every man to do his duty' and his last words were 'Thank God I have done my duty'. Oh, sorry, I didn't mean to interrupt, I'll –

—No, no, there, you see, boys. *That* is what we need to know of England. Well done, old man. And now, all right, all right, let our visitor go, I'm sure you'll hear his story soon enough. Eyes front or you'll all get six. Now, let us consider the disposition of the forces at Trafalgar. The enemy, naturally, were numerically superior, but Nelson had the weather gage . . .

—That was very good, said George. —Does that mean you're remembering?

—Not anything else, said Marley, himself baffled, —it just popped up.

—Well done, anyway. Here are the younger brutes.

She pointed to a low stockade partly shaded by one of the very few trees on the plain. Inside this enclosure, perhaps a score of children between one and three years old were playing. At the gate of the stockade a girl of about ten was sitting cross-legged, reading *Five Run Away Together*.

—All well? called George.

—Yes Miss Harcourt.

—Feeding time at the zoo soon, eh?

—Yes Miss Harcourt.

—Now, over there are the cricket and rugger and soccer and hockey pitches, of course, and there's the dorm for the boys and that's the one for the girls. The little huts are for the grown-ups.

—Don't the children live with their parents?

—Well, no, not really. When they're still on the breast they're with their mothers, of course, in the mothers' and babies' hut. It's rather jolly in there, everyone mucking in together. Obviously, no one gets left *alone with a baby*, God what a ghastly thought!

—Yes, said Marley, and for an instant he staggered as a vast, lit-up lorry roared through his mind, its headlights blinding him as he, alone in freezing rain, desperately cuddled a screaming infant . . .

—Are you all right? Jungle Jim?

Marley opened his eyes again and blinked. The vision had zipped away back into the darkness of his forgotten life, leaving scarcely an echo of blasting sound and light and misery.

—Yes, yes, sorry, I was just . . . so, what, you were saying that no one gets left alone with small children?

—Certainly not. And then they get older and well, of course they don't really *live with* their parents, no. Do children, in England? I didn't think so. Doesn't everyone get sent away to school, in England?

—I, I don't remember.

—Well, it sounds like it from all the books we've got.

—Perhaps they do, then.

—I should think so. Kids are much happier in gangs, don't you think? What kind of fun would they have if they lived with their parents all the time?

—I suppose not much.

—And how on earth would the parents ever get on with things? What a silly idea.

—Yes, I suppose it is.

—Now here's the archery range. The Headmaster's a pretty hot shot with anything really, and the Boy Scout books from the Flight tell us how to make decent bows, so we all do archery, even though we only started to run low on ammo for the rifles about four years ago.

—Ammo?

—Well, the OTC chaps brought quite a bit with them on the Flight, because the Aussies use Yank ammo.

—Do they?

—Apparently. The Headmaster rationed it very strictly, but obviously it was going to run out eventually.

—What do you need ammo for?

—For the hunting, of course. How on earth did you think we live? The boys learn to hunt as soon as they can walk. Most of them are pretty good with a bow by the time they're three and . . . Jungle Jim, are you sure you're all right?

—Three? George. Oh Christ. I've got a boy! He's three! He's called Tommy.

Marley felt his heart blast apart with light at the memory of holding his son up laughing high above his head. A son. Tommy. He grabbed George's waist in sheer delight and swung her round and round.

—I've got a son, back home, safe, in England!

—In England? So England made it?

—Made it? Yes, yes, England's, well, England.

—Well done, Jungle Jim!

—Hold on. Shh, please, George. It's coming back. Yes, yes, I was with him, on a motorway.

—A what?

—A motorway. It's, it's, well, it's a, a huge great big wide road.

—You mean one of those *autobahn* things? I read about those in the *Wonder Book of How and Why*.

—Yes, like that. Somewhere near . . . Sevenoaks. Yes, that was it.

—Sevenoaks. I've heard of that too. What a lovely name. Are there really seven oaks there? We did it in geography. It's in Kent. The Garden of England. Isn't it?

—Yes, Kent, yes, yes . . .

—And have they really got autobahns in Kent now? Golly, we've got some catching up to do. So your boy's three?

—Yes, three. He's called Tommy and . . . Oh my God and I'm called Brian. Brian Marley.

—Brian. That's a nice name.

—I'm divorced.

—Oh good. Anything else?

—No. Nothing. Well, yes. I think I've got a thing called a mortgage.

—What's that?

—I don't really remember. Something you don't want, I think.

—The Headmaster said something once about England having mortgaged its Empire to beat the Hun. And Beauvey Senior said his family had to mortgage their place in England because of the socialists. I must say I don't like the sound of those socialists. Perhaps the socialists made your father mortgage your family place, too?

—Perhaps. I don't know.

—Well, anyway, I'm sorry you've got one, whatever it is, but I'm very glad you remember your name now. And I'm so glad you've got a son. Hello, Brian Marley.

—Hello, George.

—It means you're proven stock, you see.

—Sorry?

—Oh, that's just what the Headmaster says. Gosh, I can't wait to see his face when they get back from the hunt and I tell him that England's fine! He always said we'd get back some day. You see? He's always right, in the end. I say, Brian.

—Yes?

—Well, I was thinking, since the Headmaster's not back yet, and since obviously we don't want to tell anyone else before we tell him, well, we could go back to the sweat lodge first, couldn't we? To sort of, celebrate, on our own. If you'd like, I mean. Or wouldn't you?

—Yes, yes please, George. God yes, let's.

Marley felt himself being reeled in again to her eyes and lips, his feet seemed to slide towards her across the dusty ground. But then she stopped him.

—Oh bother, look, I can see some other people going into the sweat lodge.

—Oh for Christ's . . . I mean, oh bother.

—Brian, I don't feel at all like waiting to have another bash, do you?

—No. Not at all like waiting.

—Good, she said. —I'll tell you what, let's go *almost* to the Gate, shall we? Just into the woods? I know we shouldn't, but the hunting chaps are all away, and no one will come there till they're back. Come on. I don't mind breaking the odd bound now and then. I think it makes

161

things even more, well, you know, fun. Come on then. It's terribly quiet in the wood. It's where I had my first bash, actually.

Marley let her take him by the hand and they ran over the warm, rough earth, towards the little patch of dry forest.

—George, I was just wondering, well, are you, um, having a bash with anyone else?

—Not just now. I'm a special case, you see, I'm not married so I'm the Old Maid of the place.

—You're not old.

—I'm twenty-eight, you know.

—Why aren't you married? You're very beautiful.

—And you've lost your memory. Well, you see, the Headmaster decided that obviously we were going to keep up the decencies, marriage and all that, so there'll be no *complications* when we get back to England. But then, when he could see we were going to be stuck here for quite a while, well, he realised that there just weren't very many of us, so naturally, we simply couldn't afford to have chaps and chapesses tying the knot and then not having babies after all that fuss. I mean, the Headmaster and the Padre and the Bible and the books we have about England are all pretty clear that kids are the whole point of getting married, aren't they? Not much point otherwise. So the Headmaster decided we should always try first. So when a girl's about eighteen she has her first bash. We call it Coming Out. That's what they call it in England, isn't it?

—What, um, with one of the eighteen-year-old, er, chaps, I suppose?

—God no. I told you. The young chaps aren't allowed to have a bash until they've got their blazers and they never get their blazers before they're about twenty-one at least. Here we are.

They were at the edge of the trees that led to the Gate.

As if aware of the boundary, they stopped instinctively. George looked up at Marley, her face flushed, her lips slightly apart. He touched her cheek with one hand. She pressed her hand on to his and looked down for a second, before looking up again.

—You see, Brian, it just doesn't seem to work with me. Kids, I mean. So I can have a bash with anyone I like. It's quite fun, we don't have to worry about chaps catching something unpleasant or anything like that. The Book says there *was* one chap on the Flight who had something nasty he'd caught out East, but the Headmaster made sure he didn't spread it.

—How?

—I don't know. The Book just says *appropriate action was swiftly taken*. So that's all right, isn't it? So now there's none of that sort of thing about, so I can have a bash with whoever I like. Which is nice, in its own way. Although it would be quite nice if it worked, too. Or don't you think so?

He looked into her blue eyes and saw, as clear as day, the two of them walking down a sunlit, tree-lined English street, waving happily to neighbours busy trimming hedges and washing cars, with Tommy scampering about in long grey shorts, high socks and sandals, chasing a puppy around and about the big, high, Silver Cross pram which George pushed laughingly before them . . .

—Yes. Yes it would. Very nice.

—Oh good. Because you never know, do you?

He bent to kiss her. His hand slid beneath the thin cotton of her blouse.

—Miss Harcourt Miss Harcourt!

There was a crashing amid the small trees in front of them and a boy of fourteen or fifteen came panting up, face, arms and legs covered in unnoticed scratches. He

163

was clutching an old and battered pair of military binoculars in both hands as he ran.

—Miss Harcourt Miss Harcourt I say Miss Harcourt they're coming back!

—How are they, Mainwearing Minor?

—Tip-top! *Casualties minimal hunting good* says the Headmaster isn't that bloody great sir? Ow sorry Miss Harcourt didn't mean to swear. Anyway the Head's called a jamboree for tonight.

—Wonderful. Well, cut along and tell the others then.

—Yes Miss Harcourt um I say Miss Harcourt you're looking very well today um you aren't going to the Gate are you Miss Harcourt I mean to say none of my business I suppose but I thought only us chaps were supposed to come down here and ow ouch sorry Miss Harcourt.

—You haven't won your blazer yet, Mainwearing Minor. You may have started shaving and having *that* sort of dream, but there are lots of things you don't know yet about what chaps and girls do, I assure you. Now shut up and shove off, will you?

—Yes Miss Harcourt.

—Well, we'd better hurry up then, if they're coming back, hadn't we?

—How did he know they're coming back? How does he know what the Headmaster said?

—Well, Morse code heliograph, of course. It's in one of the Boy Scout books.

—Oh yes, of course.

As they entered the cool shade of the trees, she turned and looked at him with friendly but strict appraisal.

—We'll have to get you some clothes. You can hardly come to the jamboree in that shirt, can you? I think you're more or less the same size as Armstrong. He bought it leading the last hunt and no one's been awarded his

164

blazer since. I say, that was fun, wasn't it? The steam lodge?

—Yes, great fun.

—Don't worry, you'll see your boy again soon. When we get back to England. I'm sure he's a good little chap.

They were now beneath the low branches of the small, dry, savannah trees. George turned swiftly, leaning back against one of the trunks. Marley stepped towards her, already sinking into her dark blue gaze, all other thoughts suddenly blown from his mind like the last mist on a blazing hot morning at sea. George supported herself firmly against the tree, smoothly set her legs a little way apart and let her weight sink down into her thighs with an almost imperceptible but completely heart-stopping little forward shift of her pelvis. In the total silence that followed, Marley slipped her skirt up slowly, and underneath the sound of his thudding heart he could hear, or thought he could hear, the gentle sliding of the old material against the unbelievable smoothness of the inside of her thighs. And then she said:

—Brian, who is Consuela?

Marley felt a sudden electric jolt as all his consciousness was re-routed instantly from his groin to his brain.

—You said her name, when you were at death's door. More than once, Brian. Is she your sweetheart? I'm not sure I mind, really, but I think you should tell a girl, don't you?

—Consuela?

—Ah, I was right, wasn't I? She's your girl. Is she English? Well? Hello? Brian? I just want to know. Am I just your Jungle George? Are you going to drop me when we get back to England? For this Consuela?

Consuela.

For a second the name summoned up no clear picture, but only the shreds and clues of a grand puzzle: dark

165

eyes, dark hair, a secret demand, a low, powerful calling like an echo in the hills on a still summer evening.

And then it all came back.

A big, cold wave burst upon the sea locks of his mind, blasting away his defences, a freezing wall of cold, clear memory. The door in the sunlit garden of now was blown open, and beyond it reared up the bitter past. He saw himself holding a small, weeping boy tight and hard as the boy shat in rain and darkness, lit up by blinding, rushing headlamps, his screams drowned out by a shattering torrent of noise. He knew exactly who he was again, back in England. Only too exactly. He knew everything.

He was a teacher. Not even a proper teacher. An EFL teacher.

In his mind, a horrid white plastic security door swung open, giving on to a ghastly little flat, and in lacerating detail, reality swept back over him. He knew at once all the sweaty truth about his poverty, his non-status, his endless failures, his entire lack of charisma and drive, his pathetic attempts at parenthood, his useless car. Consuela? A girl who had kissed him because she had known nothing about him. The name just stood for hopelessness and lies. And now he knew who he was, he knew he would lose George too, the moment they got back to England. He was a nobody with no hope. He had only come out here to flee himself, and to die.

—I see, Brian.

—No, George, it's not that, I only ever kissed her once, I swear, I decided not to sleep with her, she'll be gone by now, it's, it's, Christ, I've remembered, everything, I . . .

—What is it, Brian?

How could he tell her, this happy, blue-eyed girl from this impossible Eden, about the bleakness and guilt and inadequate despair that had made him go on the TV

166

show in the first place? How could she ever understand, why *should* she understand, the sheer desperation that had made him risk his life just to go on a ridiculous programme, a life so pointless and filled with shame that he had almost thrown it away, had almost *died*, simply for the pathetic chance to go on telly and maybe win two . . .?

Win? Two? Two?

—Oh my God, George. Ha! George! I've remembered!

—That's better, Brian. Hello again. Jungle Jim, I say, oooh, what on earth's got *into* you? asked George as Marley laughed loud and long, raising her off the ground, her whole weight in his arms and around his cock. He shoved her harder against the tree trunk. A golden light seemed to suffuse the world before him, as if the sun had broken through storm clouds, bringing birdsong and fresh, bright air. My God, how could he have forgotten?

The two million pounds.

He had won.

His two million pounds, waiting, in England.

He was going to live. He was going to make it home. He was going home a millionaire! No more Acton bloody Town! No more endless worry about money money bloody money. It had all worked out after all, then: his wandering, wasted life, which had seemed a logical progression towards despair, now seemed to be a meandering but inevitable journey towards triumph and happiness. Christ, he had been right all along. His mother had been right all along. Right, after all, not to have studied boring bloody law or arse-clenching accountancy, right not to have scrabbled for a steady job for ever after college, right, against all the odds, not to have crucified himself by dragging around a huge bloody mortgage ever since his twenties, right to have dumped all those girls and been dumped by all those girls, right to have come back

167

to England from Spain, right to have got divorced and given it all away. Right, incredibly, to have stuck it out. It was as if he had known. And his mother had known. She had been right, amazingly, after all, all along.

Something *had* come up for Brian Marley.

—Brian, that's, mmmm . . .

For a second, as he pushed hard into George, he saw Consuela's face again, and felt absurd guilt. But he abolished it straight away. He liked Consuela, yes. But it had only been one little kiss. He was not made to cope with that dark fire. He had been born for the bright ice of England. Not for black eyes that pulled you in like the wells of ruined castles, but for sheer blue eyes which simply bounced back any boring, troubled, un-English sort of thoughts. He was not going to explore any half-lit, mine-sown forest ever again, in search of echoing truths. Now he had found his home, at last, he would not spend his days lost in a trackless continent of black ringlets, dark skin and roaring emotions where he would never, ever feel at home. He would live in a place where he knew exactly how to be, at last, the place he had been secretly bred for from birth: he was a *real* Englishman now.

Real Englishmen do not search the world for the secrets of their existence and gaze into dark, mysterious eyes that speak of strange, big stories, eyes that would soon grow disappointed when they found no fire to answer them. Proper Englishmen do not scrabble about for insights into what the hell it is all about, this thing we call our so-called self. No, no, no. True Englishmen avoid all that. They know who they are. Oh yes. Simple. They are Englishmen. And as Englishmen, they have blonde girlfriends who do not make emotional demands on them and look great and sleep easily and cook on Agas and understand that men are different and so are never *disappointed* and do not make you feel guilty. Englishmen do not *do* guilt. They do not doubt their place on earth, their right to saunter across it, having *fun*. They have friends who come scrunching up gravel drives in quiet cars as the evening falls and the swallows turn into bats in the dark old trees, tall, untroubled friends who bring good wine and gather at long tables in big kitchens. They sleep when they want to and wake when they feel like it and make love when they choose in crisp, clean sheets and big, wide, white beds. They take their mothers to nice places at last, they have spacious houses with big gardens to play in with their sons, in the finest catchment areas, no, no, what do real Englishmen care about catchment bloody areas? They have public schools, of course they do. And nannies. They eat out merrily, free of the grinding, guarded shame of the permanently broke. They go to Brisbane if they want, these real Englishmen, they drive up to their lost fathers' bungalows, minds as cool as the air conditioning in their big hired cars, they pat the old maroon MGs on the little drives and when their fathers come out they smile, generously, like men whose lives have worked out after all and they say *Hello again, Daddy* . . .

—Christ, George . . .

—Brian, oh!

He held her against the tree long enough and hard enough for her to come as well, then let her slip down.

—I say, I *am* glad you made it here, she said.

—Rather, he said, and, —Ra*ther*, he repeated, enjoying the sound. He leaned against the tree with one arm, panting and grinning over her, gloating blatantly. As she pulled her skirts down again, he took a deep breath and looked around the little glade of trees, as if daring anyone or anything to dispute his new kingship of the forest. The whole world seemed new-scrubbed, fresh and clean. Marley surveyed his new domain.

Further into the trees, he now noticed what looked like a stockade. A Union Jack flew above it, the faded colours just visible as it swung gently in the air. As Marley's cock fell happily slack, so it seemed to him that his blood now returned to his heart in double measure, for, watching the old flag, he felt his chest swell with a pride and emotion which he had never known before. England. His England. Ra*ther*. The wooden walls. This fortress made by Nature. And indeed, the rampart of the stockade, if that was what it was, seemed to be well guarded, for he could make out, or thought he could, the shapes of watching heads against the shadowy forest.

—Is that the Gate Club? he asked idly.

—Yes. The Headmaster'll show it to you later, I'm sure. Come on. Let's tell him. Oh, I can hardly wait to see his face.

As they stepped back out of the shadows of the trees, George looked around the Colony as if taking it all in for one last time.

—It's all I've ever known, she said quite simply. —But it's all just been getting ready, really. To go home. To England. I say, Brian, I've only just really thought. You'll be pretty famous, I suppose, for finding us, won't you? Golly, that'll be fun.

—Yes, won't it? drawled Marley the English hero, standing proudly on the bright threshold of his brand new future. His failed life evaporated in the white, misty sunlight, his whole past rejigged itself so that it was now clear to see as the jolly wanderings of a man who had somehow always known that something would come up for him one day. He took George's hand and kissed her again. Now, at last, he could become what he had been born to be, what he had always been meant to be, what he had always really *been*.

At last he could be really and truly *English*.

—Papua New Guinea? Oh God, *must* I go there?

—Aye, 'fraid so, boss.

—We think it's *very* important for you to make a guest appearance on *Brit Pluck 2: The Rescue Mission*. They had 27 million viewers last night, you know. That's about twice as many as will vote in the General Election.

—Oh. Right.

—Good. Now, I'm trying *very hard indeed* to fix it so that when they find his body, or when they officially give up looking for it, you can be there. As if by chance, of course. A lot of interesting possibilities for Channel Seven when the new round of licences comes up.

—Fuck, that'd be great, eh, boss?

—I suppose, yeah.

—You can stand over his body if they do find it, obviously we'll make sure it gets disinfected and all that first, and either way you can give that speech I wrote for you about *British Courage*. Brit Pluck, you see, it all fits. British British British, that's our buzzword, remember.

—Yes, I remember.

—Right, I'll say yes to Channel Seven then. Oh, and the Chancellor and some of the other Ministers are outside. They want to see you.

—Oh God, which Ministers?

—I didn't notice. The new ones, I think.

—I'll tak' their fucking names, boss, dinnae fret.

—Must I see them?

—Well, I suppose you ought to see the Chancellor really. I'll tell him you can give him ten minutes and send the rest away, shall I?

—Would you? Thanks. Oh, I was just thinking, I mean,

I know it's not really possible, but what if this man in the jungle is actually still alive?

—Well, in that case you'll do the *Captain Scott and Livingstone and all that* speech instead. So long as you plug *British British British*.

—Just dinnae mention *England*, boss.

—Yes, yes, OK.

—Oh, and you'd better watch these tapes of the first series, so it looks like you're a fan. Mustn't give the impression that you're snooty about that sort of programme, must we? Not when 27 million people watch it.

—Oh for God's sake, must I? Oh, all right then.

*

—Headmaster, Headmaster!

—George, what the devil's the flap?

Marley and George ran into the Headmaster's big tent to find the great man arrayed in an ancient white dress shirt and striped trousers, with spats over his naked feet, selecting a collar and tie from a battered tin trunk as Tom Devereux fixed the buttoned braces to the high-waisted back of his trousers. George squeezed Marley's hand and smiled at him one last time.

—Headmaster, Tom, he's remembered, haven't you, darling?

—Have you by God, old boy?

—Good show, old man.

—Yes, drawled Marley. —My name's Brian Marley and I'm a millionaire and I can remember everything.

—Well, out with it, old boy: how are things in England?

—England's fine. We can go home right away.

—But according to the Padre, you said there were Albanians in Maidstone and our university chaps had to do their washing.

—Albanians? Ha ha, oh, no, no, *they* do the washing for *us*.

—Thank God for that, eh, sir?

—Oh, Headmaster, isn't it wonderful? England's all right! We can go home! George embraced the Headmaster. Over her shoulder, a tear glistened inside the old green eyes.

—You always said she'd pull through, sir.

—I did, didn't I, Devereux?

—You did, sir.

The Headmaster and Devereux shook hands manfully. For a moment it seemed as though the older man might even embrace the younger, but discipline held. The Headmaster turned to Marley and shook his hand powerfully.

—Home, yes, by God. Ha! Well, Marley, come on, man, tell us all about it. How England pulled through.

—Pulled through?

—The war, man, the war.

—What war?

—What war? The big one, damn it. The one with the Reds. World War ruddy III, man. What happened? Did the buggers get London? How many of our chaps bought it? Was it just Europe, or the whole world? What did the Chinks do?

—Oh, that. Ha ha. Oh no, there was no war.

The Headmaster's iron handshake froze around Marley's fingers.

—What do you mean there was *no war*?

—It never happened. The big war. World War III. There wasn't one.

Marley's hand was freed. The Headmaster took a step away and turned, leaning his weight on his trestle table as if in deep contemplation.

—No war, eh? No Red attack? No H-bombs?

—No. England's fine. We can go back straight away.

Marley put his arm around George's waist and smiled indulgently at the old man. The Headmaster continued to stare down at the rough pine of his table top, as if considering the grain of the wood.

—Headmaster, asked George, baffled, —aren't you pleased?

—It's good news surely, sir?

—Tell me something, Devereux. The locals have heard of England, haven't they?

—Heard of it, sir? Well, yes. *Missis Kwin* and all that.

—Exactly, Devereux. Some of them even speak a bit of pidgin. They're in touch with the other tribes, those tribes are in touch with their own neighbours, and so on, eh?

—Well, yes, but I must admit I don't quite catch your drift, sir.

—If there's been no war, Devereux, if civilisation has kept up, the locals would know it, wouldn't they? But they've said nothing, ever. Each time we meet them, I ask about England, of course I damn well do, and all they do is shake their blasted heads and look sorry and say *Sori heah notin bout Inglin, Hetmasta*. Same thing every time, year in, year out. You've heard them, damn it, Devereux. Think, man.

—Yes, sir, you're right. It is strange, now you mention it.

—Isn't it? What do you think, Marley?

—Me? Well, look, I'm sorry, I don't understand that either, but . . .

—Oh, but I think *I* understand. Did your lot think that none of us old chaps would be left by now, eh? Thought you could pull the wool over the eyes of the younger chaps, did you?

—Pull the wool?

Marley found himself watching stupidly as the Headmaster slowly took an aged but clearly working revolver from a holster on the table, snapped the breech open and checked that the barrel was empty.

—Um, look, I'm not sure what you mean, laughed Marley, idiotically.

—Headmaster? asked George.

—Sir? began Devereux.

The Headmaster slid a single round smoothly into one of the chambers. Marley, stunned by the impossibility of what was happening, simply watched him do so.

—George, Devereux, it's time I came clean. You see, I'm afraid the books we have out here don't quite give you the whole picture about England. And I haven't told you everything, either. About the rot that was setting in. Perhaps I should have, and if that's so, I'm sorry. But you see, when we realised we were going to be here for a while, we senior chaps agreed that to keep up morale there were certain things about England that were better left unsaid to the young chaps. Certain English names that were better left unspoken. Names like Burgess, Philby and Maclean, eh, Marley? Pals of yours, by any chance?

—Pals? I wasn't even born then.

—No war, Marley? Do you take me for a complete idiot? No war? That MiG-19 shot us down in cold blood. A civilian bloody airliner. Then we saw the mushroom clouds on the horizon a few weeks later. And no one ever came to look for us. No war, eh?

—There wasn't. Honestly.

—Everyone knew there was going to be a war. We were all getting ready for it. Spending two bob in every pound we had. Civil defence, the V-bombers, early-warning. We had to, we knew the Reds were pouring out the roubles hand over fist trying to outgun us. Yes, and we all knew there would be fifth columnists too. There were plenty of them about, I'm afraid, chaps. Blackguards, fools and ne'er-do-wells on the make who would cry foul every time

175

an English farmer defended his wife and children in Kenya but had plenty of damn Jesuitical excuses to hand when the Reds sent the tanks into Budapest. And you expect me to believe that Moscow has rolled over, without a fight?

—But it did. It all just sort of *stopped*. The Soviet Union, it doesn't exist any more, it just sort of, well, fell to bits.

—*Fell to bits?* Good God, you really know how to insult a man's intelligence. Admit it, you came here to winkle us out for your Red masters, didn't you? Because we're the last of England, aren't we?

—This is ridiculous. England's fine, it's, well, England.

The old, heavy pistol was snapped shut.

—Sir, I really think . . .

—Please, Headmaster, I'm sure Brian's not lying to us.

—My father was a Navy officer, gabbled Marley, instinctively.

The Headmaster blinked, clearly shaken.

—What? What ship?

—I told the, er, the vicar, the Padre I mean. He was on the *Eagle*. Like the comic.

—Your father was an officer on *Eagle*?

—Yes.

—When?

—Um, wait, er, 1953. Yes. The Coronation.

—Fifty-three? I was on *Eagle* in '54. Seconded to the Commandos. Off Malaya. And I never knew a chap called . . . well, bugger me. Just a moment. Marley, Marley, Marley. Good God. Now look here, Marley, I've met some damn clever Reds in my time, so you just answer me this and answer me good. If he was your father, what did he look like?

Feverishly, Marley scanned the deepest, sunless depths of his memory.

—He was, um, tall, with a blond beard. He was a sub

176

lieutenant. He did something to do with electronics, radar, I think. It's true.

There was no doubt about it. The green eyes flickered.

—He was scared of flying, added Marley, for no other reason than that this was all he knew about his own father. To his surprise, this seemed decisive.

—Yes. Yes, I remember him.

—Do you? Oh, thank God, cried George.

—Tall chap, junior radar-gunnery officer. Scared of flying. Yes. That was him. Temporary gentleman, Devereux. He was in command of a launch when they picked up a headless schoolboy after the Naples Comet crash. Very shook up, they said, wouldn't go anywhere near a plane after that.

—Yes, that's him, said Marley, quickly, reeling inwardly at the sudden knowledge that we never really know our own parents until it is too late to change anything or say anything, too late to matter. Perhaps we never know *anything* until it is too late. Perhaps *knowing* itself is something that only comes too late: we do what we do and when it is done we know what we have done but by then the tense has shifted, it is all history, the rock we have already pushed is falling into the deep well of the unknowable future, and all our late-come knowledge cannot stop the stone from hitting the dark water, whether we want it or not . . .

—That's all very well, Marley, but a son can betray his father and that still doesn't explain what the devil you're doing here. Who sent you, then? The Government? If they did, where the hell's your back-up?

—Sorry? asked Marley, stupidly. He shook the thoughts of his unknown father from him, and made himself return to reality. He looked down and saw the Headmaster's fingers growing white with unconscious pressure on the butt and trigger of the revolver, even though it was not yet aimed deliberately at him. Recently, Marley had had a colleague in the London English School, a drunken, weepy, pub-fighting Irishman who had been ordained by the Pope himself on that famous visit to Ireland, only to realise twenty years later that no one in Ireland cared what priests said any more and that he had wasted his irreplaceable youth clutching vainly at the fast-disappearing coat-tails of history while others built bungalows, motorways and businesses. Now, in the Headmaster's old, green eyes, Marley glimpsed the same inner battle being fought out, as the grizzled warrior tried to shut out the dreadful suspicion that he had quite simply been wrong all his life. Such men are dangerous, he knew. He carefully held both hands up slightly, in the ancient mime of harmlessness.

—I came on a television programme, he said, very simply and quietly. —It was, well, a sort of, a game, an adventure, in the jungle. It all went wrong and everyone died. I'm a millionaire back in England, for God's sake, I just want to go home, I've got a son. There was no war. Honestly. Everything's fine. We can go back. England will be amazed, er, Headmaster, sir. And delighted. Really.

—Sir, I think he may be telling the truth.

—I believe him, Headmaster.

The Headmaster looked from Devereux to George, and Marley saw the hand that held the old pistol tremble slightly. The barrel lowered and now pointed almost at the ground.

—Damn it, chaps, I'm not an unreasonable man. Marley, if you're telling the truth, we're all on the same side and no hard feelings. But I've interrogated Reds before, and let me warn you I am very good at telling when a man is fibbing to save his skin. So out with it, old boy. If there wasn't a war, as you claim, you tell me what the hell's happened since we came here. Well?

—Do tell him, Brian.

In the expectant silence, Marley gazed into the green eyes

as if into the well of the Truth itself. What had happened? What *had* happened, really happened, in his lifetime? What were the sepia-tinted images and shattered relics, the small evidence of the era of his, Brian Marley's, little Life On Earth, which would be dug out by anthropologists or archaeologists from dusty library vaults, mounds of radioactive waste or ice-cap-flooded cities three hundred years from now? Or, if civilisation survived and children ten generations hence were still being led, awestruck, alongside the diplodocus skeleton in the Natural History Museum, 70 million years old but by now no more dead than he, Brian Marley, would then be, what would they learn of his epoch, what scanty, easy-to-revise facts would they be taught about the final third of the twentieth century and the first years of the twenty-first? What had happened that mattered, at all, in the dark mirror of eternity?

—Well, um, yes, people did *talk* about a big war a lot. I remember lying in bed and thinking about atom bombs when I was very little. But actually, one of the first things I really remember at all is Winston Churchill's funeral.

—Good old Winston. I hope they gave him a good send-off?

—Oh yes, I think they must have given us the day off school or something. It was a big thing, we all watched it on television. And someone landed on the moon, yes, that was exciting, we all watched that, too.

—Golly, Headmaster, an Englishman on the moon?

—No, sorry, it was all just Americans on the moon.

—What, man, all?

—I'm afraid so. There *was* a war, in a place called Vietnam, for a very long time. All the time, it felt like.

—I know damn well where Vietnam is, Marley. I was in Korea with the Glosters. Did we win in Vietnam?

—It wasn't us. Just the Americans. They lost.

—Hmm, that sounds believable. Tough little sods, the

Vietnamese, chaps, knocked the stuffing out of the Frogs. So they beat the Yanks too, you say? What, and the Reds, the real Reds, the damn Russian and Chinese Reds, didn't jump at the chance to have a pop at us?

—Well, the Russians invaded Czechoslovakia, but there was no war about it.

—We just let them invade?

—Um, yes.

—Damn it all, Devereux, I can't pretend that doesn't sound all too familiar. Appeasement and Hungary, all over again. Did they threaten us with war?

—I don't think so. I was only little, but everyone only seemed interested in pop music then.

—In *what* music?

—Sort of, um, people playing guitars and singing. And everyone's big sisters and big brothers started wearing flowery clothes and talking about peace and love and taking drugs.

—What? When the devil was this?

—Um, about the end of the 1960s.

—But what were the decent people doing, for God's sake? If this was the 1960s, well, there must have been millions of good chaps only in their thirties and forties, chaps who'd been through the war and done their bit. Why the hell did they let such rot happen?

—Look, I don't know, I was only a boy, I was a Cub Scout and things like that, I didn't really notice. But I think all that stopped quite quickly, and then, well, it's hard to explain really, when I was starting to grow up and really notice the world, and think what I was going to do in it, it was the 1970s by then, and everyone seemed to have this feeling that it had all gone wrong somehow but no one knew exactly *how*. Everything was just sort of getting a bit worse and a bit greyer every year and every-thing was costing more and more every week and everyone was going on strike all the time and loads of people were being killed in Northern Ireland and there were more and more people out of work and everyone felt, well, I think everyone felt it was all just going to keep on getting worse and worse for ever and there was no point in anything any more really.

There was a long silence, which ended with a gentle thud of metal on wood as the Headmaster laid his pistol down on the trestle table.

—Sir?

—Do you believe him, Headmaster?

—I'm afraid I do, George. I'm very much afraid that I do. Some of us saw it coming. The general rot. Well, who was in power? The Government, man? Who was letting this rot happen?

—Um, well, it was Labour, mostly, back then.

—Of course, the socialists, blast them and everyone who wouldn't stand up to them.

—And then I went to university, Marley continued desperately, keen to add as many plausible details as possible while he seemed to be winning, —and people with beards taught us that nothing actually meant anything and everything that was wrong with the world was because of White Anglo-Saxon Protestant men pretending anything meant anything.

—Yes, those clever university bolshies and their rot. The same sort that said Nasser was some kind of damn hero. The sort who see good in everything but their own.

—And then Mrs Thatcher became Prime Minister.

—A *woman* Prime Minister?

—And well, then things got even worse and there were four million unemployed and there were riots in the big cities, they almost had to call the Army into Liverpool and Brixton, and then the miners went on strike for a year and –

—Stop, damn you, Marley, stop. How can I tell the chaps *that's* what we've been holding out for? Four million unemployed? Riots in south London? Miners on strike for a year? Morale will collapse, man, simply collapse. We've been sitting here keeping England going. I told them, told them all, that England would pull through somehow, that they'd come for us one day, that we just had to keep ourselves English, not go native, not give up and go to the dogs. And we have. And now you're telling me –

—That was twenty years ago, said Marley. —But lots of things have happened since then, it was –

—Brian, please, *do* shut up. I don't think he can take any more. I, oh, I almost wish you had never come here.

Sniffing back a tear, George hurried to support the Headmaster. He looked at her as if from a faraway planet. The conviction that had sustained him for so long seemed to have leeched away, and he stood before them, a mere, lost old soldier from a long-forgotten war.

—Well, well, well. No war, eh? No heroics? No last stand? Just four million unemployed and riots in London and striking miners, eh? The Red rot finally getting the upper hand. Good God, poor old England.

The Headmaster slowly picked up his old revolver again and slid it into its leather holster. He laid the holster and belt carefully on the scrubbed table, patting them straight and shipshape, as if quite certain that he himself would never need these things again but hoping against hope that someone else, a grandson yet unborn, perhaps, might one day find some use for them. Then he slowly straightened his spine by a clear effort of will-power alone.

—George, my dear, don't worry about me. I can take the truth. It's the young chaps I'm worried about. We may, yes, I'm afraid we *may* have to lie to them to keep morale up. It's not right and I don't like it, but there you are. Can't be telling them all that, can we? No, no. But we, we in this tent, yes, we must know the worst. So out with it, Marley. I can take it. What happened next? Where were we, Devereux?

—A lady Prime Minister, sir.

—Yes. Good God, have the damn socialists no sense at all?

—Oh no, she was a Tory. Very.

—What?

—And the first thing she did was have a war with Argentina.

—But the Argentines were always our pals. Polo and all that. You sure, Marley?

—They invaded the Falklands.

—Ah yes, that. Silly buggers could never let that one go. I suppose they beat us, too?

—No, we went there and took it back from them, by force.

—What, was it a proper scrap?

—Oh yes, we lost some ships and hundreds of men. But we won.

—Sent a fleet halfway round the world and won a real little dust-up? That's more like it, eh, Devereux? And then?

—Well, and then she beat the miners' strike and more or less stopped the trade unions completely.

—Did she, by God? How the hell did she manage that?

—Um, well, by charging people with police horses, mainly, I think.

—A whiff of grapeshot, eh? Sounds like quite a girl.

—And then she stayed Prime Minister for ages. The Americans started putting huge lorries carrying nuclear missiles all over England and everyone thought there really *was* going to be a big war with the Russians. I remember one day we heard that Kiev had been blown up by an H-bomb and at first we all thought it was actually the start of the war, for a few minutes everyone stopped working and stood and looked at the sky and expected to see missiles and wondered what the hell to do. But actually it was just a Russian nuclear power station blowing up, so that was all right. I mean, unless you were in Kiev, obviously. Or a farmer in North Wales, because that was where the fallout landed. And then, oh yes, well, the Russians invaded Afghanistan. We didn't do anything about that, either.

—Yes, the buggers always wanted Afghanistan, Reds or just plain old-fashioned Russians.

—They got kicked out.

—Ha! Tough little bastard, your Afghan.

—And then, well, like I said, about ten years ago it all just fell to bits. Not England, Marley added hastily seeing a flame of outrage rekindle in the green eyes, —Russia. The Soviet Union. No one expected it, especially not the university experts, the wall in Berlin came down, and in Romania they shot the chief Communist and then, well, it just sort of all, yes, just *fell to bits* in a couple of months and there was no war and that was that. And as soon as it happened, no one could believe we'd ever been scared of them and the only problem was what to do with all their rusting nuclear submarines and missiles.

—What, do you mean there are *no more Reds* left at all?

—I think the Chinese still *call* themselves Communists, sort of, but they mainly make radios and cameras and toys, these days.

—Good God. You mean we won? We beat the Red buggers? Without firing a shot? Without having to use the H-bomb?

—Well, yes, I suppose that's it. Yes, we won. We won.

—Devereux?

—Yes, sir.

—Give me your hand, man.

—Congratulations, sir.

—George?

—Yes, Headmaster?

—My dear girl, come to my arms.

—Oh, Headmaster.

—So I was wrong, eh? Well, who gives a damn who was right and who was wrong, if England won the day, eh, my girl?

—Not me, Headmaster.

—Marley?

—Yes, er, sir, Headmaster?

—Shake, old boy. No hard feelings, eh? And now, all of you, listen to me. I think this is going to be a jamboree to remember.

*

—I'm not taking her down into that bloody lot, said the Australian helicopter pilot.

—But I thought maybe I saw smoke.

—Nah, that's just the cold air from the glacier meeting the ground and coming back up. Or a geyser maybe. The only thing underneath that cloud is rocks. And rocks don't like choppers. Forget it, mate.

Below them, the strange, flat blanket of cloud lay in a bowl between the sharp clifftops, covering an area perhaps a mile square. In the tropical sunshine this white covering reflected so much light that it almost matched the glacier which lay naked and gleaming above it.

—OK, said the weary CNN anchorman, let's get back.

And so the machine swung round and they went back. Back to the baking, ghastly, ramshackle, gun-infested capital on the coast. Back to the dozens of other TV crews who were currently disembarking there from half the nations of the world. Back to the new contestants from every continent who were preparing to blunder suicidally about in the jungle alone with nothing but bread,

185

water, quinine and vitamin C, carrying their little digital cameras to record their probable deaths for *Brit Pluck 2: The Rescue Mission* (the barriers were down now and suddenly everyone on earth seemed to have agreed it was fine, after all, to die live on TV). There were so many applicants that Channel Seven and its many new world-wide licensees had all been able to drop the prize money very considerably indeed.

As they swooped away from the shrouded mountain tops, another helicopter crossed their path, sweeping the forest in the other direction, wheeling up towards the mountains.

—Well, *they* haven't stopped looking up there, said the CNN man accusingly.

—They haven't seen the cloud yet, sneered the pilot.
—Stupid fucking Brits. Let them waste their gas. Let them tear their arses off on the rocks if they want. Look, mate, that's the Hindenburg bloody Wall, OK? The Eighth Wonder of the fucking World, they call it. You can see how ruddy high it is. Fifteen hundred feet straight up from the forest fucking floor, it goes, and it's twenty-odd miles long. The crash site was down below, right? Well, you really think a dying forty-year-old bloody Brit with no gear could climb that lot even if he bothered to try? And if he did, which he didn't, do you really think there's anything under those clouds but more cliffs and more jungle and more bloody mozzies? Give over, mate. Time for a tinny.

And the pilot then amused himself by scaring the shit out of the pompous bloody Yank beside him by banking across the vast, sheer face of the Hindenburg Wall with scarcely twenty feet to spare.

*

—So, my dear, Consuela, how do you like England?
—I like very much, she replied. —But I do not like your hand so close to my leg.

186

—Eh? Oh, ha, just moving my chair, my dear girl. Baines?

—Yes, sir?

—Cognac.

—Four glasses of cognac, sir.

—Your health, Air Colonel.

—*Salud*, Sir James, *salud* to you, Sir Charles! This book, this *Best of Breed*, it is magnificent. I shall treasure it.

—Pardon me, sir?

—What is it, Baines?

—The proofs of tomorrow morning's edition have arrived sir. Will you want to see them?

—Better bring them in, Baines. Sorry, Air Colonel, my dear Consuela, sorry, Charles, but I have to keep an eye on things. It won't take me half a mo.

—Of course, Jimmy. Privilege to see the great man at work, eh, Air Colonel?

—Duty comes first, Sir Charles!

—Father, I shall go home to our hotel soon.

—Here we are. Blasted PM. If only the Party weren't in such a God-awful state, eh? Smarmy little prick can do just as he pleases, the way things are. Hmmm. Yanks throwing their weight about again, I see. Can't blame them, really, I suppose. Yes, yes, fine. Hmmm, good-looking filly there, eh, Charles? What do you think of that dress, my dear? Don't play the cello by any chance? Ah, the obits. Good write-up for O'Connor, I made damn sure he got his half-page. Hell of a fellow, Air Colonel, you'd have liked him. Gave the Reds what for when he was out with the Sarawak Rangers in Malaya.

—What for to the Reds, Sir James!

—Quite. Have to put him in *Best of Breed* Volume 2. And that won't be long coming out, the rate the chaps are going west. We shall all soon be clothed in the consolation of history, my dear Air Colonel. Once all the chaps that didn't die when they were young and brave are all dead anyway, what the hell difference does it make that some of them died in battle fifty years ago and not in a blasted rest home in Cheltenham last week, eh? Now, who the devil's this young chap, never heard of him, what's *he* done to get his two columns? Some bloody West End pansy who's big with the groundlings just because he's been on the box a few times? See, Charles, what did I tell you, the moment I turn my back that blasted idiot Harry tries to *appeal to the young* for God's sake. Bugger the young, I say. There are far more of *us* than them and –

—*Brian!* Father, look, it is my Brian.

—Oh, I say. Look here, I'm terribly sorry, my dear, I had no idea. Baines?

—Sir James?

—Hanky for the lady, sharpish, man.

—Yes, Sir James.

—It is all right, Sir James, I shall not cry. You see, I do not believe he is dead.

—Good girl, that's the stuff, eh, Jimmy?

—She certainly is the goods, Charles.

—Ah, Consuela, you did not tell me his father was an English Navy officer!

—I did not know, Father. He never said.

—Yes, that is the English way!

—Four glasses of cognac and a supply of handker-chiefs, Sir James.

—Thank you, Baines. Well, here's to him, my dear, alive or dead.

*

—O Almighty God, who art a strong tower of defence unto Thy servants against the face of their enemies; we yield Thee praise and thanksgiving for our deliverance from those great and apparent dangers wherewith we were compassed;

we acknowledge it Thy goodness that we were not delivered over as prey unto them (*rather fitting, that bit, eh?*); beseeching Thee still to continue such Thy mercies towards us, that all the world may know that Thou art our Saviour and mighty Deliverer, through Jesus Christ our Lord. Amen.

—Amen, said a rolling medley of voices, voices of both sexes and of all ages and timbres but all clearly English voices, bright, clear and confident, bathed in the curious, shadowless afternoon luminescence of their cloud-filtered colonial sky, faces glowing as well with inner brightness as they waited for the sun to set, the winds to make their daily change, and the great bonfire to be lit with flames ceremonially kindled by the Headmaster himself using the traditional bowstring and stick (as described in the *Boy Scout Handbook*, 1958), whereupon the feasting would begin and they would sing again the old songs of their race, in the shadows of the flames beneath the cold, foreign sky, arced over with half-glimpsed constellations unsung by Homer or Shakespeare.

Inside the tent, the Headmaster was waiting with his ears cocked.

—Amen, said he.

—Amen, said Marley, hastily.

Devereux stood ready to fling back the door flap of the Headmaster's big canvas tent for them to make their public entrance before the Colony. George was quickly sewing a button on to the sleeve of Marley's double-breasted dinner jacket. Outside, the Padre's fluting voice continued to read from the Book of Common Prayer.

—Now listen here, Marley, said the Headmaster, buckling on the webbing belt with the leather holster beneath his tailcoat, as easily and unconsciously as another man might button his cuffs.

—Yes, er, Headmaster sir? said Marley. He was glad of the order, because he was having problems with the black bow tie which George had merrily chucked him. He had been simply too ashamed to admit that he had no idea how to tie it, and was now secretly waiting for the Headmaster to start tying his own white tie over his wing collar, so that he could copy him, like an atheist hastily following the moves of the congregation at a church wedding.

—Morale, you see, Marley. When the young chaps, the hunting-age chaps, hear that England's fine, they'll want to rush down into the jungle and find your chaps, right now, rains or no rains. They won't stop to think what'll happen to the women and children here if they don't find your chaps and don't make it back. The young chaps never do think like that, do they? When you're twenty, three months seems like ten years. It was the same at Alamein. God, we young chaps were impatient with M'ngumry.

—Who?

—M'ngumry. Field Marshall M'ngumry of Alamein, damn it. Don't say we've forgotten Alamein?

—Oh. Yes, no, of course, sorry. *Montgomery*, right.

—Yes, well, half of us were about ready to accuse him of cowardice by the time he was ready to attack, *why the hell wouldn't he just set us loose to charge the panzers*, all that sort of thing. And of course there were some who said it was because he wasn't really out of the top drawer himself. Didn't ride to hounds, you know. Where was I?

—Um, El Alamein, I think, er, sir.

—Was I? Why the devil are we talking about Alamein?

—You said you were young and impatient.

—Was I? Well of course I was, I was twenty. Ah yes, the young chaps. You see, we never stopped to think what would happen if we didn't break Rommel there and then. And our young chaps here are the same. There's a few of them out there would just go for broke and charge down into the jungle. Got to rein them in, keep an eye on the bigger picture.

190

—But I mean, I thought the boys all sort of, worship you.

—Well, it's ruddy hard work keeping the show up, I tell you.

—The show?

At last, the Headmaster got to his white tie and Marley prepared to follow his every move. But the older man whipped it into a perfect bow at such speed that Marley had hardly got past the first bit before he was hopelessly lost. He quickly gave up and pretended to be still buttoning his shirt collar.

—Of course it's a ruddy show. Always has been. How the hell d'you think we kept India for so long? Theatrical instinct, old boy. Knowing when it's right to go a little bit native and when you've got to wear a stiff shirt and a black coat when it's ninety-five in the shade, like it or not. The Frogs and the others never quite got it right and the Yanks are bloody awful at it. How do you think you get the Other Ranks to go over the top? The same. And how d'you keep the young guns under your thumb? Same again. Show. I mean to say, look at the start of the *Iliad*, eh?

—Um, I never actually, that is . . .

—Don't tell me they've stopped teaching the classics? Well, there's young Lieutenant Colonel Achilles just back from the front line, regular fire-eater, DSO and bar and itching to get his VC, chaps that would follow him to hell and back, never lost a fight, why the devil doesn't he just march in, do the tight old sod Agamemnon and take whatever girl he ruddy well fancies? Pretty good question to kick off European literature, eh? And why doesn't he? Why can't he be allowed to? Because Agamemnon is the bloody king and his CO, that's why, and if you go around bumping off kings and COs and letting the young chaps run the place, they are going to damn well mess it

191

up, that's why. Because they're young. I was, once, and I know what it was like. You don't really believe in death when you're twenty, even when you've seen it, because the only thing that feels *really* real to you when you're twenty is the play going on inside your own head. Pride and pals and girls. No, if you let the damn twenty-year-olds take over, we'd all end up dragging each other round by our ankles, pinching each other's wives and knocking each other off, Geneva Convention or not. The Greeks knew that and no doubt that's why they liked that story so much they kept on telling it until it survived. Got to give the young chaps their *due* without giving them *power*, that's the trick. Make them feel important but make it damn clear to them that there are things they have just got to keep their mucky little paws off until they've earned their blasted turn. That's all *society* means, you know, old boy: the tricks we use to keep the hunting-age chaps busy and in their places. Dish out the privileges carefully and slowly, that's the main thing. And keep up the show.

—There, said George, tugging Marley's jacket sleeve straight and kissing him. Marley let his arm slide casually around her waist again. His hand rested smoothly on the soft swell of her hip. She smiled up at him. —Don't forget your tie, though, darling.

—No, no, of course.

—Good luck then, chaps. I'm off out to make sure everyone's under starter's orders. She slunk out of the tent. The three of them watched her go, as men. There was a brief silence as the ancient, faded canvas slapped closed behind her.

—You're a lucky chap, Marley, said Devereux.

—I'll say, said the Headmaster. —Always had a soft spot for dear old George. Hate any chap to take advantage. So, Marley, you're a millionaire back home, eh?

—Yes, actually.

192

—Good for you, never had a bean myself. Devereux?

—Yes, sir?

—Perhaps you'd better help this millionaire with his tie.

—Certainly, sir. There we are, old boy, over, under, round, back under, double her up and through, d'you see?

—Oh yes, um, of course. Thanks, er, Devereux.

The Headmaster was looking at him carefully.

—So, does nobody wear bow ties any more, back in England, Marley?

—Um, well, that is, I mean, I, yes, but . . .

—You're no millionaire, man. Don't you dare damn well lie to me again. You've never tied a black tie in your damn life, have you? Always used one of those blasted bolshie self-tying jobs, I'll be bound. Well? Not leading poor George up the garden path, are you, old boy?

—No, but . . .

—Don't 'but' me, man.

—All right, all right, look, yes, I've only just become a millionaire. I've been poor all my life. I didn't come here just for an adventure, it was for a television programme, but, well, the programme was a competition actually, a stupid, crass, moneymaking competition for idiots, to see who could survive the jungle longest. It all went wrong and everyone died but before I got lost and ended up here I won. So now I *am* a millionaire. I mean, I will be, when we get back. Honestly, that's the truth. And I really, well, *like* George, and –

—Why the devil didn't you tell us this?

—I didn't remember at first, and then, well, when I did remember, I was with George, Georgina I mean, and, I was, well, I mean, I was *with* her, if you see what I mean, and, look, I wasn't *lying* exactly, I was just, she's so lovely, she's the sort of girl I've always thought wouldn't look

193

twice at me because, I mean, I didn't want her to think I was just, I . . .

The Headmaster threw back his silvery head and laughed.

—Marley, I absolutely believe you, at last.

—You do?

—Don't worry, old boy, wouldn't be the first man to try to cover his tracks once he's made his pile. Saw it all the time in the Empire. Chaps who made a few bob suddenly inventing public schooldays they never had and Oxford degrees they never took and regiments they were never in, all that rot. Damn silly really, bound to be rumbled in the end, one way or another, but there you are, a lot of chaps do it. I see, I see. So, the long and the short of it is, your father wangled himself a National Service commission after the last war and you were brought up a bit above your station, so you ended up always wishing you had a few bob more than you actually had and you could never quite knuckle down to life as some sort of junior clerk. Or am I wrong, Marley?

Marley felt himself blushing to the roots of his soul as the story of his life was laid out before him, ludicrously simple. Was that really all it had been, all along? No mystery, no psychology, just a mere logistical puzzle that could be solved in an instant by anyone who knew the key?

—Well, I, er, yes, I mean no, perhaps you're right. Yes, I suppose so.

—Happens to a lot of chaps. No shame in it at all. In fact, when you think about it, it shows you value the things that really matter. Absolutely the right attitude. We always need new blood and if a chap can't pass for a gentleman to start off with who gives a damn provided he can by the time we've finished with him, eh? Well, you look more or less the thing now, so let's get cracking, shall we?

194

The Padre's had quite enough time to bore them all to death and warm them up. Showtime, Marley. And for God's sake put a bit of topspin on it, eh?

Devereux swished the flap of the tent smartly back, and Marley followed the Headmaster out into the public stare of the entire Colony. The buzz died and pure silence fell, expectant, in a dark crowd of bright English eyes.

They approached two ancient first-class BOAC Comet seats raised up on a small wooden platform, in front of which had been set the portraits of the Queen and the Duke of Edinburgh from the hut where Marley had recovered, now bizarrely garlanded with strange, bright flowers and big, iridescent feathers. Marley sat down, allowing the Headmaster's trousers to touch the seat of the chair before he did so. Before their makeshift thrones stood vast piles and pyramids of strange vegetables, fat nuts and firewood. On hand-hewn wooden poles were slung many and curious tree-dwelling mammals, the size of small dogs or large cats, gutted but as yet unskinned. A large number of small, hairy, long-snouted and very alive hogs snorted and bolted about in a pen of stout branches.

Nearest to the Headmaster and Marley sat the Padre and the few other surviving old men, the Founders, the survivors of the Flight. Devereux took his place amid the larger number of men about Marley's age, in a semicircular ring behind them. The rest of the Colony, some 150 people in all, Marley estimated, were arranged in what looked like strict order of age, apart from a band of males, a score perhaps, who seemed to be between the ages of sixteen and twenty-four: freshly scarred from their hunt, radiating energy, achievement and cockiness, evidently privileged, this group sat right at the front, under the eye of the Headmaster, cradling their rifles and lounging swaggeringly, smoking curiously scented rolls of dry leaves.

—For-what-we-are-about-to-receive may the Lord make us truly tha-ank-ful.

—Hear, hear, Padre. Well, chaps, here we are again. (*Applause.*) Now, you've all been talking about the news, no doubt, and cracking good news it is too, on all fronts. Marley here has pulled through like a real Englishman and he'll be giving you all the gen on the old country later on, eh, Marley?

—Um, yes, that's right, Headmaster. (*Hearty applause.*)

—But first, a few words from me. (*Loud applause, cries of 'hear, hear!'*) It was a damn good piece of work altogether down at the Sepik River crossing this hunt, even though we were quite out of season. I'm delighted to say that our Sixth Form boys lived up to the reputation established by years gone by. It was hard going in the rains but we made a damn good hunt of it in the end. You've certainly done your bit. We lost one good chap, Marchmain Junior, but his name will go up on the reredos and we'll all remember him. And when we get back to England, as we certainly shall, and soon too, now, we'll make damn sure his people know he didn't grow soft when he thought we might make it out of here, but did his bit to the end. And that's what's got us through, you know, chaps, all these years: every man and woman, every girl and boy, all doing our bit. (*Cries of 'hear, hear!'*) And that's the way we're going to keep it. (*Loud applause.*) I'm glad to say that several members of the Upper Sixth will be getting their blazers awarded later in the proceedings (*cheers*) and may thus enjoy the full privileges of our Colony's manhood (*louder cheers*). So I hope you proven girls have each got your eyes on the chap you want because as the man in the song said, tonight's the night. (*Laughter and blushes.*) Three cheers for the Sixth Form. (*Three rousing cheers.*) Splendid. Now, before we get down to the jamboree, I know you've all been waiting to hear about

196

England. England, yes. The old country, God bless her. (*Sustained cheering.*) Marley here climbed the Wall to get to us, without any gear, having lost all the chaps in his choppers, and I think he deserves a damn good cheer too. (*Cries of 'bravo!'; impromptu rendition of 'For He's a Jolly Good Fellow'.*) And the news is this. The Reds are beaten! The Reds are finished. And England's fine. (*Mighty cheers and general excitement.*) But wait, wait, calm down now, you chaps. Marlborough Senior, sit down at your place again.

The tall, athletic boy of perhaps seventeen did not sit down again, however. Instead, he stood boldly before the Headmaster, rifle in hand.

—So can we fire volleys when the next chopper comes overhead sir?

—No you damn well cannot, Marlborough Senior. Sit down. And you, De Lacy.

—When are we going down into the jungle then sir?

—Why can't we fire to attract the choppers sir?

—We should make a really big signal fire sir.

—Marlborough Senior, all of you, shut your damn mouths and put those ruddy rifles down or you will forfeit your promotions and your blazers. And you know what that means. That means no girls for you. You're not going to fire at the choppers because they won't damn well hear it. You think they will, but they won't. Have you ever been in a chopper, Marlborough Senior?

—No sir Headmaster sir.

—Well, I have and I've been shot at in one by Chinese bloody Reds and I can tell you that with all the racket in a ruddy chopper you don't even hear the round that shoots the balls off the chap next to you, let alone anything else. As for signal fires, you all know as well as I do that the air currents here will simply whip our smoke away before it gets through the cloud cover. We could try them by night, when it's clearer, but the locals all make their own fires anyway, so why should anyone flying over in the dark think twice? No one will be looking for us up here. Now, all you're doing is getting the young chaps all upset, Marlborough Senior. It's a damn bad show, so sit down. Do it, man. Do it now and we'll forget about this. And the rest of you.

—Yes sir.

—That's better. Now, what do the choppers mean? They mean that down in the jungle, England is searching for Marley here, who, modest fellow that he is, must be a chap of some consequence. But we simply can't risk setting off in the rainy season, we've nothing to take against malaria, you hunting chaps know damn well what it's like down there right now, the rivers are still rising, the crocs are hungry and it'd take us a week to get ourselves across a single gorge. And where would we be then? In the soup. We could pass a hundred feet from Marley's chaps and never know they were there. And for those of you who haven't been down there on a hunt, the Book will tell you what happened last time we tried to break out that way. Half of us died, that's what happened. Nearly damn well did for us all. That's why we have the Book, damn it, so we don't make the same blasted mistakes twice. The little ones just won't make it, so we don't go now and there's an end to it. Our job is to keep our heads for just a couple more months, get our rations dried and preserved, and then when the rains down below stop and the rivers fall and the crocs slink away and the blasted mosquitoes calm down a bit, we make the big push and strike out, one and all, hand in hand, straight and true, knowing that England is waiting for us. (*Loud cheers.*) That's the spirit. And speaking of England, Marley here is going to answer any question you may have about the England to which, very soon, we shall all be going home. (*Rustles of expectation.*) Well, old boy?

198

Marley looked round the expectant faces. He saw George smiling at him. He spoke, and found that his voice was one he scarcely recognised, yet sounded absolutely right.

—Well, what do you want to know, er, chaps?

—I say sir please sir ouch sorry Headmaster sir may I ask something sir?

—Very well, Perceval Minor.

—What do the chaps read these days in England Mr Marley sir? Is the *Eagle* still going? And the *Beano*?

—Well, the *Beano* is still going but the *Eagle*'s stopped. Half the boys and girls in England, actually half the boys and girls on earth, are reading some books by an Oxford don about dwarfs and elves and a ring of power and nice people from the West who talk properly defeating nasty little dark-skinned creatures from the East who don't talk properly.

—Mr Marley sir that sounds like *The Lord of the Rings* sir.

—It is, but . . . Oh, sorry, of course, I forgot how old it was.

—Glad to hear that one's still going strong, eh Headmaster?

—Very glad, Devereux, just the stuff to give the younger troops.

—Ripping stuff isn't it sir when they massacre the oiks?

—Um, I think it's *orcs*, actually. Although, I suppose, now you come to mention it . . . Anyway, yes, and the other half of all the boys and girls in the world are reading some books by an Englishwoman about a secret boarding school full of ghosts and things where boys and girls who are born special get taken to learn magic.

—I say sir those books sound fun Mr Devereux sir.

—Yes, they do rather, Perceval.

—Mr Marley sir have chaps got wizard electronic brains to help them with their maths nowadays sir? (*Laughter.*)

—Trust you to ask that, Hervey-Thynne. (*Laughter*.)

—Yes, actually, everyone's got computers these days. And they're allowed to use them in school. (*Cheers*.)

—Have we got a Space Fleet Mr Marley sir?

—No, I'm afraid not.

—Mr Marley sir, asked the older boy who had briefly stood up to the Headmaster, —a lot of us chaps want to join the Army when we get back. I fancy the Hussars. But I mean if the Reds are beaten hands down who are we going to fight?

—Good question, Marlborough Senior. Well, Marley, old boy?

—Ah, well, yes, you see, after the Russians stopped being Reds, people started saying that History had ended because we had won, so we didn't really need much of an army any more. But then a few years ago everything changed because some terrorists from Saudi Arabia flew some planes full of passengers into two skyscrapers in New York and killed thousands of people.

—Good God, why did they do that?

—I don't know. No one really does. Because of America supporting Israel all the time, I suppose.

—Ah, Israel still hanging on in there, then?

—Very much so.

—Tough buggers. So what did the Yanks do? Bomb Saudi Arabia?

—No, Saudi Arabia is on their side. Ours, I mean.

—But you said these mad bombers *came* from Saudi Arabia.

—Yes. I don't really understand that bit either, sorry.

—I see. So the Yanks did nothing?

—Oh no, they invaded Iraq.

—Iraq? What the devil for?

—I don't really know. The President and our Prime Minister said it was because they were a danger to us. I met a drunken American colonel and he said it was because the House of Saud was a busted flush and they needed a safe client state in the Middle East because of all the oil there and they were sick of having to support Israel *all* the time, even when a few thousand religious maniacs in hats and beards held the balance of power there. And then he said actually it was because the President thought his dad should have done it. And then he fell over, so I don't really know. But anyway, they did it and we helped them and the President of Iraq was a bastard who dropped poison gas on his own towns, so actually I don't really care why.

—No, that always seemed a good enough reason to me why someone should go and knock sense into the locals. Iraq the latest, eh? I remember we were having trouble in Iraq back in '58. Serves the Yanks right for putting the kibosh on us at Suez. Should've come in with us then, silly sods, would've saved us all a lot of bother. So the Yanks run Iraq now, eh?

—No, the Iraqis all hate them.

—Yes, the Yanks never understood hearts and minds. And we got roped into this cock-up, eh?

—Yes, quite a lot. We sent tanks, planes, aircraft carriers, everything. And we've got other soldiers in, well, all over the place really. And there are religious maniacs with turbans and beards in half the countries in the world, trying to blow things up.

—Mad mullahs, eh? Well, there's your answer, Marlborough Senior. Sounds as if there's still plenty to do out there for you young chaps. We're still pretty pally with the Yanks, then, Marley?

—Oh yes, more than ever.

—Many of our chaps get it in Iraq?

—Not many. The American air force killed a few by mistake.

—As per bloody usual. Don't suppose our boffins have come up with any damn clever new club for the bag that means we can play with the Yanks on level terms for once?

—No, sorry. We just do more or less what they want us to.

—Oh bugger. Still, can't be helped, I suppose. Winston said it was bound to come, *like the Mississippi rolling along* and all that. And as I have often said, boys, the Yanks may be swanks, yes, they may call too many of their chaps admirals and generals for our taste and their fly-boys may be cowboys who shoot at anything that moves including their own poor bloody infantry half the time, but when all's said and done, when there's a flap on, if you can't make sure you've got an Aussie or a Kiwi or a Canadian in the hole next to you, be ruddy thankful if you find it's a Yank, not some damn foreigner. Talking of which, what about the Frogs? We pally with the Frogs these days?

—Not very at all.

—Thank God for that.

—They want to make a United Europe.

—Still banging on about that, are they? Run by them, of course.

—We've joined, sort of.

—I don't like the sound of that.

—But we haven't stopped having our own pounds yet.

—I should bloody well think not. We pally with Jerry?

—Not very. We beat them and won the World Cup in 1966, by the way. (*Loud cheers.*) —They're united again now.

—Hmmm. Too bloody big for Europe, boys, that's the trouble with Jerry. Jerry can lick the rest of them put together any time he likes, unless Ivan pokes his snout in. So, Jerry started throwing his weight about again yet?

—No, they just make very good cars.

—Always did. And bloody good tanks. Didn't do him any good in the end. And you say Ivan's just Ivan again, eh, not a Bolshie any more? Not that I'd trust the bugger either way.

—Yes, Russia's just Russia again. It's a bit of a mess, I think. The population's falling every year and they're all drinking themselves to death. But they still have lots of rusting nuclear bombs lying about.

—Good thing we're still pally with the Yanks, then. Good God, I forgot to ask: who's on the throne? We still think of it as being Elizabeth, out here, but of course it can't be, can it? Is it young Charles?

—Oh no, Elizabeth's still Queen. (*Prolonged applause; cries of God Bless Her; impromptu rendition of 'God Save the Queen'.*)

—Is she really? Damn good innings. Well done, that girl. That'll make us all feel a lot more at home. Talking of innings, what about the Ashes?

—Australia, usually.

—Damn.

—But we beat the West Indies in the West Indies last time. (*Loud cheers.*)

—Rugger? Don't suppose we *ever* beat the All Blacks or the Springboks?

—Oh yes, both of them, quite often, the last few years. (*Very loud cheers.*) —You see, there's a rugby World Cup too now. We've got it. (*Extremely loud cheers.*) —And we always put thirty-odd points past the Welsh. (*Laughter and merriment.*) —The Irish and French beat us sometimes, though.

—Yes, it's an absolute mystery, boys, how the Frogs can be such damn fine rugger players and such an absolute shower in every other way. As for Paddy, I say well done Paddy if he licks us occasionally, always liked him,

203

damn good soldier, no man more ready to have a crack, shame we didn't get everything ironed out with him back before the first War, before the trouble started, should have kept him in the tribe. Could have been done, too, Winston tried damn hard. Where was I, Devereux?

—Rugger, sir.

—Ah yes, winning at rugger, eh? I must say that all sounds pretty fine, eh, chaps? God, I'd like to drive down to Twickenham again. Do they still make Aston Martins and Jaguars? Don't suppose so. Always fancied an Aston or a Jag. Had to make do with a little MG. It was rather fun, though.

—Oh yes, you can still get all those.

—Splendid. Well, Marley, I must say it sounds to me as though the things that really matter are all very well indeed. Tories still in Number 10, I take it?

—No, Labour.

—Oh bugger.

—But they've changed a lot. They hate the unions.

The Headmaster glared at Marley secretly.

—Sorry, old boy, say that again? Sure you got that right? Sure the old memory's not playing up? You just said the *socialists* hate the *unions.*

—Yes. The Labour Prime Minister wants to denationalise everything because he thinks things that are private are bound to be better than things that are nationalised and he wants to make sure rich people don't get taxed too much to pay for poor people and so the top rate of income tax anyone pays is 40 per cent and –

The Headmaster rose hastily to his feet.

—Yes, well, that's splendid, Marley. Thank you.

—But I –

—No, no, that's quite enough for now, old boy. So, well, what do you think, Devereux?

—Well, Headmaster, it sounds to me as if England got

204

into a pretty sticky patch after we came a cropper here. But it looks to me as though we've come out the other side fighting fit after all.

—Well said, Devereux, well said. Righto, three cheers for Marley, everyone. (*Three strong cheers.*)

—Padre, the hymn I think, then we'll break out the grub. We'll just take Marley inside and get him a drink to restore morale.

—But, sorry, I mean, I thought you wanted . . .

—Come along, Marley, don't make a fuss, there's a good chap.

—Oh, right, er, I, OK.

*

—Father, please! I have told you, I know he is alive.

—Your love is your honour, daughter. But our flight is closing at gate 43, and to come home now is your duty, to those who are alive not perhaps, but certainly, and who hold your hand now.

—Very well, Father. I shall light a candle for Brian every day in the Church of Our Lady of the Pilar.

—God will smile upon you, daughter. Come.

*

—Hello, Tamsin? Hello?

—Grant? Can you hear me?

—Sort of.

—What's it like in Papua New Guinea?

—Ghastly.

—What's that funny drumming noise?

—The rain on my hotel roof.

—How ghastly.

—Yes. How are our figures?

—Holding up very well. Those Romanians crashing their helicopter was good. When are your Japanese amateur climbers trying to get up that whateveritwas, *Zeppelin Wall* thing, only using ropes made of vines?

—Hindenburg. Tomorrow. Sir Ranulph confidently predicts they'll all die.

—Oh good. Grant, I'm actually calling because Channel Seven's lawyers have just told me that since Brian's dead they haven't got to pay out any prize money to anyone ever.

—Handy for them, if they can get away with it.

—Handy for us too, actually. They're going to give us a quarter of it if we don't make a fuss on behalf of his estate.

—Half a million? To us?

—Yes. I don't *think* we were planning to make a fuss on behalf of his estate, were we?

—Hmm. Not that I know of. I suppose his family would be pleased to get it, though.

—Well, that's silly, Grant. I remember we met Brian's mother a few times, ages ago. Rather posh, all Jaeger twinsets and sherry, *she* doesn't need the money. And his ex-wife got the house and all Brian's money two years ago, so his son's perfectly well sorted too.

—Yes, I suppose so.

—So *I* don't think we need to make a fuss about it, do you?

—Perhaps not.

—Especially since we'd probably lose the case anyway.

—Well, yes, in that case. Oh good. That's OK then.

—It is a bit, isn't it? A quarter of a million each.

—I suppose I should celebrate tonight really. But there's nothing to do in Port Moresby except squash mosquitoes and avoid being killed by the scariest-looking drunks you ever saw. There's a big gang of tough, straight, manly Australians in the hotel. I suppose I *could* go out drinking with them.

—Do you think they'll *want* to take a gay Englishman drinking with them?

206

—Well, they won't notice the *gay* because of the *English*, you see. They can't tell the difference.

—That's handy.

—It is, quite. What are you going to do?

—I think I'll treat myself to a weekend at the Tintern Abbey Clinic. I need a break *so* badly.

—Yes. And you can always find a friendly person to get you *anything* you want at the Abbey if you get too bored with mudbaths and salad.

—Well, exactly.

—Oh well, that's all looking good then.

—It is, isn't it? Happy mosquito-squashing.

*

The Headmaster and Devereux led Marley into the Headmaster's tent as the assembled throng struck up 'I Vow To Thee My Country' with a fine gusto. As soon as they were out of sight of the Colonists within the thin, sun-bleached canvas, however, and aurally masked by the fine, High Anglican harmonies, the Headmaster spun Marley round none too softly and confronted him, his green eyes narrowed and glowing.

—Look here, old boy, he growled. —That all sounded pretty damn good at first, about the rugger and everything, went down very well, you made England sound like a fine place. But then you damn nearly blew it, you silly sod.

—What?

—For God's sake, when I said *put on a show for them* I wasn't saying you should lie through your bloody teeth, man. They're not stupid. They've all read the books from the Flight and talked to the older chaps. They know what's what. I mean to say, really, all that rot about a Labour government that hates the trade unions and only taxes the top chaps at 40 per cent! Damn it, Marley, any fool could see through that.

—But it's all true.

—What?

—It's true. The Labour Party nowadays likes million-aires and private businesses and it hates anything that's nationalised and the Prime Minister loves being photographed addressing the troops.

—Are you sure, man?

—Of course I'm sure. I live there.

—But look here, I don't understand, Marley, aren't the trade unions kicking up rough? The miners and the boil-ermakers and the shipwrights and the footplatemen and God knows what the devil they call themselves? Even Winston had to truckle to those buggers.

—No. We don't hear much about the unions these days.

—What, no more strikes and lockouts and go-slows and demarcation disputes and what have you?

—No, not for ages.

—What about all those damn university bolshies and troublesome priests banging on about peace and disar-mament?

—Um, no, we don't hear much of them either, these days.

—Good heavens. Hear that, Devereux?

—That's a relief, sir, from what the books said.

—I'll say it is. I'll be damned. Forty per cent? Good God, it's worth a chap making a few bob again, then. I say, Devereux, I think it's time for that last bottle.

—The last bottle it is, sir.

—Johnnie Walker, sixty years by now, old boy. The Flight was tolerably well stocked, you see, and we've rationed it damn carefully. But this seems like a fitting occasion. Think I'll have a large one myself. Devereux, the Queen.

—Gentlemen, the Queen.

—God bless her.

—So, well, I mean to say, everyone must be pretty happy back home?

—Happy?

—Well, if we beat the Reds without firing a shot and we're still pally with the Yanks and we can still send our chaps in with armour and air support halfway round the world and everyone's given up on all that socialism and unions claptrap and we don't have to worry about all being blown to nuclear buggery if we put a foot wrong and good old Elizabeth is still in Buck House and we're even winning at rugger? Surely everyone in England's happy?

—Happy? I don't know. Everyone seems to be a bit sort of, worried and lost. Especially the young ones. They mostly stand on street corners and sulk about the place drinking too much and taking drugs.

—What?

—Well, you know, *teenagers*.

—What the devil's that?

—Haven't you ever heard of a thing called teenagers? I mean, hadn't people invented that when you crashed?

—*Teen-agers*? You ever hear of that, Devereux?

—Vaguely, Headmaster. Old Smithers told me about it when he was still alive. It was a new American fashion, wasn't it, Marley, as I recall? Bolshie young chaps not knowing what to do with themselves, slouching about, trying to look and sound like Yanks, hands in their pockets, chewing gum and talking big, playing in noisy skiffle bands, wanting cars and girls and dance halls, wishing they were film stars, work-shy, drinking and smoking too much, no respect for anything. That sort of thing, wasn't it?

—Well, um, yes, actually, I suppose that's it, more or less.

—Hmmm. Better not let our young hotheads hear about it. And decent people let the little shits get away with it?

—Well, yes.

—Damn fools. Boys that age aren't complicated, you

know, they just want to be up and doing, they're restless for action, it's in the blood. Why don't their fathers take them off camping or mountaineering?

—Well, lots of fathers have left home, and the rest just watch television all night.

—Good grief. Boys that age can be led anywhere, but they'll only listen to a chap who can lick the hide off them in a boxing ring and then tell them something interesting about the world while he's patching them up. Then they'll worship him. Well, I bet their National Service knocks that nonsense out of them, eh?

—No, that was stopped years ago.

—Stopped? National Service? And fathers gallivanting about the place or sitting on their fat arses watching the idiots' lantern? Then what the hell d'you expect boys to do, man? Good God, Devereux, I'm starting to think it's a damn good job Marley found us when he did. Sounds like England needs us. Still, I suppose if the trade bloody unions have shut up shop, at least industry must be doing well for a change?

—Actually, industry's pretty well stopped too.

—Industry? Stopped? My God, how many million unemployed are there now then?

—Oh, only about a million.

—*Only*? A million? A million chaps kicking their heels on the street, ripe for any sort of troublemaking?

—Well, no one seems to think that's very many, any more.

—Marley, think straight for God's sake. A million unemployed *not that bad*? Industry stopped? Are you sure, man? What the devil do working people *do* then?

—Um, well, a lot of people work in shops selling electrical things made in China by Japanese companies. The people who buy all the electrical things made in China by Japanese companies work in offices selling insurance and mortgages to all the people who work in shops selling elec-

210

trical things made in China by Japanese companies. And then all the people who work in all the offices spend the money they get from selling insurance and mortgages to all the people who work in all the shops selling electrical things made in China by Japanese companies buying more electrical things made in China by Japanese companies from the people they just sold insurance and mortgages to, and –

—That's enough, you're making my head spin, man, stop talking utter balls. Damn it, Marley, you obviously can't hold a drink.

—It's true, honestly. I think America's pretty much the same. They owe the Japanese and Chinese five thousand trillion dollars or something like that. But that's all OK, apparently, because the Japanese and Chinese use the money they make from selling us all these things to buy British and American government bonds so that the British and American governments can keep overvaluing our money so we can keep buying Japanese and Chinese things so they can keep propping us up so we can keep buying their things.

—Now look here, Marley, I'm no boffin when it comes to that sort of clever bean-counting stuff, but I don't like the sound of this at all. Doesn't sound like the kind of ship I'd like to round the Horn in. Aren't people *worried*, for God's sake?

—Well, they don't seem to be but I think perhaps they are really. Everyone has mortgages and televisions and cars and flies abroad on holidays and things, but we're all up to our eyeballs in debt. We have all these things but we know that it would only take three months out of work for any of us to lose the lot and I sometimes think everyone sort of knows it but it's just too scary to think about so no one does.

—Hmm. The sooner we get back the better, I'd say, eh, Devereux?

—The sooner the better, sir.

—Brian! cried George, dashing into the tent. She was

211

carrying Marley's little yellow camera. Behind her came a small man in a blazer, puffing at an ancient pipe. —The batteries on this thing still work. Why on earth didn't you tell us?

—What? Oh. I'd forgotten all about it, I . . .

—You OK, Marley?

Marley had indeed forgotten all about his camera, but now he stared at it with sudden unease, unwilling to take it from George's hands, as if it contained a small but highly dangerous animal. Why? He had been talking to it just before he fell, that was it. He had been recording his last message to Tommy, when he had thought it was the end. For a second, he felt his skin crawl with a million tiny, creeping legs as he remembered the horrors of the jungle; in a flash of light he saw himself again, reflected in the lens, standing there mad and dying and saying . . . saying what? What the hell had he said?

—Brian, are you all right?

—Yes, yes, I'm fine, I was just, I didn't know, I, um . . .

—Parkins, Science Master, said the small man, shaking Marley's hand. —This is wonderfully exciting, Marley. Of course, we teach the chaps a bit of science and biology from the books that survived the Flight, but we don't get much of a chance to use it. Never managed to crack electrical generating up here. But now, this is splendid, gives Science a chance to prove its worth, eh, sir?

—Never doubted it, Parkins. Always room for the boffins in any show. So what's the flap about?

—Some of the boys have heard another helicopter overhead, said George.

—And I think it's coming nearer than ever, said the science master.

The Headmaster, Marley and Devereux looked up at the faded green canvas of the tent's roof and listened. There was no doubt about it.

212

—Damn, said the Headmaster, and in a flash he had swept back the right-hand side of his tailcoat and snapped open his holster. —Are the little sods getting shirty again?

—No, no, Headmaster, said Parkins. —It's just that Beauvey reminded me about this, you see.

—About what, man?

The science master now produced a small cardboard box, illustrated with a bright picture of Dan Dare and his spacecraft.

—It's his grandfather's Dan Dare Radio Station, sir. It was brand new, a present for the trip to Adelaide. It never had any batteries, so we never bothered with it. But now, you see, with the batteries from Marley's camera . . .

—Good God, said the Headmaster, —do you really think it would work?

—Worth a crack, Headmaster.

—Marley, show Parkins how you get the batteries out of this damn gadget.

—Well, I, I don't, let me see, I'm not really . . .

Marley, still trying to work out what on earth he could have said back then that now made him feel so guilty, took the camera and turned it in his hands, looking for the button that would erase whatever it was he had recorded. Then he remembered, with a nasty feeling of helplessness, that there was no such button, since the cameras had been designed especially to allow the contestants on *Green Hell* no editorial control. Whatever he had said to it, was locked away for ever in its high-impact plastic shell.

—There, old man, said Devereux. —There. It says 'battery release'.

—Oh yes, of course, I was just . . .

—Well, hand it over to Devereux, what the devil's got into you, man? Hurry up, the chopper won't stay overhead for ever.

Marley handed over the camera. Devereux, George, the Headmaster and the science master huddled over the Headmaster's wooden trestle table desk, shrouded in pipe smoke. Overhead, the sound of the helicopter grew quite distinct now. Soon it would be directly above them. He watched them fiddle with the Dan Dare set and the camera's batteries. What the hell could he have said? Had he been raving? Had he made some insane declaration of love to his ex-wife? A reproach to his mother? An unsuitable truth for Tommy? Something, there was something stored away on that little hard disk that should not be heard, by anyone, he knew it, but . . .

—Listen, you chaps, said George.

Once again they all listened. The helicopter above them was surely still growing louder. They caught each other's eyes, making sure that it was no mere figment of the mind, and then dived back to work with renewed urgency. And quite suddenly, Marley felt a howl gather in the pit of his gut, a long, pleading cry that drowned out any petty little thoughts of whatever embarrassing confessions might be hiding inside the camera. Embarrassment be buggered. This was about life and death.

If they could not contact anyone, they really would have to leave this idyll and go down into that hellish forest. The memory of it, the dim, physical recall of how he had felt when alone and dying, made him wince and gag. It really was going to be no joke at all, trying to make it back to somewhere civilised; the Headmaster was not exaggerating, they could easily get lost, however many people were searching for them, many of these people might die, he might be one of those who died, he truly might never get home to England after all, after all he had been through, never see Tommy again. Whatever he had said to the camera back then really might turn out to be his last words to his son. It might, after all, still all go wrong.

—Hurry, Parkins, said the Headmaster, looking upwards again and listening intently.

—I think that's it, sir. Curious batteries, these, but I think I've worked it out.

—Right, Marley, said the Headmaster, handing him an ancient fountain pen and a small piece of old, lined, school-jotter paper, —better make it something that your chaps know could only be you. This could be our only chance, we don't want anyone to doubt it.

They all turned quickly and left him there to write. Devereux held the canvas flaps of the tent open so that the other three Colonists could process crabwise out,

George holding the Dan Dare Radio Station, Parkins ensuring that the wires stayed connected to the battery pack, Devereux making way for them, and the Headmaster, his thumb now hooked into his belt close to the holster, bringing up the rear, preparing himself for a big speech. From outside the tent, cheers greeted them, but accompanied by rebellious questions from the older boys.

—Calm down now, all of you, barked the Headmaster. —That chopper won't hear small-arms fire, I've told you that, but we're going to try to reach him with a Morse code signal. So quiet all, and think of England. Get a move on, Marley.

—Yes, yes, called Marley from inside the tent. He wrote hurriedly:

Message to Grant Brodie of Channel Seven Television UK vital vital it's me Brian really I'm alive up above that huge cliff thing there are always clouds over the whole place but at night you might see a bonfire anyway for God's sake come and get us there are loads of English people here and you can land safely in a helicopter this is really repeat really Brian Marley.

Then he stepped quickly out.

The entire Colony was stopped dead still to watch the group crouched around the Dan Dare Radio Station. They all looked up as Marley came out. Devereux checked the contacts one last time, then turned to Marley and held out his hand for the paper. The Headmaster took it from Marley, as if merely intending to check it quickly while handing it over to Devereux, but he stopped at once and cried:

—For God's sake, man, are you a complete idiot? It'll

216

take half an hour to send this lot! He's not going to stay overhead all day and there's hardly any power. Something else, man, just make sure they know who you are and where you are and make it damn short and snappy.

—Brian, do, please.

—Sorry, um, well, I . . .

Marley scribbled fast, hotly aware of 150 pairs of eyes staring at him in the stillness. He handed his note to the Headmaster, who frowned.

—*Arse?* You sure, old boy?

—Look, he'll know it's me.

—Devereux, send it.

—Yes, sir. All set, Parkins?

—Chocks away, Devereux.

The Colony, Marley too, stared upwards at the clouds again, to where the sightless chopper was bustling and clattering nearer, as though the collective aura of their longing could reinforce the feeble batteries. George came over and took his arm, as if she could not bear to be alone for this moment. Together they held their breath as the science master held the wires to the battery and Devereux began to tap out the message on the terminal marked 'Colonel Dan Dare'. In the absolute silence, the little squeaks of their desperate dots and dashes could clearly be heard coming from the antique toy. The tiny bulbs on its Bakelite towers flashed in time to the code.

.- --. .- .- .-. ... . ..- -. -.. . .-. -.-. .-.. - - - ..- -.. ..- -.-. .- -. .-..

.- -. -.. .... . .-.. .-.

Devereux stopped tapping. The lights on the little radio station stopped flashing. The science master still crouched, sweat gathering on his forehead, holding the wires tight in place, fingers whitening visibly. The clouds remained silent. The lonely earth spun beneath them. Seconds

217

passed, then minutes. No answer came. Devereux began to tap out his signal again, but after the first .- --. .-, the tiny lights merely blinked weakly, then died.

—I'm afraid the batteries are really almost completely dead now, sir, said the science master, very quietly but very distinctly. —We can't send any longer. Perhaps we can receive for a few more minutes, but that's it. I'm sorry.

—Good show, Parkins, said the Headmaster, firmly.

Marley looked around at the upturned staring faces, the hands held in others' hands, the stiff but shivering upper lips, and felt his heart pleading along with them. His wish was their wish.

England *had* to hear them.

England *had* to reply.

He held George's hand closer. He felt her trembling.

Very softly, the Padre's choirboys began to sing 'Jerusalem'. The sound of the helicopter was fading, surely? The almost-adult boy who had argued with the Headmaster shifted his grip on his rifle and eyed his comrades.

—Steady now, lads, growled the Headmaster, and moved his hand to the butt of his revolver.

Time hung fire. *Nor shall my sword sleep in my hand.* The whole Colony, Marley too, were staring towards the receding noise in the sky, at the place the longed-for message would have to come from. It was as if they believed they might be able, by sheer force of their joint longing, to make the radio waves corporeal, visible to the yearning human eye; as if they might, if they gazed hard enough heavenward, actually see the reply to their entreaty burst through the clouds and thunder down upon them, winged and glorious, a message from England descending in chariots of fire. They stood there and prayed, a tribe of long-lost, pale-skinned primates, gazing at the unblinking clouds, pleading for the gift of meaning.

But the metallic clattering of the unseen helicopter was undoubtedly dying now.

In England's green and pleasant land.

Dying.

Dying.

They were all so intently fixed skywards that when the toy receiver on the dusty ground began to flicker and twitter, it took a good two seconds for people to blink and look round at one another in wild surmise, hope, and the fear of the loss of hope. And then to look down at the machine. The choir hung fire and stuttered.

—Put a sock in it, Padre! roared the Headmaster, as Devereux dived for the set and fixed it with both eyes from six inches away. As the signal came through he scratched hastily in the baked dirt. The flickering and tweeting stopped and he lay there, frozen, staring at the fragile, aged plastic and the message it had received.

—Well? demanded the Headmaster. —Devereux man, come on, what did it say?

—Marley, old man, Devereux asked, waving him to the set, voice trembling, —can this be right? It's rather strange, sir. I'm not sure it's even English.

Marley, the Headmaster and George quickly knelt down to look at the words cut into the dust. They said:

w8 4 us 2 cum 2 u.

Marley looked up into the green eyes once again, more closely than he had ever done. He could hardly speak, and could hardly hear his own voice when he managed to make it work. The sound of George's tense breath in his ear almost drowned out his own words.

—Yes. You see, that's how people say things, these days. It, um, it means, well, it means they're coming back.

There was another silence as the Colony turned to the

219

Headmaster for orders. He stayed for a long moment, staring at the little radio set, apparently checking thoroughly to see if he needed to shave his chin. At last, Devereux asked, —What do you think, sir?

—What do I think, Devereux? he said, quietly. And then he winked at Marley, before rising slowly to his feet, dusting himself down and standing to address the Colony. —What do I think, chaps? Eh? Well, as my father said on VE Day, I think it's time for a spot of good old English maffiking!

And, eyes wild, he whipped his revolver into his hand and began blasting shell after shell into the heavens above.

*

—Tamsin, where are you?

—Grant? Really, I'm just, well, you know, *freshening up* in the loos at the Abbey Clinic, actually.

—Well, get on to the PM's team. Brian's *alive*.

—Alive? He can't be.

—He's sent a Morse code message from some unexplored place in the mountains, Christ knows how, but it's definitely him, he said *aga arse under clouds u can land help* and that could only be him.

—But what about our half a million pounds?

—For God's sake, Tamsin, don't be such a slut. He's our friend and he's alive and he's going to be rich. And anyway, it's our show, we'll make our money one way or another. If we can get the PM along to be in on the rescue we'll even be on the Honours List next year. Either way, we're made men. So stop snorting and get going.

—Right. (*Sniff.*)

*

—Fuckin' hell, turn the telly up, George. That mad old cunt's made it. Fair play to him.

*

—My Brian! He is living!

*

—Daddy! Daddy!

*

—Brian? Alive? Oh. Ohhh.
   —Mary, Mary, are you all right, my dear? Quick, Janet darling, get the sherry. Under the sink. No, better make that the brandy.

*

To Brian Marley, mass hysteria had always been power-fully tinged with an unspoken dread. Useless at soccer and rugby as a schoolboy, having had no one to teach him, never picked for their teams by the self-elected captains of the playground until the cruel, public, make-weight end of each choosing session, he had been unable to make the mental leap to stand, fatherless, in the beery, piss-ridden, still-unseated seventies terraces of Loftus Road and cheer people he did not know doing things he did not understand. As a shy young teenager, unsuccessful with girls, he had found himself unable to join in the delights of Disco Fever, and even less able, later, to dive, spiky-haired, into a packed, deafened, gob-flecked mass of other young people without feeling that something incalculable but terrible was surely about to happen. He had never been able to bring himself to stand in a crowded stadium and, along with ten thousand others, worship some distant git with a guitar, or allow the sheer press of shouting, cheering, whistle-blowing people to lift him

221

bodily from the ground and away into the insane blare of the Notting Hill Carnival. The Ing-er-land frenzy of World Cups left him cold. Bemused, he had watched footage of what looked like mass, indiscriminate copulation in the bars of Edinburgh and Cardiff when the Devolution votes were declared. He had never known the unreflective joy of unthinking union, the loneliness of his travelling years abroad had in reality been no lonelier than living in his so-called homeland.

And now, on a mountain top in Papua New Guinea, he found it all at last.

At the Headmaster's cry of 'Mafeking!' all the barriers of Englishness tumbled away. George was in Marley's arms, kissing him wildly. In his ear the Headmaster's revolver fired on into friendly clouds, joined by volleys of rifle fire. Hands grabbed him, slapped his back, arms embraced him, passed him bottles of spiced, burning drink, lips kissed him, he felt unknown skin, hair, features in his own hands, warm breath, hot cheeks, salt tears of joy. And then the world was only George and him, lips on lips, no words, no looks, no questions, just warmth and damp between her legs, yearning and wild need in him, hands clawing and teeth banging together, falling together into the tongue-filled darkness back where we came from, the jungle and the night and the dark, thick, inseparable blood, the haunted yearnings of all our lives, the mighty tides we vainly fabricate with drugs and pounding sounds, for real for ever now as all around them pulsed the strong, sweet rhythm through endless veins conjoined in the oneness of us, of we, of home at last, of England.

IV

ENGLAND EXPECTS

Histories of Colonialism generally fail to mention that of all the major states of Western Europe, one alone, in the second millennium, spent several centuries under the complete dominion of a distinct minority which was *not*, in the end, overthrown in a national revival. The Moors never controlled all Spain, and were ultimately ejected. The Austrian-Germans, Magyars and Turks between them could never eliminate Southern Slav identity. Poland always rose again, whatever the Prussians or Russians did to her. England, the greatest coloniser of all, was unable ever fully to abolish even despised little Wales, let alone truculent Scotland, never mind troublesome Ireland. It is, it seems, virtually impossible to extirpate a rooted nation. But in one case and one alone, a major, established European culture, for centuries recognised by popes and princes, with all the panoply of a solid coinage and book-written laws, biblical translations and infant secular literature, was *entirely and permanently obliterated* by a small foreign military caste. So profound was the transformation of 1066, so glaring the cleft between the conquerors and the conquered, that a thousand years later, whenever an Englishman gives a French-sounding, hard-to-spell name, his countrymen will assume that he is somehow privileged.

Every society has its castes and gradations of ranks, but Hastings built Class into the English language (and hence, the English mind) itself. This unique dislocation crossed the oceans along with Empire. To this day, the very act of acquiring full mastery over *his own language* sets an English-speaker automatically apart from the mass of *his own people*. By any normal linguistic yardstick, the world-wide English-language tabloid press is quite literally written in a different tongue from its broadsheets. The ordinary Frenchman, Spaniard or German knows when he is being spoken to by a more educated countryman, to be sure, but he recognises the language as a higher form of his own, which, with a little effort, he can make out and, indeed, appreciate. But when the ordinary English-speaker hears an educated countryman, he hears a foreigner or traitor speaking a cunning half-Latin jargon which he could never deduce from his own words and the cultured Englishman feels nowhere so utterly foreign as amongst his feral compatriots. It is thus simply *not possible* for an English, American or Australian politician to woo a mass-electorate with the full resources of language (and hence thought). He must at all costs avoid 'talking fancy', that worst of crimes amongst those who are able to speak (and hence think) only in the wretched half-language that was socially and culturally decapitated in 1066; and he, in his turn, will necessarily despise his voters, just as Norman barons for centuries scorned their wretched, clod-hopping, forelock-tugging English vassals. Hypocrisy and sound-bite culture is thus built into 'Anglo-Saxon' [*sic*!] public life in the democratic era; we find that the greatest colonising culture in history is itself still riddled with a classic post-colonial self-hatred for which we may all pay the price.

Professor Kieran O'Conor,
Foreword, *The Unconquered Conquest:
Englishmen, Normans and Ireland,*
Dublin, 2002.

—Go to sleep children, or the White Man will get you.

Parental warning, Papua New Guinea.

—Mr Brodie, may I assume this line is secure?

—Well, it *was* your own Special Branch men who set it up.

—Of course. We'll be landing in a couple of hours. Now, the Prime Minister must *absolutely* be there *right* at the moment when you find this Marley person. I don't mean we're asking you to tell *lies*, of course, we would never suggest that, but we would be very happy if the pictures could *suggest* that it was the presence of the PM himself which led to us finding Mr Marley alive.

—That's a bit steep, darling.

—So could the fuckin' fee for Channel Seven's wee licence renewal be after the next election, Grant. D'ye want me to call them and tell them you're playing hard wi' us?

—Looks like you've got me over a barrel.

—Yes, I suppose we have. I believe it's called being *in power*. So that's agreed then? How very kind of you. And, if I may say, purely as a personal opinion of course, how very *responsible* you are being. A shining example of our great British broadcast media at its best.

—Aye. The shite-hot grasp of wha' really fuckin' matters.

—Thanks.

*

—Father, I must go to England!

—Ay, Conchita, this is the man for you! And now he is rich also. That is good.

—Father, I do not care about his money.

225

—Of course. Only the wretched care about money. The only good thing about a man having money is that he does not have to care about money. That is why it is good that a man should have money.

—Father, you are wise.

—Daughter, I am old. If I were not also wise, what would I be? Yes, we shall go to England once again. And now let us turn on BBC News 24 so we may see the latest updates.

*

—I think we should put this Marley chap on the front page, don't you?

—Absolutely.

*

—Come in, come in, my darling little boy.

—Granny Granny Granny Daddy is coming back!

—Yes, darling, I know, isn't it *wonderful*? And guess what? The television people are flying you and me to Australia to meet him. Well, well, you *are* getting big and strong. Now, let's have some ginger beer to celebrate, shall we? And Mummy, of course.

—Are you having ginger beer too, Granny?

—Do you know, I think I'll have some sherry instead. What about you, my dear? Ah. Come into the kitchen for a minute please. Just one moment, Tommy darling. Come in and shut the door. Right, there's a kitchen roll on the side there, pull yourself together.

—I'm sorry, Mary, I don't know, I can't think, all I can think is, is it too late for us, after all? Is it, Mary? Do you think?

—What, now my son is a millionaire, you mean? Much. But I'm sure he'll, how should I put it, *sort you out*, I believe is the modern phrase. For Tommy's sake. Now

226

really, stop making such a *scene* in front of the poor little boy.

—Oh.

*

—Oi, George, four pints and put the telly on to that fuckin' jungle thing, willya? Wish I'd fuckin' betted on the mad old cunt. Never thought he'd fuckin' make it.

*

—Come on, chaps, get those torches along here. At the double!

Some primeval instinct in Brian Marley, some relic of the deep old ordering of things that enables a baby to sleep through loud music and laughter (which means that the tribe is nearby and alive) but wakes it at a soft, suppressed cough in nearby stillness (which might be a hyena or a rival humanoid in the night), detected the urgency in the shout-whispered command. His hormones obeyed this ancient call and he leapt back into conscious-ness, out of his drunken, post-sex sleep, like a whale bursting up for air after hours in the sunless depths.

Leaping fires and racing shadows in the night. He tried to sit up, but his body was only half working; one of his arms and one of his legs were immobile, pinned. He fell back again, and as his eyes recovered from the yellow burst of light and reset themselves for night running, he saw above him, between the thin night-time clouds, a patch of black infinity littered with unknown, uncaring stars. He panicked at the sight, as if he were about to fall, impossibly, headlong upwards into that cold eternity. He gasped for air, choked with the attempt to swallow past his sandpapered tongue and throat, then immediately shut his eyes tight again as a rusting trainload of hung-over pain crunched into the buffers of his skull.

Hurrying feet landed close to his ears as they ran loudly through the dry undergrowth. He saw torches held high by the running figures and realised that the sounds which had awoken him and the light that had blinded him were not part of some confused dream, but the seepings-in of the real world about him.

He looked around again in the darkness. Shadowy figures leaped and bounded through the night, laughing, flaming torches in hand. In the shifting torchlight he saw the unmistakable silhouette of the Headmaster, his hand raised in stern command, and the looming, blue-eyed shades of a dozen tall, square-shouldered youths. The hunting party. In the distance, he could hear the sounds of many engines in the sky, reverberating from the mountainsides. Craning his neck back towards the huts and tents of the Colony, he saw the flashing red and white lamps hanging in the darkness, and the ghostly searchlights sweeping the inky cliffs. But far more alarming were the flickering lights deep inside the Headmaster's eyes as he turned and saw Marley lying there.

—Aha. So you *did* come here, old boy.

—What?

—Now look here, Marley, I saw your eyes on that damn clever little camera of yours. Wondered why the hell you wanted it so badly. Started thinking. Those TV fellows are little better than a set of damn Reds in my experience. Sell their own grandmother to cause a stink. And quite frankly, you're New Money, Marley. You may be a millionaire now, but in my experience New Money is always on the lookout for more. Thinking of taking a few more pictures to sell to the BBC, were you? Or are you actually *in* the BBC?

—No, no, my mother just lives near it, gabbled Marley, half awake and half terrified. —This is the first time I've had anything to do with the telly in my life. I'm not *making* the programme, I was only *in* it.

228

—So you weren't thinking about poking about down here with your damn clever little camera, were you?

—I don't understand, moaned Marley, through his pin-sharp hangover. —I wasn't going to poke around anywhere . . . and anyway what's to poke around in?

—That's the stuff, Marley. So you're not going to bleat?

—What?

—I don't know, though. You say that here and now, but there's no knowing what a chap will do once he's got used to hot baths and daily newspapers and tea parties and chattering blasted womenfolk again. I've seen it all before. You sure you won't bleat? Paws off the lady and stand up then, man.

Marley looked round and saw that his left arm and leg were fixed to the ground not, in fact, by paralysis or gravity, but by George's snoring body. He was dragged smartly upright and George rolled off him with a sweet grunt and a little stretch but without waking. The Headmaster laughed and pulled her dress roughly down over her thighs again.

—Damn fine girl, as I recall, he chuckled.

—What? said Marley blearily. —You mean, you mean, you . . .?

—Well, who else do you think has the first bash to see if a girl's good stock? *Droit de seigneur*, old boy. Didn't she tell you? Yes, that's right. Half these chaps are *my* natural sons, whoever's name they have. Or grandsons. I rather forget who's which sometimes. Mr Chips just isn't in it, old boy. Yes, I've had a rather better innings down here than I would have had back at home. Well, close your mouth, Marley. I thought as much. Easily shocked. That was always the trouble. Bloody misty-eyed do-gooders at home banging on about England's Mission who never had the foggiest idea what has to be done out in the Colonies just to keep things ticking over. And no doubt there'll be some of them turning up here in the morning. So it's time we tidied things up a little bit down at the Gate. And just in case you ever have a mind to bleat on about things to your pals who work on the idiots' lantern, you're going to help. Stand up and be counted and all that. Come on. Leave her, she'll be fine. Good strong girl.

His arm held by Devereux's hand, Marley was hoisted upright.

—What are we tidying up?

—The Gate, said Devereux.

—What, where you go down into the forest?

—Exactly.

—Why has it got to be tidied up?

—Ask the Headmaster, old man.

—We are simply going to light another big bonfire to guide our rescuers down, said the Headmaster, smiling widely. —And if we can clear the place up a bit while we're at it, so much the better, eh, chaps?

—Yes sir, chorused his acolytes, laughing.

—Oh, come on, Marley, let's not play games. You've seen the stockade. Don't think it'll go down too well with the ladies and pinko queers of London, do you?

—What won't?

—Oh. Oh, you *haven't* seen it? Damn, thought you must have. Well, too late now, old boy, here, take a good look.

The Headmaster thrust Marley powerfully forward into the trees and held his own torch high. At his signal, all the other torches were raised.

Marley staggered, almost tripped, regained his balance, looked up and leapt back in fright and disgust, a short yelp of sheer animal terror in his mouth. He would have run wildly off into the dark forest had he not collided immediately with a pair of muscular youths. He hit them at full pelt, but they scarcely budged an inch; it was like running into two man-sized sacks of potatoes. Marley recoiled from the impact and stumbled, winded, flat-back upon the earth, at the foot of the wooden stockade.

It had not been the heads of defenders he had seen on the stockade when here with George. It had just been heads. Heads on stakes, woolly-haired, dark-skinned heads smashed horridly open by stakes that pierced them from jawbone to cranium. Most of them were very old; some were not old enough to have yet become comfortingly archaeological, and a few of them, most horribly, were so recent, so very, very clearly new that they still displayed the vacantly decaying features of the recently living. Marley gagged and whimpered.

—Can't take it, eh? said the Headmaster. —Yes, I suppose it takes more than one generation to breed the right sort. Look up. I said look up, Marley. It's nothing except reality, you know. We'll all look like that one day, more or less. The head-shots are mostly mine. I said look up. If you can't even look up, I'll have to assume you're going to bleat when you get home, old boy. And I can't allow that, you know.

Marley looked up.

*

—Grant, can you hear me? Have you taken off yet?

—Yes, just, and it's still half dark and I'm scared shit-less and I'm going deaf without my ear-defenders and I can hardly hear you, so this had better be *bloody* impor-tant, Tamsin.

—It is. For God's sake don't let anyone say anything to Brian about *winning the show.*

—What? Why the hell not? That's the whole point of the programme.

—Channel Seven aren't paying the prize money. They say he didn't win.

—Didn't win? Of course he fucking won.

—If you say so. A dozen lawyers at Channel Seven say *not*, but if you say so.

—How can he *not* have won?

—Well, they say no one can *prove* that Welsh schoolteacher was about to give in, can they? And you know, they may be right, Grant.

—Oh come on, you saw the footage just before the heli-copters ... Look, I don't like to bloody *think* about it, while I'm flying in this horrible thing. That Welsh bloke was *crawling* towards the landing site.

—He might have just been avoiding the rotors. Very sensible. Make sure you don't forget to do it as well.

—He was screaming.

—Singing. To keep his courage up. They do, you know, the Welsh.

—His leg was black.

—Perhaps it was just covered in mud. We'll never know, will we?

—Brian was just standing there and saluting. He looked fine.

—Well, I don't know about you but that doesn't sound very *fine* to me. Sounds to me more like he'd totally lost his mind. Saluting, in a jungle?

—Well, yes, I suppose.

—Perhaps he was sort of *surrendering*, you see. The fact is, Grant, we don't *know* he lasted longest and he *didn't* stay in the jungle for a week on his own.

—Yes he did, Tamsin. Fifteen days, now, actually.

—But the radio beacon was destroyed. He had no *choice*. That was the whole point, wasn't it? What's so, well, *plucky* about just surviving when you've got no *choice*? We might as well have just dropped six people in the jungle with no food and no water and no radios to see who *lived the longest*, if that's your idea of a game-show contest. Hmm. Not bad actually. Very cheap. Anyway, the point is, Channel Seven

232

say all bets were off the moment the choppers crashed, oops, sorry to bring that up again, Grant. And they're serious.

—Fuck. That means we'll have to sort Brian out from *our* cut.

—We can't give him two million pounds of *our* money, Grant.

—Well, not two million, maybe, but . . .

—I agree we have to help him, somehow, obviously, but a million would be, well, almost a *quarter* of our whole profit.

—Ye-ah.

—And we're talking about our investment capital here, you know. We need it to develop our next shows. Half a million now could be worth ten to us in a few years. I might need a nanny one day, you know.

—He nearly bloody died, Tamsin.

—Loads of people died, Grant. Some good friends of ours died. Well, some people who worked for us, anyway, and that's nearly the same thing, isn't it? At least Brian's still alive.

—Yes, and so he won. Come on, Tamsin, you know he did. We'll have to give him *something*.

—Whaddya mean *we*, paleface? No, of course we'll help him out somehow, but it doesn't have to be *hundreds of thousands of pounds* though, surely?

—Well, I just mean, on principle.

—You're so honourable. If you want to give Brian whatever, a hundred thousand bloody pounds or something, just because he *happened* to survive a helicopter crash, oh God, sorry, there I go again.

—Would a hundred grand be enough?

—Enough? God, he'd hardly believe his luck if he got fifty. Grant, seriously, what was he before this? A schoolteacher? Not even that. An EFL teacher for God's sake, a glorified tourist guide. Fifty K would be what, two years' pay? All at once? Tax-free? Just because he got lucky? God, I wouldn't mind two years' pay in a lump sum just for going on a crash diet for a few weeks in an amazing, unspoiled place.

—No, I suppose.

—And teachers have a steady income. We don't. We don't get paid holidays. Or subsidised pension funds. Yes, we're doing well *now*, but maybe in five years' time fifty grand will come in very useful thank you. I have to think about the IVF baby I might have one day. A year's pay, all at once, would change his life and not bankrupt us.

—He could hardly complain at that, I suppose.

—Complain? Grant, if we played by the *bourgeois fucking rules* he'd get nothing. And think of all those interviews and exclusives he'll get. Would he have got those without you? Of course not. He'd still be just a teacher, daydreaming of fame. You've changed everything for him already. Knowing you was the biggest break of his life, you've given him something far more important than money. Won? He's *already* won, Grant. You've given him his chance on a plate. He wasted his life and ended up as a grotty EFL teacher and now *you* have sorted him. If he can't take this chance himself, now, when he's going to be the most famous man in the country for *at least* a whole weekend, why on earth should *you* be expected to bail him out yet again? I don't understand you. Especially when he's such a bloody homophobe.

—Brian? Homophobic?

—You heard those last few pieces he did before the crash. Going on and on about his son and how kids were all that mattered really in the end and all that reactionary shit.

—Um, is that homophobic?

—It's hardly what *I'd* call gay-friendly. Personally, as an unburdened woman, *I* find it downright insulting, to be quite frank. And if having brats is all that matters to him, well, he doesn't need our money, does he?

—Perhaps we could help him get the press coverage.

—We already are, Grant. We *made* him. But yes, we could pull strings. It might use up a few of our favours, but I can see you're determined to do this.

—We'll set him up with Baz Bingley's PR machine to make sure he gets the best price for his story.

—There, you see? How many teachers ever get that? A story to sell *and* Baz to sell it for them? My God, there are *minor soap stars* out there who'd be glad to get that. So I'll call Baz, shall I?

—Yes, do. Brian'll get much more than a year's pay out of it, one way or another, won't he?

—Much, God, definitely. Well I'm glad *that's* sorted.

*

—Please . . . *please*, said Marley, who was convinced that having seen, having been forced to stare at, this grove of horrors he must now surely be doomed to die himself as an incriminating witness.

The Headmaster, however, did not shoot him on the spot, but merely waved his young followers to their work, watched for a moment as they began to burn the stockade, checked the direction of the wind, sat down beside Marley and lit up his pipe, puffing out small, rhythmic clouds of sweetly fragrant, curiously heady smoke. Marley sat frozen. As the old skulls crumbled in the flames and the fresh heads shrivelled and steamed in the heat, the Headmaster clapped him on the shoulder.

—Always things done at the front that are best kept to ourselves, eh, Marley? Tell me, this newfangled thing called psychology still going strong back home?

—Psychology? Well, um, well, I think so, I think . . .

—What a lot of bosh, eh? I remember after Korea these damn fool German-sounding boffins started asking the chaps how they felt about it. How they *felt*, would you

235

credit it? What the hell has how anyone *feels* got to do with anything? It's what we *do* that matters, not *why* we do it. No doubt the ruddy Nazis *felt* they were in the right, and no doubt they could quote Nietzsche and sing Wagner while they were doing it, but they *did* things that made them the scum of the earth. Same as the Reds. I'm sure Karl Marx was a brainy type and meant well and no doubt they all *felt* that history was on their side and all that rot, but what they actually *did* was stand people up against the wall a hundred at a time and put one in the backs of their heads. Who gives a damn what anyone *feels*? Bloody Hampstead Bollinger Bolsheviks banging on about how some chaps were affected by the war, by what they'd done and seen. My father and his brothers and all their pals went through the Somme and lived in trenches made out of other chaps' guts and saw their school chums being blown into meat paste and all that vile, rotten stuff, and if these *psychologists* were right, well, they would all have gone stark staring bonkers one way or another, wouldn't they? Some of them did, it's true, but not very many. Do you know what most of them did after the Great War? And the second show? Almost all of them? Just ruddy well got on with things and stayed decent chaps, that's what. And didn't bang on about it.

—Ah, said Marley. He was concentrating on keeping his eyes fixed on his own feet and trying to blank out the awareness, or even worse, the imagination, of what exactly had, or might have, just made that dull, popping, bursting sound, what precisely had just splashed hard on to his sleeve.

—So you see, all this stuff here at the Gate doesn't mean we've gone to the dogs and become a gang of damn headhunters. It just means that there were things we had to do to get by, so we did them, but we shut up about them and we kept it from the women and children. Of course, there's no denying the thrill of the hunt and all that, especially for the young chaps. Remember myself the first time I led my chaps in with fixed bayonets at Alamein, I was only nineteen and yes, it was damn exciting what with the pipers and all and I'm not saying we took many prisoners in the heat of it. But when the shooting stopped we dressed their wounded just the same as ours. Which is the whole bloody point. It only goes so far. It *doesn't* rot the soul, not for most chaps. You see, Marley, war is like whisky or actresses or having a crush on an older boy at school.

—Ah, said Marley, again. He could think of nothing else to say.

—Most chaps can take a couple of drinks and then put the cork back in the bottle; most chaps can have a bit of fun with a good-time girl and then go home to the memsahib; most chaps grow out of that sort of schoolboy messing about. And most chaps can go to war and see things no one in their right mind would want to see, then come back on leave and have a game of golf. And most of us do. The ones that get into queer street thanks to war, or whisky, or boys or a dancing girl's stockings, well, they were going to end up there anyway, one way or another.

—But heads on stakes isn't bloody *decent*, that's . . .

—The show, old boy. We knew from the start that we could never really defend the Gate for long if the locals all got together and decided a spot of white man would look good on the dinner table. Had to make them think we're damn near all-powerful. Most of all, we had to get *one* lot on our side. You see, those aren't just any old locals' heads. They're all Miyanmin. The Miyanmin are an absolute shower of headhunters. They live off the other chaps, the Altbalmin and so on. I'm not saying that our Altbalmin pals would say no to the odd slice of a chap now and then, if they got the chance, but that's just par for the course round here. The Miyanmin, though, well, they've got the worst patch of jungle land and they're regular terrors. I mean, look here, old boy, have you any idea what they get up to round here? I suppose you think it's all noble savages and that sort of Hampstead rot?

—No, no, I mean, I've no idea, I . . .

—Exactly. Well, I'll tell you how it works. These chaps you see on the sticks here, the Miyanmin, gang up together from all their villages, across the other side of the big river, the Sepik. Happens every three years, we've worked out, just long enough for them to forget what happened to the last lot. They build a rope bridge across the gorge, fascinating to watch, clever as hell, takes them weeks to get it all set, then they cross into Altbalmin country, our side, d'you see? A hundred or so of them, usually. They find a small Altbalmin village, they always choose one a bit set away from the rest of the villages. They creep up by night, surround the place and then, at dawn, always the best time to attack, dawn, these chaps don't need any damn fool at Sandhurst to tell them that, well, at dawn in they go, set the place on fire and do the lot of them, men, women and children, as they come running out of their huts. They do it like this, generally, d'you see?

—Glaarg, Christ! gasped Marley, jumping, cowering then freezing as the Headmaster whipped a leathery arm around his neck so that a sharpened bone was now sticking into Marley's flesh, almost piercing the skin, between his shoulder blade and his collarbone.

—Now, I thrust down sharply, pierces the lungs, and that's your lot. That's how the Miyanmin do it, anyway. Well, then of course they take off your head with a bamboo knife and wrap it up in banana leaves. Off with your arms and legs next, then they gut and bone you, roll you up and carry you off just as if you were a rucksack, with your legs and arms slung over their shoulders. Terribly neat, really, obviously been doing it for ever. They do keep the very small babies, the ones that are too young to remember, the ones that won't grow up thinking about how their supposed Ma and Pa ate their real Ma and Pa. Good for tribal numbers, you see. The babies hereabouts mostly don't make it to their first birthday, so a healthy one-year-old who's got over the killer diseases is a damn valuable thing. But otherwise they scoff the lot of them.

—But you stop them?

—Exactly, Marley. That's where we struck lucky. Back in '58, just after we came back, half dead, after we tried to get out through the jungle, Tom Devereux's old man and his pals spotted the Miyanmin building their clever little bridge. We decided to watch what they were up to. It was pretty clear after a bit, and so the upshot was that when the Miyanmin started their attack on the Altbalmin village, we were waiting for them. The ambusher ambushed and all that. We bumped half of them off before they could make it back across the gorge. Well, as you can imagine, the Altbalmin were pretty damn impressed and grateful. We gave them to understand that we'd come down here from the clouds to protect them and that so long as we were here and fed and happy, their own days of ending up in a Miyanmin cooking pot were at an end. Stuck the heads on the stakes to show it, and of course to drop the hint that if they didn't damn well treat us like their saviour gods, they might get what for. Been doing it ever since.

—But don't the, whatyoucall them, Miyanmin, know what's going to happen to them now? Why don't they stop attacking?

—Well, the lucky thing for us is that none of the silly buggers round here can read or write. So each generation on both sides just think everything is a sort of force of nature and if anything goes wrong it's because they didn't make the right sacrifice to the right tree, that sort of rot.

The Altbalmin just sit there and pray to the local ju-ju that it's not their own village's turn next time, and meanwhile the Miyanmin keep up the chants as they build their bridges. And we keep doing them in and putting their heads on stakes and the Altbalmin keep the rations coming up to the Gate. Very good arrangement, really.

—You just live off the natives?

—Well, how on earth else did you think we live up here, old boy? Farming? Not us. We're not clodhopping earth-grubbers, for God's sake. Different caste. Soldiers. Who won both World Wars? We did. And we didn't do it so we could dig up bloody yams and feed chickens. No, no, we fight, they farm, we keep the bad chaps away, they cough up.

—You were hunting . . . *people*?

—Miyanmin, yes. Best game. And don't go thinking it's us with guns against them with arrows. We hardly use the guns, these days, not enough ammo left. But we don't really need them. Clive didn't have better guns than the locals in India, he was just better at war. We train hard, plenty of sport, weapons drill and tactical exercises, and best of all we know in advance that every few years or so the young bloods over the river will feel they've got to earn their own blazers by putting man-flesh on the menu for their tribe again. We know the signs that they're getting ready, because we write it all down in the Book and we've been doing so for forty-five years. Whereas they start from scratch every time. Simple, really: our intelligence is better, our morale's better, and we have a slight edge in firepower. So we win.

—But, um, do you really need to take their heads?

—Well, you have to use the sort of war your enemy uses, don't you, unless you're planning to lose. And that's the first law of war, old boy: *don't lose.* They wouldn't give Bomber Harris his due after the last show, no one wanted to talk about firestorms and civilian casualties,

240

but my father always said that if bombing Dresden showed Adolf the door just one day earlier, or saved a single company of our chaps, it was worth it. And as for us and the locals here, well, when it comes to war, old boy, quite frankly you can't get much more *total* than eating the other side, can you?

—But you don't, I mean, you don't . . .?

—Good God no, what do you take us for? No, no, we leave them to the crocs. This is just our little trophy room. The Altbalmin love it. Pleases them no end. They come up and have a good laugh and mock the heads and chuck rocks at them, that sort of thing. Borrow them, occasionally, and sit them on the table on their own feast days, so they can gloat to the dead chaps about all the lovely grub they're scoffing this side of the veil. Bit much, I admit, but our own grandfathers were doing much the same thirty generations ago, no doubt. The point is, best not to mention it back home, eh? They tend to get shirty about that sort of thing west of Suez, always did. They just don't understand: if you're going to have an Empire, if you want to send chaps out overseas to set the locals straight, if you think we really ought to occasionally knock sense into undesirable murdering lunatics and stop fellows burning their sisters when they get widowed and eating each other and all that sort of thing, well, then you can't expect your chaps to do it without getting their hands a bit dirty, going a bit native occasionally. If you don't want all that, well and good, we can all sit quietly at home like a bunch of fat-arsed Swedes, smoking our pipes and playing golf and not caring a damn about who's invading whom where and who's burning his sister and why. And as far as *you* go, old boy, the question is very simple: are you one of us or not? I think you are. I find I can always tell by looking a chap in the eye. Look up, Marley. I said look up.

Marley felt the green eyes scanning behind his own

pupils, peering into the vast caverns of his mind. He was utterly unable to move, or even to blink.

—Yes, I think you're one of us, in the end. You may not be yet. But you will be. Pick up that stake and chuck the head into the fire. Do it, man. Behave like a white man. Almost dawn, they could be here any time now. Do it. You'll forget about it soon, you'll see.

—Will I? Marley was still transfixed by the green rays.

—Well, if you don't, that just means you were one of the chaps who was always going to come to a sticky end anyway, one way or another, doesn't it, old boy?

—How can you tell?

—Tell? You can't. You'll get over it or you won't. That's how you tell. But I assure you you're not walking out of this wood until you've got your hands dirty. I've a feeling they're going to like our story, back in England, and I'm damned if I'm having you bleating and messing things up for us after all this time. Do it. That's an order, Marley.

Marley closed his eyes and grasped the nearest stake. It tore out from the earth like a rotten tooth. He turned his head away and held his breath, trying to lock the iron, bombproof doors of his mind against the knowledge of what was drooping and wobbling from the end of the pole. Jumping away, he flung the horrid thing into the consuming flames. The Headmaster clapped him on the shoulder and led him, stunned, out of the fire and the smoke and the beastly smells.

—Good man. See? Not so bad, was it? Come on then. Chin up, Marley, we're going home. And you're going to be a hero. Look, here comes the sun now. By God, listen, and that's a chopper coming down. More than one of them. Come on. Think about it, old boy: the next sunrise we see will be in England!

*

242

—Grant, what the hell are these pictures coming through? Is this some sort of joke?

—I know, Tamsin, it's fucking impossible. But it's there.

—My God, Grant, if this is real it's . . .

—I know, Tamsin. Stay on this line. Security? Helicopter one, do you read me?

—Loud and clear, Mr Brodie. Landing site secured and descent-control IR equipment set up, but Mr Brodie, you never said nothing about a hundred-odd people with guns, I can't guarantee the PM's safety and I profession-ally advise that we should consider –

—Sod the PM, he's got his Special Branch men to look after him. And sod safety, I want everyone searched right now for private equipment and I want them searched again on the way out of here.

—Searched, Mr Brodie?

—This is the story of the decade and this is my footage and these are my recordings. I want the lot, no one takes a frame or records a byte or a word for themselves on my time and my money. Do it well, and I'll let you sell your story.

—Will do, Mr Brodie.

—Over and out. Right, everyone, listen in, just keep everything rolling no matter what. All my life I've been making crap. I think we are just about to go down in history. Roll all the cameras until the batteries are flat, and sod everyone. And anyone who mentions *winning the show* to Brian is sacked on the spot, OK? You hear all that, Tamsin?

—God, Grant, you're good.

—So get off this line and get on to international sales.

*

—Granny, said Tommy, perched on his big, club-class seat and gazing at the little TV screen on its clever

243

metal arm, —why are all those people waiting for the helicokters? I thought Daddy was lost in the jungle.

—How extraordinary. It looks just like a big Scout Camp.

—What's a Scout Camp, Granny?

—A very nice place, you'll go to them later, now shush for a moment and let's see if we can see Daddy down there, shall we? Oh yes, my dear, thank you, another sherry would be lovely.

*

—Um, I thought I was supposed to be, y'know, rescuing a dying man, said the Prime Minister, looking anxiously out of the third helicopter at the impossible scene unfolding below them as they descended through the last banks of cloud cover. The entire Colony was drawn up in dead straight ranks, with the faded Union Jack flying in their midst. —Or wasn't I?

—Ye-es, said his Best Friend. —What do you think? he asked the Prime Minister's Press Officer, who was glaring down with suspicion that was clearly about to brew into fury.

—Ah think Ah niver cleared this fuckin' photo opportunity. Ah dinna like it.

—No, no, I don't think it's a set-up.

—Ye're no' saying it's real?

—I think it is. And I think it's the most wonderful thing we could have asked for. Look at that Union Jack.

—Shite, yeah.

—Quick, call London and announce we're bringing the General Election forward as far as possible.

—Aye, great.

—Er, sorry, I just wondered, are you sure that's wise?

—Yes.

—Oh. OK, then. So, um, what do I do when we land?

—What do you do? You do what you do *best*, of course.

—Aye, boss, just keep that big smile comin'!

*

—What the devil are they all doing, Marley? Who's in charge? Why are all these damn telly people buggering about with their kit while we stand here like lemons on parade? What do they think we are, bloody actors? What are they waiting for? Who's that ghastly chap in the latest chopper? Know him? Looks like some kind of arse-licking hotel manager with his bellboys in attendance. But those other chaps with him are security bods, or I'm a Dutchman.

—I *think* it's the Prime Minister.

—Listen here, Marley, exactly what kind of top brass *are* you?

—I'm not, it's just, these days, if you're on the telly, well, you see, everyone important is on the telly, and people sort of get confused and think it works the other way too, so now we all think anyone who's on the telly must be important. And I was on the telly, so I suppose the Prime Minister thinks everyone will think I'm important.

—Good God, what rot. What sort of people do we have as Prime Ministers these days?

—Um, people who think whatever they think people want them to think, I think.

—Well, *I* think it's time we had a word with him. Socialist, eh? Devereux?

—Yes, sir?

—Would you mind terribly fetching me my cane, there's a good fellow?

—Of course, sir.

*

The Prime Minister, his face fixed in a nervous and slightly lunatic smile, emerged from his helicopter, flanked by his

Best Friend, his Press Officer and several Special Branch men in dark glasses, to find the entire Colony on parade before him, smiling politely and brandishing the faded portraits of the Queen and the Duke of Edinburgh, while the choirboys warbled 'Land of Hope and Glory' under the conducting of the Padre.

—Which one's Brian Marley? asked the Prime Minister's Best Friend, who had a lifetime's practice in smiling even as he plotted.

—Yon gowk standin' by that mad-looking auld bastard wi' the stick. The one wi' his arm round the waist o' that wee blondie.

—Right. Come with me, Prime Minister. And remember, he added from the side of his mouth, —it's all live.

—Oh, ah, OK, great.

—Now, how do you *do*, Mr Marley? May I call you Brian? This is sensational, the Prime Minister's *so* excited about meeting you.

—Hi, Brian!

—Oh, hello. Look, I think the Prime Minister should talk to the Headmaster, not to me.

—The who?

—Well said, Marley. Now stand aside, there's a good chap. You're the PM, eh?

—Ah, well, yes, actually. Hi!

—Well, I'm the Headmaster of this place. So is it true what Marley here tells me, that you Labour shower have dropped all this unions and nationalisation and disarmament claptrap? Well? Finally admitted you lot were wrong all the time?

—Sorry? I, ha, well, look, really, it's not *about* dropping anything, what the New Labour project is *about* is . . .

—Answer the question, man.

—Eh?

—Thank you so much for your interest, that's quite

246

enough for now. This way, Prime Minister.

—And just who the devil are you then?

—Me? Oh, I am simply the Prime Minister's adviser. I'm sure the Prime Minister will be delighted to answer all questions to your complete satisfaction later on, so if we could just, please –

—He'll damn well answer me right now. We've been waiting here the best part of fifty years, keeping our end up, and I want to know what's going on in England.

—I'm sure that's a most interesting point, but, this way, Prime Minister –

—Don't you *but* me, you slimy little suburban sod. I speak for my whole Colony. And Marley here too. Right, Marley?

—Um, yes, er, Headmaster.

—So spit it out, man, and stop bellyaching. (*Cheers.*)

—If you don't mind, Prime Minister, this way, I think we should – Ow! ouch! what on earth are you doing you crazy old – Yikes, help! Someone take that fucking *cane* away from this madman. Grant, if this is on live, I swear I will personally – Ow, ouch!

—Ha ha ha!

—Hey, wha' the fuck d'ye think ye're doing?

—Mind your tongue, man, there could be children or ladies listening. Another six for your smarmy little pal, I think.

—Ouch, ow, help me!

—Grant, stop yer fuckin' cameras! Cut!

—Come on, you Sixth Form chaps, cried George. —That rotten little Jock's using sergeants' mess language to the Headmaster. I think you should de-bag the rotter, don't you?

—Righto Miss Harcourt!

—Ha ha ha!

—Ah, fuck, ye bastards, ye, hey, ma troosers, no, shite!

247

Security, over here, ya bastards, dinna stand there laughing, fuckin' help me!

—You fellows with the damn fool Yank sunglasses, reach for those pistols and my chaps will shoot you like dogs.

—That's the stuff, Devereux. Well done, George. You there, yes, you with the ridiculous leather trousers, damn you, point that blasted camera at me when I'm talking to you. This so-called Prime Minister has *not* answered my question. But he will. And all my other questions. And if he won't answer them now, he'll damn well answer them when we get home, to England. (*Cheers.*)

*

Amazing, eh, Jimmy? Front-page stuff for you, I suppose?

—Front *and* inner, Charles. I say, *what* a splendid-looking girl. We'll sign *her* up straight away. Good God, Charles. Look. The chap calling himself the Headmaster. Look at those eyes.

—That can't be . . . Hugo Quartermain, can it?

—It bloody well is. Baines? Baines, where the devil are you?

—Sir James?

—Get my editor on the phone, will you? Tell him to hold the front page and get his bods to look up Hugo Quartermain, MC. He got a paragraph or two when that Comet went down in '57, or was it '58? Anyway, wake him up and tell him to get on to it. And bring us two more whiskies, will you, there's a good chap? Big ones.

—Yes, Sir James.

—God, Jimmy, look at old Quartermain go.

—Good old Hugo. Hell of a fellow. Beat the living daylights out of me at school.

*

As the Headmaster gave the Prime Minister's Best Friend a thrashing and his Sixth Form boys stripped the Prime Minister's Press Secretary, Marley retreated instinctively from the chaos. He saw Grant Brodie, shouting orders into a microphone in one of the helicopters, and set out to greet him. He had not taken two steps, however, when he trod on his own little yellow camera. It was simply lying in the short, dry grass near the Headmaster's tent. It must have been dropped there during the sending of the Morse code signal.

For a second, Marley looked down at it blankly. Then his last speech to Tommy began to pour queasily up on to the light of his memory, like water backing up from a flooded drain. He began to realise why he had felt so uneasy earlier, seeing them all holding the camera. England. Yes, he had said some things about England, that was it. Some not very good things. Things the Headmaster would not like. Or George. He was not sure exactly what things, but whatever they were, they belonged to the bad old past, not the bright new future. He knew he had not had time to press SEND before he fell, so the bad things had never gone off, they were all still locked within the hard disk inside the camera. They would have to go, just in case.

He looked around as unsneakily as possible, and found that, naturally, no one was looking at him any more. Every cameraman and Colony member was rushing to see the fun. The Prime Minister's Best Friend was limping from the scene, trying to pull his trousers and pants back up over his cane-reddened buttocks as he hopped away, screaming tearfully at the cameras to leave him alone, while George was watching, holding her hips and shaking with laughter, as the Sixth Form boys tossed the now naked Prime Minister's Press Secretary in the old Union Jack.

In a flash, Marley whipped the camera up and under his blazer. He walked slowly towards the flames that still blazed at the Gate. When he was a short distance away, he broke into a slow, loping run. Clutched to his chest, the little yellow camera seemed to grow heavier and heavier, as if it contained the distilled, dark, heavy-water essence of all his failed and futile past. This was it, his final tie with the hopelessness of his old life. He reached the place where the Gate had been and stopped before the raging fires.

The Headmaster was right. No one would ever look for severed heads here. Or for a severed past. And whatever they found could be explained away. This was where the truth died and was consumed, the phoenix pyre where his life would be reborn as a free-wheeling myth, without fear of discovery. This was the cleansing flame.

He tossed the camera into the very heart of the fire, and watched. The bright plastic lay for a few seconds deep amid the flames, curiously untouched. For one nasty moment, Marley wondered if it could possibly be fireproof. Then it began to blister, melt and collapse. All at once it reached some mysterious threshold of ignition and belched silently into blue flames and clouds of black, oily smoke. Marley smelled a brief, acrid eddy of poisonous modern hydrocarbons in the whirl of hot, timeless woodsmoke, as if his bitter past was wafting heavenwards and away past his head. And then it was all simply gone.

Whatever he had said or not said about England, about his life, about anything, back then, was lost for ever now. He could spin his past as he liked, play with it as light as air, juggle it until it fell into step with his glowing future. He turned his back on the fire and walked away, his face hot, feeling his shoulders rise and broaden with every step. Free at last, he strode back towards the helicopters and the scrum of activity around the Headmaster. George was turning to look for him, tears of laughter streaming down her cheeks. She saw him, waved, and smiled. She walked towards him, running her hand through her short, golden curls.

—There you are, darling. Where on earth have you been? You're missing all the fun. I don't think that silly little man will be able to sit down for a week. The Prime Minister's locked himself into one of the helicopters and he says he won't come out until he gets the Headmaster's word that he won't get six too.

His hands fell easily around her slim, strong waist. Through the thin material of her blouse he felt his thumbs resting, as if by evolutionary command, against her lowermost ribs; he looked down into her bright blue eyes.

—Well, you're looking happy to be going home, she said just before he kissed her.

—Rather, smiled New Marley.

*

—'Ere, I tell you wot, boys, I'm fuckin' goin' along to fuckin' Heathrow to watch these fuckers get back, what you reckon?

—I'm up for it, Mikey.

—Me too, Mikey.

—Well get 'em fuckin' in then.

—Ha ha ha!

—Look at 'em with those ancient fuckin' guns. They don't give a fuck. Yeah, I reckon these blokes are goin' to light some fires under some arses. About fuckin' time too.

*

The Altbalmin and Yaifo hunting parties came upon each other on the jungle track near the foot of the Hindenburg Wall. There being currently no burning feud, territorial clash or culinary ambition between the two tribes and the groups here present being of such parity in size and weaponry that neither side could realistically expect to

251

carry off the other's heads without themselves suffering the sorts of wounds which would mean lifelong cripplement if not lingering death by infection, they swiftly came to an unspoken agreement not to fight. Soon, they were warily sharing the contents of their little skin hunting pouches, prized varieties of bitter leaves, mildly appetite-suppressant and very slightly hallucinogenic.

Each group possessed a unique and ancient language, in which they could recount the endless genealogies of their forefathers, chant strange epic poems of the creation and doom of the world, of the deeds of heroes or the jealousy of the spirits, and sing vast encyclopaedias of long-garnered forest lore. But although their territories were separated only by a single ravine, these languages were completely unrelated, so that when they wished, as they did now, to discuss the arrival of the helicopters and the sad unravelling of the joint foreign policy which had united their tribes almost since the oldest man now living in either valley could remember, they perforce did so in a less poetic but more useful idiom.

In fact, the words of their slow and solemn discourse differed little, had they but known it, from those being used in most of the millions of emails and text messages fizzing digitally, at this very moment, unheeded by these doughty Stone Age warriors, across the measureless depths of the godless skies above them.

—*Waitpela antap mountan go haus bilong em.*
—*Ya. Hetmasta go see missis kwin.*
—*Mi sapos hetmasta heah Inglin orait. Nau em go.*
—*Yaifo tellim samting?*
—*Na. Altbalmin tellim samting?*
—*Na. Altbalmin laik mekim stap long taim. Altbalmin no tellim notin.*
—*Yaifo no tellim notin. Yaifo sori em go.*

252

—*Ya. Altbalmin sori em go. Hetmasta gut. Hetmasta bugerap Miyanmin gut.*

—*Ya. Em kilim Miyanmin gut. Ha ha!*

—*Ha ha! Em putim het antap stik gut!*

—*Ha ha!*

—*Ha ha!*

The happy reminiscing subsided and a gloomy pause followed.

—*Gut taim stap nau.*

—*Ya. Trabol nau.*

—*Hetmasta go haus, Altbalmin bugerap.*

—*Hetmasta go haus, Yaifo bugerap.*

—*Miyanmin kam eatim up Altbalmin na Yaifo.*

—*Ya. Nogut oltaim bek.*

—*Ya.*

*

No one in their right mind gets out at Port Moresby: tall, tanned, beef-fed young Caucasians on adventurous diving holidays transfer immediately at the airport to small prop-driven craft that will take them to distant beaches and reefs despoiled only by the $200-a-night lodges in which they have Internet reservations, while those others who have come, carefully equipped with myriad innoculations and insecticides, for scarifying but photogenic encounters with rainforest tribesmen only recently converted from cannibalism, just as quickly flee the merciless reality of this hideous, all-too-modern place and fly onwards to the newly penetrable interior.

Marley and the Colonists had no choice in any case, for, having packed their almost non-existent belongings into their fifties luggage (Marlborough Senior had been secretly but severely caned by the Headmaster for attempting to conceal a shrunken human head, surreptitiously saved from the flames, in his brown leather school satchel), they were

253

all whisked off in helicopters and then slipped without delay or customs at Port Moresby into small Fokker jet planes now heading for Darwin. This was not done out of consideration to them, but at the insistence of Channel Seven and its Exclusive Newspaper Partner, the Anglo-Australian-American Tabloid News Company, who were determined that no rival journalist should address a single world to Marley or any of the Colonists until they cleared customs at Heathrow, thus giving them a thirty-six-hour window to scoop the world. The Prime Minister's Best Friend was right behind them in this, since it gave him, in his turn, a thirty-six-hour window to decide how to spin the fact that he had been seen live on TV, by about half a billion people, being caned thoroughly on his naked back-side by an elderly gentleman while handsome, bronzed youths with ancient rifles and big shorts stood about and laughed at him. He was already writing his next letter of resignation, on the grounds of a Severe and Bitterly Regretted Error of Judgement, so as to take the heat off the PM. He could be quietly reinstated in a few months' time.

Marley flew and dreamed in the noisy little plane. He had already turned down an exclusive deal for £250,000, on the advice of someone called Baz Bingley, to whom he had spoken on Grant Brodie's phone, and who was apparently already working on the book deal. So he said nothing to the journalists but just sat next to George, happily sipping champagne and eating titbits. Occasionally he saw, or rather felt, the Headmaster watching him, but he had no intention of mentioning the heads on the stakes to anyone, including himself. Indeed he was managing to persuade himself that, even if that had ever really happened, it had happened a long way ago and a long time away and far from himself and home. Home. England. Marley closed his eyes and half dreamed happily of his new life.

The clearest of these honey-coloured, warm-lit visions

was set in that locus of every Englishman's dreams and nightmares, that place outside whose windows every Englishman born after 1960 has so often paused and stood, disbelieving, his astonishment tinged either with half-shifty delight or with half-despairing outrage: an estate agent's office.

Into this particular estate agent's office (it was larger and airier than most of the ones he had actually ever dared go into in real life) sauntered the new Brian Marley, dressed in soft, heavy corduroy trousers, a jacket of one of those mysterious, lustrous tweeds, almost as soft but even heavier, and resplendent brogues. At his side strolled George, blithely exuding English healthiness. They wandered the serried ranks of photographs, idly perusing five- and six-bedders with granny flats and the like, until one of the estate agents asked him in an agreeably fawning manner whether he *needed any help, sir?* Instead of blushing and saying *Um, just looking actually* (as he had so often done), Marley in his fantasy spun slowly on his well-cobbled heel, looked at the estate agent as if mildly surprised to find one here of all places, and smiled, with the effortless grace of one who knows he can now answer the oft-dreaded question *And what sort of price would we be lookin' at, sir?* with the answer *Oh, around a million or so, I suppose. Cash, of course.*

—What did you say, Brian? yawned George, raising her voice above the roar of the little plane. —Or didn't you?

—Oh, he smiled back, —I was just thinking about the sort of house I'm going to get.

—Haven't you got one now?

—Only a flat, actually.

—Oh yes, I think one of the books said something about unmarried men only having flats in town. I suppose that goes for divorced men, too.

—Well, I want to get a proper house now.

She opened her blue eyes properly and looked carefully at him.

—Does that mean you think you might not be unmarried very long?

—I was thinking about it.

—Were you thinking about not being unmarried with anyone in particular?

—Yes, actually.

—Mmm. Tell me more about the house you're going to get.

—Well, I was thinking about Kent.

—Not too near that autobahn thing you were talking about, I hope.

—Oh no. I won't be commuting to London so we, I mean I, could live a bit further out. I was thinking about an old place with six or seven bedrooms.

—That sounds nice.

—And a big garden.

—Of course. In the Garden of England.

—Yes. And some outbuildings. I could make them into sort of cottages for friends to stay in, and a big old garage so I can have an old English car, and –

—Oh, I see, is *that* how you say it?

—Say what? Car?

—*Garridge*.

—Garage?

—I thought it was called a *garaaj*. I'm sure the Teachers called it that when they read to us from the Books. It's a thing you keep a car in, isn't it?

—Um, yes.

—Oh well, the Teachers must have got it wrong. How funny of them. I must tell the Headmaster. How he'll laugh. *Garridge*, not *garaaj*, I must remember that.

—No, I mean, yes, I mean, no, I think *some* people do call it that, *garaaj*, I mean.

—Golly, that sounds complicated. What sort of people? I thought all proper English people were the same. I mean, obviously there are cooks and nannies and so on, and they have their own way of speaking, they're nice and well, *funny*, aren't they? Perhaps *they* say *garaaj*? And I suppose there are horrid dirty smelly people who don't talk properly, like the baddies in *The Famous Five*, but *they* don't count, do they? So, do real people, I mean people who matter, say *garridge*? You must tell me, Brian, I shouldn't want to make a mistake and have people hear me talking like some ghastly social climber or a Jamaican nigger, should I? Is there anything else like that I should know? Or is *garridge* the only one? Brian? Are you all right? Really, you are looking rather *intense*. Is it flight-sickness? Gosh, you've gone all white. Poor lamb. That's it, close your eyes. You'll soon feel much better. Oh look, we're going down. Is that Australia? How exciting. And to think that was where the Flight was going in the first place! Do you think we'll see kangaroos?

*

—Will we see kangaroos, Granny?
    —I expect so, my darling.
    —Is it far now, Granny?
    —Not very far, my darling. Oh look, there's another cartoon coming on your little television. Put your headphones back on. That's it. Now, I'll just put this funny little mask on and have a little rest, I think . . .

*

Dear Prime Minister,
It has been the greatest pleasure and privilege of my life to have been asked by you to help you serve the British people over the last few years. I have not, perhaps, always acted wisely, but any errors on my

257

part have sprung from an excess of zeal for your great mission to reform and rejuvenate Britain . . .

—You see, I've made sure it says Britain, Britain, Britain.
—Tha's fuckin' good.
—Gosh, thanks. I don't know what to say.
—You don't have to. Leave that to me.
—Great!
—And this bit is rather good as well.
—Aye, go on.

It was foolish of *me* to attempt to discuss *your* great project rationally with a group of half-starving, isolated, backward-looking, violent reactionaries. I should have left them to you, who have always been our guiding light. *You* could have shown them the error of their ways; *I* merely played into their sordid hands. But my actions prevented you from dealing with them as you surely would have done, and for this sin of omission I must pay the price. I therefore ask you, with heavy heart, to accept my resignation, and to assure you that, whatever great concerns of State may occupy you in your crusade for Britain, if you chance in future to glance at the benches behind you, you will find, in me, at least one quiet voice for whom loyalty is honour.

—Heh heh heh.

*

—Father, look, there is my Brian in Australia! Oh, oh, but it is not possible!
—Aha! He has found an English girl.
—No, I will not believe it!
—Daughter, he is kissing her.
—It is not possible!

—He is a man, daughter.

—But she looks like a boy!

—The English are strange, daughter. Victorious, but strange.

—I must go to him!

—No, daughter. He has found one of his own kind. That is the way.

—Oh, Father!

—Come, daughter, come to me. All will be well. He has found one of his own, and you shall too. There are many young officers in Argentina. Tomorrow night is a ball at the air-force base. You shall have a new dress. Yes, it is time. You shall have a brave husband who desires a true woman. You shall have many children.

*

Enflanked by large, suited men belonging to Channel Seven or to Anglo-Australian-American, they were shepherded swiftly through transit in Darwin, a small lost white tribe. The women nervously hugged the small children tight; the older children carried the picture of the Queen and Prince Philip bravely before them, like peasants displaying an icon in time of plague; the older boys scanned the airport, unarmed now but still prepared for anything, while Devereux and the men kept up appearances stoutly and the old men, the few survivors of the Flight, pointed out the marvels of the changed world to one another. The Headmaster strode onwards, his eyes fixed on his timeless ideal, untroubled by the mere surface apparitions of the world.

—It's not very like in the Books, said George.

—No, but don't be scared.

—Oh, I'm not. It's all such fun.

Marley held her shoulder protectively and they continued on their way. Now and then a few rogue photographers or journalists managed to get into the transit lanes, but they were quickly silenced. One person was allowed through: a short, fat, shiny individual, his face alive with the vengeful anticipation of a man who has been poor and despised, but who now finds himself reading the splendid menu in a famous restaurant before ordering a dinner for which someone else will be paying.

—Brian, Baz Bingley. Good to see ya, mate. Now, you didn't do anything daft like sign up with them? Great. We can get double that if we play our cards right. Sorry, Frankie, no, you have *not* got an exclusive. Not yet you haven't. Brian, come with me, yes, and you love, very nice arm-candy too . . .

—Brian? Who on earth is this?

—Oh, he's just, he, sort of, he's helping me, um . . .

—Right, Bri', the cameras are waiting. Just look amazed and happy.

—Amazed and happy? Why?

—This is your fifteen minutes, mate. If you want to make hay, you do it now and you do it my way. Here we are.

—OK, OK, I . . . Oh my God. Tommy. Mum. *Dad?*

—Daddy! You are alive!

—Tommy!

—Welcome back, darling, I always knew you'd make it.

—Lovely pictures! Just like that, please. And like this. Lovely. Smile.

—Dad?

—Brian, look, I saw you on the box, I, well, I told Gudrun about you.

—Better late than never, I suppose, Frank dear.

—She was pretty pissed off, I can tell you.

—You poor dear.

—I just, look, I just needed to see you again, mate.

—Daddy is this your daddy does that mean he is my grandad?

—Yes, um, yes, he is.

Marley, stunned, held Tommy tight. He felt the unre-membered weight of his father's now thin arm on his own taller shoulder. But now the brief photo-opportunity was completed and his whole family were being shep-herded onwards by the security men, politely but firmly, as if they were very minor stars at an Oscar ceremony, to the British Airways departure gate.

—So this is your boy, eh? said the Headmaster, over-taking them. —Fine young chap. You must be Mrs Marley. Well done.

—Oh, well, thank you. Brian, would you?

—Sorry, this is the Headmaster, Mum. And this is, er, George.

—Hello, Mrs Marley.

—Oh, hello, my dear.

—Ah, and Marley Senior, eh? Well, don't you recog-nise me, old boy? I was on *Eagle* too, man, in '54. Ah, now you remember me, eh? I say, didn't we de-bag you in Singapore for sending the port the wrong way round? I'm sure we did. Ha, ha, the old days, eh? We'll have to crack a bottle and have a chat.

—Oh, ah, yeah, said Frank Marley, with a look of dawning recognition and horror. The Headmaster now casually plucked Tommy from between his father, grand-mother and grandfather in order to toss him high in the air.

—We'll make a good soldier out of this one, eh?

—Um, actually, er, sir, Headmaster, he's not used to, I mean . . .

—Mummy, Mummy! screamed Tommy, in terror of the unknown, grizzled male face and the dizzy height. Dumped swiftly back on the ground by the surprised and disappointed Headmaster, he looked wildly around and dived for the nearest set of skirts, which happened to be

George's. He hit her just below the knees as she walked, with the embrace and impact of a miniature rugby tackle. She, taken by surprise, almost fell on top of him and, having heaved him up by the collar from underneath her feet, spanked him once, quite firmly, on the bottom.

—Don't *grab* at girls, darling, it's not done.

Tommy stood for several full seconds, mouth frozen open, face blank with shock at his first experience of corporal punishment.

—Bloody hell, said Marley's father quietly.

—Um, oh God, er, George, said Marley.

Tommy's eyes flickered wildly towards his father and supposed protector. Seeing there that his outrage was somehow reflected and confirmed, he allowed out a hideous wail of pain and injustice and demand for vengeance.

—Oh really, laughed George.

—Now now, darling, there's no need to make such a scene, flustered Mrs Marley. Her own youth had included mild beatings as a matter of course, her bringing up of Brian had still involved the occasional tap on the thighs, and she was not entirely convinced by modern notions of education in the young, so she was unsure how to react to George's slap other than to comfort her grandchild. Marley stared and kept walking, and allowed George to take his hand as though nothing had happened. He dared not turn and catch Tommy's eye. No, that was no good now, but it would be OK, he could explain it later, Tommy was old enough to understand, he would forget about it soon, it was nothing really, just a slap, no harm done, no . . .

—*Dadddddyyy!!*

—It's OK, darling. Come here, come here.

—What a fusspot, laughed George. —He'll have to grow out of *that* before he gets sent away to school, won't you, Tommy? Golly, look, what an enormous aeroplane. Is it ours? I say, Tom, chaps, look at the size of this kite!

—Golly!

—Brian, son, this is it for me. Got to go back. Don't forget, sit up front if you can, boy, said Frank Marley, as he quite suddenly almost dived forward and embraced his son at the gate. —Sorry, mate. G'bye.

Marley felt, with helpless embarrassment, a tear on the old cheek that rested briefly on his own, then was gone. He knew he would not see his father again. When he could focus properly again, the old man was already gone into the crowds and they were entering the tunnel towards the waiting jumbo. But on his other cheek his son's tears were still pouring down.

—Why am I getting sent away to school Daddy? Sorry I won't grab ladies again please don't send me away to school Daddy!

—No, no, no, it's OK, it's OK, it's all OK, oh Christ . . .

*

—I suppose you *should* really tell Brian before he finds out.

—I suppose. Couldn't you?

—He's *your* friend and you *are* on the phone with him.

—I suppose. What if we tip off someone and let *them* tell him? Then we could pretend it was nothing to do with us, couldn't we?

—It *isn't*, Grant. *We* didn't decide he didn't win the money. Channel Seven did.

—Oh yes, I keep forgetting.

—I'll talk to someone. Don't forget to stretch your legs now and then.

—They'll be stretched out all the way in First, won't they?

—Oh yes. Well, *bend* them now and then, then. Did you get everything anyone shot out there?

—Everything. I had security frisk everyone.

—Good. I've already negotiated the book and documentary rights.

—Oh good.

—The PM's people are furious with us, of course.

—Do we care?

—I don't think we do, do we? I mean, we're *the media*, aren't we? And the election's coming up. So if there's any doubt at all who's going to win, *they* have to make *us* happy, not the other way round, don't they?

—Yes, I suppose. Is there? Any doubt, that they'll win, I mean?

—Well, I don't know, Grant, but they're sounding all sort of *anxious* suddenly.

—Oh good. I like them much better that way.

*

They were somewhere over white mountains. Tibet, perhaps. At any rate, they had been flying over nothing else for an hour and Marley was busy watching the snow-capped peaks to see how long it would be before there was any visible sign, however circumstantial, that *Homo sapiens* actually existed at all on planet earth.

Behind him, his mother and Tommy slept, as did George; she had curled up again like a cat on the fat club-class seat. He dozed. Awoke, drank, dozed, awoke. He stared out again and again into the angelic, inhuman blueness, at the impossible but undeniable curvature of the earth itself. He listened to the endless hissing of the jet engines. He ran his finger around the window surround to feel for hairline cracks like those which had destroyed the early Comets. He wondered what ludicrous little fault would be found to have made this particular aircraft crash, if it did crash. He worried about the effect of solar radiation on Tommy's little brain. He worried about Tommy and George.

It was not her fault that she had hit Tommy, of course, everyone hit everyone in the Colony. It had seemed quite natural out there, even to him, though now he thought

264

back he could not see *why* he had thought it normal. Well, he would just have to explain to her, that was all, and she would see. And as for Tommy, well, even if it took Tommy a bit of *getting used* to George, especially after that slap, well, he, Tommy, would have to get used to someone sometime, wouldn't he? He, Marley, could not allow him, Tommy, simply to force him to stay bloody single for ever, could he? Of course not. Anyway, once they were settled down in their wonderful new house, Tommy would soon like her. Who could resist George, after all? They would have a fine new life, and for Tommy that would make up for everything, in the end. He looked down, happy again, at the impossible, tight blonde curls of her hair. Yes, and then again, what about poor George? God, she was going to be lost when they got back to England. Yes, she would need looking after. He would look after her and be strong and English. In a big Georgian house. With plenty of money. And everything would be fine and wonderful.

It was a pity George would never really understand how huge the change was for him. Not that he wanted to dwell on the past, of course. That was dead and gone, thank God. It was just, well, it was just that he sort of wished he could tell her about how bad things had been for him, before. How far he had come. But he couldn't. Obviously. Her eyes would simply stay as blue and bright as glass and *How funny of you, Brian*, she would say. And she would yawn. Gorgeously. For Christ's sake, did he want to lose her or something? Drive her away with his, well, *damn whingeing*? No, no, no. Everything was fine, for God's sake, who cared how or why it had happened? Anyway, after all, he would have plenty of space to explain things, if he wanted to, in all the interviews he was bound to give. Yes, that would be good. A grand explanation of everything he had ever done and why, a message to whoever would understand, not a *whinge*, of course, no, no, simply a smiling explanation of why he sometimes felt, well, you know, a little bit stunned and . . .

> With the stunning Georgina at his side and his delightful son, Tommy, on his lap, Brian Marley smiles as he describes his quiet, fatherless, lower-middle-class childhood, his shy, untrendy teens, his speedily wasted twenties and his barren thirties. He can afford to smile now, of course, but there is something truly engaging in the frank way he admits to having been an utter waster all his life, pathetically scared of anything that might seem remotely like reality or . . .

No, no, no.

Marley blinked out into the icy void beyond the thin little window. What was the point? There wasn't one. Yes, but that was not what mattered. What mattered was the telling. He stifled a groan. It was no good. What does anything matter if no one hears it, if no one *understands*? He had miraculously broken out, escaped his past scot-free, but now, like a cunning gangster who has made his big hit and got clean away, he felt his brain rage with the helpless need to *tell* someone, to stand in a quiet bar, to drink deep, to collar someone and talk to them and watch the strange light of understanding dawn in their eyes as he spoke of what he had done and been and become. Of his journeyings. And quite suddenly, as they crossed the Channel at last and the excited Colonists, George among them, crowded the windows to catch their first sight of the White Cliffs they had all read about but most of them never seen, Marley knew that there was someone he had to see, someone he could talk to, someone who would understand.

Her course would have started again after the New

Year by now. If she had come back. He checked his watch. It was only morning, in England. She would be at the London English School in Piccadilly right now. He saw again her dark eyes, and knew that yes, she would understand. Then she would go home, of course, they would say goodbye for ever and he would have got it all off his chest, he would be happy, he could be English for ever, afterwards, with George. Yes indeed. Certainly for the best. Just to say goodbye, really, just to make sure that nothing haunted his English idyll to come.

And so when George looked round from her window and cried, —They really are white, aren't they? Oh, how wonderful. Brian, I say, Brian darling, where are you going to take us in London? he smiled back happily at her, full of innocence and happy duty, and said, —Well, I was thinking, have you heard of the Ritz?

—Yes, it was in the Books. It's a café, in a place called Piccadilly, isn't it?

—Yes, that's it.

—*Ritz in Piccadilly*. I always thought that sounded such fun. Like *piccaninny*. Is it? Fun, I mean?

—Let's see, shall we?

—Let's. I'm so glad we've got you to show us round, Brian.

—Me too, George.

*

Really, Tamsin? You sure? He's not going to get a *penny*? And he doesn't know? You mean we can break it to him *live*? Fuck me, thanks for the tip. I owe you. Bye! Quick, Sid, get a spare camera crew out to Heathrow, top priority. And call all the news stations. We got ourselves a scoop.

*

At Heathrow, the Colonists were led to Immigration; Marley's passport had been destroyed in the helicopter

267

crash and he too had to wait. He said goodbye to his mother and Tommy.

—Well, I must say she seems a very nice girl.

—Yes.

—No she doesn't Daddy I hate her she hit me I'll kill her she wants to send me away to school.

—Yes, well, goodbye, look, I'll see you both tomorrow.

—Yes, you go and relax and enjoy yourself, darling. You *deserve* it.

—Thanks, Mum. Bye, sweetheart.

Then they were both kissed and waved goodbye. As he walked up to Immigration, Marley tried to listen to Baz Bingley as he spoke of deals and figures and tactics, but he was secretly looking for a phone box and wondering if he could sneak to one now, to get hold of Consuela. Then he caught sight of George again, looking unutterably gorgeous, standing beside the Headmaster as he examined an anti-terrorist policeman's Heckler & Koch machine pistol, the officer having handed it over under what seemed to be some form of atavistic hypnosis.

—So that's our strategy, right, Bri?

—Eh? OK, er, Baz.

—Right. Sign here.

—What?

—My contract. Forty per cent of whatever we get. It's industry norm, Bri. Lovely, ta.

—Um, Baz, can I have some money now please, I haven't got any, you see, obviously, and I need to –

—Sorry, mate, don't advance cash to clients. Unethical. I'll call you.

—Oh. Bye. Grant, hey, Grant, Grant, over here, Grant.

—Oh, ah, hello, Brian, I didn't hear you. Ha. So, well, look, I can't really stop right now, I should be . . .

—Grant, I know this is silly, but have you got any money?

—What? Sorry? Money?

—Can you lend me a bit till we get the prize money sorted out? It's crazy, I've got to take some people out, to the bloody Ritz, and I haven't got a penny.

—Money? The Ritz? Oh, um, well, the thing is, um, Brian, are you sure you want to go there, I mean, the Ritz?

—Well, I've never been able to go there before so I'd quite like to look at it once. I think I can afford one big night out, eh? I mean, out of two million quid?

—Ha. Well, yes, yes, yes of course, Brian, money, um, money, yes, take this, um, yes, take it all, look, I've got to shoot off right now, but I'll, no, no, it's just our petty cash, don't worry, please, take it, yes, well, bye . . .

—Thanks, Grant, said Marley, taking the large and hastily offered roll of banknotes, but Grant Brodie was already off through Immigration, waving his passport and almost breaking into a run. Marley put the money into the deep pocket of his big shorts and looked around. George was striding over towards him. She looked heart-stoppingly lovely again.

—Well, I must say your television people have been very helpful, they've managed to get us all sorted out. Though I must say these passports aren't half as nice as the ones the founders have, are they? Although it's really a lot of rot, isn't it? I mean to say, what on earth could we be *but* English? And one of the inspectors was a nigger, can you believe that? He had the nerve to *question* us. Tom Devereux nearly laid the black bugger out.

—Ah. Um, the thing is, George, people don't actually say that nowadays.

—What, bugger?

—No, um, nigger. *And* black bugger.

—Oh. All right, so what's the fashion now?

—Oh, just, well, *black*, it's really just . . .

—All right. Though I must say I can't see the difference myself, and I think it's a damn cheek some insolent black asking a chap like the Headmaster if he can *prove he's English*.

—Yes, well, oh God, so, so, right, can we just pick up our passports and go?

—Yes. To the Ritz?

—Yes.

—Oh, Headmaster?

—Ah, George, there you are.

—Brian's taking us to the Ritz, will you come too?

—Is he? Good man, Marley. No, no, I'm going straight to my club, old girl, as soon as we've got everything settled. Find my old chair, see if . . . Good God. Jimmy?

—Hugo. I knew it, damn it.

—Jimmy, by God.

—Hugo, well *done* the other day. We were all delighted when you gave six to that little . . . I say, Hugo, *do* introduce me to your charming friend.

—George, this is old Jimmy. We were at school.

—Hello, old Jimmy.

—He*llo*, young George.

—But what the hell are you doing here, Jimmy?

—Well, I run a big newspaper, actually.

—Do you? How funny.

—Isn't it? We're going to make this young chap rather famous, eh, Marley? And we'll want you too, Hugo. We all loved the way you whacked that ghastly little creep. It's caused quite a stir, I can tell you. We've started an appeal for you chaps, in case some of you end up without a bean. Loot absolutely pouring in already and we're putting the screws on this ruddy so-called government to come up with some too.

—Never mind me, Jimmy, I've had a good innings, all

I need is a quiet place to pitch the old tent and a bottle of decent Scotch. You sort my chaps out first.

—Of course, Hugo, of course. And tell me, my dear George, have *you* ever thought of writing for a newspaper? Look here, you lot, my car's outside, let me give you a lift.

—Hold on, Jimmy. Devereux, I say, Devereux?

—Yes, sir?

—Transport and billets sorted out for the chaps?

—Yes, sir. The newspaper bods are laying on cars for us. A few of us are going to the Ritz, isn't that right, Marley old man?

—Um, yes, yes.

—They're putting us up in the Dorchester. Nurses for the kids, the whole show. Apparently all the big hotels in London are empty these days because the Yanks are too damn scared to come to London in case the Arabs knock them off.

—Mmm, bit low on the old moral fibre, the Yanks. Still, handy for us, the Dorchester's not too bad, as I recall. Righto then, Devereux, I'll toddle along with Jimmy and we'll rendezvous in the bar at the Dorchester at, say, twenty hundred hours.

—Yes, sir.

—Lead on, Jimmy.

The Senior Editor led them to his Bentley and they swooshed Londonwards.

—Is this your famous autobahn, Brian? asked George.

—Yes.

—I think it's rather ghastly, really.

—Yes, it is.

—I say, Hugo, you know there's a General Election coming up?

—What, is that little shit standing again?

—Well, exactly, Hugo. That's the spirit. Look here, the fact is, the Party's in a bit of a mess, but I'll tell you what,

I'm going to call a couple of my chums, if you don't mind. Good chaps, big in the Party . . . Jenkins?

—Yes, Sir James?

—There seems to be a car following us. TV crew by the look. Thought I saw them chasing us when we got in. Lose them, will you, there's a good chap, I don't want them snooping around when Hugo meets my pals. Not just yet, eh, Hugo?

—Jimmy, what the devil are you getting at?

—England, Hugo, England. Now, my dear George, let's talk about *you*. Don't suppose you play the cello, do you?

*

—Consuela Martinez? said the London English School secretary. —What *class* is she in, Brian? She isn't *in* any class, Brian. She left at Christmas and she isn't coming back.

—Oh. Well, did she, I mean, did she, leave any message? For me? Or anything?

—No-o, she didn't leave any message, Brian.

—Look, Sandra, I don't suppose you can tell me, I mean, just for once . . .?

—Sorry, Brian, you know we *can't* give out the home addresses of students to teaching staff, certainly not to ex-teaching staff. Not even if they're millionaires! I get asked that a dozen times a year by various men, you know what EFL teachers are like, and with our staff turnover we simply can't check everyone. If we started giving out the girls' addresses, well, we all know where that would end, don't we? Down-at-heel, middle-aged, infatuated Englishmen knocking on the doors of nice young girls in Acapulco. *Not* good for the school's reputation, Brian.

—I just wanted to, you know, say goodbye.

—Of course you did. No, sorry, Brian, can't be done.

Still, I don't suppose you'll be heartbroken for very long, will you? Not with all that money. I wouldn't be, I can tell you. Don't suppose we'll be seeing you back *here*, anyway, ha ha!

—No, probably not. Look, isn't there . . . OK, OK, sorry.

—Happy spending, Brian! Oh, and I think you should buy some clothes first thing tomorrow, don't you? Those shorts are a bit . . . long, aren't they?

Marley stood in his long shorts with cold knees on the steps of the London English School. The evening sessions were about to begin, and a river of international youth passed him on the steps, scarcely breaking to flow about him, wealthy youth from every country, creed and colour, united solely in their desire to pass their time exclusively in the company of other wealthy youth, and expressing this simple wish in the international pidgin which was all they wanted or required.

—You like, like, to go see Beatles show?

—Oh yeah, I, like, love to go. You guys, like, going?

—Yeah, we, like, going tonight. You like, like, to come?

—I like very much come.

—Is, like, very cool, I think.

—I, like, think too.

—Yes, very cool.

—She love you yeah yeah yeah.

—Cool.

—Oh, I too am like iPod.

—Yeah, iPod 128.

—Cool.

—We share taxi.

—Cool.

Marley looked across the wide street to the Ritz. He could clearly see George through the big windows. Her hair was glistening under the chandeliers, her head was thrown back, laughing. Around her were many young men, tall, pink, firm-jawed, expensively dressed young men who had been appearing, summoned by Christ knew what social instinct or network, ever since he and George had arrived. A waiter was bringing yet another magnum of champagne.

He crossed the road, took a deep breath and went back into the warmth and light and high-ceilinged babble.

—Hello, darling, did you see your pals? Now, here are some new pals of *mine*. This is Charles and this is Tarquin and this is Drogo and this is Ivo. They're all in the Guards. This is Brian, chaps. *His* father was a Navy man.

—Hello, said Charles and Tarquin and Drogo and Ivo.
—Well *done*. They were all several inches taller than Marley, ten years younger, and much fitter.

—Hello, he said manfully.

George suddenly kissed him on the cheek in a way she had never kissed him before. He wondered what was different about it, then he realised that she was smiling over his shoulder at someone as she was kissing him. She held the smile and turned his shoulders gently round. Flashguns blitzed in his face as she kissed him again.

—Don't worry, darling, it's just some people from the *Tatler* and *Harpers & Queen*. So they're obviously still going. Have some more champagne. Do you know, I've decided I rather like it. It's fun, isn't it, the way the bubbles go up your nose? Cheers, darling. Oh yes, apparently I've got hundreds of cousins and so forth, isn't that fun? One of them is an earl, he's coming along soon, I'm sure you'll like him, he sounded great fun on the phone. Did you know everyone nowadays has little telephones you can carry about? Dear old Jimmy's going to get me one straight away so we can chat whenever we want. I'm so glad you brought us here, darling, you're so clever, and I must say it's rather a relief.

—A relief?

—Mmmm. I mean, when we were driving along on that autobahn thing, and then through all those wretched places, what were they called? Southhall and Ealing and Acton and Shepherd's Bush. Well, I must admit I felt a bit funny. You know, as if England wasn't at all like the books after all. Actually, I know it sounds funny, but I got rather *depressed*. But then it got better, I started to recognise things from the pictures, Marble Arch and Buckingham Palace and things like that, do you remember how excited I was when dear old Jimmy took us round there in his car, darling?

—Yes, yes I do.

—And now we're here and, well, everything *is* like in the books after all, really, isn't it? I mean, as far as I can see, things are pretty much the same.

Marley blinked, then looked again, as if with new-scrubbed eyes, at the countless tables of the laughing rich, at the hordes of servile waiters, at the empty bottle before him which must have cost what the Government deemed sufficient to feed and house a small unemployed household for a week.

—Yes. Yes, I suppose things *are* pretty much the same, really.

—Oh, and by the way, darling, can you tell me again about *garridges* and *niggers*?

—Sorry?

—Well, perhaps I got it wrong, but I *thought* you said people *did* say *garridge* and *didn't* say *nigger*. But everyone here says *garaaj* and when I was talking about our Colony and how we dealt with the locals, I did let *nigger* slip out once or twice but no one seemed to notice. In fact, I'm sure Drogo said it too. It's very complicated, isn't it?

—Yes. Yes it is.

—Well, I'm sure I'll get the hang of it. Jimmy's offered me a job on his newspaper, isn't that fun? He wants me

275

to keep a sort of diary thing and write all about all the things I think are ghastly about England these days and all the things that are really just the way they should be. I think that'll be great fun, don't you?

—Yes, I'm sure it will.

—We're going to his club next. I'm sure *you've* been to it before, but *I'm* terribly excited because they don't usually let girls in but they're going to change the rule just for today, especially for me, which is really rather fun, isn't it? You will come, won't you?

—Yes, of course. Look, George. I might just have to, er, pop across the street again first, I, um, forgot to say something to my old pals. Perhaps I'll follow you on a bit later.

—Are you all right, Brian? I must say you do look a bit, well, *serious*. Is it just too much champagne? Please don't be a *bore*, darling. We're home. In England. And everything's fine. Oh, look, I've finished the bottle again. Well done that girl, eh? Can we have some more?

—Yes, yes, of course.

—Oh good.

—Oh good, said Drogo and Ivo and Tarquin and Charles.

Marley drank. Then he drank some more, and tried not to panic at how expensive it was going to be. He had to keep reminding himself that it didn't matter, not any more, at least, not today. Everything was going to be all right. Everything. There. Yes.

But then he stood up so suddenly, downing his newly filled glass as he did so, that his knees flung Ivo's drink into Drogo's lap.

—Oh, really.

—Oh, really.

—Are you all right, darling?

—Yes. I'm fine, I'm just going to get some air. Sorry, Ivo.

—So, can we have another bottle, then?

—If you pay for it, yes, Drogo.

—Oh.

—Brian?

—Back in a minute, George.

Marley strode towards the door that led out again to Piccadilly, hampered only by a slight rubberiness in his champagne-filled knees. But at the door he stopped. This was crazy. He was drunk. He couldn't just run off and leave George like this, alone in the modern world. Slowly, he turned to go back to her. But as he neared the table, unseen by them all, he saw Tom Devereux lean over to her.

—I say, George, what the hell's got into Marley?

—I don't know, Tom. He's really being rather a bore.

—Ah. The thing is, George, he told the Headmaster and me, he's only just made his money, you see. The fact is, now we're back home, I can see that he isn't *really* the thing.

—Oh, Tom.

—Ah, said Drogo and Ivo and Charles and Tarquin.

—Don't worry, old girl, the Headmaster says it often happens, a chap can seem perfectly clubbable east of Suez, but when you get home you realise he isn't really the thing after all. Bit of a cheek, though, really, making a girl think he is, if you ask me.

—Oh dear. What should I do, Tom?

Marley spun round quickly and now almost ran towards the door, smiling with relief. That was OK then. No need for guilt. He could escape.

Where to? To a normal bloody country, that was where. To anywhere he could get by in the language, and that meant pretty well anywhere in Europe, to any place where people judged you by what you said, not by the accent you said it in. Yes, true, it would mean he would be foreign for ever, but no more foreign than he was here, in his supposed homeland. Ha, yes, he knew his ex-wife only too well; if she was offered the choice between Marley buggering off and leaving her alone in England with her work and Tommy or getting, say, half a million quid and coming to, say, Spain to live nearby and swim, there was not much doubt what she would do. OK, then, he would buy her off. He would buy Tommy's freedom from England. His son would grow up able to speak English, of course, like every educated person in Europe, but he would grow up to *be*, to be *thinking* in, French, Spanish, Italian, German, Dutch. Anything but English.

Spanish. Yes, Spanish. Because Consuela might come with him to Spain. And he was going to get her, right now, he was already halfway across Piccadilly, paso doble-ing boldly through the traffic like a bullfighter on song, heading for the London English School once again. And this time they would not say no to him. This time, he was going to bribe and threaten and beg and scream and sit down and bite the carpet and kick and kick until they gave him her number and if they *still* refused he was going to get on the next flight to Argentina, and then on into Patagonia, he was going to hire a car and put adverts in the papers and posters on telegraph poles and just drive and drive until he found her, he knew her name, he knew her father was an air-force officer, that would help, it did not matter if he spent ten thousand pounds finding her, twenty thousand, more, he did not care, he . . .

—Brian Marley?

—What?

Another pretty young female journalist, complete with her team of lights, cameraman and boom swinger, had inserted herself in his path. He sighed. Baz Bingley had said he should do this kind of little TV interview, without giving anything away, to make the papers want his big story more tomorrow. Well, OK then. After all, the more money he made tomorrow, the more there would be to bribe his ex-wife, to buy a place in Spain, to find Consuela, to start to *live* at long last . . .

—Nice shorts, Bri'! Bit chilly on the knees, ain't they? chirruped the newsgirl.

—Ha, ha, yes, back home, you know. Look, I'm really sorry, I'm in a bit of a hurry.

—So, did you do it just for the money, Bri'?

—What?

—*Brit Pluck, Green Hell, Two Million*? Just for the money, was it, Bri'?

—For the money? Good God, no, not at all really, drawled Marley instead, reeling out the prepared lies Baz Bingley had suggested. —I've been travelling most of my life, you see. It was simply for the adventure. The challenge. The sheer experience.

—Right. So it wasn't just for the money, Bri'?

—Like I said, not really.

—In fact, Bri', you'd really have done it for no money at all?

—What? Yes, yes, I told you. Now, please, I really have to go.

—So, really, Bri', you won't be worried if you don't get it?

—Don't get what?

—The money.

—Ha ha, goodnight. Excuse me.

—But what if you don't, Bri?

—Look, this is all very silly, isn't it?

—What, you mean you haven't heard the rumours?

—What rumours?

—Is this the first you've heard of it?

279

—Of what?

—Channel Seven aren't paying out, Bri'.

—What?

—So, how does it feel, Bri'?

—What do you mean, they're not paying out? Of course they are.

—No, Bri'. They say you didn't win.

—What?

—They say no one won, Bri'.

—That's ridiculous. *I* won.

—That's not what they say. They say they're not paying.

—This is rubbish. This is . . .

—We got a link to Channel Seven here, Bri'. You want to ask them? You can ask them right now if you want. Bri'? Bri'? How does it feel, Bri'?

V

ANOTHER COUNTRY

It may be that we must regard ourselves in future not as a European power looking towards the East, but as the eastern extension of a Western block centred on North America.

Clement Attlee,
Cabinet Meeting, 1946.

The unspeakable truth was that by 1941 we were a defeated nation, whose conquerors had neglected to invade us. Impoverished, beaten in Flanders and Malaya, condemned as it seemed to grey years of sacrifice with no certain end, we were invaded by our allies instead.

Peter Hitchens,
The Abolition of Britain,
London, 1999.

Our enemies claim that we in the West have nothing on our side but superior weapons technology and productivity. True, in these we rightly place much of our trust. Throughout history, the better-equipped battalions have generally been the lucky ones and we have been so good at equipping our battalions that we have rarely *needed* a 'mobilizing ideology' to win the day. But where we have been genuinely endangered or outraged – England in 1940, America in 1941 and 9/11 – the answer has never been lacking. So I say to our enemies, beware: if your murderous hatred ever truly arouses us, you shall find another Winston S. Churchill, another JFK, another Martin Luther King who will make our language ring across the world in tones of fire. And then you shall meet the West truly ablaze, superior technology and productivity united with a mobilizing ideology called Freedom. And you shall stand in fear and trembling, and it shall come to pass with you as it came to pass with Sodom and Gomorrah.

General W. Paul Jones Locksmith,
passing-out address at West Point, March 2003,
quoted in *Prospect* magazine, June 2003.

England, Two Months Later

—Ah now, to fock, lads, would you's give it up, it's too late to be kicking off focking fighting now, slurred the half-Irish, half-Jamaican voice.

There were in fact no Irishmen or Jamaicans present in Godolphin Road, London W12, nor anyone remotely of such extraction, nor anyone who was drunk. The only person this end of the street was Brian Marley, coming home late but sober in the March darkness to his mother's flat, and he was talking like this to himself because he did not at all like the look of the four large male shadows whose heads he had just glimpsed beneath the sodium light, through a gap in the hedges.

—Oh bollocks and shite, attempted Marley, sliding into a bizarre form of sub-Glaswegian as he continued to practise the accent which he hoped might persuade the four unknown men, should they choose to engage him in night-time banter, that he was, in fact, a tough, hard-drinking, working-class male of indeterminate but credible ethnic origin to whom the odd scrap after the pub was no great shakes, and who just happened to be wearing a tweed jacket, a shirt without a tie, plain jeans, dark socks and rather expensive leather brogues.

If only he had kept that bloody paint-stained boiler suit on! But he had not wanted to bring the mess and smell and general low-level industrial pollution that is Home Improvement with him into his mother's ordered world (Tommy was staying the night there once again), so he had changed into his English-teaching clothes for tomorrow.

These two dress codes, second-hand tweed and dirty overalls, defined Marley's life nowadays. He was working once again at the London English School, where he had by now more or less ceased to be the object of solicitous and condescending interest, teaching Oxford, Shakespeare and suchlike. His spare time was taken up with Making a Home for Tommy, which now seemed the only possible reason not to just give up and go to the pub for good one afternoon along with the many other Destroyed Men of London. Instead of loathing and avoiding his flat and wishing, like ten million other Englishmen, that he owned a large Victorian Home with Many Original Features, Marley had taken up the manly challenge of home-making and now lavished upon his unloved property every spare moment of his time and every spare pound of his money, basing his transformations, in theory at least, on the latest fashions in interior design. A bright, modern home for Tommy. He was not deterred by the fact that the value of his flat was almost certainly still falling, or at best flatlining despite his investments in it, because he was not doing it up to increase its notional resale value. He was doing it to give his son a Modern Space in which to Develop His Lifestyle. It was true that at present the result was a building site pure and simple, completely unin-habitable, but Marley did not care. He hacked away and knocked down and measured up, on and on. It was also true that he sometimes found himself suddenly taking his finger off the trigger of whichever cacophonous, half-understood power tool he happened to be using at that particular moment and, in the sudden electro-mechanical peace, gazing blankly at his work, dazed, as if he had just walked smack into a plate-glass door, unable to stop himself asking what the hell he thought he was doing and what the hell was the point of it. But at such moments, he recovered by pointing out to himself that the same question might be asked of any of us, about anything we do, at any time. So then he decided that if he was spending so much time doing up his flat, then obviously, by a neat reverse logic, that must mean that he had a future. So then he went back to work.

Marley's mother was vital to his project. She seemed to have gained a new lease of strength from that brief meeting with her ex-husband in Australia, perhaps because, having seen this still-shy, still-English, hen-pecked old man, she was no longer haunted by the thought of a handsome young ex-officer leading a joyous life of sexual abandon in the unrationed sunshine. Moreover, any suspicion that her son was a mere waster was now thoroughly dispelled, replaced by the righteous certainty that he had been appallingly cheated by life. Filled with new energy, she was very happy indeed to have Tommy stay with her while *Daddy got on with his jobs*. On these evenings, Marley came back to her flat already cleaned up, and they had sherry. Then, when she had gone to bed, he would kneel down low on her carpet and crawl down in between the little forest of slender oak barley-sugar columns beneath her little Edwardian-Elizabethan gateleg table. He would feel on his face the fringes of the chenille she used to cover the polished oak, just as he felt it thirty-five years before. He would plug his Internet lead into his mother's phone socket and surf eBay for *Eagle* annuals and Collectable Toys he had once had. Thanks to eBay, there was no need to have lost his past at all, here it was, stored in other people's attics, just waiting to be summoned down and brought back to life. In this new world, nothing was ever truly thrown away, no past ever truly got rid of. It was all there, just waiting, whenever you wanted it and were ready to pay. It could all be had back. When he was not busy reassembling his childhood, allegedly for his son's benefit, Marley would Google-search for HMS *Eagle*, or find strange little forums on Papua New Guinea and the habits of its natives. Like every Internet session done by anyone anywhere in the world, Marley's made him feel less sad, weird and lonely because after all there *were* clearly other people out there who shared his interests. He was not alone. OK, maybe it was only a few hundred people out of half a billion, even so . . .

But now, here, tonight, in Shepherd's Bush, the world was not going to be denied. As he spied through the scraggy hedges, still thin from winter, to try to get a closer look at the four men who were approaching his line of walking, Marley felt the full, insistent weight of its non-virtual reality.

He continued to walk half resolutely on, but kept watching the little street as he approached the corner where it met his own path. He felt his heart begin to race, his hackles rise, his balls withdraw. He caught sight of the four shadows again for just a second, then they were hidden again by another section of the tall, neat-cropped privet. But that one second was enough, for in that time the heads of the four shadows changed shape: their profiles disappeared and eight backlit ears were now visible, standing clearly out from short-cropped heads. They had turned towards him. He could not see their eyes, but he knew that they were looking his way. He could feel their unseen, predatory, binocular gazes zeroing in on him, and detected a tiny but just percep-tible change in their stride as they shifted pace to fall in ever so slightly more closely with each other. They had spotted him spotting them. They now knew that he knew that they knew that he knew their paths were going to cross. Marley felt ancient wiring looms and gear wheels fire into life in his mind as his primate-derived scanners lit up.

Marley's hominid radar was simply the normal human

equipment, which meant it had grown only in the last few hundred thousand years from out of chimp-like stock and had been built by nature for calculating the odds in murderous, zero-sum wars of territory with other pre-humans. Hard-wired into the young Marley's head, it had developed culturally in the nasty little unsighted corners of English state-school playgrounds of the 1960s and 70s and been honed in cheap, dodgy bars all over Europe in the final two decades of the second millennium. This radar now kicked in, its natural superconductors firing bright as day, triangulating the situation in all its logistical and sociological aspects as swiftly as a tennis star intuiting the direction of an impossibly fast serve. Marley's brain, thus instinctively informed, came swiftly to a linked system of grim but unavoidable conclusions:

(a) that the four men were a self-conscious group of some kind, not a mere chance aggregation;

(b) that this solid gang of unknown (and thus prima facie hostile) males would sally out from their side street and into Godolphin Road just before Marley himself reached the corner where the streets met; and

(c) that a small pack of adult male *Homo sapiens* roaming a dark street late at night when decent people are all abed are

(i) virtually certain to be fuelled by drink,

(ii) statistically a safe bet to be from the Tough Classes and hence

(iii) structurally likely to decide that since they can obviously kick the shit out of the lone, unknown, rather older and less aggressive male who has just emerged from the darkness before them, without any significant risk of injury to any of themselves, they might as well do it just for the hell of it.

Fight being out of the question against such odds,

Marley now considered his defensive options. First, he thought about tacking over to the other side of the street to avoid the otherwise inevitable moment when they would meet on the pavement and he would have to yield the footpath to them, which would naturally be the moment that would provide the excuse for the psyching-up barrage of mockery. But he knew this would be no good: just as his defensive sensors had marked the four men, their offensive survey would be sure to spot his evasive manoeuvre and interpret it (correctly) as fear; he would have given up the small chance of pretending he was so drunk (and thus harmless) that he had not even noticed them, without putting any real barrier in the way of their possible attack. By acting like prey, he would ensure that he became it.

Next, he thought about turning back up the ill-lit little road and returning to the main street of Shepherd's Bush. He could mime having forgotten something, for example. But this U-turn would be so shamefully blatant a flight, so undeniable a blow to his hominid pride and sense of self, that he was not sure that he could face the sheer truth of it, even in his current pride-stripped state.

The last two months had not been kind to Marley.

There was no hope now of his ever getting the two million pounds. He had visited every no-win no-fee solicitor in Shepherd's Bush and found that none of them, knowing how many QCs, and how eminent, would represent Channel Seven, thought his case worth risking their time for, however great the potential earnings. The consolation prize of media attention and lucrative sales of ghost-written articles about *How I Survived Green Hell* or even *How I was robbed!* was not to be either, because the public, fed on a diet of allegedly important would-be stars doing supposedly extraordinary stage-managed things on so-called reality shows for so long, had leaped at the chance to read about the Colonists, about genuinely unusual people to whom something truly remarkable had actually happened for once.

For the first few days, Marley's tale had been buried in endless emotive family dramas, as distant cousins were united, long-forgotten wills reopened and trust funds thrown into turmoil by incorrect suppositions of death. But all this, in its turn, had been forgotten when the Headmaster, having spent an evening or two at his old club in the company of the Senior Editor of the *Intelligencer* and several influential figures, and upon learning that the Conservative Party under its present leader was judged to have no chance whatever in the coming election, had declared his intention to oppose the Prime Minister (to whom he had taken an instant and highly personal dislike) if the Party would immediately accept him as its chief.

The Party faithful had quickly forced their parliamentary representatives to accept. The Headmaster, having had a mere three weeks to campaign, had done so on the simple slogan *Let Us Sort Things Out* and had resolutely refused to set out a single policy other than that of common sense and decency. This tactic had at first merely amused the Prime Minister's clever Best Friend, but had resulted in the memorable live television exchange, considered by many seasoned observers to have swung the result, in which the Prime Minister's mocking attack had rebounded disastrously.

—But sorry, I mean, come on, what exactly do you *mean* by common sense and decency? What do you mean by *sorting things out*? These are just empty phrases.

—Yes, old boy, I suppose *you'd* hardly know, would you? *I* know what common sense and decency are, and *I* know what needs sorting out, and the people of England know, and if the Prime Minister doesn't, God help us.

Any boy in any school of mine who didn't know what those things meant would get six, and if you ever dare come to my study alone so will you, you two-faced, pompous little shit.

The spontaneous laughter and cheers from the studio audience which had greeted this vision first alerted the Prime Minister's Best Friend to the possibility of disaster, but, like every avalanche, this one was only audible when it was too late. Support rolled in irresistibly from the press, the City and the Services. Some people complained that the official mailing of its three million members by the National Trust at the last minute, with a scarcely disguised plea from the Duke of Norfolk to vote for the Headmaster, was not really fair, but older observers recalled the time when the BBC satire *That Was The Week That Was* had done much the same on Harold Wilson's behalf. This could not, though, have accounted for the entire swing to the Headmaster. No one really knew the reason. Perhaps it was the fact that the Chancellor's *ongoing downturn* in the property market was still going on down; perhaps it was because the Headmaster was the first Prime Ministerial candidate since Churchill who could be photographed addressing Guardsmen in some foreign hotspot, from the turret of a tank, without appearing ridiculous; or perhaps England was simply bored and fed up and ready for change, as it had been in 1945 and 1979 and 1997. It might also have been the speech which the Headmaster made in his last Party Political Broadcast, a plain, undecorated address in which the Headmaster was flanked by the entire England World Cup-winning rugby squad, who had endorsed him to a man after a brief meeting during which it turned out that the Headmaster had played for the army at number seven and had missed his own England cap in 1954 simply because he had been otherwise occupied in the jungles of Borneo.

Well, here we are. It is near on fifty years since myself and my friends were shot down by that Communist fighter. For all those years we believed that England was engaged in a life-and-death struggle with a potent and deadly enemy, that England was, once again, forced to lay herself, and her sons and daughters, between that enemy and his wicked dream. What was the enemy's dream? we thought. Why, the same dream that all of England's mighty enemies have had, of course, since the great Spanish Armada appeared off the coast of Devon. The dream of Philip II of Spain, of King Louis of France, of Napoleon Bonaparte, of Kaiser Bill, of Adolf Hitler, of Joseph Stalin. The dream of a Continental Empire, encompassing all of Europe, dominating all the world. That is the foe which, in our little jungle clearing, we believed England was once more fighting, perhaps had died fighting, perhaps, with her loyal cousins and powerful allies, the old Commonwealth, and the United States of America, was fighting still, tooth and claw, for freedom.

And we thought that England might need us. That was what kept us going. That is why we did not go to the dogs. So that we would be there, if England needed us.

Well, we are back, and it may well seem that we were wrong. It may seem that we had been saving ourselves, aye, and training ourselves too, for a battle which was fought and won without us. After all, the Red dream of Socialist Empire has been defeated, not indeed by force of arms, though the eternal and implacable readiness to arms was vital, but by the forces of its own sheer impossibility. Surely our country, which we in our little tropical redoubt, our little corner of England, thought embattled, is in reality safe and sound, its borders unmenaced, its skies undarkened, its people secure?

No, we were not wrong. England is indeed in danger, mortal danger, not of defeat merely, but of extinction itself! Our Parliament, the Mother of Freedom, soon to be merely a subordinate talking-shop, our forces, the finest in the world, to be instructed by a cabal of so-called generals from Luxembourg and Belgium, our once-proud youth, whose grandfathers defeated the dark legions of the Nazi SS or smashed twenty times their own number of the Communist hordes at the Imjin River, intoxicating itself, week in, week out, into swinish, drugged oblivion in order to escape the grey vista of an aimless future. Perhaps we were the lucky ones. Our lives in our little jungle clearing, far from home, never knowing if we would see England again, were hard, spartan, and sometimes short, yes, but perhaps we were indeed the lucky ones. We few escaped what the rest of us, what you, our brothers and sisters, were made to endure. Shall I say the words? Do we ever want to hear them again?

I am afraid I must say those words. The sixties. The seventies, dear God. The drip of hopelessness. The creeping malaise that strips the heart. The despair of betterment. The waking up each day to find that those in power have allowed yet another value to go lost, yet another idiocy to be embraced, yet another self-evident truth to be denied, yet another corruption to go unpunished, yet another, and yet another, and yet another *question to be fudged*. And now, here we are, it is the third millennium, and still it goes on, and on. Yes, we were indeed the lucky ones, because we were allowed to keep our belief. Our belief in honesty and decency. Our belief in ourselves.

Our belief in England. And we have kept it. And we keep it still. And we know that in your hearts of hearts, you, like our proud rugby team, share that belief. Come with us. Believe, with us. And with God's help, together, for England's sake, *let us sort things out*.

Eighty-three per cent of all eligible voters over the age of forty turned out, on a rainy day in early April, in every English county south of Chester. So that was that, of course. Following a number of speedy (but vain) attempted defections from the former front ranks of the New Labour Party, the Headmaster had found it rational to rename his administration the National Government. Life since then had become interesting in England.

Not, though, to Brian Marley. He had scarcely noticed the election. What difference did it make to him? It was just politics. All he wanted was to earn his living and make a home for Tommy. Hoping to regularise his future earnings pattern and get a pension, he had applied to retrain as a proper schoolteacher. He found, however, that politics is hard to ignore, because teaching, which for as long as Marley could remember had been the last resort for Englishmen who thought themselves too intellectually distinguished for mere productive work but could find no one else who shared this opinion of them, had suddenly become a highly desirable job.

The National Government had immediately introduced into every school at least one full-time specialist disciplinarian, ranking equal with an assistant head, generally of military background (—*Better an MC than an MA*, as the Headmaster put it), who had the power immediately to exclude any pupil over the age of thirteen and transfer them to the care of the local Prison Service, with no appeals to anyone. Two hours' PT a day had been prescribed by law for all schoolchildren (which naturally meant several hours' work a week less for all other teachers). School dinners had been made compulsory and a uniform menu adopted across the country, consisting simply of a daily, nourishing stew of meat or fish and vegetables, the recipe for which had been passed as kosher and halal by the respective bearded authorities, who had recognised, in the Headmaster's doubt-free green eyes, bristling moustaches and complete lack of any discriminatory instinct whatever, a man worthy of treating with. (—*I've fought alongside many men*, he had said in his first post-election news conference. —*White, brown, black, yellow and most of the mixed-up stuff in between, and I'm damned if I care what name a man calls his God, provided he is scared of that God and nothing else on earth, and I'm damned if I care what colour his hide is, provided he is willing to risk it, with a smile on his face, for Queen and country. But I will not be the Headmaster of a place that is breeding up a generation of fat-arsed layabouts whose only gods are their stomachs and wallets and whose only heroes are a shower of grinning young chorus girls and gigolos prancing about on the idiots' bloody lantern.*) Finally, all schools had been reconstituted as Partnerships, along the lines of NHS medical practices, many subordinate duties, such as the keeping of registers, had been devolved to semi-trained staff, and Teaching Partners were to wear their gowns whenever they entered a classroom. The Headmaster himself was known occasionally to descend on a school without any prior warning, cane in hand, caring nothing for any directives by anyone on the use of corporal punishment. Teaching once again had status and the teacher-training courses were all full to the brim, especially now that everyone knew they had been stripped completely of the hideous sociological guff which the last four decades of trainee teachers had been forced to endure. No one wanted a forty-something EFL teacher thank you very much. So that was that. Marley was doomed to teach English in England for the rest of his life.

He had thought about signing on instead, and devoting himself to his home improvements. It seemed quite an attractive option. But when Marley investigated his Social Security prospects, he found that things had changed here too. The National Government had abolished all benefits for healthy single people, using the money thus saved for massively increased early-years childcare schemes and for generous Child Benefits paid in the form of vouchers for specific Government-approved foods. The single unemployed were now assigned immediately to the Territorial Army or to the new Civic National Service programmes, where they were housed in barracks and spent their days planting oaks and beeches (this single policy had entirely won over the Green movement), mending hedgerows or digging pensioners' gardens in return for comradeship, healthy activity and another careful selection of food tokens. This had resulted in a large increase in applicants to the Army and a large decrease in the number of young, single foreign men appearing in England claiming to be at risk of their lives if they could not get in. In any case, even proving this risk would not have helped them for, as the Headmaster said, *if things are so ruddy iffy, what the devil is any fit young chap doing, buggering off from his country and leaving his sisters and mother in the lurch?* Single young men appearing in England, destitute, from countries where the National Government judged the regime to be Wrong, were henceforth to be given six weeks' military training and then sent back, if need be by parachute, under certain circumstances equipped with light weaponry and always armed with the Headmaster's personal assurance that HMG, and by extension NATO, would smile, developmentally and militarily, on any new regime once they had *damn well sorted things out for themselves.*

295

Marley had left the DYB office (that is, Do Your Bit, the new name for Jobcentres) and had stood in the street, dizzily aware that he had become mere history. The world had changed as swiftly as it had in the weeks when the Berlin Wall came down. Everything before suddenly seemed like the distant past, and Marley was part of *that*, not part of *this*. He had been left behind, that was all. His habitat had been lost, his climate had changed and, unable to adapt, he was evolutionarily doomed. And now, it seemed, he was physically doomed as well.

—Sod it then, said Marley to Marley. —Might as well get bloody beaten up.

Yes, a week or two in hospital would be quite restful, it would be almost like when he was back with the Colony, in bed, being tucked up by George . . .

George.

Consuela.

The names almost brought Marley to his knees, his head spun at the certainty of unimaginable loss.

—Pull yourself together, Marley, you contemptible little apology for a man and a father! snapped that well-known voice inside his head.

Yes. That was better. He would work and work and work, his one mission in life was to maintain some semblance of normality for Tommy until Tommy was old enough to want to strike out on his own, into his own, unknowable future, far away from the very minor socio-archaeological phenomenon that had been his father. He would do his duty, that was all. And part of his duty was to avoid getting the shit kicked out of him right now. He had to avoid a serious beating, whatever depths of play-acting or grovelling he had to embrace.

He looked up again to check that he was still fated to cross the paths of the four large men. He could only see them as shadows dappling against the sodium light, behind a tall privet hedge, but the vectors were unchanged and inevitable. As the men approached the junction of the two streets, the hedge on their side gave way to a waist-high wall. Now, Marley's primordial sensors were able to fully survey his potential aggressors, and what they found was very slightly relieving.

The four of them did not have that alarming, high-stepping, slightly spiky gait with that nasty hint of strut and roll; there were none of those too-quick movements of the head and neck as they swapped incomprehensible but audible comments, and the tones of their voices were long confident of their own bass depths, in no danger of breaking out into the hideous chimp-cackle of scarce-broken, unhousetrained youths. This was not so bad, then. They were men, yes, and they were all wearing dark leather jackets with many pockets, but they were not *young* men. They were adult bull-males, already established. They were still a band of males out late, true, but however skin-headed and aggressive they were, whatever reasons they might find to think Marley comical or unlikeable, any violence they offered would be merely to confirm their already won status. They could be anthropologically negotiated with. Marley would have to take a bad joke or two about his posh clothes and crawl slightly though undeniably, but probably the worst that would happen would be loss of face, maybe a slap or two and a scornful kick up his supposedly posh arse as he fled gratefully away. So much less dangerous than if it had been a genuine hunting party, a war pack of unproven youths out to test, show and feel their strength. The situation was not pleasant, not at all, but it would very probably not, after all, mean a staggering, blood-boltered trip to the nearest A & E ward.

The four men were almost at the corner now, and still on a collision course with him. Marley swallowed, kept his head down, started to whistle an old-fashioned, absurd tune, trying to radiate the general impression that he was absolutely without status and thus not worth bothering about. Then the men reached the corner, just before he did and, to Marley's surprise and deep discomfort, straight away spread out blatantly to stop him, in what amounted to a miniature parade-ground manoeuvre, covering the whole width of the pavement with a wall of heavy-built, confident manhood. And there they stopped, waiting for him. Their identical leather blouson jackets gleamed dully in the weak street light.

Marley had not expected anything like such decisive and well-oiled aggression. He felt his throat jam up all over again. He had been fatally wrong. He had missed out some vital part of the primeval calculation. This was now potentially very bad indeed. When a gang of fully-grown men actually decide, consciously choose and *decide* to attack another lone man, not in mere sudden teenage obedience to some dim, testosterone-driven instinct but as a deliberate enactment of their power, things are not going to stop at a few half-aimed kicks. Marley kept his head down and tried to hold on to rationality.

What could they want? Why had they picked on him? Visions of male gang rape, of methodical carving-up, of slow death in some basement den, slipped greasily between the shutters of his mind. This was very bad indeed.

A hard, black object was slapped against one of their palms. And another. Then stillness. The silence eventually compelled Marley to risk a glance upwards. On all the four jackets he saw the initials *NFR*. A powerful torch blinded him, and he looked quickly down again, to avoid both the beam of light and any dangerous eye contact.

At this point he saw that all four of the men were wearing big, long khaki shorts with perfectly creased turn-ups, thick, grey, knee-high woollen socks with small red tabs hanging smartly from the turn-downs, and heavy, polished black brogues.

—'Ello, sir, they said as one.

Marley laughed aloud with relief.

—Evening, sir. Sorry? Sorry, something funny, sir?

—No, God, no, no, sorry, it's just that I'd completely forgotten about the Neighbourhood Foot Reserve patrols.

—Forgotten? Where you been, sir?

—Oh, just, I've been very busy, you know.

—Not one of them as don't *like* the NFR, are you, sir?

—No, God. Hi. Brian Marley, I'm visiting my mother, she lives just up the road, number 48. Um, I, er, don't think we've met.

—Evenin', neighbour. Nah, don't think we have met. Don't mind if we ask to see your ID card?

—Um, no, well, of course.

Marley smiled vaguely, and began to search his pockets for his passport.

—Lovely evening, he said.

—It certainly is, neighbour.

Spring was indeed well in the air, the daffodils were already wilting, the blossom already out on the fruit trees, but this spring was not merely one of climate. England was basking in itself, admiring itself with a touch of incredulity, its half-disbelieving self-examination encouraged by the hordes of foreign media representatives who, whether they approved or not of recent events, showed indubitably, merely by their presence and their stunned fascination, that at last, for the first time since the Falklands, England was doing something that really mattered in the world again. Yes, there was a real spring in England's step once more.

As Marley searched his pockets with gradually increasing worry and felt the first metallic pre-taste of

299

panic rise at the sides of his mouth, three of the Neighbourhood Foot Reserve patrol stood relaxed before him. They were all stout and fit mortgage-holders over twenty-six, as the Law required them to be, and were unpaid save in respect among their fellows, in the warm consciousness of zeal and in the knowledge that their car-insurance premiums were substantially lower, and the values of their homes noticeably higher, because they lived in a registered NFR area. They were armed only with large metal torches but, Marley knew, were also equipped with radio panic buttons connected to, and electronically traceable by, the nearest police station. This would ensure an immediate response from the regular police, who had far more time for chasing really dangerous people now that Home Secretary Devereux's reforms had relieved them of most deterrent patrols and almost all paperwork. The fourth member of the patrol, the Recorder, filmed the whole proceeding with his little digital infrared-lit camera, which was (as a prominent, luminous sticker proclaimed) the property of the police. This camera, Marley now recalled, had an unalterable time-code display which was burned into every disk used by every patrol; each patrol was obliged to film the whole two-hour tour of their streets from beginning to end and hand the disk in to their local police station at the end of their duty, on pain of imme-diate disbanding. It was supposed to make the public feel that no abuse of the new system could ever happen, but Marley could not help feeling an uncomfortable sense of lurking guilt.

—She lives just up the road, you see. My mother. Number 48.

—Yeah, you said, sir. Nice to see a bloke visiting his old mother, even this late. You 'ave *got* your ID, haven't you, neighbour?

—Yes, of course, just let me . . . Ah! Here, sorry about

that, he laughed, relieved. The first NFR man looked at Marley's slim red EU passport for some seconds. Then, silently, he passed it on to his comrades and looked up again, steady and slow.

—Fought you said you 'ad a ID card, sir?

—Well, no, but I mean, ha, my passport's still just as good. Um, isn't it?

—'Aven't you *got* a ID card, sir?

—But, I, my passport's just as good. Isn't it? Still? repeated Marley, idiotically.

—Oh yeah, sir, that's quite all right. Still *legal* for a good month. But you should really get a ID card, you know.

—*I'm Doing* my bit, are you doing yours? said the second patroller, jokingly wagging a figure at Marley as he quoted the well-known slogan from the National Government's poster campaign.

—Still, you don't look much like a illegal immigrant to me, I got to admit.

—Ha ha ha.

—Not finking of running off to the EU, were you, sir?

—Ha ha ha.

—God, no, laughed Marley overloudly.

—Not Welsh or Scots, are you, sir?

—No, God.

—It's just, some Taffs and Jocks want to hang on to their old UK EU passports. Dunno why. Fink they can appeal to the European Court of Human Rights or somefink.

—Ha ha ha.

—No, no, said Marley, —I just, you know, haven't, got round to swapping it yet. I'm English. Completely English. I've been meaning to get an ID card, I'll do it tomorrow.

—Well, it just feels so much more *English*, don'it, sir?

301

It did indeed. The new English ID card was rather more than a mere card. It was a substantial affair, deliberately large, dark blue and leather-bound, in order, so Home Secretary Devereux had declared, *to give a chap a sense of pride again when he feels it sitting there in his pocket. As it shall henceforth do at all times in all public places.* This ID card was not only larger than the red EU passports, but was soon to replace them entirely, for England had withdrawn from the EU ten days before.

It had been England only which had withdrawn, for when the Welsh and Scots Nationalists and their allies had mounted a constitutional objection to the UK's withdrawal (backed, of course, by the French), the National Government in London had unilaterally declared Wales and Scotland to be independent, Ireland to be reunited and itself henceforth to be simply the Government of England, Anguilla, Bermuda, the British Antarctic Territory, the British Indian Ocean Territory, the British Virgin Islands, the Cayman Islands, the Falkland Islands and Dependencies (South Georgia and South Sandwich Islands), Gibraltar, Monserrat, Pitcairn, Henderson, the Ducie and Oeno Islands, St Helena and Dependencies (Ascension and Tristan da Cunha), and the Turks and Caicos Islands. The British Commonwealth had been dissolved, but most present members had already applied to join the new English Language Community.

Queen Elizabeth had at first been inclined to mount a spirited defence of the UK, but, faced with the sudden and suspicious enthusiasm of her son for the Celtic Rim, and it having been pointed out to her that her beloved position as Monarch of Scotland was in any case hereditary and hence constitutionally independent of the Act of Union and that no one really knew how, when, why or indeed whether England and Wales had ever truly been united in the first place, she had quickly and publicly

302

agreed to the new arrangement. For a heady two days or so, Edinburgh, Cardiff, Belfast and Dublin had hummed with the expectation of vast financial support from Europe (Paris had clearly hinted they would get it) and of some liberal uprising in their favour from within England itself. Neither had been forthcoming, nor would they now be, for within the past few days the German electorate had realised that with England out, they would now have to foot the bill for every olive grove in Greece, every dairy farm in Normandy and every sugar beet in Poland. Berlin had demanded an immediate and complete end to the CAP, at which a drunken French delegate had accused Germany of wanting to enact genocide on French farmers and an impassioned Italian member had reminded his large constituency that many of their grandfathers had been massacred by Germans in 1944. In order to save its own skin from popular outrage, the German Government had yesterday followed the example of England and seceded from the EU. And so that was that. The German Chancellor was negotiating bilateral trade and defence agreements with the Headmaster, under the aegis of NATO, and most of the smaller countries of Europe were clamouring to follow suit. The larger ex-members were not in good shape: France had, as usual in its history, greeted the discomfiture of a grand foreign policy by relapsing into virtual civil war; Spain was swiftly re-examining notions of a transatlantic Hispanic culture; and three different Italian governments had been sworn in and brought down in the last week. Ireland alone, among the formerly keen states of Europe, had experi-enced an unexpected dividend from England's depar-ture, because the Loyalists of Northern Ireland did not know who they were supposed to be loyal *to* if the UK had ceased to exist. They knew very well that they were not wee sneaking perfidious Englishmen, but to claim homicidal overseas loyalty to an independent Scotland was too obviously absurd even for them. So they gave up and admitted they might be some kind of Irishmen after all, uniting that green little land in self-government for the first time in eight hundred years. After the initial euphoria had worn off, however, Dublin realised that now it could no longer offer German and Dutch firms tax evasion within the EU and had been shorn of the massive UK subsidies to the North, it was going to be in deep shit. Together with Wales and Scotland (both bankrupt, racked by linguistic and sectarian strife respectively), Ireland was frantically trying to establish what they called the Federation of the Anglo-Celtic Archipelago. London had so far shown no interest whatever in the project.

—Oh yes, Mrs Marley at number 48, nodded the first patroller, at last finding Marley's name in the despised little reddish booklet. —We've just been sorting out her noisy neighbours for her. Lot of nice sound-system gear we impounded back there. Should make a good few bob for the Headmaster's Charitable Fund at the next NFR seizures auction.

—Oh, great, thanks, said Marley.

—Don't mind showing us what you've got in your pockets, do you, Mr Marley? Of course you don't.

The second patroller held out a stout bag of fine nylon mesh and the cameraman closed in somewhat as Marley emptied his pockets out in order to show that he was not carrying duty-evaded tobacco, proscribed drugs, or more than one hundred pounds in cash. This last was, of course, illegal now that the Headmaster, with the vocal support of the banks and the tax authorities, had introduced his new anti-drugs legislation, under which anyone carrying more than one hundred pounds in cash was deemed, by that act, to have themselves provided the prima facie case for an immediate police search of their homes, cars and bodily orifices without the need for any further warrant. While this measure was deeply unpopular among taxi drivers and members of the building trades, no one could reasonably deny the force of the Headmaster's argument: *Look here, when did you last hand over more than a hundred pounds in cash, eh? Unless you were hoping they'd knock the ruddy VAT off? Come on, let's stop whingeing and get on with driving the drugs out of town.*

Marley, it turned out, was carrying £15.73, so that was all right. The patrollers decided that judging by his dress, age and general demeanour, there was no need to ask him to take an on-the-spot multi-drugs test. Anyone who was asked politely to do this by a Neighbourhood Foot Reserve patrol, and who was filmed refusing, was liable to immediate Neighbourhood Arrest followed by exhaustive and intrusive custodial testing by the police themselves, under the new laws which had declared that the mere *actus reus* of Being Under the Influence of Proscribed Substances outside of one's principal abode would henceforth constitute a criminal offence, and that this Strict Liability should extend, with penalties of property seizure available, to any owner, part-owner or shareholder of any residence or conveyance where three or more people, or any non-residential land or premises where ten or more people had been found to have gathered under such influence. The National Government had shown its seriousness in this matter the previous Friday night, by sending in five hundred police officers with dogs, backed up by two companies of the Grenadier Guards, to stop, search and test every person in the Ministry of Sound club at 2 a.m. Several thousand people had been formally cautioned and informed convincingly that they were for the high jump if ever caught again. In the past few days, hundreds of clubs up and down the country had declared that they would not be opening for the foreseeable future, since everyone knew that none of their countless sub-genres of dance music were of the remotest interest to anybody who was not taking the requisite drug. Tickets to the next Glastonbury Festival were widely available at well below face price, but all flights to Corfu and Ibiza were booked for months to come. England had become a quiet place once more. Even the morning milk-delivery round was coming back now that one could reasonably expect one's milk not to be pinched by gangs of thirsty young people wandering the streets at 5 a.m.

—Thanks for stopping, sir, said the first patroller, and —*Safe home, neighbour*, the whole patrol chorused, as they strode off again on their ever-varied path around their own, well-known streets.

—Ha, yes, thanks, said Marley.

*

The newly unmothballed Army barracks in Kent was cold, clammy and fart-ridden. And yet not, in its way, unmerry.

—The Sarge said we'll get the first six fuckin' pints free. On the Government.

—An' the Corporal said there's loads of birds in Maidstone gaggin' for it. Albanian tarts, an' all.

—If we make the fuckin' grade tomorrow.

—Course we'll fuckin' make it.

—If it fuckin' kills us.

—Fuckin' hell, the Sarge is a hard cunt.

—But he's fuckin' fair.

—I s'pose.

—Hey, Macksie, you remember when you called him 'sir' first day here?

—Ha ha ha.

—Ha ha ha.

306

The largest of the five youths who had been sent here together the week before grinned and sucked on his night-light fag as he started to tell again his well-known story to his happy sidekicks.

—Yeah, fuckin' right. *Don't call me 'sir', you little cunt,* he says, *I earned these three fuckin' stripes and no little cunt is going to call me a fuckin' wanker now.*

—Ha ha ha.

—Fuckin' great.

—*You call me 'Sergeant', you little cunt, save the fuckin' 'sir' for Lieutenant the honourable Rupert Montmorency de fuckin' up the arse Villiers-Smythe or some other wanker. Now you can give me fifty and clean out the shithouse or we can fight it out here right now, no ranks no reports no comeback.*

—An' you fuckin' did, Macksie. You 'ad a fuckin' go.

—I fuckin' did too. Kicked the fuckin' shit out of me, he did.

—All right to us after that, he was, though.

—Yeah. Tell you what, boys, I thought I'd fuckin' hate this place. I thought fuck that, I did. But I don't mind it now, me. See their faces when we marched down the town this morning? Fuckin' nice, that was.

—Here, Macksie, what you reckon to the stuff they're saying, about how we're goin' to get sent over to have a crack at the French cops if they don't let our lorries go?

—Sooner the fuckin' better, mate. Fuckin' French cunts. Me, I want to win my first stripe. Roll on fuckin' Friday, mind. First six pints free! Right, I'm going to score some fuckin' sleep. Any cunt that wakes me up with his wankin' I'll cut his fuckin' cock off.

—Ha ha ha.

—Ha ha ha. G'night.

—G'night.

*

307

As Marley approached the little steps that led down to the door of his mother's flat, he wondered who the hell round here could afford the vast, low, British-racing-green Bentley, the latest model, parked at the kerbside, all curves and chrome and wire mesh and other such references to the great designs of the late fifties. Christ, to think that he too could have had one of those cars, if only those bastards at Channel Seven had . . . No, no, no, that was pointless. All gone. But he could not resist patting it wistfully, even so, as he passed it by.

—Goes like shit off a shovel, old boy, I can tell you. Must say cars have got a *lot* better while we were away.

Marley froze, and only after some long seconds dared looked down to where the voice had issued up, as if from the bowels of the earth itself. In his mother's doorway, the Headmaster was knocking out his pipe on his heel. Behind him, Mrs Marley was standing, looking as if she had just emerged from a mental wind tunnel, her eyes shining, her smile rigid, absently holding the old black-and-white photograph of Marley's father before her chest as if it were some sort of religious icon.

—Headmaster. I mean, Prime Minister. I mean, Headmaster.

—Thanks for the sherry, Mrs Marley, and for showing me the picture. Took me right back. Fine grandson you've got there. I'll bring your son back to you in half a mo, just need to have a little chat.

—Yes, yes, of course, she said.

—Mum, I mean, Mummy, is that OK, I mean, are you . . .?

—Yes, yes, of course, she repeated blindly. —Off you go.

—Hop in then, Marley. In the front. I always drive myself, you know, and I'm damned if I tell my security chaps where I'm going most of the time. Don't hold with all this ruddy mollycoddling. I drive where I want and I walk where I want and I go into any school I damn well like, and if anyone wants to bump me off, they can have a crack if they like, I carry my old service revolver and if I'm quicker on the draw than they are they'll end up singing castrato, eh? I've had a decent innings as it is. Don't bother with the seat belt, old boy, buggered if I ever do.

Marley sat cautiously on the vast leather seat. The squeak and smell reminded him of his youth. He reached dreamily forward and touched real, solid wood on a car dashboard for the first time in thirty-five years.

—What do you, I mean, um, why are you, is there something . . .? he began.

—Fine woman, your mother, very sound on the question of television. She was very pleased when I told her we're banning all popular music and all presenters under the age of twenty-six on children's programmes. Channel Seven are going to lose their operating licence tomorrow, by the way. Simply not high enough standards, we decided. And far too pally with the last lot at Number 10. Thought you might enjoy that. Your mother certainly did. You know, Marley, I keep finding it quite extraordinary, the way people react to us. It's as if no one's actually been *listening* to what people *want* for years, in England. Just gassing with their ghastly West End cronies in the papers and on the box. Very strange. Still, that's all over now, eh? Ah, here's the Neighbourhood Foot Reserve, good show, glad to see them stopping all comers.

—Evening, neighbour, thank you for stoppin', sir, very nice motor if I may say so, don't see many of them about, don't mind if we ask to see your . . . Crikey, sorry, sir, Headmaster, sir.

—Not at all. Doing a splendid job. It'll be noted. I'll be off then.

—Yes sir Headmaster sir.

The vast car pulled seamlessly away.

—Good idea, those chaps, eh? Doing the world of good if I say so myself. Now then, old boy, let's get down to business.

—I haven't told anyone about the heads on sticks, honestly I haven't.

—I've decided you need a job, Marley.

—A job?

—A place, rather. In the FO.

—The Foreign Office?

—Yes. You'll be Second Secretary to the Committee for the Special Relationship.

—Me? But I don't, I mean . . .

—Oh, don't worry, we're not looking for some damn clever little boffin. It's a bit of a cushy number, frankly. Staff posting back at HQ, if you see what I mean. The boodle's no more than par for a middle-ranking office wallah but they say the pension's good, if you care about that sort of thing.

Marley did not turn his head. In the corner of his eye he could see the Headmaster's eagle-like profile in the soft glow from the big white dials. He cleared his throat and looked straight ahead, out into the night.

—Is this, I mean, is this because I didn't, you know, *bleat*? About the heads on the sticks, I mean?

—Good God no, old boy, laughed the Headmaster. —Never thought for a moment you would. And we'd know if you *had*, eh? No, no, not worried about anybody *bleating*. Not any more. Of course, you don't know, do you? We had the Army in there at first light on day one of my administration. Turns out there was some rather hush-hush gadgetry on board the Flight, that's why the Reds shot us down. Wouldn't want that getting out, eh? And we want to get things ready for the well-heeled tourist. Extraordinary, we had a mob of bizarre-looking young

310

people banging on in Trafalgar Square about our new heli-port damaging an indigenous culture. The last lot left us some very useful special police powers, so we'll give them what for if they hold up the traffic again. Isn't that the most absolute drivel you heard in your life, Marley? For God's sake, the Roman bloody Empire went west, and our own too, come to that, and mankind seems to be jogging along quite merrily, so I can't for the life of me see what's so important about a couple of blasted mud huts, can you? Sentimental hogwash. Where was I, Marley?

—The Army at the Colony. Preparing it for tourists.

—Yes, yes, of course. They're generally *cleaning the place up a bit* while they're at it. Good man in charge, distant cousin of mine as it turns out, learned his stuff as a young chap in Londonderry, very sound. All ready for the tourists now. So you see, if anyone tried to make a name for himself by having a drink too many with some damned bolshie scribbler and talking subversive rot about what went on there, well, he'd just be making trouble for himself, wouldn't he? Not that anyone will, of course, eh? We're *we* people, Marley, not *me* people, and we think of you quite as *one of us*. Well, what do you say?

—Oh. Well, I mean, a job, God, um, well . . .

—George is expecting, old boy, and it's yours.

—George? Expecting?

—Yes, she's rather chuffed about it. Seems she was right about needing new stock from England. Perhaps the old gene pool *was* getting a bit murky out there, rather my own fault I suppose. Anyway, the point is she's having your child. Obviously, you'll marry her.

—Sorry?

—I assume you want to give your child a father and your name, Marley?

—Well, yes, of course, but, I mean, does George, does she want, does she . . .?

311

—She wants a decent place and her child's father for her child, of course, old boy.

—But I don't know if we, I mean, she and I, whether we . . .

—Look here, Marley, I hope you're not going to spout any damn middle-class rot about love and marriage?

—Well, no, I mean, yes, I mean, well . . .

—Never understood that rot. Love's a damn fine thing and no man who hasn't risked a knife in the bazaar for a crack at his girl is a man in my book, and marriage is a damn good institution and my Government is backing it to the hilt, but only mooning poets and spineless clerks get them mixed up. I don't suppose for a moment George intends to be your regular middle-class Kent memsahib, far too much spirit, but who the hell would want that anyway? I'm sure the two of you will work things out in a pally sort of way, not scare the horses, *pas devant les enfants*, that sort of thing, eh? Of course you will. Now, old George hasn't got a bean, of course, just what Jimmy pays her, though I believe her cousin is going to let her have some half-decent old rectory or other on his land, so we thought we'd better set you up in a quiet sort of way. Never realised how many plums a PM can dish out on the QT, but I must say it's coming in rather handy, what with my blasted offspring all needing a leg-up now we're home. Anyway, this one's yours, old boy, congratulations and all that, here's the bumf if you can be bothered reading it.

Marley took from the Headmaster a large, stout manila envelope marked FOREIGN OFFICE and turned it stupidly in his hands several times before taking out a contract printed in impressive characters on snowy, weighty paper. He tried to read it but the letters merely danced and swam about on the blinding-white vellum, waltzing with Agas and rectories and orchards and George's blue eyes,

312

a crazed whirl of unlooked-for, late-come hope, echoing to the sound of the Headmaster's voice.

—You won't have to turn up every day at half past nine, naturally, we don't hold with that nonsense. In fact, you wouldn't have much on your plate if you *did* turn up every day, to be quite frank. So I shouldn't worry about it too much if I were you. We'll let you know if there's a flap on and we need chaps to come up and man the trenches, but I don't suppose there will be. Just sign there, old boy. Hello, Marley, are you asleep, man?

—No, no, I just, look, this is all a bit sudden, I mean, can I have a think about it?

—A think about what, old boy?

—I don't know, I just, a think, I . . .

—You're on the books as active and drawing pay from today. Your first salary should be in your bank next week.

—Oh. Um, sorry, how did you get my bank details?

—How? We're the *Government*, old boy. Funny question.

—I just, I just want some time to think.

—Look here, Marley, George is pregnant. What's to *think* of? And we're offering to make you *really* one of us. Frankly, I don't know that I'm terribly pleased that you have to think about it once, never mind twice. Perhaps you really did mean all this rot?

—Rot? What rot?

—This rot, Marley, this rot.

Marley felt himself quite clearly turn white as the Headmaster produced a digital minidisk.

No, oh God no, it wasn't possible, he had burned the camera, he had seen it melt and catch fire, it was all gone, all burned, it was . . .

—Your queer pal Brodie on the telly brought it back from the Colony. His security chaps found it in your little camera. Which then disappeared. I wonder where it went, don't you? Really, Marley, have you any idea what damn Red rot

313

you were talking? No? No, I thought not, of course, although Devereux did wonder. Let's take a look, shall we? Sit back, old boy. Got all sorts of wizard gadgets in this jalopy. There, in it goes. Are we all sitting comfortably? Then let's begin.

Marley sat carefully back and swallowed hard. In the Bentley's vast, polished walnut dashboard, a small screen lit up.

*

—Well, I think tweed suits you wonderfully, Grant. And I *love* the brogues.

—I should think so, they cost a bloody fortune. God, Tamsin, do you know what I feel like, going out like this, at *one in the morning*, ha ha, I can't believe it!

—What do you feel like?

—Nervous. Me, nervous again! Thank God. I feel so *wicked*, grrrr! Christ, this feels so *right* somehow.

—I know. Such a *relief*, in a way. All those years of trying to be half-baked Californians. My Icelandic poet says he feels quite at home in England, nowadays. I must get back to him, the poor little iceberg.

—*You? Going home?* At *one*?

—Yes, funny, isn't it? But actually, it's because I'm going to have a baby.

—*You? A baby?*

—Yes, funny, isn't it? We're going to have a few, actually. It's really almost *lucrative* these days, you know. I must say I can't fault the Government on that.

—Oh my God, Tamsin, are you sure? You'll never be able to go out again.

—Well, I was getting rather fed up with it, to be honest. I only kept on doing it because everyone else was. And now, I don't know, it just feels as if everything's changed suddenly. The Zeitgeist or whatever you call it. It's a bit like the way all those Hungarians and Ulster Loyalists and

Russians all stopped breeding, as if someone told them it just wasn't worth it any more. Only the other way round. It seems worth it, for some reason, now. No, you go on and celebrate, I'm going home to drink Horlicks and brood in peace. And the terrible thing is, when I say that, I'm all sort of *excited* about it. Will you be all right here?

—God yes. This is absolutely thrilling. Look, him, over there, I'm *sure* he is. He must be. He looked at me. And that dinner jacket, it's *so* camp, no he's *got* to be. Oh my God, it's Lucas. I didn't recognise him at all, out of leather. *Hel-lo, Lucas, old boy!*

—Hello, Grant. Very smart. Hello, Tamsin, *love* the twinset.

—Did you tie that bow tie yourself, Lucas?

—Of course, old man, God, what do you take me for, some kind of pinko homo? There was an article about how to tie them in *Real Men* last week, actually, major nightmare, took me hours to learn it. But I think it worked in the end. Or doesn't it?

—It's great. God this is fun, isn't it, Lucas?

—Bloody wonderful. It's like a fucking masked ball or something. I don't recognise anyone at all. It makes things all so lovely and secret and brave. I mean, you can't be *quite* sure, can you? Funny, isn't it? All these years of dark rooms and complicated games, and all the time it was staring us in the face: the ultimate perversion is repression.

—I know, no wonder the Victorians conquered half the world. They must have been bloody terrifying.

—Well, must toddle off to the bar. What's your poison, old boy? Stop it. Don't you *dare* giggle, Grant, the whole *thing* is to keep a straight face and a tight pelvic floor.

—Goodnight, boys. Leave you to it.

—Goodnight, Tamsin darling. Happy breeding.

*

—*Daddy here*, the disk began, with the little flat screen softly lighting up the car's dark interior and glowing bright in the Headmaster's eyes. Marley saw himself in the jungle, a horrible wreck, filthy and dying in the hideous green half-light.

—Daddy here. Not much time now. I, well, I, er, look, I'm sorry I missed Christmas with you, sweetheart. But really, I just wanted to explain to you why you haven't got a daddy. A dad. For God's sake, pull yourself together, man, OK, OK. There, I'm trying, I . . . You should have some money, anyway, that'll be more good to you than I would've been. Christ, though, I wish I could see you growing up. Teach you to ride a bike. Teach you to swim. Hear the things you say. Feel your hand growing bigger, till you stop wanting to hold hands and then one day shaking hands again and your hand stronger than mine. But if I'd stayed it wouldn't have been like that. You'd have seen I was a sad, useless waster, this was my last chance to have another chance and I blew that too and now I'm done for. Sorry, Christ, guts gone again, sorry, sorry . . . OK, the thing is, Tommy, look, you'll have a few bob behind you. A few bob. Shit, that's what they said when I was a boy, you see, and I still say it, no one under forty knows what the hell it means, I can't help it. Bob, funny. Look, I didn't mean to die. I meant to live. I was going to be a better person. For you, for Consuela. Ah, yes, Consuela. You'll never meet her now. Oh Christ, Consuela, sorry, Tommy, I can't help it. OK, that's better. Ugh, leeches, ptthw. Sorry. Look, Tommy, all I want to say is: please please please for Christ's sake don't buy a Georgian house or an Aga. Promise me? Oh shit, this is so unfair, I don't want to die now I've only just realised what

316

was wrong with my bloody life. Sorry. There. It's England that's wrong with me, Tommy. England. When I was a boy, Mum, your gran, I bet she won't admit it now but she used to say: England will never be free until there are oak trees growing in the ruins of Buckingham Palace. Ask her. I dunno. Maybe when you get this everything will be different. Oh shit, Christ, sorry, sorry, just couldn't breathe then for a sec. Tommy, Tommy, little Tommy, maybe it's just me and the stuff they still filled our heads with when we were kids, maybe you'll be fine and England will just be a normal bloody country and everyone will forget all that balls about it mattering how you talk and us being better than everyone else in the world, Christ, that would be good! Maybe that'll be your England. But I dunno, Tommy. Sometimes I think England is just too far gone. If I'd made it back I would have tried to get you away, so you wouldn't have to have that round your neck. We could've . . . ah, ooops, oh Christ, shit, sorry, ugh, hmmm, hard to get up. No, wait, don't go. I'm still here, wait a sec. Ohhhh God. Yeah, look, listen, Tommy, if I'm going to get this to you I'd better go now, before . . . you know. Sorry again, and goodbye. Just don't forget to live, that's all. I was so busy being English I nearly did. Hey, so at least I got somewhere, in the end, even if it was only here! Bye, Tommy. Love you.

The picture died. There was a church-like silence in the big, leather-smelling car. Marley tried to swallow without making any sort of noise. He failed, miserably. The Headmaster sniffed by way of reply.

—Extraordinary rot, Marley. Of course, one mustn't forget you weren't terribly well.

—I was ill, I was hallucinating, I was nearly dying, I . . .

—I'm surprised at your mother, I must say.

—She never said that, I didn't mean that, I was just, I was bitter, I was scared, it's rubbish, all of it, I was, yes, in a bad way, it's all, all, well, it's, yes, rot.

—Isn't it? Utter rot. Well, I'm so glad you think so too. And do you know, I think it wasn't just you, Marley. It seems to me there's been a lot too much rot about in England generally since we left. But now the old place has come back to her senses and so have you, eh? That's the spirit. So now we know where you stand, would you like to borrow my pen, old boy?

Marley thought of the green eyes again. He thought of skulls on sticks. He thought of his life as it was, and would now inevitably be. An English deal with George. No horses scared. Was that all there was? For a second he saw dark eyes again, alive with deep, big feelings.

But then he thought again, of a life where he would never have to worry seriously again about his bills or his mortgage or his job or his mother's old age or his son's future. Where he would have a beautiful wife admired by other men and another child to love. Where he would be free to think about, well, just to bloody *think* for once, to relax for once, to step back off the never-ending mouse-wheel and quietly decide what to do with his life, for once. And suddenly he broke into a grey, clammy sweat at the thought that he might lose all of that for nothing, for some vague, insane fear of the loss of freedom (*freedom for what, you mad, overgrown, teenage arsehole? Freedom to be poor? To be lonely? To be disregarded and despised?*), or for the loss of some emotional potential (*potential for what, Mr Profundity? Potential for whingeing? Potential for gazing deep into your own navel?*). Shit, he was actually about to do it again. About *not* to study law, about *not* to get a proper job straight after college, about *not* to get a mortgage and fix up a pension when he was young. All over again. Even now, at over forty, he had learned nothing about the sad reality of the world. Incredible: he was, quite seriously, at his age, still thinking about *not* marrying a gorgeous girl who was going to have his child. And why, for God's sake? Just because he did not think they actually *loved* each other. Insane! What the hell was wrong with him? Who did he think he was? Was it too late already, yet again?

—Yes, yes please, Headmaster, of course, ha, thanks, thanks very much, oh, nice pen, of course, it's just, wow, it's such a shock, you know, I, hold on . . .

—Here. There. And there. And there. Good man. That's your copy. And this one, yes, this is mine. Well, that's that then. Welcome on board.

—Er, thanks, er, Headmaster, sir. Ha.

—Pop in when you feel like it, no hurry at all. You'll want to call George, of course. Shouldn't do it tonight, she'll be asleep by now. Try her in the morning.

—Yes, of course, Headmaster. Oh, um, when I call in, to work, I mean, what office should I ask for . . . what was it again, the Committee for the Special Relationship?

—Oh yes, that. It's all in the bumf. Not public yet, still hush-hush, but you've signed the Official Secrets Act and you're one of us now, eh? Yes, the Yanks are pretty keen. They wanted us to run the EU for them, apparently, but now that's all rather fallen apart, we sat down with them to see if we couldn't sort out something a bit more solid. And do you know, I think we have. We'll be called *Old England*, you see.

—Old England?

—Rather fun, eh? We'll be the biggest single State in the Union, so we'll get at least as many Senators and what have you as New York and California, and then they'll have to chuck money at us before every election, which is pretty well all the time, the way they run things over there. I know it sounds a bit iffy at first, Marley, but

319

I mean to say, it's not as if we ever do anything much anyway without checking it out with them first, as things stand, is it? We can't, really, can we? Haven't been able to since the last show. Best to be honest about these things. Would have saved us an awful lot of trouble and money back in the fifties if we'd been honest with ourselves about where we really stood back then. You see, Marley, if you think about it, you'll find we'll be a damn sight freer and have a lot more clout as a state in America than in a United Europe. And this way, at least we'll be dealing with our own sort in our own language, not with the ruddy Frogs through wop interpreters. In fact, I think that this whole EU business was a pretty narrow squeak, don't you? 1805 and 1940 all over again, rather. So yes, we're going the whole hog with the Americans now. Just as Winston always wanted it, really. The Scots and Welsh will be desperate to follow suit, of course, and very welcome as far as I'm concerned provided they toe the line. Good chaps, so long as they don't forget who's in charge when push comes to shove.

—But, I mean, what about, well, the Queen and stuff?

—Oh, Her Majesty will stay on, of course. Good God yes. The Yanks love her. She'll be Queen of Old England, don't worry about that. They've got musty provisions for Indian Chiefs and that sort of thing in Yankland; there's no big constitutional issue. The Prince of Wales did think about banging on about it for a bit, apparently. He seemed to think that one of the papers would still give him the time of day even now, but Mama told him pretty sharpish that he'd find himself playing on a rather sticky wicket one way or another if he didn't put a sock in it. So he has.

—But do *they* want *us*?

—Well, yes, actually. Between ourselves, I think they rather like the notion of another thirty-odd million white-skinned, English-speaking voters. Might help them to *win*

America back, the President said. And we think that about a million of our, what do the boffins call them these days? Ah yes, *C1s*, well, our chaps reckon about a million of *them* will want to emigrate to Florida straight away so they can chew gum all day and drink Coca-Cola with that abominable sweet Yank whiskey in it. Each to his own, say I. The President and his family are very happy about *that*. Florida's a bit iffy for them, it seems, and they seem to think that your average English C1 is a natural GOP voter. The better sort of East Coast Yank will naturally want a decent Georgian pad in Old England, of course, to go with the family ranch in New England, the ones that haven't got one already, that is. So in the end, you see, we'll lose a whole army or two of our frankly rather scaly Other Ranks and get a few battalions of their top-notch chaps and girls who can appreciate a well-bred horse, a good shotgun and a stiff, peaty malt. Not a bad swap, I'd have thought. The Yanks are rubbing their hands rather at the thought of us jumping ship from Airbus to Boeing, of course. God, the Frogs will be hopping mad at that, eh? Our Services will get all the latest Yank gadgets and we'll supply chaps who won't insist on complete air supremacy and can take a few casualties if need be without banging on about it. The Canadians and Aussies and Kiwis are already thinking about coming in, too. And I can't see the Irish staying out for long either. I mean, why on earth would they, when half of New York claims to be Irish anyway? And very welcome, damn good soldiers. And of course, everyone's quite excited by the idea of us lot having the same immigration and asylum laws as the Yanks, which is to say, taking none of the buggers at all as far as I can tell.

—So . . .

—Exactly. So there we'll be, d'you see, Marley, just like the good old days. The whole tribe pulling together again.

321

Free trade among ourselves, no one much able to say *boo* to us when it comes to the ships and the men and the money and all that sort of thing and well, I mean to say, I should think that will be that, rather, as far as the world goes, for the foreseeable, shouldn't you?

—Well, I, I mean . . .

—As I said, no need to concern yourself too much with it really. And mum's the word pro tem, eh? Drop in when you feel up to it. On second thoughts, better phone first if you do decide to come, just to make sure your desk's ready, might take a while to find space for you. Tell you what, we'll call you when we need you, how about that? You speak a lot of foreign languages, don't you?

—How do you know that? Oh, yes, of course. You're the Government.

—You're getting the picture, old boy. Yes, I can see that might come in handy over at the FO, soothing the odd troubled dago brow over cocktails, you know the sort of thing. They *do* rather like being spoken to in their own jargon, don't they, even though they all speak perfectly good English. Silly, really. Perhaps we'll drag you in now and then for that sort of thing. Well, anyway, glad you made it through to us, Marley. God, I remember when you turned up, eh? We really thought England had bought it, up till then. Couldn't have been more wrong, as things turned out. Yes, you did your bit all right and it won't be forgotten. Keep in touch about the wedding day. I'll do my level best to be there for you and old George. We'll have a bit of a shindig, eh? Well, here we are, your mother's place. Have a drink to celebrate, why not? Say thanks again to your mother for me, will you? Very sound woman, I thought. Surprised if she really said that about Buck House. Still, as you said yourself, you were talking rot. That's the point. So let's just have no more rot, eh, old boy? Goodbye, Marley. And congratulations. Damn fine girl, George.

—Thanks. Goodbye, Headmaster.

Marley staggered from the big green car and watched it hush away into the darkness; the engine was eerily silent, but the vast, fat tyres gave off a strange ripping noise, as if a long sheet of vellum was being torn slowly in two.

—Well? said his mother, who, it seemed, had been waiting at her front door all this time. He turned to her, light-headed, his contract flapping heavily in his hand.

—Um, can we have some sherry, Mum? Something's come up.

*

—Was that fun, Harry?

—God, absolutely, George.

—Shall I call room service for more champagne, do you think?

—Do you think we should have *more*? I mean, if you're pregnant?

—No, I suppose not. That's a bit of a bore, isn't it? Talking of which, I'm going to marry Brian. The Headmaster's giving him a half-decent job. We're going to live in Kent.

—I can't see you and Marley living happily ever after.

—Well, I think he'll be a good father. In fact, I'm sure of it. And he *did* make it through to us, you know, from the jungle, so there's something to him. He can be a bit of a bore, that's all. Too *intense*, sometimes. Comes from living too long abroad, I suppose. But I don't see at all why you and I should stop having fun, do you?

—God, no. Absolutely. Let's not stop. George, you, you're like, I don't know, you're like someone from a, well, just, someone from a *better place*.

—Me? How silly you are, Harry. I'm just a good old-fashioned Englishwoman.

323

—Do you know, George, I think that's just what I mean, in a funny sort of way. Oh, righto. God, George.

*

—'Night, Baines.

—Goodnight, Sir James. Shan't you be wanting your car, Sir James?

—No, I don't think so. I think I'll take a stroll, perfectly safe at night now the Foot Reserve are out, and to tell you the truth, Baines, I rather like to go and look at Number 10 in the dark, these days. Just to see the lights on and think that good old Hugo's inside, keeping a lookout for us, batting for England. Makes me feel everything's all right again. And do you know, I really think it is. I really do, Baines.

*

Marley, well sherry-ed, lay down on his mother's sofa bed, under his mother's well-kept 1950s woollen blankets, in his mother's flat, with his mother, satisfied at last in her son's life, reading by a small light in the next room and his own little son, the son now of a man no longer poor and disregarded, a son due to have a sibling and a new stepmother and a new life, lying a mere stud-wall away, spreadeagled in the matchless relaxation of infant sleep. He laid his head on his pillow and felt again for the contract beneath it.

No one could blame him. George was pregnant, after all. He was doing the right thing. And for Tommy, too. Making his future secure. And his mother was happy with him at last. Something had come up. No more worries. Well *done*, Brian Marley. All right, it was not really *love*, strictly speaking, but of course he would marry George. Why on earth would he not want to? It was as if he had indeed placed an advert in the *Intelligencer*:

324

Normal Englishman (early 40s), senior civil servant (FO), well travelled, now happily settled in England, proven stock, Aga-friendly, clubbable, seeks beautiful, normal Englishwoman to glide through life with, sherry in hand, and be survived by children.

And as if that advert had been answered. What more could anyone want? And Tommy would get used to it. Well, he would just have to. He had no choice anyway. Well, that was not quite true, of course, there is always a choice, yes, yes, very philosophical, very undergraduate, but he was forty-three and his mother was getting old and he had lost Consuela anyway. OK, true, he had never actually flown to Patagonia to find her. Perhaps he still could? Yes, and offer her what? He had seen the green eyes, he knew what would happen to his job if he did not marry George. So, yes, he could always run to Patagonia, broke, middle-aged, and stand on her doorstep and offer her what, exactly? A flat with a white plastic door, that was all. Choice? There was no choice. And George was pregnant, anyway, so what could he do, no one could blame him . . .

*

—That's old George fixed up then, sir?
—Yes. I'm glad. It would have been a shame if we'd had to deal with Marley some other way. After all, he did find us.
—Funny, that sort of chap, sir. Almost the thing, but not quite.
—Takes a couple of generations, Devereux, that's all. George'll make sure the kids go to a decent school. By the time they're grown, no one will care whether their grandfather was a socialist Cabinet Minister, a National Service lieutenant, an Armenian moneylender or a field marshal. They'll sound the thing, and that's what matters.

325

Because if you *sound* the thing, that means you *think* the thing, and that means you *are* the thing. Doesn't matter if a chap hasn't got a bean, so long as he's the thing. That's why we have to keep the things that matter going, Devereux: so the next lot of chaps become the thing too. Like making new chaps part of an old regiment, really, that's all. That's the trouble with the Yanks, d'you see? They talk too much damn sentimental rot, all that Low Church nonsense, so they *think* too much sentimental rot, so they can't take a few casualties without bellyaching. Not the thing at all. Which means they need us, eh? When's my flight to Washington?

—Seven in the morning, Headmaster.

—Glad we got Concorde back into service, eh? Fine kite. Of course, we'll get clearance to fly her to any damn place in Yankland now. What are you up to tomorrow, Devereux?

—Oh, I'm doing that speech where I tear up the whole Social Work Appointments Supplement of the *Paper* and announce that all funding for that sort of nonsense has been stopped at once and is going straight to the Stable Family Tax Rebate.

—Oh yes, that. Yes, that should be a good show. You know, Devereux, I'm amazed no one seems to see how easy this democratic politics is, what with the idiots' lantern and all. Really, you just have to treat them the way we used to treat the locals in the Empire: nothing too complicated, put on a bit of a show, never let them see you blink. Well, better turn in then. You popping next door for a nightcap?

—Number 11? No-o, they're having some sort of boffins' brains-trust meeting, something to do with the switch to dollars. Or it may be the latest stink about OPEC. Not my cup of tea at all.

—Nor mine. Leave them to it and good luck to them.

326

The stink will blow over, Devereux. I've been reading up. This Thatcher woman, now, she was the most unpopular PM in history. Four million unemployed. Then she won her war and everything was all right. So if there's too much of a stink about anything, we'll know what to do, eh? After all, that's what we're *good* at, really, isn't it, Devereux? Always keeps the oiks happy. Thought those damn OPEC sheikhs would've learned their lesson from Iraq, but perhaps not. Ah, fresh air, that's better. Bracing tonight, a bit. Funny, never thought of this place as having a half-decent garden, but it is, rather, isn't it?

—It is, sir. Shall I have a cup of hot cocoa sent out to your tent before I shove off?

—Good man, Devereux.

*

Mrs Marley surveyed her flat contentedly. Two generations of her blood sleeping soundly. An interesting job in the Foreign Office. She went quietly up to the sofa bed where her son was sleeping beneath the picture of his father on the aircraft carrier. He was thrashing about a bit so she waited until he was still again before taking the contract from underneath his pillow. It was easy. She did it exactly as she had so often slipped a milk tooth out, in this very flat, before popping a sixpenny piece neatly back underneath. He did not even stir. She took the big envelope back into her small bedroom, got back into bed and settled herself down to read it. *Hush-hush* indeed! He would not mind. He would not grudge her the shared pleasure. He was her son. It was for this that she had dodged the doodlebugs and never remarried and worked and worked and worked. The *Foreign Office*. Yes, that surely justified a quiet gloat . . .

*

Marley, still trapped sherry-deep in his dreams, fought blindly to throw off the overheating blankets and snouted his head wildly into the now damp pillow.

He dreamed that little Tommy was at the door to his bedroom, a bedroom he had never had, a tall, high room with mouldering paint and stained plaster. Tommy was hammering at the door, screaming to get in to Daddy. There was something out there with Tommy, something terrible, but Marley could not get out of bed to go to the door, his limbs were dull, his hands flapped uselessly in front of his eyes. *Daddy! Daddy!* Then Tommy opened the door and stood there, crazed with fear. Behind him a horribly tall, hideously thin figure came lurching into the room, its green eyes shining and a cane jutting from the top of its shattered skull.

—Hello again, old boy. Time your boy went off to school. Make a man of him. Make a soldier out of him!

Marley awoke, jabbering silently with mortal terror, and found that it was morning. Rain battered against the semi-underground bay window of his mother's basement flat. A grey morning, like so many before. Another day of teaching English. Another hangover. As he lay blinking, champing his dry mouth, still fighting the retreating tendrils of his nightmares, his mother came in from her little kitchen with a steaming mug of tea.

—Are you all right, darling? You were making an awful lot of noise in there. Still, you didn't wake Tommy up, so there's still time for us to have a little chat.

—Eh? muttered Marley blearily, taking the tea from her automatically, as he had done countless times before. —A chat?

—Yes, dear, about your job.

—My God, I'd forgotten! Ha. My job, yes.

Marley's nightmare was wafted away like a summer mist, leaving only sunlit uplands in view. The job. His job. His future. Ha. He sipped the tea. Mmm! Ah yes, his new life, God, how could he have forgotten? George. George in his bed. Tra-la, the flowers that bloom in the spring. He would go into town, slap down his resignation from the London English School, walk along Piccadilly, a free man with a fat pension, Marley of the FO. He would swing blithely into Jermyn Street and buy, at last, a real, proper, brand new, made-to-measure tweed jacket and wool trousers. Hmm, perhaps he should go to a gym a few times first, he was a bit overweight, but now, yes, now it was *worth* getting thin again. OK, he would wait to buy himself new clothes, yes, of course, today he would take his mother to buy clothes for *her* instead. They would go to Jaeger, he would take Tommy out of school today, they would ride in a big red bus, outside the rush hour, and feed pigeons and look at the diplodocus skeleton and . . .

Before he could suggest this plan to his mother, however, a large and stout manila envelope flumped down on to Marley's blanket-covered lap with unspoken but clear reproach. Marley looked up at his mother over the rim of his mug.

—Well, Brian? The Committee for the Special Relationship indeed.

—What?

—You haven't actually *taken* this job, have you? Oh, really, Brian.

—But, I . . . Mum, have you been reading my bloody contract?

—Don't swear at me, Brian.

—Sorry, sorry, but –

—I did take a little peek, yes. And a good job I did too. I know, Brian, I know, they're hard to resist, that old bastard had me talking so *far back* yesterday evening that I was practically trying to swallow my tonsils as I spoke by the time he'd gone. That's their secret weapon, you see. It was the same in my day, we all had to learn to talk like them or we had no chance at all, the sods. *Headmaster*, indeed.

—Mum? Are you OK?

—I am now. And yes, a lot of what he's done so far has just been common sense. But I've seen through him now. He's just another bloody-minded old upper-class bugger with a heart as black as Newgate's knocker. I've always said that what this country needs is a proper bourgeois revolution at last. Karl Marx was right about that, though of course he was quite wrong about everything else.

—What? Um, Mum, I –

—Don't look so shocked, darling. What on earth do you think we talk about at the Esperanto Café? Victoria bloody sponges? Really, Brian, don't tell me even *you* have fallen for this modern idiocy that says old people, especially old women, are no use and know nothing? My dear boy, I have seen bombs fall and tanks roll and states collapse and men run off to Australia so I have learned a thing or two and I am *still* considerably younger than the average Chinese Communist Party Chairman thank you very much indeed.

—Of course, Mum, I was just, but –

—And I know that you are *not* taking this ridiculous job. Become part of America? What nonsense. No, no, over my dead body.

—But Mum, it's a good job, it's the Foreign Office, it's –

—You are *not* taking that job, Brian.

—I'm not?

—No. What have you got on the old bastard? Come on, don't lie to me. I can always tell when you're lying. I'm your mother, I used to change your nappies, remember? So you can tell me why that bloodthirsty old militarist is trying to bribe you. He's trying to shut you up, isn't he? Well? What really happened out there?

—No, Mum, look, it's, it's because he wants me to marry George.

—George?

—Georgina. The girl I met there.

—Oh yes. She seemed nice. But now she writes that dreadful, snooty tittle-tattle in the *Intelligencer* magazine. Well, that's all it is, you know. But what else can one expect in a country where we're all supposed to roll over and grin like twits every time we catch a glimpse of a silly old bag who's only interested in her bloody corgis and racehorses? Where was I, Brian?

—Mum, Mum, listen, please. George is expecting, and it's mine.

—Oh. Oh really, Brian. Don't tell me this is another of your *little accidents*?

—Well, yes, actually, but –

—Of course, I'd love more grandchildren, but there's no reason you've got to marry her, not these days. Unless you love her, of course. Do you?

—Sorry?

—You heard, Brian.

—Well, I mean, I *like* her, she's very, you know . . .

—I see. You don't love her. Really, Brian, you're just too weak.

—What?

—So they're trying to buy you off to make that silly prattling girl respectable? No, no, no. In any case, I'm going to call the *Paper* right now about this Old England nonsense. We shall demonstrate. If there's one thing the buggers don't like, it's old birds demonstrating. They can't just bash *us* over the head, can they?

Mrs Marley moved towards the phone, waving the envelope in her hand as if it were an order paper that could not be ignored. Marley dived from his little sofa bed, realised he was naked, snatched the envelope back from his mother and covered his groin with it as he tried to stop her picking up the receiver.

—Mum, stop, you can't, he cried, pointing to the Foreign Office logo which now hid his shame. —This isn't just any old job for Christ's sake. I signed the Official bloody Secrets Act.

—Oh Brian, you didn't? Well, I'm sorry, but that's just too bad.

—What? Mum?

The doorbell rang.

—Now, who on earth's that at the door this early? If it's that old bugger again, you are to tell him you're *not* taking his job. *America* indeed. The bloody Yanks made us pay cash on the nail for every last bullet in the War, and they only came in after we'd run out of money *and* the Japanese had attacked them. For God's sake, go and get a towel round yourself, Brian.

—Don't answer the door. Mum, you don't understand. If this gets out I'll go to prison.

—I understand perfectly well, Brian. How on earth do you think any of us poor ordinary buggers ever got the bloody vote in the first place? By people going to prison. Why do you think we aren't being run by a bunch of scar-faced, jackbooted Prussians? Because people were prepared for far worse than prison. Prison indeed! My dear boy, I have told you before, this country will only be free when there are oak trees growing from the ruins of Buckingham . . .

— . . . Yes yes yes, but, Mum, stop, please, think of Tommy. He needs a father.

—I *am* thinking of Tommy. He'll have a father he's proud of. Best thing a boy can have. You never had one and look what it did to you. I'm sorry, Brian, but it's true, I always hoped you'd make something of yourself, but you were always, well, a little bit wet. Of course you were, you had no father to look up to. To be quite frank, I was always really rather relieved you didn't turn out to be a poof.

—You were?

—But now Tommy will be proud of you and so will I. Yes, I think something interesting really *has* come up for you at last, darling. Do get some clothes on before I let him in.

—Mum, shit, I'm not going to bloody prison just for some mad fantasy of yours, I'm too old, this is my last chance. Christ, Mum. I'm naked, I, wait, I . . .

—Hello? Oh, hello. I'm sorry, my dear, we're not buying anything.

—You are Brian's mother, *señora*?

Marley stood rooted for a split second, then spun wildly out of the room and jammed himself against the wall in the corridor, his heart yelping and leaping inside his ribs. Frantically, silently, he sneaked along to the bathroom, to at least find a towel to wrap himself in.

—Oh, I'm so sorry, my dear. Are you a friend of Brian's?

—Yes. I was. He is here, yes?

—Well, yes, I'll just . . . Brian? Brian? I don't want to shout too loudly, my dear, my grandson's still asleep and I, just a minute . . . no, no, this is silly, you must come in, you can't stand out there in the rain, you look like death warmed up. How long have you been out there, you silly girl?

—I am expecting a long time.

—Expecting? What, *you* as well? Oh, really. Brian, come here at once!

—No, no, not that kind *expecting*, Mrs Marley. Waiting, and hoping.

—Oh. I see. Well, um, ha, *entrir in me domo*, said Marley's mother, blushing, in hopeful Esperanto.

333

—First please, Mrs Marley, you must tell me true. I have run from my father, who has been my life, because I do not believe Brian loves the English girl who looks like a boy. I am going to the English School in Piccadilly Street and I am crying and crying until they give me your address. I am waiting outside to gather my courage. Before, I was sure, Madam Marley, but now I doubt, and now I must know.

—Brian, where on earth are you? Now come inside this minute before you catch your death of cold. As for that other girl . . . you must excuse me, my dear, I'm in a bit of a tizzy, I'm going to have to go to the Esperanto Café to tell everyone we must do something about it.

—About?

—We're not bloody Americans. Guns and Bibles and Hamburgers? Hell's bells and buckets of blood, I should think not. We British are Europeans. Of course we are. At least, I bloody well am. We won the referendum three countries to one, you know.

—Sorry, I am not understanding, Mrs Marley.

—Brian? Brian? He must be with Tommy, he'll be back in a moment, now you just sit down and get your wet things off and – Who's this at the door now? Really, it's like Euston bloody Station here this morning, it's – Oh. Hello. Georgina, isn't it?

—Good morning, Mary, darling. I may come in, mayn't I? That black cab's waiting for us. I've come to take Brian for champagne at the Ritz. To celebrate our engagement, you see.

—So I heard.

—You must come too, of course. Oh. Hello. Let me guess. You must be . . . Consuela.

—Yes, it is I. And you are name?

—Me? Oh, I'm George.

—This is a boy's name.

—How funny you are. What a sweet dress. So . . . *bright*.

You do know Brian and I are getting married?

—I do not believe.

—Brian, are you there? Brian, I think you should come out. He'll be out in a minute, my dear. My dears, I should say. Where was I? Is it too early for sherry? Yes, of course it is. Perhaps I should make some tea. Brian?

Marley, his loins now safely wrapped in a long towel, but his brain locked in panic, stood flattened against the corridor wall.

On the wall opposite him hung a large, framed black-and-white picture. It had always hung there. It showed himself, aged six, with his mother, standing shyly before the breastplated cavalrymen in Whitehall in a home-knitted jumper, shorts and long socks, clutching in his small hand a little flag which said I'M BACKING BRITAIN. Marley stared at it, and saw his own forty-three-year-old features, wide-eyed, floating like a ghost in the polished glass, reflected dimly back at him over the frozen tableau of his thirty-odd-year-old mother and his six-year-old self. Absurdly, he realised that he had never before stopped to wonder who had taken the photograph, and that it must have been his father. That meant his father had seen just this, just then.

Time kneaded and folded itself about him once again, and he realised now that it would always do so, whenever he let it, because the past is all we know, the future is always obscured by cloud, we hack our way through it towards nowhere we know, and whenever we tire of the endless exploration, as well we might, whenever life seems absurdly short and the horizon no closer than when we set out all those years ago, it is the past that is always lying in wait for us, tempting us with the infallible promise of the trusted, the explored, the warm and the safe, the only real home we shall ever have. Waiting to tuck us up tight.

—Daddy?

From the other end of the corridor, Tommy appeared,

dazed with sleep, and stood looking at him, blinking, still half in the world of his dreams.

—Daddy?

—Hello, darling. Come here, everything's all right.

—Who are those ladies talking with Granny?

—Ah, well, ha, yes, I suppose we'd better go and see, hadn't we?

Marley swept up his little son, close and bed-warm, swung him around on to his chest, then turned to start down the corridor, towards the three women. He felt like a man going bravely to face the Gestapo firing squad. Then he wondered just how on earth he should think he knew how a man felt, going to face a Gestapo firing squad. Then he wondered why the hell he even thought about things like the Gestapo and firing squads? But by now it was too late to wonder any more about how the hell it had come to this, because he had come to the end of the corridor. Another stride would take him out and into the room and to his fate.

—How silly you both are, he's joining the Foreign Office and marrying me. It's all arranged.

—Always he talk me of leaving England. With him, I go anywhere.

—My son, leave England? He would never leave his son and his mother.

—And he's hardly going to jilt *me*, you poor thing. He's one of us, now.

—He will find the way for do all thing right, Mrs Marley. Because he is man, your son, I know.

—Yes, well. And as for you and this *baby*, my dear, and this *job*, well, I'm afraid . . .

Mr Brian Marley

Brian Marley, who was torn to pieces by several women yesterday, saw the light of day in the early

1960s, which were in practice the late 1950s, in England. Born into a country unsure whether it should keep its global responsibilities or simply pay its way, into a generation unsure whether it should cleave to a happy vision of unstoppable progress or a gloomier vista of impending cataclysm, and into a gender unsure whether it should prepare itself for Englishly dutiful sacrifice or Californian personal fulfilment, he had some trouble settling down to a normal life. He contrived to exist for several decades without ever quite knowing what he should be, and thus never did anything much that might have given anyone at all the slightest reason to love him. He is survived by a son, and by his own shame.

Marley stepped out from the corridor, through the open door to his mother's best room and into their midst, with Tommy held high against his chest, as if the presence of his son and his own evident, loving fatherhood might serve as a sort of emotional flak jacket against the worst of their accusations. The three sets of female eyes met his, each glowing with expectation. He boldly set back his shoulders, pulled in his stomach and opened his mouth to speak deeply and firmly. Then he became horribly aware that the towel, released from the pressure of his relaxed belly, was unwinding itself from his waist and beginning to slide gently downwards. He hastily unleashed his stomach again and grabbed for the towel with one hand, almost dropping Tommy as he did so. But it was too late. The soft white cotton wafted heavily down over the hairs on his legs, over his ankles, and away.

—Oh, sorry, um, shit, oh God, George, Consuela, thank God you, I mean, you came back, you, Mum, could you . . .? George, look here, we need to . . . *lo siento, Consuelita*, um, Tommy, could you just stand there, no,

337

just *there*, in front of me, while I, oh Christ, Mum, sorry, I just want to get behind the settee, I mean the *sofa*, I mean oh for God's sake who cares what it's bloody called? Sorry, Tommy, I wasn't shouting at *you*, I was shouting at *me*, sorry, everyone . . .